In the Company of Darkness

In the Company of Darkness

Marshall Pickens

Corvid Publishing

This is a work of fiction. All characters, organizations, and events portrayed in this novel are either products of the author's imagination or are used fictitiously.

In the Company of Darkness

Copyright 2022 by Marshall Pickens

To my parents,
Jack and Angelyn,
For letting me get a Writing
And Literature degree in college.
Their support means everything.

Chapter One

"I would like to open up this time to testimonies." The pastor said.

James sighed. The church he was sitting in was small by any standard, and he was already dreading the greetings and well wishing's, and invitations to lunch of all the people whose eyes he'd felt on him throughout the service. Big churches you could blend into the crowd, and even if they did have an official greeter you could avoid them just through the sheer mass of people. This church, however, held, on a good day, ninety souls. There was no way he could avoid the proverbial, and literal, rush after the service.

Tuning out an older woman who had started to ramble on about her son setting her up on Facebook and how it had connected her to a sick friend in Ohio, James looked around the church for the thousandth time that morning. He knew he was being a bit judgmental, and he mentally apologized to the woman, but he was starting to run out of patience. He'd been so sure he would find what he was looking for here.

It was a nice enough church. The ceiling was a beautiful cedar that ran down in great arches to the floor, and, of course, there was a great big wooden cross hanging on the wall directly behind where the pastor stood to give his sermon. James always found it a bit strange, or ironic, that people now worshiped, and wore around their neck, a great big instrument of torture and execution. Aesthetically there was really only one problem with this small Alaskan church. One thing continued to draw his gaze. It was so out of place with the cedar ceiling, and the old wooden cross. Who in their right mind had decided to put in a see through Plexiglass pulpit? James would have loved to be in on that church meeting.

He could almost hear the conversation, "But the plastic doesn't go with anything."

"Yes, but the people need to be able to see the worship band on stage."

"Why?"

And on and on the argument would go until someone suggested they all pray about it.

He'd been chasing and almost catching up for two years now, and honestly he was starting to question his reasons for trying so hard. Naive was the only term really coming to mind when he thought about his first few days with the power. Sighing he changed that to the first year with his powers. So much had happened so fast that he hadn't really taken the time to stop and consider the why behind any of this. At first he charged ahead with his half formed ideas of doing what was right worn like armor, and when it turned out his armor wasn't good enough to protect those around him he charged on with anger and revenge filling in the new chinks in that armor. After the first year of trying to catch the monster, and he wasn't being metaphorical with himself, the thing really was a monster, his motor had run down a bit. After the second year he was simply continuing on because he was too stubborn to quit, and because he simply didn't know what else his powers were for. Belief fueled them, and he did believe they would work, but eventually, and he worried this would happen at the worst possible time, he would run into the problem of what he believed in. Right now, he believed in catching this thing and destroying it. Revenge might not be the best of beliefs to cling to, but at this point it was what he'd whittled it down to.

As far as the chase itself had gone it wasn't so bad that he'd missed his guess about where his prey was going to be. This wasn't the first time and he was sure it wouldn't be the last. He was just glad to finally have figured out the pattern, and now had a place to start looking. Letting his eyes roam around the well-lit sanctuary James tried to peer into every shadow. You would think with more light there would be fewer shadows, but James had learned the opposite was actually true. The more sources of light, the more shadows were created. Any one of them could hold his quarry.

His instincts had led him here, and over the last few years of chasing the Darkness he'd learned to trust them. In which case, James thought, he must be too late and the Darkness has already fed and moved on. The Darkness was a soul-sucking parasite that fed on the negatively overcharged emotions of its host. It wasn't just that it lived in shadows, as far as James knew; it actually was part of the shadow.

The more it fed the stronger it became, and the stronger it became the more of its environment it could control. Conceivably, if given free reign, it could become strong enough to control any number of people around it and then physically manifest itself into God only knows what.

And sitting here in this church James wondered if God really did know. So far, James had been able to hound it enough that it hadn't had time to continuously feed, or at least James hoped it hadn't. He really had no idea how strong it was, or could get. He just assumed since it seemed to be running it must be weak enough to fear him.

The voice James was tuning out changed, and something about it grated on his memory. He'd been raised in churches just like this one, and in each there had been one of these voices. She always knew what was best, and she was always pecking you into going in the, what she called, correct direction. She was the kind of hen who would never accuse you of something but would always say something along the lines of, "but have you prayed about it?" She went to conferences about the Holy Spirit, and the healing power of prayer. But when it came right down to it she was just a hen, and all she really did was peck, peck, peck.

"I am afraid Pastor." She was saying. "There are so many distractions and voices calling out to our youth these days. It's bad enough the world throws evil in the faces of our teens every time they turn on the television or go shopping, but we need to make sure this church is a safe haven for them. They need to know this is a safe place for them to run to in times of trouble."

If James had a trick knee it would have been acting up, but in his case the hairs on his arms actually stood on end. His scalp tightened and a tingle ran down his spine.

"When these distractions and evil come into our very church we need to be strong and stand against them." She turned and looked around at the crowd, "The world would try to talk to you about tolerance, which is all well and good, but there comes a time to say stop. To draw a line in the sand and say this is as far as we'll be pushed." She turned back to the pastor, "Myself and some others have been praying."

James groaned at this. This was a church language all to itself. Understanding the language of the church was like learning to speak Spanish. In this case if someone said they had been praying about something it really meant there was no way to contradict them, because you hadn't been praying about it, and even if you had prayers never contradicted each other. So in effect she'd just said that she was right no matter what because she'd been praying about it, and if you said differently you weren't hearing the voice of God and you needed to pray about it more.

She turned and looked toward the teens, "We feel some of this worldliness has crept its way into our church and is threatening the spiritual lives of our teens."

For the first time that morning James took the time to look at the teens in the church. He'd noticed them when he first came in, and had been slightly surprised to see they were all sitting in the front two rows of the sanctuary. In his day they sat as far back as their parents would let them so they could pass notes or secretly hold hands with their girlfriends. But now, taking the time to really look at them, he noticed something. One of them looked different. Most of them were t-shirts and jeans kinds of kids with a few better-dressed ones thrown in, but one of them stood out. Her hair blended faded pink with a newer layer of green. And poking through the shoulder length multicolored locks he was fairly sure he could see the metal studs of a dog color.

"Grace," the hen said in a sad, but loving voice, "we would like to have the church pray with you this morning."

Grace shifted her shoulders a little but refused to look up at the clucking.

"Grace," her voice lost even the hint of loving veneer, "we need to lay hands on you and ask God to remove the demonic forces that are trying to control you." She paused for dramatic effect, "Won't you let us Grace?"

Now that was a loaded question if James had ever heard one. If Grace refused then she was obviously possessed by a demon, but if she said yes then again she was admitting she had a demon she needed to get rid of.

Grace finally turned to face her accuser, and James had a slight idea what it must have been like to sit through the Salem witch trials. When she spoke her voice was quiet, almost a whisper, "Are you judging me based on the clothes I'm wearing?"

"No dear," the hen replied.

"Oh," Grace said, "then you must be judging me by the color of my hair?"

The hen sighed as if Grace just wasn't getting it, "Of course not dear."

"Then what?" Grace stood up and squared her shoulders at the hen, and James almost started clapping for her. "What are you judging me on? My propensity to gossip? No, wait, that's you isn't it."

Wow, James thought as the congregation gasped, I would buy tickets to see this. He turned in time to see the expression on the hen's face change from exasperation to hate.

"This," the hen gestured at Grace, "is exactly what I'm talking about; divisiveness." Spit actually flew from her lips as she said the word, "The devil seeks to divide our flock." As she stepped out from her pew into the center isle James noticed something.

It wasn't that her shadow was wrong, or off, or slightly different. It was all those things. With all the lights of the sanctuary blazing around them her shadow was too dark, and moved slightly off key from the rest of her. James wasn't even listening to the argument now. He vaguely noticed the hen had raised her voice and Grace hadn't. A part of James' mind cheered and thought, good for you Grace. Her attitude and posture reminded him powerfully of his former girlfriend Kate. It had been her death, caused by the very thing he was hunting, which had first led him on this crusade. Over the past few years he'd done a fairly good job of not thinking about Kate. It was still too fresh and painful, and he didn't want to get distracted from the task at hand. This time it was a bit more difficult to push the memories away. It wasn't just a pang of guilt that tapped him in the brain, it was a whole tidal wave of it. He'd never really confronted the feelings surrounding his inability to save her. She was his girlfriend, and wasn't it his job to protect her from things like this? James realized if he let this past tense train of thought go on too long he would lose his chance in the here and now, so he decided part of his mind had to be blocked off to allow the rest of his senses focused on the too dark shadow of the church hen. He allowed a forced smile to spread over his face as he stood and squeezed past the others in his row and out into the center aisle.

When they finally noticed him he was standing right behind the hen. It wasn't a big church, but all the attention had been on the two women arguing in the front. His looming presence stopped the talking and just before the hen could say something James lifted his right hand and put his index finger to his lips in the universal sign for quiet. He wasn't surprised that it worked. They were shocked a stranger would do this, and the shock would work to his advantage, but it would wear off soon enough, and the Darkness would realize what was going on.

James mentally reached into himself and found a core of belief. Belief could change the world, alter lives, and if applied correctly could change the physical world around you. Just over two years ago James had learned if you truly believed something, like believing you are going to breathe again, or the sun will come up the next day, then you could harness it in a way he would only call magic. These days it came easy to him. Two years ago, not so much. It had been easier for him than it would be for your average American because James had been raised on a steady diet of fantasy novels and comic books. But still, believing in magic, real honest to goodness magic, was a hard thing for someone who had been raised to believe some things were real and others were just fantasy. He'd been lucky to have seen someone do magic in the days leading up to him learning how. Seeing is believing isn't just a trite statement. If you see something done chances are you are going to believe it can be done. And right now he truly believed.

His hand tingled as he reached into the hen's shadow and grabbed the Darkness. With an effort of will he pulled, and she screamed. It felt, strangely enough, like pulling off a giant strip of Velcro. James wasn't sure how powerful the Darkness had become over the last two years, but he didn't think it was more than he could handle. Why else would it be sucking bad vibes off some lady in small town Alaska?

When he finally pulled it free he felt a subtle shift in the world around him. From his peripheral vision he could see pure white eyes open in almost every shadow in the sanctuary. At the same time James could feel the whispers begin. They weren't audible, but more of a pressure on his mind. He knew the Darkness was talking directly to the minds of every person in the room. It was trying to make something happen.

Holding up the piece of shadow in his hand James turned to the congregation, "Don't listen to it." Having grown up in the church he knew the right words to use, "He is the father of lies."

James wasn't surprised when the whispers stopped. This was a room full of true believers. They truly believed in the existence of demons, and they believed demons would whisper lies to you. They also truly believed in the existence of God, and had been raised to believe nothing could overpower God's people in His holy church. The belief might not be directly channeled like James', but just the overwhelming existence of it could shut down the Darkness.

This was going easier than he'd expected, he thought, then shook his head for a naive fool as shadows all around the sanctuary came to life whipping out. People, pews, flower arrangements, and even a guitar flew through the air. James dug inside himself and extended his power. He held in his mind the true belief that he could stop the objects in mid air, and they did stop, but the human mind is limited to how many thoughts it can hold at the same time. For James' power to work he needed to be able to picture it in his mind, believe it could happen, no matter how crazy, and then put some effort into making it happen. In this case James had unconsciously extended his hands to stop everything from hitting him in the face. This had the unfortunate side effect of allowing the piece of shadow to slip away.

James unceremoniously dropped everything, including the people, as more things flew at him. Blocking these, he came to the realization he hadn't thought this through as well as he should have. His brain started talking to him as he continued to picture stopping the barrage of objects in his mind's eye.

So how do you fight a shadow?

Well, James replied to himself, I was able to grab it when it was on that lady.

Oh right. The one you so kindly referred to as a hen.

Hey now, this is no time to go pointing mental fingers.

Oh really? And isn't the good guy, i.e. you, supposed to be nice to people?

Look, you, this really isn't the time to get into my inclination to sarcastically skewer people in my mind.

And why would that be?

Really? You have to ask that? Are you not paying attention right now?

To... oh right, flying objects, and oh, look at that he can sharpen his own shadow and try to stab you with it. Now that's a handy trick.

Oh seriously, now is not the time! How am I supposed to fight this thing if it's a shadow?

Don't think of it as a shadow dummy.

James almost didn't dodge the incoming razor sharp shadow as the thought hit him. Why was he thinking of it as a shadow? It was obviously substantial enough to pick up pews, and real enough to sharpen itself to slice through the piano. James grinned at his new mindset, and with a force of will he pushed as much junk in the room out of the way as possible. People and pews alike were shoved to the back of the sanctuary as James faced the main bulk of the Darkness.

With his smile fixed James extended his hands palm out and fire leaped from them in liquid streams hitting the Darkness and causing it to steam and pop. In his mind he covered his back with a curved wall of air to ward off the shadow knife attacks as he burned the Darkness across the front of the sanctuary. James' left hand might have slowed just for a moment, and he might have cheered a little in his mind, as the flames melted the Plexiglas pulpit into a bubbling mass.

The ninety or so members of the congregation were trying to push their way through the debris to the double doors at the back of the sanctuary when the Darkness changed its tactics. Hearing the screams James turned to see people being picked up by the arms of shadow. He didn't hesitate and started cutting the arms off with scissors of air as fast as he could picture it.

"Stop." The voice of the demon crawled over his nervous system and the room tilted slightly for a moment. "I will kill them," and shadow arms turned into knives at the throats of three teens.

The boy on the left was gangly with overly big hands. His growth spurt had outdistanced his parents' ability to buy new pants for his go to church black suit. The addition of a thin black tie over a white shirt made him look like a bad version of a wild west mortician.

Right next to him a shorter blond boy had a shadow razer hovering slightly above the neckline of a professionally tattered Abercrombie and Fitch shirt. James was momentarily jealous of the kids comfortable jeans and sneakers since fighting a ticked off shadow demon in his own dress slacks and loafers was a bit uncomfortable.

Then there was Grace. When the shadows grabbed her she'd initially tried struggling but after a glance at James, and with a bead of blood dripping from where a shadow knife nicked her neck, she'd settled down. Grace had a delicate look to her and under her colorful hair her skin was pale with soft features. Her clothes looked threadbare but in an over worn and personal way with the cuffs of her jeans fraying from being walked on and the collar of her shirt showing holes in the stitching. In reality it wasn't her he was seeing standing there but an afterimage of Kate, and failing her a second time wasn't an option.

Lowering his hands slightly James nodded, "There's nowhere for you to go."

The voice turned sharp and raked across James' mind, "You will let me leave, or..."

"Or you kill them. Right." James paused, then looked at the teens. "You three believe in heaven?"

Their eyes got very big. "I know, I know," James said to them, "there's a big difference between believing in heaven and actually thinking you're about to go there."

James sighed and shook his head, "I'm sorry but getting rid of this thing is more important, and you'll go to heaven so you really don't have anything to lose, right?"

Abercrombie and Fitch, passed out. The mortician swore, and James wondered if his parents knew their sweet Christian boy could say those four letter words. Grace just looked at him and nodded slightly.

The voice slid back into a whisper, "You're bluffing."

James shrugged. On the inside he was frantically hoping the demon would flinch and give him an opening. In so many cop shows the bad guy has some hostage and you're just screaming at the TV to just shoot the guy. His head is sticking out, and you're supposed to be some amazing cop who just last scene shot the face off a paper target at the firing range, so why can't you shoot the bad guy who's only five feet away? The part of his mind he'd blocked off broke free and screamed at him to not let it happen again. He'd lost Kate to this monster and he wasn't about to lose Grace. But a bluff is only as good as your willingness to go through with it so he gave a little wink at her and started to raise his right hand.

The Darkness screamed and windows shattered. A tendril of shadow flicked out and carved a line in the air. James hesitated not knowing what was happening, then hesitated again as he watched the Darkness pull on the line as if it were the edge of a door. His mind spun. There were no doors here. James knew where both doors into and out of this world were, and this was not one of them. His mind flicked over possibilities while trying to settle on the right thing to focus his belief on.

The Darkness flowed through the partially open door faster than James thought possible, pulling the three teens with it. His instincts kicked in and he grabbed the edge of the door.

It felt wrong. It was thinner than paper, and the harder he tried to hold it the more his fingers slipped. Closing his eyes James formed a solid picture of a door in his mind. He believed there was a door there. He believed he was pulling it open and stepping through it. And his belief made it real. The door opened, he stepped through, and fell.

Chapter Two

The dark tentacles the demon had wrapped around them pulled and the world shrunk to a small point of light. For a moment Grace's body rebelled at the lack of air causing her lungs to spasm. It quickly passed and dust flew up as they hit the ground. Laying there she sucked in a mix of dirt and air while part of her mind yelled at her. She blinked trying to clear the dust from her eyes and pushed herself up to her knees.

Looking around she saw two boys off to her left. One was stretched out on the ground and the other was squatting over him shaking him. Recognizing them she felt a moment of relief that something was normal. Unsure of just about everything she got to her feet and tried a hunched over walk that Hollywood had taught her would keep her safe in almost any situation.

"Mitch." She half whispered at the black suited boy.

A full body twitch sent him a step away. One hand came up in a confused attempt to figure out whether it wanted to punch or possibly block whatever might be coming.

"Wha?!" He looked at her and lowered his voice, "Grace?" He gestured wildly around them, "What the," he paused and she could tell he really wanted to use one of his few known curse words, but his upbringing wouldn't let him, "what is going on?"

"Why should I know?" She loudly whispered back.

Mitch looked around and unconsciously loosened his tie, unbuttoning the top of his white shirt, "Where are we? What happened to the church?"

Grace followed his gaze, and found herself not wanting to. The world she found herself in seemed devoid of life. Her quick glance saw no grass, bushes, trees, or in point of fact anything at all other than dirt and rocks. They seemed to be situated in a small cleft with mountains rising up directly around them. "It doesn't matter."

"It doesn't matter?" He kicked at the ground and they both watched as finely powdered dust settled on the still form of the other boy. "Look around Grace. Ray is unconscious, the church turned into a bad version of the set of Mad Max, and," he pointed up, "there's no sun."

"Well," taking a quick glance up she realized how much she didn't want to prove his point, "we can't do anything about the sun, but we can at least check on Ray." Taking a step toward Ray, something grabbed her shirt from behind pulling her back.

"Welcome," The voice rasped behind her then let out a string of coughs. Trying to catch Mitch's eye she was hoping he would let her know what was going on but all she could see was him staring over her shoulder.

Something thick wrapped around her waist and a very disconnected part of her brain had flashbacks to jungles and large snakes, then she found herself flying to the right and landing hard. Sometimes things take a while to become clear while at other times everything seems to fly together of its own free will; in this moment it all came flooding back. The thing made of shadows in the church. The man facing it with fire flowing from his hands like twin snakes. She'd been going to church for as long as she could remember, and while she hadn't always fit in she'd generally been a believer, but no one really believes in certain things no matter how much they say they do. Flaming hands and shadow monsters fit into that very specific category of things you say you believe in but secretly think is only for radicals and nut jobs.

Looking up she expected to see an inky blackness flowing across the dirt and rocks like some evil octopus had inked itself, but instead she saw a man, if he could be called that. He was maybe four feet tall and most of that was made up of protruding elbows, knees, and shoulders. He was disproportionate to a ridiculous degree with some parts of him reminding her of paintings from lessons on the black death while other parts looked more like thick tree branches, gnarled and twisted. He was dressed like a monk from Monty Python in a rough brown robe with bulky sleeves, a hood, and a rope for a belt.

"What have we got here?" He rasped leaning over the still form of Ray, who even unconscious and laying in the dirt could pass for an Abercrombie and Fitch model with his perfectly tousled sandy blonde hair and a strangely symmetrical face.

The disproportionate man leaned over Ray and poked at him, "Not dead. Good. You!" He pointed at Mitch without looking up, "Wake him up, we need to move."

Mitch stared at him, then straightened his wiry fame, "No."

16

Finally looking up, the thin man looked at Mitch and smiled, "Ahhh," he breathed in deeply and Grace, for a moment, thought she saw a dark mist float away from Mitch and toward him. "Thank you for saying no."

Stretching his arms above his head as his twisted frame would allow the man leaned from side to side until his shoulders and neck popped loudly. "It's been so long since I was," he paused and wiggled his fingers in front of his face, "corporeal. I needed a reason to stretch myself before moving on, and if you were all nicely compliant there'd be no fun in kicking you down the hill."

"You don't scare me." Mitch forced the words out and actually managed to slightly sound like he might mean it, if given enough lead up time.

The man stretched out his right arm and started walking toward him. "I am Kron'ael, you and," he pointed with his other hand to Grace and Ray, "those with you are mine. I will consume you from the inside out as I drag your worthless husks across Purgatory. You will," Mitch tried to swat his advancing arm away, assuming the pile of twigs making up the little man would be easy to push aside, but with a flick of his wrist Kron'ael grabbed Mitch's arm and pulled him until their noses were almost touching, "you will be scared little human. I have been one with the music of the stars, and you are nothing compared to that."

He flicked his arm like brushing away a fly and Mitch flew across the clearing and disappeared over the edge. Grace could hear him scream along with the sounds of rocks clattering. This time she knew she wasn't seeing things, or to be more correct, she was seeing something as a mist rose up from where Mitch had disappeared and floated to Kron'ael where he breathed it in like an addict looking for a fix.

When he turned and looked at her she couldn't stop herself from flinching, and when she saw the mist rise from her she held her breath not wanting to accidentally suck it in. Laughing, Kron'ael advanced toward her and she realized she was scooting away through the dirt and forced herself to stop knowing it wasn't going to do any good.

"Since your friend seems to be indisposed at the moment it falls to you to wake your compatriot. I do not wish to be in this place any longer." She watched as his gaze drifted to the left and following it she found herself looking at a rectangular hole in the sky. It seemed to float a few feet above the ground and every few seconds shimmered like a mirage.

"If you need any more motivation," he looked back at her, "I would be more than happy to do what is necessary to move this process along."

She stared at him, then looked back at the hole. A noise like glass scraping across rock made her jump and look back at him. Little black blades extended a few inches from each of his finger tips, "You don't need all of your skin to be useful to me."

Scooting away a few steps more she pushed herself up and ran to Ray. When she reached him he still hadn't moved. She was relieved to see the man had been right and he was visibly breathing. Remembering he'd fainted in the church when the other man had suggested he'd be willing to sacrifice them to destroy the monster she realized the twisted pile of bones behind her must be that same monster. It must have pulled them into whatever this place was to get away from the man with the flames back at the church. That must be why he was so intent on leaving as quickly as he could.

She hesitated over Ray and considered trying to stall long enough for him to show up. Maybe it would only be a few seconds. She glanced around at the land and the dust and realized it had already been way more than a few seconds. If he was right behind them, and coming through that door to save them, wouldn't he be there by now? If she waited too long she was sure bad things would start to happen, and right now it was more important to survive, and help her friends survive, than to stall and hope someone showed up to save them.

Looking at Ray she raised her right hand and realized it really wouldn't bother her to slap him as hard as possible. He'd never been nice to her, and had always been part of the click trying to ostracize her. In fact, she was fairly sure he wouldn't even know what the word ostracize meant. Bringing her hand down with a solid smack she saw Ray twitch and heard the monster chuckle behind her.

Blinking hard, Ray sat up and looked around. She wanted to explain what was going on, but couldn't think of a good way to start. Should she start with how some kind of monster pulled them through a hole in the sky into... where?

She started to look around again and was stopped by pain shooting through her back as the thin man drew back his foot for another kick, "No time for sightseeing missy. Move it."

Scrambling to her feet she reached out for Ray's hand to help him up. He grabbed it and continued to sit in the dirt. The monster stepped up and she watched as he raised his right hand. The fingers merged together, elongated, and thinned becoming a skin toned knife attached to his arm.

"I will start by cutting off your ears since you don't seem to use them, then your nose," he took a step closer, "after that I'm not sure. I like to leave room for creativity."

Grace yanked on Ray's arm, pulling him up by sheer force and dragging him in the direction she'd see Mitch disappear. After a few steps Ray seemed to finally wake up. Pulling his hand away from her he started to really look around.

"Where are we?"

Grace twitched at the volume of his voice. She realized, in some part of herself, that it really didn't matter but it felt like they should be whispering. It was partly the feeling of not wanting the monster holding them hostage to hear them, but it was also their surroundings. She was just now realizing how silent everything was. She could hear each step, the breathing of the thing behind them, even the light tumble of rocks from somewhere ahead, but what she couldn't hear subconsciously bothered her. There should be other sounds. Sounds of life. And not just that, there should be a whole range of sensations to go along with those sounds. A breeze should brush the hairs on her neck, or the heat from the sun should warm one side of her face. The lack of these bothered her.

"Seriously?" Ray poked her in the arm. He looked over his shoulder and lowered his voice finally catching the same feeling, "What's going on? Did that guy just grow a knife out of his arm?"

"Yes." Of all the questions Ray could ask in that moment it was the only one she could answer definitively. That thing, who or whatever he was, had most definitely just grown a knife out of his arm. Why it wasn't bothering her more she really couldn't say, because, on reflection, it should really be freaking her out.

After a few steps the ground started dropping in front of her and she could just make out the top of Mitch's head. A few more and she could see he was sitting on a rock, which was disturbingly the exact same color as everything else, his elbows resting on his knees and his head cradled in his hands.

"Good," the voice from behind her was slightly deeper than she remembered it, "you were smart and waited for us."

Mitch looked up and Grace followed his gaze over her shoulder. The monster, Kron'ael or something like that, didn't just sound different he looked different. It was hard to tell under the loose structure of the robe but his steps fell in a strange pattern and his right foot drug along the sand as if it was slightly longer than the left.

"Well, up and at 'em." He waved his hands to shoo them all forward, "Time waits for no one." He chuckled a bit, "Except here I suppose."

Mitch stood and faced Kron'ael, "I'm not going anywhere until you tell us what is going on."

Nodding Kron'ael stepped forward, brought his hand back, then jamming it forward pushed his fingertips into the left side of Mitch's abdomen. Ray screamed. Mitch gasped and staggered backward pulling himself off the outstretched hand. Blood bubbled from the wound turning the white shirt bright red.

"I understand," Kron'ael reached out with his left hand and steadied Mitch, keeping him from falling over, "you're curious, and you're trying to be protective. At other times those traits would be admirable. In another life I would have respected them. In an entirely academic way I still respect them."

He patted Mitch's shoulder, "But here, and now, I just need you to understand that I'm in charge and you do what I say." Looking up into Mitch's face he nodded for effect and waited for Mitch to nod back. "I understand you're not really in a talking mood right now, so a nod will do."

Reaching out with his bloodied right hand he pressed it against the still bleeding hole in Mitch's stomach, "Fortunately for you, I need you alive. You literally are no good to me dead here, and aside from that I have no idea what would actually happen if you died here. That's a moot point however since I'm confident I can keep you alive for as long as I need."

Mitch gasped and stepped back from him. His hands went to the dark wet spot on his shirt. He poked at it and winced, expecting to find a bloody gash then looked up at Grace when he realized it was gone. Grace nodded at him, silently saying let's keep going for now, we can figure it all out later. He nodded back.

"Great," Kron'ael said, "Now that you've all agreed to not die right now. We need to keep moving downhill until I can see where we came out."

They walked along a thin strip of a path heading in zig zags down from the mountains in silence until Kron'ael said, "I suppose it wouldn't hurt to let you know where we are. I was trying to figure out the most effective way for me to handle this, and that in itself was strange. Things are usually so clear, but I've never been in this situation before. In fact, it's been a while since I've even been solid."

He absently kicked at a stone and watched it clatter down the uniformly colored landscape of the mountain. "Sometimes it's better for the chaos and tension of the situation to keep people in the dark, literally and figuratively speaking depending on the situation. However, I decided it would actually promote a better reaction if you knew what was going on. The delicious expectation of it all would add to the overall flavor."

He paused as they all looked back at him. Grace didn't look for too long as a rock rolled under her foot almost twisting her ankle. Her mind reeled and whirled with every new situation. Normally she considered herself a grounded individual. She understood how other people would think it was a strange description for her, with the colored hair and slightly old school punk rock dress code, but those were just a little bit of rebellion against the establishment she found herself in. It wasn't even sub-conscience, she knew she was doing it to be rebellious. She wanted to tweak the nose of those stuffy church people. It didn't mean she didn't like things planned out and regimented. If you looked at her sock drawer you would have thought she was seriously obsessive compulsive. All of this flowed though her mind as her thoughts reeled and whirled, and it bothered her. She didn't like not knowing what was going on.

"Well," the monster flourished a twisted hand, "I'd like to welcome you to Purgatory."

They all stopped and stared at him.

He shook his head and put a hand out to stop them from saying anything, "Keep moving sheep."

Sliding a few feet down the side of the mountain he stepped onto a new trail heading at a different angle down the mountain. Stopping he grunted with the effort of opening his arms wide as if to embrace the countryside spreading out below them. The mountain range they stood on spread out to the right and left encircling a valley floor covered with uniformly shaped blocks of construction. There seemed to be no specific pattern to the overall layout, but within each block they all were the same. Each had a stone wall surrounding a small city. The buildings within the city were laid out in a perfect grid and none of them were over two stories high. Everything seemed to be built of the same burnt umber colored stone, with square edges and straight lines dominating everything. Each city, if they could be called that, was separated from the others by rocky outcroppings or sand dunes for hundreds of yards. At the edges it all seemed to blur as if a heat mirage stopped the eyes from seeing perfectly what lay beyond.

They stumbled down the slope to the trail and stopped beside him trying to take it all in. Without looking at them he said, "Purgatory is the repository of most of the world's souls. They wait here until judgment day where it will be decided what their eventual resting place will be. I," he turned and looked at them, "don't want to be here. In fact, other than back there with that mad man, this is the worst place for me to be. I'm all," he gestured down at himself in disgust, "wrong here, but you will make everything all better."

His form seemed to blur for a moment and without moving he stood in front of Ray. With a jerking motion he grabbed the front of Ray's fashionably distressed t-shirt and pulled him down until they were face to face. "You see, pretty boy, each and every one of you is a gateway for me. Inside each of you," he reached up and grabbed Ray's face with his free hand and cupped his chin turning his head left and right as if to inspect a product before purchasing it, "is a spark. You're born with it. Some of you fan it into a flame while others simply learn to ignore it."

Shoving Ray away he watched as he stumbled back and fell into the dirt, then turned to the others, "You're evil. You're born evil. You've been marked with it and you stink of it from the day your great, great, ancestor decided to stand around and do nothing while his wife got talked into eating the wrong fruit. And you know what's always cracked me up?"

He turned and looked at Grace, "They always blamed the woman. That, in and of itself, has been a boon to my kind. We've used that blame to start wars, to burn people at the stake, and to ostracize entire sections of humanity. But really, honestly, who was the warning given to? To her? I think not. You know how I know?" He blurred again and poked Grace in the chest, "Because I was there. Looking down."

He pointed up, then his eyes slowly followed his own quivering arm up to the tip of his finger then up to the off color sunless sky. "Another reason I hate this place. No stars."

Pushing with the finger still pointing at Grace he watched as she fell. She felt like screaming at him. She just wanted to know what he was doing, why they were there, what he was planning, but all he wanted to do was talk. Fear kept her from speaking. The image of him pushing his hand into Mitch was still very fresh in her mind, and while he may look like a boxer crammed into a too small container she knew there was something there she didn't want to face.

"That spark of evil each of you is born with? That's my way home. Each of you is full up of potential. So many possibilities. Some lead to glory, but some," he turned and smiled at Mitch, "some lead to Hell."

Mitch took an involuntary step back then stopped himself as he saw the puff of black smoke rise up from him and drift toward Kron'ael who sucked it up. Grace watched as Mitch clinched his jaw, tensed his legs, and visibly straightened his back. She didn't know weather to applaud him or tell him to stop being stupid. Bad things happen to people who choose to stand up to evil. But it also made her want to stand up a little bit straighter. It made her want to not be scared.

"Now, now," Kron'ael chuckled and patted the air in front of him, "it won't hurt at all."

He blurred sideways and jabbed his hand down at Ray's chest, "Besides some make better doors than others."

A shriek split the air and Ray threw his head back. Kron'ael plunged his second hand down and started to pry Ray's chest open. Grunting with the effort he stepped onto Ray's thighs and dropped onto his knees knocking the air from Ray's lungs. Ray's mouth hung open as he tried to scream but no sound came.

Grace wanted to close her eyes but couldn't look away. From the corner of her eye she saw Mitch twitch like he was trying to decide what to do, but in the moment of his indecision it ended. Kron'ael pulled his hands free and stood. Stepping to the side he started kicking Ray.

"Stupid, stupid, stupid..." he screamed and screamed as he kicked.

The screaming broke Mitch from his frozen moment and he rushed forward balling his fists as he went. Kron'ael took a step back and swung his right fist in a backward sweeping arc. Mitch tumbled like he'd run into a lead pipe, his momentum causing him to tumble through the dirt and rocks of the trail.

"I hate this place." Kron'ael whispered to himself. "Fine, we'll just have to take the long way."

Smoke rose from Ray like a bonfire and Grace watched as Kron'ael breathed it in and grew a few inches. Then he turned to her, extending a hand. She felt something invisible grip the front of her shirt and yank her to her feet.

"I wanted to avoid him, but it seems I'll have to talk to that self pitying excuse for an angel after all." He dropped Grace on her feet, "Pick them up, and if you so much as think of back talking me I swear I'll tear your head off."

Grace twitched toward Ray then toward Mitch, not quite knowing who to help first, when Kron'ael turned to Ray and said, "Seriously boy, you're not even hurt, pull yourself out of the dirt."

Not even hurt, she found herself thinking, I just saw you stick your hands into his chest and pull him apart. But she wasn't in a state of mind to stand up to whatever this thing was so she turned to Mitch and tried to help him stand. When he was up and leaning on her she turned to see if Ray needed help only to find him dangling in the air next to Kron'ael.

Mumbling to himself Kron'ael twitched one arm forward and sent Ray tumbling down the trail. Without looking over his shoulder he said, "Well, my little lambs, are you waiting for an invitation?"

Chapter Three

Pain blossomed through James' knee and he tried to tuck as much as possible before his shoulder slammed into the ground followed quickly by his right ear. He hacked and coughed as dust coated the inside of his mouth.

"Ow!" Swear words were useful at certain times. They helped emphasize what you were talking about. In other times, however, even four letters were too much effort. His shoulder, however, decided to use some very creative swear words and screamed at him when he tried to roll onto his back.

"Ow, ow, ow..."

James decided since no one had tried to kill him yet it would be better for all involved, and since it was just him for the time being, to simply lie in the dust until he stopped hurting so much. Finally, being a smart boy, he rolled onto his left arm and pushed himself into a sitting position. He spit, then tried to create more spit just to get the taste of the dust out of his mouth. Looking down he tried to assess his situation. He must have fallen a few feet at least because his right knee was bleeding through a rip in his Dockers. Flexing his right leg he decided it wasn't too bad. It would ache for a while as he walked but that was about it. His other problem was his shoulder. Rolling it and wincing he came to the uniformed medical opinion that it was simply bruised.

Well, he thought, this was turning into a great rescue wasn't it. At least this time everything was much more cut and dried. The first time he'd met up with the Darkness everything had been muddled. One of the professors at his University had decided intolerant politics and religion were ruining the world, so when the Darkness had whispered in his ear promising power enough to change things he jumped at the chance. The professor, after secretly committing murder and trying to have James killed, had lied and convinced Kate to join him. Everything had gone down hill from there. Kate died, James retaliated and killed the professor, and the Darkness had snuck off with no one the wiser. Eventually James had realized something else had been behind, and most likely possessing, the professor.

This time, however, he knew what he was facing. He knew who the bad guy was. Unfortunately he didn't know where the bad guy was. The Darkness was obviously a ways ahead of him or else he would've attacked James while he was lying face down on the ground. His right leg made the decision it would be best to look around his immediate surroundings preferably while sitting since, really, the extra six feet he would gain by standing wasn't going to change the lay of the land. So James looked.

He was a bit confused as to how he got here, not that there was a magical door, that didn't confuse him. After the last two years not much on the weird scale could surprise him anymore, and seeing the first of the doors connecting worlds together had been one of the trigger events setting him on this path. He'd dropped out of college and set off on his one man demon hunt hoping to catch the thing and destroy it before it found the other door and moved on to another world.

The thing that confused him was the presence of a door in the middle of a church. As far as he knew, and granted it wasn't really all that much, he didn't think you could have one of the doors in the middle of a building and not have anyone notice it. They were invisible but still functionally there. You could reach out and touch them. Both of the doors he'd come into contact with had been strange for sure, but not like this had been. It was like the door hadn't been there at all before the Darkness opened it.

Other than his confusion at the door, his immediate surroundings were nothing special. He was in a thingy that cut back into some mountains. His father would be a little disappointed in him right now for not knowing the word for it. His dad was the kind of person that gave directions using North, South, East, and West instead of left or right. If you asked him where the bathroom was in the local mall he would tell you it was in the northwest corner of the building. How that helped, James didn't know because who brings a compass into the mall? Canyon wasn't the right word for this place. Maybe it was a draw. You would think after reading all his dad's Louis L'Amour books he would know stuff like this.

The draw, he decided to call it that just because it sounded right, wasn't very wide. It sloped down out of sight presumably to a valley or some such at the base of these mountains. James pushed himself up with his good arm and flexed his right knee a few times just to make sure it was actually working. As he straightened up something that had been nagging at him the whole time finally hit him. There were no plants. He looked around again. None. Not a blade of grass or a bush. Nothing. And also, slightly disturbing, was the fact that everything was the same color. The dust covering his clothes, the rocks, and even the mountains themselves were all a dirty orange in color.

Where was he, James wondered? Obviously another world, but what kind of world wouldn't have any plants and would be all orangeish? He looked up to check the position of the sun and realized even the sky was the same dirty orange, only a little lighter. It was like looking up into an overexposed picture of sand in a proverbial sunbaked desert. On top of that, or literally in that strange sky, he couldn't find the sun. It wasn't like it was hiding behind a cloud because there weren't any, and he had the feeling if there were any they would, strangely, be orange. Maybe it was behind one of the mountains, he thought, then stopped himself because, really, why did he need to find the sun? It wasn't as if knowing a direction would help him with anything. From all he could tell he'd stepped onto another world entirely, so finding what direction was west wouldn't exactly lead him home.

Well, James thought, first things first. Establish an escape route. He needed to find the door he'd come through and mark its location so if he needed to get away fast he wouldn't have to hunt around for it. Tracing back from his body imprint in the dust he found where his knee had hit the ground first. He then extended his hands and started walking toward where he expected to feel a door he couldn't see. That was the way with these door things he'd found. Whatever, or whoever, had put these doors in had, for some unknown reason, made them invisible and freestanding. With this one, it seemed, whoever had put it here had either done a terrible job or just thought it would be funny to put the exit a few feet off the ground.

Waving his arms around and limping he made three sweeps of the area before coming to the irritating realization that there was no door. "I knew it." He said to the orange dust. "I knew there was no way one of the doors could be stuck in the middle of a church and no one would notice it."

He flexed his bruised knee again, "So how am I..." He trailed off as too many how am I's wound through his head. How am I supposed to get back home was first but quickly followed by, how am I supposed to eat, drink, save the teens, and destroy the evil demon without an exit.

"Well," he looked up at the orange sky, "as someone once said, focus on what you can do not on what you can't."

James headed off toward the mouth of the draw hoping to find tracks the Darkness had left behind. He could at least get the teens back, and maybe even destroy the Darkness. Then he would have to figure out a way home. Because, honestly, staying here in orange dust world was just not an option.

Exiting the draw, the valley stretched out before him. A packed dirt road ran down from the mountains and split off to feed into walled cities. Each city looked like it could hold a few thousand people, but there were so many of them dotting the valley that, as a whole, they could hold over a hundred thousand people. It was the strangest set up James had ever seen. Some cities were almost close enough together for their walls to touch, and yet they definitely had walls to divide them from each other. It was almost like looking at a model for ancient Greek city states all crammed together into one area.

The cities were uniformly square and dusty orange. The buildings, from up here on the mountain, all looked like they were made from the same square cut sandstone. He couldn't see too many details but what he could see was a personally disturbing sameness to everything. The windows and doors were all the same size. The city walls were all the same with no details to set one city apart from another.

As James descended the side of the mountain range heading for the road he kept hoping for a capital city of some kind to come into view just so this all would make a little more sense, but it never did. As he got closer and was able to make out a few more details he noticed that each little city had, at its heart, a square castle. So maybe each city was its own state, but how would that be possible, he thought. Where would they get the necessary resources with only that much room? Come to think of it, James looked around the valley again, where did any of them get resources? The valley was as devoid of vegetation as the draw had been.

James looked down at the area around his feet then worked his way out from himself until he was scanning the horizon as far away as he could. He noticed a few oddities in the mountains off to his left and right far off in the distance, but the one thing that seemed to be true of the entire area was the lack of vegetation. There didn't seem to be a tree or even a random tumbleweed anywhere, and everything was the same dirty, dusty, orange.

So, he thought, I've stepped through a door that shouldn't be there into a world that seems to be totally dead.

Well, his brain replied, *maybe they killed it off then left.*

"What," he let himself speak to the air just to fill the uncanny silence, "like a war or something?"

Have you seen anyone moving around?

"Now that you mention it, no, I haven't." He squinted at the cities, "Huh, with no one around it might make it easier to find the Darkness and the kids."

Or, you might just have to search every single one of those cities to find him.

"Wow, you sure are optimistic aren't you?"

You know me. Just trying to balance out your pessimism.

"So, onward then?"

Can't go back.

"True enough brain," James said to himself, "true enough."

James slid and struggled down the side of the mountain until he reached the packed dirt road. It wasn't amazing but it was a sight better than just sliding down a dusty mountain.

After rounding a few bends in the road he saw a few houses ahead. Shrugging to himself, he knew there was no way he could have seen them from up the mountain since they were, not surprisingly, built from the same color rock as everything else and blended perfectly into the background. What did surprise him were the faces he saw peering out the windows.

He actually stopped and stared for a few seconds trying to wrap his mind around the fact there really were people here. His mind raced over the possibilities and he couldn't come to any kind of answer about how they were surviving here.

There was no food, no vegetation of any kind, and so far he'd seen no rivers or water anywhere. But this was a different world. Maybe everything was underground and they had entrances to it from their houses. That would explain a lot, James thought to himself as he gave his best smile to whoever was looking out the window at him.

Raising both of his hands with his palms facing out to show what he hoped might be the international sign that he meant no harm James said, "Hello." And the faces disappeared back into the house.

James took a deep breath and thought about what his next move should be. He was a stranger, and he knew that could mean bad things depending on what the people were like. In the brief time he'd looked at the people in the house he hadn't been able to really tell anything about them. There didn't seem to be any kind of lights on inside, and so they'd been mainly in shadow.

After standing there for a bit longer just in case they were making sure he wasn't a threat, he decided to move on. Now that he knew there were people around he would have to change his plans. Someone must have seen the Darkness pass by. Normally that wouldn't be the case since the sneaky little parasite could jump from shadow to shadow, but that would be impossible if he intended to keep his hostages with him.

James hadn't seen any of the teens left behind so he knew they were all still together with the Darkness. Even if the Darkness was hiding in one of the teens' shadows the people around here would definitely have noticed a group of three strangers walking along.

At each small home James found the exact same scenario repeated. He would see someone looking out at him, he would say hello in the best way he could think of, and they would vanish back into their home as if he carried the plague. James had almost decided that at the next house he would simply open the door. If the people were hostile they would have done something already, and he really needed to know if they were heading down into some underground city or something else unexplainable from his current point of view.

The road swung to the left around a bolder and split. James had been expecting it to fork at some point because of the multiple little cities he'd seen from farther up the mountain. He'd just come to the decision to take the left fork for no good reason except the need to decide on one of them, when he noticed a person on his hands and knees in the dust beside the road. He wasn't surprised to have missed the man because the clothes he wore were the exact same color as everything else, and he was covered in a fine layer of the orange dust that seemed to coat this whole world giving him a certain amount of de-facto camouflage.

James opened his mouth to say something but stopped when the man raised his hand as if to say, just a moment please. So he waited. The man couldn't have been much over five feet tall, and from what James could see he was what someone would call as thin as a rail. He wore a floppy hat that hid any hair he might have had, and his skin color was absolutely impossible to tell under the dust.

"Aha!" The little man said as he stood up, "This one should do nicely." Turning to James he held up a rock for inspection, "See how round it is?"

"Sure." James nodded slightly and unconsciously raised an eyebrow.

"I've been out here searching for God only knows how long for one like this." The little man sat down on a large rock beside the road, "You see," he gestured around vaguely, "there are no rivers. And that makes it unbelievably hard to find a nice round rock. So I thought to myself," he tapped himself on the side of his head, "self, where else would you find the right conditions for a round rock? And you know what I said?" He stared at James waiting for a reply.

James shrugged and thought this wasn't turning out at all like he wanted, "I really have no idea."

"Exactly!" With that the little man produced two other rocks from his pockets. They were approximately the same size and shape as the one he'd just found, and he began to juggle them. "I'm not a rock doctor, or whatever you would call someone who studies that kind of thing. I had no idea where to look."

The three rocks kept up a steady pace weaving their way through the air from one hand to the other. "So I thought again to myself. Fine, self, since you were no help with that one maybe you could be of more help with this question." Switching all three rocks to his right hand while still keeping them flying through the air, he tapped again at his head with the index finger of his left hand. "So I asked myself this question. Where would you find a lot of rocks? Because if you could find a lot of them then the chances of finding the right one go up by, well, a lot." He looked at James again, "So what do you think myself said to myself this time."

James smiled openly this time, "The mountains."

"Double exactly!" All three rocks flew high into the air as if to punctuate his statement. "Mountains, after all, are made up of rocks. And what'd you know?" He grabbed the falling rocks out of the air and held them out for James to see.

James nodded, "Perfect rocks."

The juggler shrugged, "Well, not exactly perfect. Mainly for the fact that they're rocks and not actual juggling balls." He eyed them as if they had personally offended him, "And it would be better if they were different colors." With this statement he looked around the world at large then back at James, "But, hey, what're you gonna do? You gotta work with what you have." He winked knowingly at James.

All through this strange interaction James' mind had been whirling. First, this juggler spoke English, which in turn made him think of all the science fiction TV shows he'd ever watched and wondered why all the aliens spoke the same language. Questions piled up in James mind like a train wreck until one broke free of the others, "Who are you?"

The juggler gave him a dashing smile, "That question really has no point my friend." The juggler looked around the world again, "In this place who a person is no longer matters. Your name, your family line, all of that is pointless. Here what matters is what you did with your life. So it's more what you are that counts here rather than who you are." He pointed back up the mountain, "Some of these people have been here for so long I bet they don't even remember their names, but they remember what they did with their life. What choices they made, or didn't make as the case may be."

"Then," James frowned at the juggler slightly, "where exactly am I?"

The juggler cocked his head to one side, "You don't know?"

"That would be why I asked." James said.

"How is it you don't know?"

"I don't know that either." James was getting a bit frustrated now, "Isn't that kind of the point of saying I don't know."

The juggler nodded at that, "Yes, yes it is. It's just that, well, I've never met anyone here that didn't automatically know where this was, and why they were here."

"Well," James said, waving his right hand in the air in a distinct get on with it gesture.

"This is," the juggler looked at James as if he was trying to think of a way of explaining the color blue to a blind person, "Uhm, well, the only name I've ever heard for this place is Purgatory."

"Purgatory?" James said.

"Yes," the juggler sounded slightly confused at this point, "the place where dead people go to wait for judgment day."

"Purgatory?" James said again.

The juggler shook his head, "Wow. I've never seen someone deny their own death before. This is, well, just wow."

"Deny my death? What're you talking about? I'm not dead."

"That is exactly what I'm talking about." The juggler sat back down on the bolder at the side of the road, "I've met people from just about every faith here, and even some from faiths I never even knew existed. Lots of them have no concept of purgatory, and some even outright denied its existence. But they all knew they were dead." He just stared at James for a second, "But you, wow, you're a first."

"But," James looked around the world, "but I'm not," he started putting all the pieces together. There was no sun, no clouds, and no vegetation of any kind. "So," he noticed again the absence of water anywhere, "there's no underground city where everyone's growing food and swimming in underground lakes?"

"What are you talking about?" The juggler looked around as if looking for something he was missing in all this conversation, "No. No underground anything."

"Where do you get your food from? And your water?"

"Food?" The juggler stood up again and walked over to James, "We're dead. Why would we need food, or water." He poked himself in the chest, "I died once," then he reached over and poked James hard in the chest, "and you must be dead if you're here."

"Ouch," James rubbed at his chest where the juggler had poked him. A thought struck him. "Do dead people bleed?" he lifted up his pant leg and showed the juggler where his knee had gotten scraped up when he fell through the door.

The little juggler stared at the dried up blood on James' leg for a few seconds. "That," he looked up at James then back down at the knee, "that's impossible."

James dropped his pant leg back into place and let out a heavy sigh, "At least we both agree on something. This is impossible."

"So you're really not dead?"

"No. I'm really not dead. And this," James waved his hands at the strange dusty orange world, "is really Purgatory?"

"Yep."

James looked out over the expanse of the valley below, "So every human that ever lived is down there?"

"Not exactly, no." The three rocks started doing their tumbling dance between the jugglers' hands again.

"What'd you mean not exactly? I thought Purgatory was where people waited to be judged at the end of time."

"Yes, it is." The rocks continued to fly between his hands.

"Then..." James didn't exactly know what to say.

The Juggler smiled at him. The smile said he knew a joke, and he would share it with you some time. "You see, not everyone has to wait, and this isn't the only valley, so some are in other valleys on the other side of the mountains."

"Not everyone has to wait?"

"Sure." The juggler changed the pattern of the flying rocks, "Some go directly to their eternal reward or damnation, while others have to wait to be judged."

"That's," James realized this conversation wasn't really helping him at all. "Why would he come here? I mean, it answers some questions like why the door was there but not because it wasn't a normal invisible door to another world."

"Uhm," the juggler spoke up, "can I interrupt you right there?"

"What?" James looked over at the juggler, "Oh, sorry, I was just thinking out loud."

"About what, exactly? Because honestly most of that sounded..." he wagged a finger in a circle around his ear while keeping the rocks going in the other hand.

"Well," James started, then realized it would take way too long to explain the whole thing, "I was tracking a criminal, and he kidnapped some kids and fled here."

"Here?" The juggler looked at James through the middle of the spinning rocks, "The only way a criminal could flee here is by dying."

"The criminal used magic."

"Magic?" The juggler shrugged, "Why didn't you say so in the first place. I've met a bunch of people down here who could do magic before they died. One old fellow from the new world said he would regularly bring dead bodies back to life to do work for him."

"Yes, well," James thought about that for a moment then shook his head, "anyway, I was just trying to figure out where he'd gone with the kids, and why he would bring them here of all places."

The Juggler looked at him and whispered conspiratorially, "Did he have any connection with angels or demons?"

"Yes, actually." James thought about it all for a moment, "He might have actually been a demon, but I'm not exactly sure on that point."

"Well, in that case," the juggler caught the rocks, tucked them into his pockets, started walking down the road, and motioned for James to follow him, "you have two options."

Following him down the road James said, "And those would be?"

"The towns or the gates."

"And what does that mean exactly?" James said.

"If your criminal has friends here he might head for the towns to trade the kids he has for a favor."

James looked out over the valley again at the hundreds of little towns, "And where would I start?"

"If he came out in the mountains like you."

"He did," James added.

"Then he would be headed to the town directly in front of us."

"All right," James said, "what about the gates?"

"On the one side," the Juggler pointed to a range of mountains to the right of the valley, "you've got your eternal reward, Heaven, Elysium, the Fields of Aaru, or whatever you want to call it. On the other side," at this he pointed to a stretch of desert to the left of the valley, "you have eternal punishment, Hell, Hades, Xibalba, etcetera."

"I doubt he'd head toward," James gestured to the right, "and with the teens in tow he probably wouldn't go straight for Hell, so..."

"So the town it is."

James nodded, "I'll start there."

The juggler stopped walking and said, "Good luck to you."

"Oh," James said as he stopped, "You're, uhm..."

The juggler smiled and pointed to the town, "I'd have to be crazy to go into that place, and I know for a fact people might have considered my decisions a bit strange at times but I'm definitely not crazy."

"Is there something wrong with the town?"

"Lots." The juggler nodded. "They scoop you up and put you to work building and digging. It's not natural down there. If you ask me, things have gotten a little bit out of hand and someone is going to need to do something about it."

He looked at his hands, "My hands are works of art. I've juggled worlds in these hands and once I even juggled for the Pope himself." He winked at James, "He thought I was just a street performer." He shook his head, "No way I'm going to let them use these hands to hold a shovel."

James nodded, realizing he shouldn't have expected any more help from the little juggler. "Well, thank you," he paused for a beat to wonder at the oddity of the entire situation. "Thank you very much."

The juggler smiled and bowed with a little flourish, "I would say a little blessing for you my mom taught me but we're in Purgatory so I really don't know how much help that would be. But," he gave the same big inside joke smile, "it couldn't hurt."

He put one hand on James' chest and said, "Mi sheg'molkha kol tov, hu yigmolkha kol tov. Selah."

The Juggler nodded, "I have the utmost confidence it will come true."

James smiled at him, feeling strangely better for the encounter, then turned and started toward the town.

People operate on expectations. Some might call it judging others, or even stereotyping, but in reality it is simply a set of expectations. When you leave a restaurant there is a set of expectations for the interaction with the hostess. When you walk into a fast food place there is a different set of expectations for interactions found there. Some expectations are good, some are bad, but we all operate with those expectations in place. If that weren't true no one would ever drive a car. We expect the other people to obey the stoplight while we turn in front of them. In James' case he'd built up a set of expectations about the world he was walking through, if you could really call it a world.

James was convinced the juggler had been telling the truth. The Darkness hadn't had any other means of escape. In that church with all the belief around it holding it in, he'd been effectively trapped. The Darkness had used the only option it could to escape. James expected it would have opened a door straight to hell if it could because James was fairly sure, at this point, the Darkness was some kind of demon. The only explanation he could think of in this case was that the Darkness couldn't open a door to hell from the middle of a church, so he opened one as close as he could and ended up in Purgatory.

So far no one had bothered him, and if the juggler were to be believed no one really cared what James did. They all were just waiting for the end and the final judgment. On the other hand the Juggler seemed to think the Darkness might have some kind of contact here in Purgatory. Maybe someone whom the Darkness had worked with was still waiting on judgment and the Darkness would be able to influence them to help out. But no matter what the situation, one thing the Juggler had said made James sure he could handle any situation that came along. The Juggler had said he knew people here who used to have magic. That meant they no longer did. James guessed when you died you no longer had access to whatever source the power came from. That was something he'd never learned. Two years ago a monk named Rupert had taught him about the power of belief, but the whole problem of the Darkness had cut short any real lessons other than how to use it. James had no idea where the power came from, or how it really worked. It was like using a smartphone. He could use it, and even use it well, but if someone asked him how it actually worked he would have no clue.

In this case, however, it gave him an advantage. No one here could use magic because they were dead. James was not dead. He was absolutely certain of that. A large portion of that certainty came from the aches still emanating from his banged up knee and shoulder. He was certain if he was dead they wouldn't hurt any more because pain was your body's way of telling you to get something fixed before it could kill you, and if you were dead it would no longer need to tell you that. Since you would already be dead. It made perfect sense to him.

So the short of it all was that James was alive and had magic while everyone else was dead and only had slightly orange dust and rocks to work with. This actually put a smile on his face as he walked through the gateless door in the wall of the town. He wondered what was the point of a wall if the door had no gates on it?

The small city seemed deserted. The buildings were all made of the same dusty orange stone, and there seemed to be no rhyme or reason to the layout of the town. James wondered if this was all built in preparation for dead people or if they had to build it when they got here? And why did they need buildings anyway? There wasn't going to be any rain. And if it did rain how rude would that be.

The street he was on continued straight into the heart of the city, and somewhere up ahead James heard sounds. In a normal world he would think people were doing construction, but here he had no idea what it could be.

"Oy, a new one."

James jumped at the sudden sound of the voice. Turning he saw four men emerging from a side street.

"Good," the one on the left said, "we could use a fresh back for the new section."

"Excuse me," James said, "I was wondering if you had seen..." Before he could finish, two of them jumped at him and grabbed his arms. "Hey," he said as he fixed the belief in his mind that they were light as feathers and he was as strong as a gorilla. With the power of his belief fueling his muscles he flexed to throw them against the wall of the nearest building. Nothing happened.

"Now don't struggle," one of them said as they pulled his arms behind his back.

James pictured in his mind a wall of force blasting out from him in a circle knocking them all away. He believed this was possible because he'd done it before. He knew it would work just like he knew the sun would come up in the morning. Again he pictured his belief triggering the power and he pushed out with his arms to give a physical push to the magic, and again nothing happened.

Handcuffs of some kind clicked into place on his wrists behind his back, and the four men started taking turns shoving him down the street in

38

the direction of the sounds. Something had gone wrong. Maybe, James thought, he hadn't believed enough. His teacher had told him the belief could only change the world if you totally believed. Like a fish believed it could swim or a bird could fly. James looked up into the sky, like you believe the sun... With that thought he paused. There was no sun here. No one here took a next breath of air. He slumped as the reality of the Jugglers words hit him. Magic didn't work here. Not because they had lost the ability when they had died, but because this wasn't a world. Belief, no matter how strong, couldn't change what this place was. James' world was a world of change, constant change. Over time mountains would fall and oceans would shift. But here, in Purgatory, nothing changed. Here you were done. James remembered a Bible verse he'd learned as a little kid about the three greatest things; faith, hope, and love. Purgatory was the permanent end of two of those.

James slumped and let the men drag him down the dusty street. There could be no faith in a place where everything was seen, and all you were doing was waiting to be judged on what had already happened. And hope? No. This place was the end of all things. Here hope had no place. And in a place without hope, and without change, belief was nothing. His advantage was gone.

The street narrowed then opened out on a city square. The noise had grown steadily and when James raised his head he saw what had been causing it. Hundreds, possibly thousands, of people were digging. One of the men unlocked his handcuffs, shoved a pickaxe into his hands, and pushed him toward the pit in the center of the square.

Chapter Four

Stone is heavy. It's also scratchy and awkward, but mostly heavy. Have you ever tried to just pick up the biggest rock you could find? It isn't always that it's too heavy, or amazingly heavy, but it's just too heavy for you. You always have a sense that someone could pick it up, and maybe you could if you could just get a better grip on the thing. But no matter what it's just heavy. And after lifting half a dozen or so very large rocks the weight seems to become proportionately worse.

James had learned early on that your head actually pounds when you lift stone. The knob on the back of his head was throbbing as he tried to pry another stone loose from the orange soil. It was a constant reminder of his first escape attempt. For the millionth time he wondered what God had been thinking when he made this place orange. It just wasn't right. If you're going to have people waiting for what could be thousands of years to be judged then why not give them some variety of color. This was just mind numbing. He stuck the end of his pickaxe under the rock and pried it loose. His head throbbed just looking at the thing knowing he would have to haul it out of here somehow.

He hadn't expected the guards to be so fast. When they'd first pushed him into the pit and told him to get digging he figured he would just wait 'til the first break then make a run for it. An undetermined amount of eternity later he realized dead people don't take breaks. So he changed his plan. He'd been working out lately and was in, what he considered to be, fairly good shape. While the guards were dead and were not in any shape at all that he could determine. He knew they were strong from his brief encounter in the street, but they couldn't have endurance.

He dropped his rock on the foot of the nearest guard and ran. He heard swearing from behind him, then his head exploded and his face had the opportunity to introduce itself to the ground. Thinking back on it he was fairly sure one of them had hit him with a shovel. It hurts to be hit by a shovel. It also knocks you unconscious.

When James had woken up they had given him his pickaxe back and pushed him back into the hole. And here he was. Learning about the proportional weight of stone versus the tiredness of the person trying to lift it. He had to do something soon or he would be too tired to do anything. They might be able to go forever, literally, without a break, but he wasn't dead. Something was going to give. If they figured out what he was then what? Would they kill him? And what happened to you if you died here? Did you just pop right back up in the exact same place except dead?

He wasn't sweating, and that had struck him as strange. Of course strange was also proportional like everything else in this hole. He wasn't sure how long he'd been working. It was hard to tell time since the light never changed, but he was sure he should have needed a drink by now, and he didn't. He hadn't needed to go to the bathroom. He wasn't hungry. Maybe this place took care of those things. Maybe since nothing changed he was exactly as he had been when he came through the door in the first place. But if that was true then why was he getting tired? That wasn't fair. If he didn't get hungry then why get tired?

"Hey!" A guard yelled down at him, "Get back to work!"

"Or what?" James yelled back, "You'll kill me?"

"Listen wise guy there are things worse than death that the boss can do." The guard stepped closer to the edge of the pit.

"Like what? Make me work in a stinking pit till judgment day. Oh wait," James waved a hand around, "I already am," he snapped back.

The guard stepped to the very edge and looked down at James. Before he could say anything James hooked his pickaxe around the guard's ankle and pulled. Using the leverage James hauled himself out of the hole while pulling the guard down. Before the guard could get back up James kicked him hard in the head not caring how much it would hurt because, hey, the guy was already dead anyway what harm could it do. Another guard ran at him and James swung hard with the pickaxe catching him in the right temple and sending him sprawling.

Sprinting toward the narrow city streets his eyes darted back and forth trying to make sure none of the guards got behind him again. Two of them came at him from the right and James threw the pickaxe horizontally causing them to slow down, and dodge, to avoid being hit. Another came from his left swinging a shovel at his head. Not wanting to have a matching knot on the other side of his head James turned, lowered his shoulder, and charged the guard. The shovel swung through the air where his head had been a moment before just as James' shoulder knocked the wind from the guard's lungs. I guess that means the dead breathe, James thought as he pushed away from the falling guard and sprinted toward the nearest street.

The buildings didn't really rise on either side of him when he made it to the street. They were, at best, two stories tall with most of them being one story. They reminded him of pueblos in the American southwest. They had the same adobe sandstone style, and everything was dusty. Turning a corner at random he expected to see people in the street but it was empty. This whole town felt empty. Or maybe a better way to put it was that it looked empty. There was no one to push past as he ran down the street. No one stood in their doorways to watch the crazy man run by. No one closed the shutters on the windows to keep from being involved. But James knew people had to be here, or what was the point of the houses. Were they all working at the quarry he'd just run from?

Turning another random corner his mind popped from being occupied about the strangeness of Purgatory towns to the not so strangeness of the row of guards waiting for him in the middle of the street. Shifting his weight and trying to turn around proved more difficult than he'd thought as his feet slid out from under him and billows of orange dust kicked up from the street. His left hip hit the hard packed dirt. He grunted with the impact, rolled to his stomach, then tried to get his feet back under himself. Just as he was starting to push off with his toes a guard landed on him, then another, and another, driving the air from his lungs, and pushing his face into the dust of the street.

They wrenched his arms behind his back and shackled them. Being yanked to his feet by the shackles and pushed down the road James had to wonder what they were going to do with him now. "You have to admit," James said, "that was a pretty good try."

"Huh," one of the guards snorted. "Right."

"Actually," a guard behind him said, "that didn't even rate in the top ten, I would say."

"What?" James said, "But I got away."

"No, you didn't," said the voice behind him.

The guard holding his right arm said, "You didn't even make it halfway to the walls."

"Almost halfway," the guard behind him added.

The guard on his right pointed back to where they had caught him, "If you had kept on straight instead of turning you'dve had a better chance."

"Well," James said, a little annoyed at being told he hadn't done as well as he'd thought, "what do you have to do to make the top ten?"

"One bloke," the guard on his left spoke up in a lower-class British accent, "you remember his name?" He asked as he looked around at the other guards.

"Which one?" Asked the guard on his right.

"The one who got up onto the roofs."

"Oh, right."

There was a pause from all the guards before the one on the left continued, "Anyway, there was this one, whose name at present none of us seem to be able to remember because really, there are so many of you it becomes a bit ridiculous after a while."

"James," James said.

"Huh, what?" The guard looked a bit shocked to be interrupted in the middle of his story.

"My name. It's James."

All four of the guards looked at James uneasily as the one on the left continued, "Well, we didn't ask now, did we? Anyway, as I was saying before I was so rudely interrupted, there was this little bloke who made it up onto the roofs and jumped from one to the other until he made the walls."

"What happened to him?" James asked.

"Don't know. He's the only one who's ever gotten away."

"Now," the guard behind him added, "we have people on the rooftops for that kind of problem."

"Good to know." James said as they continued to pull and push him down the empty streets.

After a few more turns James saw what must be the central keep. It rose three stories high in a grand expression of sandstone orange cubism. It reminded James, in a way, of a step pyramid, but it tried to look a little like a castle at the same time. It wasn't large by any standard. On his single trip through Europe a few years before James had seen keeps three to four times the size of this one. "So, we're going to see the boss?"

"Yep." The guard on his right said. "He's the one who decides what to do with your kind."

"So, how did you come to be a guard?" James asked.

They all looked at him like he was slightly crazy and the one behind him answered, "It's who we are," as if that should explain everything perfectly.

Right, James thought, because when all is said and done and your life is over, you are who you are. All your choices have been made. This was Purgatory. The waiting place. Here you just were who you were and that was that. He guessed these men had been guards in their life and so were guards in death because you can't change anything now. Nothing changes here. That seemed to be the point of this place.

James was led through the open gateway of the keep and down the main hallway. A few doors led off from the hallway along with stairs. Most of the stairs went down James noticed. Maybe that explained the lack of size for the keep. Maybe the majority of it was underground. There were no decorations on the walls. No paintings or tapestries. Nothing broke the simple monotony of color and form. Everything continued being square, and dusty.

They entered a large central chamber and James looked up to see if the ceiling was a dome. He chuckled to himself with a lack of surprise when he saw that it was flat and square and, of course, the same monotonous color. It would have been better, he thought to himself, as the guards pushed him into a seat in front of an empty throne, if it had been the orange of the fruit. But no, this was the orange of dust, of sand. This was the color of boredom.

Looking up at the empty throne at the front of the room, James wondered who would be in charge of a place like this. All the leaders of history were here somewhere. He mused that at some point they had started building their own little kingdoms. If you were who you were, like the guards, then Alexander the Great would be a king. Maybe this little town was run by Genghis Khan, or Julius Caesar. That would at least be interesting.

The room shook. A light shot its way into James' brain. He closed his eyes against it but it burned through his eyelids. He smelled flowers. His mind tried to make sense of what kind of flowers but gave up for lack of caring. After a few seconds the light seemed to become bearable, not that it was any lighter, but he felt now he could at least open his eyes and look without being blinded. When he did open his eyes, what he saw took his breath away.

Sitting on the simple throne in front of him was the most magnificent being he'd ever laid eyes on. It glowed. James tried to think of a better way to describe it but it was all that came to mind. Light seemed to well up from inside of it. Like if a person was one of those chemical light sticks, and you shook them up.

From somewhere in the room a voice called out, "Behold," the voice cracked then recovered, "and kneel before the lord and protector of this poor circle of Purgatory," hands from behind him pushed James off his seat and onto his knees, "the Archangel Jah-diel!"

James looked up and his mind began to blather.

An Angel?

Uhm, was all James could think in reply.

Maybe he'll help us?

Uhm, well, we are chasing a demon, aren't we?

And aren't Angels supposed to fight those things?

That does seem to be what you normally hear.

And he doesn't seem too busy here, does he?

Not really, no.

Brilliant. Then we'll ask for his help.

But we just beat up some of his guards and tried to run away.

Oh for Heaven's sake, and I actually mean that, he's an Angel. By definition he has to forgive you and help you fight a demon.

Well, things are looking up a little, aren't they.

James made eye contact with the angel and flinched. Blue spots danced across his vision and tears welled up and ran down his cheeks. He thought of Galileo going blind by looking through his telescope at the sun, and wondered why anyone needed to be warned not to do that.

"So," the voice of the angel actually tinkled like wind chimes, "another soul who thinks it's too good for work."

"No," James started to say.

"Silence."

James watched the angel out of the corner of his eyes since looking directly at him didn't seem to work. The angel leaned back in its throne, "You come here thinking you are important because you were someone important in your short life. Kings, priests, and lately senators all end up here. You think you are too good to work for the betterment of every soul in my keeping."

"I need your help." James blurted, "A demon kidnapped some kids and..."

A blast of force knocked James from his knees onto his back, "I said silence." To James the angel now sounded like an angry little wind chime and his mind wondered how anyone could be taken seriously with a voice like that until another blast of force wrapped itself around him and lifted him from the ground. Right, James thought, that's how you get taken seriously. The angel motioned with one finger and James floated closer.

"Thousands of you come here to me, and you all have your problems." The angel briefly glanced up, "What did I do to deserve this?"

He stood and with a flick of his hand James slammed into the wall across the room. "For millennia after millennia I have been here listening to your whining prattle about how you need to go back because someone is in danger, or your nation can't survive without you." He walked to James, reached out and picked him up, "Well, now you are mine, and you will dig and you will build. I have been left here long enough, and for what?"

Again he looked up. "For what!" His voice was a hammer blow to James' chest and small cracks appeared in the walls.

"I am an Archangel. One of the first of creation, and here I sit with crawling worms like you eating away at me like a corps. But I have found it."

Unable to look away, James' mind turned, as it did in times of crisis, to sarcasm.

Crazy eyes.

Ya think?

I'm just saying. Behind that nice glow, that angel has crazy eyes.

Jah-diel raised his hand and James floated higher, "I found a way out, and I will take it."

Turning to the guards Jah-diel threw James at their feet, "This one irritated me. Put him in the darkness for five hundred years. That should teach him what his place is."

The guards touched their fists to their hearts and said in unison, "Yes, my lord."

The angel turned and was simply gone. The empty room was dark without his presence. The guards reached down, grabbed him under his shoulders, and lifted him to his feet. As they pushed him out the door James muttered, "Just had to be a pissy angel, didn't it."

"What'd you say?" the guard behind him poked him between his shoulder blades.

"Just commenting on the grace and mercy of your angelic master," James said.

"Well, you'd be a bit out of sorts, too, if you were stuck overseeing this place for all of time, wouldn't you?" The now-familiar guard on his left said.

"So," James tried to think of what to do next, "that gives him the right to abandon his duty and start abusing souls?"

"It's not like he's going to kill anyone," said the guard behind him.

"That's true," James said and thought at the same time.

I can't spend five hundred years in the dark, whatever that might mean, he thought.

And it's not like you can kill any of them.

This is true.

So what does this mean?

Well, I could, uhm, hit them with, uhm...

Right. Still wearing handcuffs, aren't we?

Yes.

"You know." James said, "Mr. Boss man angel didn't say anything about these handcuffs. And it's not like I'm going anywhere."

"Right." All four of the guards laughed, "You must think we're stupid or something. Nope, they stay on."

Great, James thought and wiggled his wrists around in the cuffs. They cut into him and blood started trickling down into his palm.

Ouch.

Yes, but sometimes you just have to do what you have to do.

I know, but still, ouch.

At least they won't expect it.

And why is that?

Dead people don't bleed.

James pressed his right wrist hard into the cuffs and turned it until the metal bit through his skin. Blood ran down. James moved his hand around trying to get the blood under the cuffs on all the sides. Finally squeezing his hand together as tight as he could, he pulled. He twisted his hand again and grunted at the pain.

"You can't get out of those." The guard on his right said, "We perfected them over a vast amount of time, you might say."

Right, James thought as his hand popped free, but you never tested them on someone with active blood flow. He twisted and shoved one of the guards away. Turning he raised his left hand with the cuffs still attached and swung it like a medieval morning star. It cracked satisfyingly against a guard's head. Turning and running James wondered which direction to go this time. He remembered from his first view of the city that the keep was at the center, but he also remembered there was no discernable pattern to the streets.

A guard jumped out at him from a side street and James ducked and swung the chain hard at his knees. There was a crack of something breaking and the guard tumbled over the top of James. He decided to go as straight as possible, mainly because turning required him to slow down. Two more guards dropped down off the rooftops in front of him and James lowered his shoulder and sped up. Hitting the guard on the right just under the sternum and hearing the breath whoosh out of his lungs, James rolled over him and lashed out with the chain in the general direction of the other guard.

The guard caught the chain and yanked James forward and into the dust of the street. James knew he had to finish this fight quickly. The longer he took the more guards would show up.

Long ago, in what now seemed like a different life, his Dad had taught him how to fight. It hadn't been much really, just a few lessons on how to stand and how to throw a punch so things would actually work. Mainly the lesson consisted of learning when to fight and when not to fight. It was one of the memories that had stayed with him all these years, and one of the many reasons why he looked up to his Dad so much. He could still hear his Dad say, "You should never start a fight, but if someone starts one with you I want to make sure you're the one who ends it." Unfortunately, in this situation, none of those lessons helped. He was facedown in the dirt with one hand chained and held by a dead guard that worked for an irritable angel.

So he did what any human does against an aggressive male attacker. He rolled to his side and punched straight up into the guard's crotch. James felt a twinge of regret as the guard rolled onto the ground twitching. Pushing himself up his right wrist screamed at him and James was sure some permanent damage had been done. At the least he was sure he would have a scar, and he had no idea how he was going to patch it up once he'd escaped. There wasn't exactly a hospital around the corner.

Ahead of him James saw the wall of the city. Turning right, he vaguely wondered if this would get him in the top ten of escape attempts. He saw four or five guards blocking the street and beyond them the open gate of the city. James looked to his left and right and didn't see any alternative. The surface of the city wall was smooth and it was too high to jump up and grab the edge. The houses next to him were also smooth. They were shorter but James still didn't think he could grab the edge of the room and pull himself up, especially with his right wrist and hand the way it was.

As he charged in, one of the guards leapt for him and James smashed him in the face with the whipping chain on his left hand. Another guard tackled him from the right and James rolled with it until he was on top of the guard and looking down into his face. James smashed his forehead into the bridge of the guards nose and heard a crunch. Starting to push off the third and fourth guards kicked him in the sides at the same time. On the second kick James was able to grab the foot of one of the guards and pull him over him causing the other guard to try and stop his kick mid swing. James shoved the newly fallen guard into the legs of the other one causing him to fall. James got to his feet, kicked the ever-present dust into the gasping faces of the two guards, then turned and ran for the open gate.

The world boomed and turned white. James found himself sliding on his back through the dusty street until a house stopped him. Shaking his head he blinked to clear his eyes. Looking up at the gate his heart dropped when he saw the Angel blocking his escape.

Chapter Five

They drug him through the streets. Blows from guards knocked him into unconsciousness any time he tried to look up. When his eyes finally opened all he could see was the polished stone floor of the keep. James' foggy mind stuck on how clean the floor was compared to the rest of this dusty world. Hands pulled him off the floor and stood him up.

Jah-diel sat on his throne. His back was straight, his palms rested on his knees, and his eyes burned. "You have injured my guards. You have insulted me."

The Angel stood. Glowing white wings appeared from unknown dimensions and spread behind him. The edges brushed the walls, the ceiling, the floor. "You think this place is a playground for your amusement?"

The wind chime quality of his voice was replaced by invisible pressure like a hand pressing on his sternum. "You think you're here because you're better than others?" The Angel stepped down from the raised dais, "You are a fly. You are less than a fly." He reached out, grabbed James by the throat, and lifted him till they were eye to eye, "I am master here, and you will obey me."

Dropping James to the ground Jah-diel gestured at the floor and a block of stone rose waist high. The guards grabbed James, dragged him to his knees, and shoved him against the stone. His mind was still foggy and slow from the beating he'd received coming back from the gate. All he could do was stare at the stone and wonder what it was there for.

One of the guards went around the stone to face James while another grabbed his right arm and pushed it across the surface of the stone. Facing each other across the stone they held his arm in place. A light from his left caused James to flinch then look up. Jah-diel was holding a sword. Fire flickered where a blade edge should have been. James looked from his arm stretched across the stone to the burning length of the sword and back. Finally a thought fought its way through the fog in his brain, and as the realization of his situation dawned the Angel brought the sword crashing down. Pain blossomed through his arm and exploded in his brain. The world shrank to a small white dot then vanished.

Chapter Six

Coughing and spitting dust he woke up. Rolling onto his side he started to push himself up and pain shot up his arm causing him to collapse and curl up into a fetal position.

"Slow down there, mein freund." A voice drifted through the pain. "You're going to need to take it a little bit slow for a while."

Finally when the pain subsided to a dull throb James opened his eyes. Unwavering light poured into his eyes from the dull amber sky. He could tell he wasn't in the citadel anymore, but beyond the sky above and the dirt packed hole around him he had no way of determining his location. The floor was hard packed and ended a few yards away at a solid dirt wall. He lay there taking deep breaths and trying to figure out the situation. He had no idea where he was or how he'd gotten there. Someone behind him was saying something but since they didn't sound panicked James decided to ignore them for the time being and take stock of himself.

How'd I get here?

I don't remember, his brain replied.

What is the last thing I do remember?

Running, being caught.

Right, I was trying to escape.

I kinda remember something else. His brain said hesitantly.

So do I.

The Angel.

A block of stone.

An honest to God flaming sword.

And then...

James rolled onto his back, and held his hands up. He swallowed, took a slow breath and looked at the blank space where his right hand used to be. His mind was blank. A voice continued talking somewhere in the distance but inside him nothing stirred. Slowly he bent his elbow and looked at the burned stump. Reaching over with his left hand he gently touched it and a slight flare of pain ran up his arm.

"They cut my hand off."

"You're lucky." The voice behind him said, "The man who was in here before me had his feet cut off."

"What?" James looked around to see another man sitting a few feet away.

"His feet." The man pointed at his feet to reinforce his point. "I guess they think it's fitting to cut off whatever you used to try and escape. The one who was in here before me could run like the wind. So they cut his feet off."

James just stared at him. Even in his state of shock, James recognized the man. "You're..."

"Nein," The man held up a hand to stop James, "I know who I am."

James slightly nodded at him then looked back at his arm.

"So," the man said, "I've been down here for a while. I must have missed some fun up there if you did well enough to warrant getting your hand chopped off."

James looked slowly back over at the man, then around at his prison. It was a hole in the ground. It looked to be around fifteen feet across, but James wasn't sure. He'd never been good at judging distance. It seemed to be about the same depth at about fifteen feet.

"I," James hesitated, "I slipped out of the hand cuffs and used them to knock the guards out of the way."

"Ahh," the man said, "How far did you get?"

James looked at the man, stared at the recognizable features for a moment, then said, "How far'd you get?"

The man shrugged, "Maybe three or four blocks." He looked up at the indistinguishable sky, "I was..." he sighed. "Well," he gestured at himself, "you obviously know who I was."

James nodded and slumped back again.

"I wasn't trying to escape from the city, you see," he paused and looked down at the dirt. "It was the stares of all the people around me." He looked up at James, "Do you understand?"

James nodded again.

"So, how far did you make it?"

James slowly put his left hand on the ground and pushed himself into a sitting position while holding his right arm against his chest. "I was at the main gate."

"Well," the man looked amazed, "that's the best I've heard since I've been here. How'd the guards stop you?"

"They didn't."

"Then..."

James looked up from staring at his arm, "The Angel blocked the gate."

"Oh." Was all the man said.

"So," James hesitated for a moment, "did you really commit suicide?"

The man snorted, looked down at his hands for a moment, then nodded.

James looked away and said, "I'm not dead you know."

"Right." The man said, "And I'm not Adolf Hitler."

James started to say something but the man held up his hand to stop him, "Look, we all have to face it sometime. We end up here and it comes crashing down on us. I lied to myself for most of my life, and I even lied to myself when I chose to end my life, but I can't lie anymore."

He waved at the ever-burnt sky above them. "This place makes it impossible to lie. Your whole life gets spread out before you and all those places in it where you convinced yourself what you were doing was right or necessary get shown to just be lies." He sighed and poked at the dust, "It's why I ran. I couldn't stand the accusations in all those eyes, because I knew they were right."

The man looked up at James, "You are dead. We're all dead. That's what this place is. It's the end. Is that why you ran? You thought you could get away from it? Go back to being alive? Fix the problems and the lies?"

"No," James shook his head. He couldn't take his eyes off the spot where his hand used to be. "But I'm not sure it matters any more."

He lay back down and covered his eyes with his arm to block out the ever-present light. Did it matter? He needed to catch the Darkness. He needed to save the teens. But why did it matter? It mattered because that monster had gotten Kate killed. It mattered because Grace was out there and he couldn't let it all happen again. But there was nothing he could do now, nothing for him to be. He couldn't be the good guy any more. Not like this.

He tried sleeping but it didn't go well. His arm throbbed, his mind played tricks on him, and so many things you do automatically while trying to get comfortable, especially laying on the ground, involve your hands.

Reasons, excuses, and complaints all warred for attention. He tried to ignore his own voice in his mind, but in the emptiness of the sky above and the silence of the hole eventually he had to face it. What rose to the top and silenced all the other voices was anger. It bubbled up and his muscles tensed. He wanted to strike out, to smash and beat something, but even that reminded him of his missing hand.

So his anger turned inward.

Stupid.

I had magic. I had power.

Still, his brain screamed at him, *who did you think you were, a superhero? Did you think this was a comic book?*

No, I just...

Just what James? Just thought it would be one of your fantasy books? One of your sci-fi movies?

That's not it at all!

Then what? Did you not realize when you run into dangerous situations you get hurt? Did your mom not teach you that?

But I had magic!

And now what do you have? No power, no way out, you have nothing but dust.

I have to save those kids. I have to save her.

What?! Really?! You're broken and stuck in a hole and you think you still have a chance? No, no, not even a chance.

"Shut up!" His voice echoed off the walls of the hole.

He pushed himself up with his left hand and ignoring the other man began to pace back and forth across the hole.

"Why did I end up here anyway?"

He turned to the other man and raised his only hand, "and I don't want to hear from you because I am still alive."

James stomped across the hole and punched the wall, turned, and raised three fingers, "Three teens. Heck, I don't even know if they're teenagers, I just assumed they were because of where they were sitting."

He yelled at the hateful sky and kicked a rock, "I could've just let him take them, but no, I had to be a hero, didn't I?"

Tears rolled down his cheeks and he raised his right hand to wipe them away before remembering he didn't have a right hand anymore. Staring at the red scarring stump his mind went blank. Eventually one thing filled the emptiness. A simple question of why.

"Why?"

He continued to stare at the stump of his arm, "Why me, why this, why did I, why didn't I?"

He looked at the other man in the hole with him, "Would you do it differently if you could?"

The man made eye contact with James and held it for a long moment, "Anger drove me to do what I did. I don't know if I could do it differently. If you put me in the same situation with the same people and the same events, I really don't know. We are who we are."

James slumped to the ground exhausted. "We are who we are." He laid his head back into the dust, "Who am I?"

His mind turned over and over the picture of those three teenagers being drug through the door by whipping arms of shadow, and each time he wondered if they were really worth it. He didn't know them or their families. They might have been terrible kids who teased and bullied. It might have been better for the world to let them get dragged into Purgatory. Each time he tried to justify letting them go, and each time he remembered Grace. The look on her face when he had openly considered letting them die had stuck with him. People constantly talked about doing the right thing, but words were like dehydrated water to a thirsty man. When it really came down to it he hadn't jumped through the door to do the right thing, he had jumped through to save her.

Eventually he drifted into a half sleep with dreams of his family drowning in orange dust. Noises woke him and he looked over to see the guards pulling his fellow prisoner out of the hole.

How long have I been here? James wondered.

It's hard to tell with no night or day.

My fingernails don't grow, and neither does my hair.

That's kind of a bonus, right?

What should I do?

I don't know...

Depression washed over him slowly. He couldn't escape. His power didn't work anymore. And, he looked for the millionth time at his arm, his hand was gone. A tear rolled down his cheek and dripped into the dust. James reached out with his left hand and pushed it around making a little muddy depression. Sighing he started to write a letter to his dad.

Back in college, before any of this had started, before he knew how to use the power, and before he knew anything about the Darkness, he would write letters to his parents every week. They would call every once in a while too, but it was fun to write to them. He would tell them about his classes, the people he met, and how everything was going. Now, James wrote out his depression. His frustration poured into the dust. Looking at the little ball of mud from his tear he couldn't help but think from dust we come and to dust we shall return.

In his mind his dad told him to keep trying, there was always hope. But nothing changes in Purgatory. Hope is dead in a place where nothing can or ever will change.

His father's voice in his mind then said something strange, "A place doesn't change on its own." Oddly his father's voice sounded a lot like the little Juggler he'd talked with, "Nothing changes unless we change it, and sometimes you have to make your own hope."

Thoughts started tumbling through James' mind so fast he wasn't even thinking in complete thoughts. He would get halfway through one and know what it was before it was done. There was a thought about how the definition of insanity was doing the same thing over and over and expecting different results. There was a thought about sometimes you have to make your own luck, and how God helps those who help themselves.

"These are all wonderful," James said to the dust, "but how do they help me?"

"Who you talking to down there?" A head poked over the edge of the hole.

James looked up at the guard, "Don't you ever get bored?"

The guard looked down at him and shrugged, "What you gonna do? I'm a guard, so I guard."

James nodded and said, "What's your name?"

"Why's it matter?"

"Because," James said, "if I'm going to be sitting here with you for who knows how long it would be nice to know who I was spending so much time with."

"Well," the guard paused and thought for a moment, "Octavian."

James eyebrows went up at that, "You mean Octavian Caesar? Emperor of Rome Octavian?"

"Ha!" The guard swung his legs over and sat on the edge of the hole, "Don't I wish. Then at least I would have some great memories to relive while I wasted away in this sand trap."

James nodded knowingly, "Where are you from Octavian?"

"Thrace."

James thought for a moment trying to place the name on his modern mental map. All he could remember from his western civ class was it was somewhere to the east of Italy in the Roman Empire. "So you are Roman then?"

"Yep," Octavian put his elbows on his knees and rested his chin in his hands. "I served in the legion under Hadrian himself."

"Did you make it all the way to the north of…" James was about to say Scotland but realized they wouldn't have called it that during Octavian's time so he finished in a questioning voice, "Britannia?"

"Na," his voice was a touch sad, "I died on the march through Gaul."

"I thought Caesar had pacified that area long before Hadrian marched through it," James said.

"Yeah, that's true. I didn't die in battle."

"Oh," James paused to see if he would add anything, and when nothing more came he asked, "What happened?"

"It rained for weeks on end, you see, and my feet just got worse and worse." He shrugged thinking about it, "There wasn't anything the surgeon could do once the infection had set in."

"That," James paused, "sounds like a horrible way to die."

"I remember laying there thinking how I just wanted to get it over with and die already so I could move on to something better," Octavian said.

"And you wake up to this." James gestured around at the world with the stump of his right arm.

"Exactly," Octavian replied.

"I don't think this is the way it's supposed to be." James said.

Octavian shrugged, and James continued, "This is supposed to be a place where you wait and reflect on what your life was before you're judged at the end, not a place where you build a castle for an irritating Angel who seems to be ticked off just by being here."

Octavian snorted, "He is an irritating cuss, isn't he? You should hear him grumble about how bad he's been treated, and how he's better than this place, and what did he ever do to deserve being put here." He shook his head, "As if we have a choice about being here."

Taking that as a cue James decided it couldn't hurt to try one more time, "Speaking about having a choice in being here. I didn't actually die to get here."

"Right," Octavian said.

James was expecting that, "I have a job to do Octavian. I came here, to Purgatory, to finish my job."

"Right," Octavian said again.

James shook his head, "I'm not doing a very good job of explaining. How 'bout I just give it to you straight." James stood up, took a deep breath, and said rapid fire, "I was chasing a demon who kidnapped three kids to use as hostages. He took them here. I followed him and was captured by the guards and brought here. I need to get out so I can get the kids back and destroy the demon."

"Right," Octavian stood up and dusted off his pants, "I'm gonna stretch my legs a bit. When you think up another story, let me know." Octavian disappeared over the rim of the hole.

"Do you enjoy being here?" James yelled. "Do you enjoy doing what that angel tells you to do? Do any of you enjoy being here?"

"Of course we don't enjoy it," Octavian looked back over the edge. "Isn't that the point of it?"

"Who said so?" James said. "Who said you're supposed to be unhappy here?"

"Well," Octavian paused, "nobody has to say it."

"Look, I don't care if you believe me or not, but I have something I need to do. I think you can help me. And I think you would be a lot happier helping me than just sitting here listening to," James waved his stump of an arm, "that maniac angel ranting about how bad his life is while he cuts off peoples' body parts."

Octavian just stared at him then said, "What are you suggesting?"

"I'm..." James paused and thought for a moment, "I'm not sure actually. You were the soldier, not me. What do you think needs to happen?"

"You just wanna get out of here so you can do whatever it is you think you still need to do. What does that have to do with me?" Octavian said.

A thought struck James and he smiled, "It has a lot to do with you, and with everyone around here."

"And how's that?"

James smiled up at Octavian, "I want to get out of here, but I can't with the angel still in charge. You want some peace and quiet, some time to rest while waiting for the final judgment, right? You can't do that with the angel still in charge."

Octavian stared at him for a while then finally said, "You want to overthrow an angel?"

"What I want," James' voice turned hard as he bit into each word, "is to get my hand back." He paused and took a steadying breath, "But that's not going to happen so, yes, I want to get rid of the angel."

"Were you crazy when you were alive?" Octavian shook his head and walked away.

"Wait!" James yelled, but this time no one answered. For a moment James had hoped. He thought he would be able to convince Octavian to help, but thinking back on the conversation it seemed crazy now. How could he hope to convince a dead guy that attacking an angel would be the right thing to do? It really was crazy to think about trying to overthrow a being of unknown power. Hope was a dangerous thing. It could destroy you as easily as save you.

James sat. He kicked at the dirt. He tried counting and every sixty seconds he would make a mark in the dust. Time here was meaningless but if he didn't do something to occupy his mind he would start thinking about his hand. Even so, after two hundred and sixty five marks he gave it up and just flopped back to lay in the dust and stare up at the always slightly burnt toast sky. Finally the sound of footsteps made him look over at the edge of his hole. He had to roll out of the way when a rope dropped down. Looking up he saw Octavian and two other guards watching him over the edge of the hole.

"Well," Octavian said, "are you going to grab it or are you just going to lay there?"

James smiled then looked from the rope to his one hand. He wrapped the rope around his right forearm then grabbed on tight with his left hand. Looking up he nodded to the three and they pulled. Pushing with his feet while they hauled him up he quickly rolled over the edge onto his back. His right arm was throbbing terribly but he didn't have time for that right now. James smiled at the thought. This place, Purgatory, didn't even have a concept of time, and yet he was in a hurry. Well, he thought, of course he was in a hurry. He had angels to overthrow, hostages to rescue, and demons to destroy. He smirked at the thought. Maybe he was insane.

James made his way to his feet and looked at his rescuers. Octavian stood in the middle of the three and was easily the shortest. James would have been surprised if he topped five foot six. He had brown eyes, short cut curly brown hair, and skin the color of a nice tan. To James' left was a man he could only describe as burly. He had black hair and a mustache that drooped below the level of his chin. His broad shoulders and thick hands looked capable of ripping small animals in half, and the expression on his face said he might just enjoy doing that. The man on James' right was easily as tall as his six foot two inches. All he could really think when looking at him was how thin he was. His nose was thin, his face was thin, he was a poster child for thin.

"So," James dusted himself, "who are your friends, Octavian?"

Octavian nodded his head to the one with the impressive mustache, "This is the Hun, and," he nodded to the thin man, "this is the Israeli."

"No names?" James said.

The Israeli shrugged and said, "This isn't the place where names mean much."

"Well," James looked at the three and thought it wasn't too bad of a start, "did Octavian tell you what's going on?"

The Hun nodded, "We're getting rid of that blight-cursed angel."

James nodded once and looked at the Israeli, "What's the point of this place?"

The Israeli looked at the hole and said, "You pissed him off and he tossed you in to teach you a lesson."

James shook his head, "No, I mean," then he frowned, "well actually that's a great place to start. Uhm, so..." he trailed off. "Look I can't just go around calling you the Israeli. What's your name?"

"Why does it matter?" the Israeli said. "We're not here to make friends. We're not here for any other reason than to wait on the judgment of God."

"Exactly," James said. "But, honestly, if we are going to plan the overthrow of an angel, it would be nice if I could use your name."

"Mishael."

James' eyebrows slowly went up, "Wow, you mean like *the* Mishael?"

"No. If I was him do you think I would be," he gestured around at Purgatory, "here?"

James shrugged, "Well, when you put it like that, I guess not. Anyway, back to my original comment. I asked you what the point of this place is and just a moment ago you answered my question. You said that Purgatory is a place of waiting and reflection."

Mishael nodded, "Yes. You see, in life our memories dull over time, or we are able to color them by convincing ourselves that what happened was for a good reason. No memory in life is perfect."

The Hun cleared his throat, "You may call me Uldin." He bowed slightly to James. "This forgetfulness in life is for a good reason. You must be able to function and your past can," he paused here and let out a breath slowly, "stop you from doing what needs to be done."

Mishael looked at them both, "My friend is right. But here in this place all those barriers are removed and you see all your life as it really was."

"So," James paused, "you are given a chance to reflect on your life before being judged on it. Is that so you can have a chance to defend your actions?"

Octavian shook his head, "I don't think so. I think in a way this is the judgment. We are judging ourselves. There is no lying or hiding from the truth of your actions or how they affected others. I believe by the time the end comes there will be no need to tell us where we will be spending eternity we will already know."

"Then what is the point," James held up the stump where his right hand used to be, "of doing this?"

Mishael made eye contact with the other two then looked back at James, "There is no point."

Octavian shrugged, "This is why we're here. Things like this keep happening and we," he gestured at the other two, "among others, don't think this is the way it should be."

James nodded, "I got the feeling, during my little conversation with his high and mightiness, that he is not happy to be here." They all nodded back at him and James continued, "I assume he was put here to, in a way, oversee Purgatory and he took the placement as a slight."

The Hun twitched his chin at the far-off castle rising from the city center, "Many of us believe he was put here as a punishment for something."

Mishael shrugged, "I disagree, but our personal beliefs on the point of the existence of angels can wait for another time. Right now we need to talk about what you have in mind."

James smiled. "It's simple really. Ants."

They all stared at him for a few seconds before Octavian waved his hand at James, "We all know what they are but what do you mean?"

James' smile grew. "Have any of you ever seen a colony of ants defend itself?"

Chapter Seven

Moving toward the city as quietly as possible James wondered about the ability to sneak in a place like Purgatory. If everyone knew what was going on they would surely notice the one thing that was out of place, right? Or, maybe, they all had their heads down hoping so hard not to be noticed by Mr. Crazy Wings Angel that no one would even see them, or if they did no one would say anything about it.

They were moving through an empty space between a few of the smaller cities of the valley and they paused at the top of a small rise in the ground. His three new friends needed a moment to discuss where to go first, and he wanted to take a look around. He hadn't really had a chance since his first view of the place coming down from the mountains where he'd entered this world, if you could call it that. Closer up he could see paths between the cities and even people, from time to time, moving between the cities. As his gaze crossed over the never changing landscape one thing jumped out to him.

"Hey," he tapped Octavian on the shoulder.

Octavian looked over from the animated but whispered conversation he'd been having with the other two, and James wondered what was the point of whispering. They were scheming against an Angel. Either he would be able to hear them no matter what or, and he took a split second to look around at the sheer emptiness of the area around them, no one would hear them at all out here even if they shouted their plans.

Octavian cleared his throat in the not so subtle unspoken way of saying, hello, you tapped my shoulder, what do you want? "So, you've been here, relatively speaking, for a while, right?"

Shrugging Octavian glanced at the other two, "If I believe you about what year it is for you then, sure, I'm fairly old compared to others."

"Well," James pointed to a spot in the distance, "could you tell me what that is?"

Octavian turned to see what James was pointing at and paused. He stared at it for a while then turned to the other two, "Hey," he shoved Uldin and pointed to what James was looking at, "you know what that thing is?"

Uldin and Mishael shaded their eyes from the sun that didn't exist is this place and James was struck by an internal sigh and chuckle about habits that last beyond your lifetime.

Uldin gave a grunt that seemed to be a mixture of confusion, annoyance, and curiosity. A man and his whole society must grunt a lot to be able to convey all that, James thought.

Mishael looked longer and finally without saying anything started to walk in the direction of their find.

From the top of the rise all it looked like to James was a difference in the pattern of the place. Something about it looked out of place. Like seeing a Wal-Mart in the middle of the forest this was something that was man made in a place that was not. As they came closer they started to notice how some of the trails from city to city now ran to it instead of to the next city, and once they crested the next ridge and could see down into that section of the valley they saw the people.

People were lined up from the closest cities passing stones from hand to hand. With the lack of any kind of other material there was no hope of ever making a cart or wagon so it looked like a bucket brigade but with cut stone. The structure itself was incomprehensible to James and when he looked at the others their expression seemed to agree with him.

Mishael gestured for them to move forward but along the edge of the rise so as not to gain more attention than necessary. At the worst, James thought, they were guards and could pretend to be guarding him and taking him somewhere.

The land of Purgatory was not flat. From looking at it up in the mountains he expected it to be even and coated with a fine layer of dust, but down here he saw that it rippled like a frozen mis-colored oceanscape. By staying just below the top of the rise they could work their way closer without being exposed to the eyes of whomever was supervising the building.

After a few checks and more moving, Mishael motioned for them to crawl and they squirmed up the sandy hill and peaked over the edge. The lines of humanity stretched away like spokes on a wheel, and at the center of the wheel was a square that was trying to look like a circle. Because of the uniformity of the stone it seemed the builders were having a hard time getting the shape they wanted. It looked to James like they were trying to make an arch, but things weren't going quite to whatever plan they had to be using.

In his medieval history classes at the university James remembered how wooden structures would be used to hold up the curve of the arch until the keystone could be put into place holding it all together. Here, however, there was no wood. Which also meant they couldn't build scaffolding which meant they had no way to get up and work on the structure easily either. This led to stair steps of stone being piled up on all sides of the arch and an argument between what must be the foreman about how to support the arch until the keystone could go into place.

Into this argument walked a twisted little man dragging three people behind him. They were shackled together and shuffled or tripped along behind him. Dust covered all three and the foremen ignored them as just more human flotsam crashing against the immensity of Purgatory. The little man hobbled up to them on his twisted legs and poked one of them in the chest. James couldn't hear the conversation but obviously the man in charge didn't like being poked at, and James' brain started adding in the words to the unheard argument.

Hey, ugly face, what for did you poke me for?

Well, tall, dusty, and stupid I have something that is obviously more important than what you're talking about.

Really? Cuz I'm talking about how to make a human pyramid large enough to hold up this whole ugly mess until we can finish that arch, and that's the most important thing in this ugly world. Literally.

Whatever had really been said obviously didn't agree with the foreman because at that moment he picked the ugly little guy up with both hands and threw him back into the three prisoners behind him. Two of them fell and the third went to a knee and started trying to help them up.

The twisted little guy slowly pushed himself up from the dust and brushed off. Straightening as much as possible he glared at the foreman. James' stomach convulsed as a familiar feeling washed over him. Just at the edge of hearing whispers started. If he concentrated he could ignore them enough that they became just a slightly irritating buzz. The foreman wasn't as lucky. Around him the eternally unchanging light of Purgatory seemed to dim ever so slightly and the foreman clamped his hands over his ears.

James didn't wait to see what happened. Sliding down the small hill he ignored the whispered queries of his new friends and sprinted around until he came into sight of the closest line of people. None of them blinked or questioned him as he pushed his way into the line. He grabbed a stone with his good hand and passed it down the line then repeated the motion three or four more times until he assumed he was blended in enough. Stepping out of the line he glanced around and seeing no one looking he moved down the line five or six people. He knew this might take a while, and it had a fairly good chance of getting him caught again, but it didn't matter. Grace and the others were there and he had to get to them.

Every time he tried to think about what to do when he got them his mind broke. He had no power, he had no hand, and no plan was coming to mind. Against those odds he didn't know how he would win, but there was no argument inside of himself. It didn't matter right now. What mattered was getting to them.

But why?

Because I have to.

I'm not saying you shouldn't do it. I'm just wondering why.

What does it matter right now?

Because we aren't always going to be right now. Eventually this will be over, for good or bad, and something else will happen. What then? Another excuse? More statements about how right now isn't the right time to think about it?

No, it's because.

Because of what?

James remembered his temporary comrade in the hole and what he'd said.

"Because," he whispered to himself, "it's who I am."

He passed stones then moved. Three more times he handed stones down the line then would move. Daring to glance up he saw that he was maybe twenty yards away from the twisted thing that must be the Darkness. Something must be different here in Purgatory for him to manifest as more than just a smudge of darkness with eyes. Or maybe it was that there were no shadows here for him to manifest in, and this was what he really looked like.

James unconsciously weighed the stone in his left hand against the mental possibility of hitting the ugly thing over the head with it. He dismissed the idea when he saw what was left of the foreman convulsing on the ground. Obviously the Darkness hadn't lost its power when making the jump to Purgatory.

Stealth might be his best bet, he decided. The Darkness was distracted by his interaction with the man the foreman had been arguing with, and none of the people in the lines, including what James now saw as guards, were looking that way. It seemed everyone was very pointedly not looking that way. He decided to slowly slide up to the three teens and work them into the mass of people. Using the work going on as cover he should be able to get them away before the Darkness noticed.

He passed the stone down the line and moved five more people closer. His movement caught the attention of one of the shackled teens. The boy looked right at him. Under the dirt a now truly ragged Abercrombie and Fitch shirt struggled to stay together and James was sure these were the kids he was looking for. He decided they would need to be ready to go when he got to them so he winked as obviously as he could, hoping the boy would get the universal signal for doing something sneaky.

The boy elbowed the one next to him and whispered something. That boy looked at him and James was forced to wink again. Causing yet another elbowing and more whispering. He sincerely hoped all the commotion wouldn't alert the Darkness to what was going on. Then Grace turned to him. She looked terrible, but not any worse than a trek through the desert would leave someone. A sparkle of hope built in the back of his mind. His fears of them being tortured and dismembered, or eaten by something terrible hadn't come true. Maybe they could walk out of this with minimal emotional damage. If he could find a way out.

He didn't want to think about that.

Grace smiled at him and his worries temporarily vanished. Right now it didn't matter about the long term plan. Get to them, get them away from the Darkness, and figure the rest out from the safety of somewhere else.

He nodded slightly to Grace in what he hoped was a sign for, let's do this, and started to shift his weight when something akin to a sonic boom knocked him from his feet. His ears ringing he rolled over and looked toward the teens.

Across from the Darkness stood the Angel Jah-diel himself. His mind spun and fractured into multiple parts all arguing with each other over what to do and what was going on. One part was sure that an Angel, no matter how crazy he seemed, showing up to confront a demon was a good thing. There should be some righteous smackdown coming pretty darn quick, that part of his brain said. Another very loud part of his brain was mentally running in circles waving its arms around and screaming about his hand being cut off. This part of his brain effectively stopped him from standing up and doing anything to distinguish himself from the crowd.

Jah-diel spoke. The voice of the angel convinced most of James' higher brain functions to take some time off, just in case, because, seriously, it's an angel talking. "What are you doing here?"

James expected the Darkness to just kind of shrivel up and die at that point but the opposite happened. He drew his twisted form up to its maximum height and tried his best to look the ten foot tall glowing being in the sparking electric eyes. "Per the gateway agreement," his voice didn't come from his mouth but bubbled up, hissing, all around like bad surround sound, "I seek passage through your territory."

Jah-diel rested his hand on the pommel of his sword and stared down at the little demon for what seemed like five slow minutes. "You dare show up here at the gateway itself and demand anything of me."

"The agreement clearly states that in times of need..."

The angel slid a few inches of blade free from its scabbard, "Don't quote the agreement to me fallen one. You may have been of the second rank at one time but no more. Your presence here could disrupt the entire project."

Holding up his hands in a placating gesture the Darkness replied, "The definition of an emergency is what it is, Jah-diel, and I would like to leave here as quickly as possible for my sake and yours."

James brain functions finally kicked back in and the part that had been running and screaming now just stood there dumbfounded and watched the continuing conversation. It was soon joined by all the distinct parties of James' personality as they had a mentally refreshing drink of water and discussed the improbability of the current situation.

That angel is talking to that demon.

Yes.

Should that be happening?

Well, granted my experience with these kinds of things is a bit slim, but I don't think so.

Yeah, that's what I thought too.

So...

We could try and take advantage of the situation and grab the kids.

True, except if you take the time to look around...

James looked around. Every person, or soul, was flat on the ground trying its best not to be noticed by the crazy angel. If he tried to make a grab for the kids now he would be the most noticeable thing in all of Purgatory. But he was so close. He couldn't just sit here thirty feet away from them and not even try. He knew, however, that if he tried now he would only die in the attempt, and what good would that do.

Looking back toward them he caught the eye of the dark haired teen he thought of as the mortician and felt bad for a moment for not even knowing the kid's name. The best he could manage now was to let them know that he would keep trying. He could give them some hope, even if it was slim, that someone was coming for them. James gave a little smile and a shrug that was supposed to mean there's nothing I can do right now but I'll keep trying. The problem with wordless communication in a situation like this was not knowing if the message actually got across. The kid's slight nod was the best he could hope for.

His ears popped and the light changed around him. James sighed and let his forehead fall to the dirt for a moment. Maybe now with Jah-diel gone his original plan could still work. As people around him started shifting he took a bit more of a chance and got to his knees. The angel was definitely gone but along with that, in some sort of defiance of physics, the Darkness and the teens were now far enough away that his brain assigned the term miles to the distance.

Standing he let out a resigned sigh when a hand dropping on his shoulder caused him to jump and start to swing a punch with a hand that didn't exist any more.

"Whoa, whoa," Octavian held up his hands and took a step back.

"Sorry," James turned and looked again toward the vanishing teens, "but I need to..."

"You need to come and talk things out my friend." Octavian took James' arm and pulled him back toward the hill where the others were waiting.

Mishael looked him up and down, "That was stupid."

"Yes," James replied, "but necessary."

"The angel will know if you interfere with that thing."

Uldin nodded, "We still need to remove him. Tactically speaking he is the eyes, and if you don't want to be seen or interfered with then you need to poke out the eyes."

"That is a creepy analogy," James replied, "but, yes, you are correct."

He turned and looked at the now too distant figures of Grace, the Mortician, and Abercrombie. "I just hope I don't fall too far behind."

Chapter Eight

"We've got to try again, Ray."

"No, Mitch," Ray whispered back, "we don't have to try again. You know..."

Mitch poked him in the shoulder, "We don't know anything. This place," he tried his best to indicate all of Purgatory with a simple nod of his head, "bends things. He was right there. You saw him, and then..."

"Poof." Grace whispered.

"Yeah," Mitch nodded toward Grace, "poof, we were, like, ten miles away."

"But he was there." Ray quietly argued, "Not like the last time. All we have to do is nothing and he'll catch up. You saw what he did back at the church. He can handle this thing." He looked at Grace for support.

She grimaced and for a few moments she simply listened to their feet. Each step was a sigh as the deep sand dragged at their feet. The dunes surrounding them had risen up slowly until their vision was filled with little mountains.

"I don't know," she said.

"What do you mean, you don't know?" Mitch said.

"Mitch," she looked at him, "I mean I don't know. If we actually get away we have nowhere to go. We don't know where we are, and even if we can get back to those cities, you saw what happened. That Angel," she paused, surprised at her use of the word, "agreed to help him."

"But if we stay..."

"Yes," she nodded, "If we stay, eventually he will do something and it's not going to be good."

Ray shook his head and stopped listening. They didn't understand how this worked. This wasn't the movies. The bad guys didn't give you a chance to make it a more exciting storyline. They were going to die. He was sure of it.

He looked down at himself and was amazed at what he saw. His shirt was ripped from sliding down the trail after the monster threw him. His pants didn't look much different, with the rips having been there anyway. Only the dark stains where the cuts on his knees had bled caused them to look any different. Then there were his favorite shoes. He'd worked on his mom for months to get the all white Jordans. He made sure to carry them to school in his backpack so he didn't scuff them, and he'd only worn them to church because the weather was good enough. Now, the leather was scuffed beyond repair and the color had devolved into the definition of dingy. They were a total loss, and he knew his mom wouldn't be willing to get him another pair for at least another year.

"Look," Mitch whispered as forcefully as he could without alerting Kron'ael, "if we stay with him we know we're going to die. If we get away at least there's some possibility..."

Ray let Mitch's words buzz around him like flies. He couldn't even find the energy to swat them away. The buzzing continued and some part of him knew they were talking either to him or about him, but he just didn't care. He slowly pulled his gaze up, from watching the puffs of dust settle onto his once perfect shoes, to Mitch and Grace quietly arguing about the best way to add pointless hope into this hopeless situation. As he looked away he reached up and rubbed at a persistent ache in his jaw. It took a bench press of mental effort to unclinch the muscles in his jaw.

He didn't realize he'd stopped walking until Grace bumped into him. With the quickness of a darting mouse he saw fear dart across her eyes. They all knew what happened if Kron'ael caught them straggling.

Tugging at his sleeve she quietly said, "Come on Ray."

His jaw clenched again as he took a step. They were treating him like a little kid. Pulling him along, trying to convince him that everything would be okay. Her tone of voice reminded him of his Mom dealing with his little brother. A spike of pain shot through one of his molars and he twitched. Clenching his fists he stared at the ground. Puff, the dust settled onto his Jordans. Puff, perfect white turned to grit. Each speck of dust was an insult to everything he'd worked so hard at, and now, now...

Something grabbed his right arm and yanked him sideways. His clenched teeth were the only thing that stopped him from screaming. Mitch pulled him to a run and without looking back said, "I don't care how you're feeling right now. You need to run, or I swear I'll pick you up and carry you, cuz I'm not leaving you behind with that thing."

Ray looked around and saw they'd come to some kind of actual rock formation instead of just the never ending sand dunes of depression they'd been crossing for the past few... his mind tried to say days, but here there were no days. No sunrise, no sunset, nothing to mark the passage of time except footsteps in the dust.

His legs pumped faster and faster out of sheer habit. Countless basketball drills, and soccer fields flying under his feet had burned a perfect memory into his muscles. He knew to the foot how long he could go at this speed before his lungs would start burning, and he knew how much farther he could push before his thighs started to give out. For a moment, even in this place, he was able to toss off the ache of clinched muscles and just run. Running for any distance needed a pace, and without thinking about it his eyes slid past Mitch and focused on Grace. He'd never noticed her before now. That wasn't exactly true, if someone had asked him he could have pointed her out. Her existence to him was simply a function of the small size of the church, not any friendship or common interests. He was vaguely aware she went to his school, but he didn't hang out with people like her. Maybe if she'd played a sport or done something he would've noticed.

Letting his legs do their own thing he started trying to remember if he'd seen her do anything, and the only thing he could even slightly bring to mind was her running, maybe, with the track team. It would make sense since she seemed to be doing fine keeping up, and even set a good pace. It wasn't a flat out sprint, but it also wasn't just a slow jog. The pace was a good one for eating up distance while still leaving enough in the tank to make a sprint if necessary.

His eyes glanced quickly left as Mitch fumbled along. Ray watched as Mitch caught his foot on a rock sticking up a few inches and barely managed to catch himself before pitching headlong into the dirt. Ray felt his jaw clinch again. It would serve him right to fall on his face, he thought. Acting like he was better than everyone since they'd ended up here. Constantly pushing the monster and trying to get Grace to side with him. Looking at Mitch he wondered how he even kept himself going. It reminded him of Woody from the Toy Story movies.

From the corner of his eye he saw Grace skid and take a sharp right through another gap in the rock. His eyes took it in and without slowing down he angled toward the crack, extended his left hand, using it and his foot as a spring board he shot around the corner. Grunts and rocks clattering sounded behind him and he smiled to himself knowing Mitch hadn't made the corner.

A few strides later they broke from the rocks and Ray was forced to skid and lean to the right to avoid hitting Grace.

"What're you doing?" He said between gulps of air.

She pointed past him, and turning to look he was greeted with something he hadn't expected. A gray stone building rose from the dust of the open plain. It resembled a badly made two layer cake with the bottom layer being a simple unadorned square, and the top layer being a slightly offset and angled square. It gave off the feeling like someone had accidentally bumped it and never fixed the problem. It stood out like a wedding cake at a funeral, with the gray of its stone against the perpetual sunset orange of the sky.

Mitch skidded to a halt next to them and bent over putting his hands on his knees, "That," he sucked in a few deep breaths, "looks weird."

"Thanks for that Mitch," Grace put a hand on his shoulder and looked at him sideways, "You gonna be okay?"

Nodding, he reached up and patted her hand, "Sure, there's just not much call to run like that in band."

Of course, Ray thought, he would be in band.

"What do you think we should do?" Grace asked.

Ray was about to answer when Mitch straightened up and started walking toward it. Looking over his shoulder Mitch said, "We're looking for some way to get out of here right? Might as well try the one place we've seen that isn't the same color as everything else."

The only opening into the strange squat building was a simple rectangular opening, as if someone had forgotten to include the stone for the wall in that section. There was no frame and no hint that any type of door had ever been attached.

Mitch stopped and flattened himself at the edge of the door and peered in, "Besides," he whispered, "it's either this or keep running, and I'm not sure I could've done that."

Grace leaned against the wall behind him and poked him in the back, "You're telling me the plan, your plan by the way, which was to run, was entirely based on the hope that something amazing would happen before you ran out of breath?"

Mitch smiled over his shoulder at her, "Hope springs eternal."

She smiled back, "But apparently your breath doesn't."

Ray flexed his fingers, popping his knuckles, as he leaned his back against the wall on the opposite side of the door. He wanted to wipe the smile off Mitch's face. Did he realize where they were? Did he forget what had happened? That thing back there, which was definitely coming after them right now, had thrown him down a mountain.

"Here goes," Mitch said and tried to slip through the door as quietly as possible.

Everything in Ray's mind screamed at him to get away, to do something else. This place was weird and nothing good ever came from weird. You didn't walk into the only strange building hoping something good would happen. It was like... It was like sticking your hand into a bag full of cats. Well, not like that. He wasn't quite sure what it was like, but he felt that something bad was going to happen, and it was stupid Mitch's fault.

Ray watched as Grace followed Mitch into the darkness and realized he couldn't stay out here by himself. Looking around he had to decide if he was going with them, or if he was going to take his chances with more running. Beyond the gray building everything was flat and empty. The monster would be able to spot him from miles away, and he wasn't going to head back into the rocks and dunes.

Grace's head poked out of the door, "Come on Ray, you need to see this."

So much for running, he thought, and tried to be as quiet as possible going through the door after Grace.

The small amount of light spilling through the door did little to illuminate the interior of the building, but after a few moments his eyes adjusted enough to realize they were standing in a single large room. Dust from outside had blown in adding grit to the simple stone floor, but other than that the space was devoid of anything. Rolling his eyes he realized they had just walked themselves right into a trap. There was one way in and no way out. He knew they shouldn't have tried to run. Maybe if he explained that Mitch had literally dragged him along the monster would only hurt them.

"Come on," Grace walked confidently into the space, "You can't really see it until you get closer."

"See what?"

After a dozen steps a rectangular structure started to resolve itself out of the gloom. Ray saw Mitch walking around it, running his hands over it, and pushing on it. He was about to ask Grace what it was, as if it mattered since they only had a few more moments of freedom anyway, when he realized it looked just like a door.

He could just make out the wavy wood grain pattern running the length of it. It reminded him of the pattern in the fake wood door to his bathroom back home. Why would a door, here of all places, look like the one from his bathroom?

"It looks like..."

"Yeah," said Grace, "I know, right."

Mitch turned and looked at them with his right hand resting on something, "It has a door knob, and since we really don't have time to argue about it..."

Words bubbled in Ray's mind trying to put themselves into some semblance of order. He knew what Mitch was going to do, and he knew it wasn't a good idea. Watching as Mitch opened the door he wished with everything that he could just be back home where things still made sense.

As the door swung open he expected to see the gray stone wall beyond, but all he could see was darkness, and he watched in horror-filled fascination as Mitch, then Grace, walked forward, slipping into it like a swimmer sliding off the dock into the cool water of a lake. He knew he should move, knew he should do something but he was frozen. He didn't want to be here. More than anything he didn't want to be here, but that door, that rectangular pool of blackness, was the shadow of an oncoming car to a deer.

Somewhere behind him a rock clicked its way down the path, reminding him a choice had to be made. After another moment's hesitation in which his brain reminded him what exactly would be coming up behind, he walked toward the door. At the threshold he realized he couldn't make himself step into the darkness.

"I wish Grace was here." His whispered words were swallowed by the mouth of the door standing open waiting to devour him.

He closed his eyes and imagined her hands on his back pushing him. There was no rush of wind past his face. No ice cold shivers or a feeling of being dunked into water. His ears popped, then someone's hands grabbed him. After a few moments of sheer terror believing something was going to eat him he opened his eyes and found himself back in the church. Destroyed pews piled against the walls and scorch marks flared out like rays of a black sun.

Events squeezed together in his mind, too many and too close together to properly spread out for inspection. Days passed, his parents fawned over him, doctors checked him, and a certain code of silence seemed to descend over the group. A realization that no one would believe what had happened settled on them without the need of being spoken.

It was decided by his parents that he should take a week or so off from school, but after just a few days he insisted on going back. It was his life. It was all he'd wanted while suffering through the place he would never name out loud. He needed the basketball team cheering him, and his friends grinning at him over an inside joke. It took a few days to convince his parents he wasn't going to pull a Humpty Dumpty, but eventually he found himself standing in front of his locker fifteen minutes before the first bell.

Sighing he reached out and ran his fingers over the blue metal, feeling the dents the years had left. He turned the padlock almost without a glance, muscle memory remembering exactly where to stop in order to pop the handle. The numbers weren't exact in these old things. You needed to know the trick of it, to feel it catch just a bit beyond the final number. In that moment it was a holy experience, and he fully realized the metaphor of it all. He was opening the door back to his life, and not just opening a dented blue locker. Everything would be back to normal now.

High school life starts when you get to your locker. The trip to school and everything before it was just an endless repetition of actions and faces; always the same and always boring. It was when you got to your locker that everything truly began. The population started flowing past like salmon in a stream as they came in from the parking lots and bus lanes, and he knew his friends would all be rushing to see him. This was his world.

The crowds of people parted and Ray looked up in time to see Mitch and Grace walking toward him. The smile on his face dropped as they got closer. Running through half a dozen excuses not to talk to them, he realized he'd intentionally been avoiding them since that day in the church. The last thing he wanted right now was to be reminded of that nightmare.

The tension in his back eased as, smiling and talking to each other, they walked by without noticing him. Simultaneously, his smile tugged back up as he saw his guys coming around the corner up ahead. He knelt down and reached into his locker to pull out his Jordans but had to stop himself, remembering they wouldn't be there today, and maybe not ever again. They'd been expensive the first time around, and after the hospital bills he doubted his parents would be able to get him another pair. Those would have made this a perfect day, but when his friends got here he knew it would be forgotten, at least until tomorrow.

Grabbing his books for his first period class and straightening up he wondered what was keeping the guys until he heard a familiar laugh. Looking down the hall he saw they'd stopped to talk with someone. Shrugging he wove his way through the normal muddled crowd trying to tell himself he could go to them as easily as they could come to him. But he couldn't shake the feeling of irritation. He'd been through Hell, almost literally, and even if they didn't know that they still knew he'd been in the hospital. They should at least have come to ask why and how he'd been doing. After all, when Shaun had broken his hand and been out for two days they practically threw a party for him when he got back. Shaun's locker had been decorated by the cheer squad with get well notes stuffed in the edges, and he wasn't even a starter like Ray.

His feet stopped at the same moment as his thoughts, both hitting a metaphysical roadblock when he saw who his guys were laughing with. Mitch had his head thrown back ,mouth open, laughter exploding out. His arm was casually draped across Grace's shoulders. She was reaching up and holding his hand against her cheek pretending to use it to wipe tears away. Ray's chest twitched like he was a guitar and someone had plucked the wrong string. It hurt, but he refused to admit why, and even to a certain extent that the feeling even existed at all. After all he, the starter on the basketball team, the one with all the friends, had no need to feel anything toward those two. Even if Grace was pretty and smart.

Ray pushed his way through his unwanted thoughts and the crowd around his guys with single minded determination. This situation didn't fit his reality and he was going to fix it.

"Hey, guys." Ray playfully punched his closest friend in the shoulder, but instead of the customary smile and fist bump he found Mitch pushing his way in between.

"Hey, Ray." Mitch turned and gestured at the surrounding crowd, "Hey, guys, it's Ray."

Grace stepped over, "Hey, Ray, I didn't think you'd be here."

"Yeah," Mitch chimed in, "after everything, we kinda thought you'd prefer to stay home where it's safe."

Stepping toward Mitch, Ray felt the color rise in his cheeks, "And what's that supposed to mean?"

"Well," Mitch looked toward Grace for help.

"Ray," Grace reached up and put her hand on Ray's shoulder, "you didn't exactly help us out over there. In fact," she paused for a beat, struggling over the right words, "in the nicest way possible, you were a complete wuss, Ray. You were scared of everything, whined about every step, and generally were as helpful as wet cardboard."

"Yeah." Mitch nodded, "I might not have added the wet cardboard part, but she nailed it."

"Wha..." Ray stepped back and bumped into someone, "I thought we weren't going to..."

"What, Ray?" Grace shrugged, "You expected us to just forget the fact that you couldn't stand up to a grasshopper if it jumped at you? Much less that we were fighting for our lives and you completely gave up?"

"But that was..." He looked around at guys he'd been friends with since sixth grade, "Come on guys. You know me. You know I'm good."

"Do we Ray?" They all replied in unison. Their combined voices creating an irritating swarm effect.

"Mitch!" Ray turned toward him wanting to scream, "You said you wouldn't tell anybody." An unwanted tear slid from his left eye. "You promised."

"So you're going to blame it on me?" Mitch stepped back and settled his arm around Grace again. "It's my fault people finally saw through you? Saw you for what you really are? I think not Ray."

"Grace? I thought we were friends? At church..."

Grace frowned, "Church? You think that because we happened to breathe the same air at church, where you ignored me for years, that we're friends. No, Ray."

"Well guys," Mitch's voice cut through a background buzz Ray hadn't noticed until then, "it seems to me there's only one way to deal with this."

Ray looked around at his guys and watched in horror as each pulled a knife from their pocket and said in unison, "It's what we do to cowards Ray."

He watched Mitch and Grace turn their backs on him and walk down the hall as the first blade bit into his back. Soon they were blocked from his sight by the swinging arms of his former friends as the knives rose and fell, each cutting away at his reality until nothing was left.

Nothing but a sound. It tugged at his mind and wouldn't stop. Screaming, ragged and shoved full of pain, echoed around his head. Then fire bloomed on his cheek and his eyes snapped open.

Mitch knelt over him, hand raised, "Are you awake?"

Ray sucked in a breath and the screaming stopped.

"Sorry bout the smack." Mitch sat causing a puff of dust to rise around him. "I tried shaking you, and yelling at you, but..."

Ray's breath rattled through the gravel of his throat, "It's all right," he managed to whisper.

He looked around, and the empty desolation of the world matched his soul, "Where's Grace?"

Mitch nodded to a pile of broken sandstone, "Over there. Throwing up I think."

"I..." Ray stared at the dust settling around Mitch and noticed a single wet spot. He stared at it fascinated until another drop hit slightly to the right of it. Looking up he saw Mitch's hands covering his face, a slight snuffling sound coming from behind the screen of his fingers. Farther to the right he could just make out the gagging sound of someone who has nothing left.

"How many times do you remember?" Ray whispered.

Mitch sniffled and ran his hand across his nose, "Five."

Nodding at Mitch he realized couldn't remember each event specifically, and he was glad of that, but he could remember these moments. Mitch waking him up, or Grace waking him up. Once he'd woken first and could only sit and listen to them scream, not knowing what to do.

"Well, my lovelies," the Monster's voice fairly purred at them, "up and at em."

Ray's head twitched to the left in time to see it, the Monster, rounding the corner of another pile of rock. His back was straighter, and Ray could see muscles ripple beneath what looked like a black silk shirt. Where once there had been a decided limp the monster now strode toward them with the purpose of a jailer ready to drag his charges back to their cages, "Dinner time's over." The Monster gave them a wicked smile, "for me, at least."

Ray's teeth creaked and he relaxed his jaw. Standing he saw Grace come from around the stones wiping her mouth off. He glanced at her, she met his eyes for a moment, then she went and helped Mitch up. The memory of his nightmare surged over him briefly. Them laughing together, him the outsider, but then Mitch turned and wrapping an arm around Ray's shoulders pulled him along. A lump welled up in his throat and threatened to press out through his eyes.

Why, he wondered as they staggered arm in arm behind the Monster. Why were his nightmares like that? Sometimes, over the past innumerable days Mitch and Grace would give a glimpse into what they saw, what their nightmares were. Grace's were unthinkable, literally. The one time she started to talk about it, both he and Mitch stopped her. There were some things it was better not to remember, or ever have in your head at all. Mitch's were generally based around people he loved dying in front of him in various ways while he was stuck, unable to help. So the question remained, why were his the way they were? They were always the same, with minor changes.

He was home, things were back to normal, then everyone turned on him. Normally Mitch and Grace were there leading the charge, or being cheered on by his friends while they killed him again. Was it such a bad thing to want what he wanted? To be liked, to have friends, were these the stuff of nightmares?

Mitch squeezed him so he looked over, "Don't worry man. While we're still alive we have hope, right."

Ray gave a fake smile. And why did he hate Mitch so much?

"It's like juggling."

"What?" Mitch glanced at him.

"I..." Ray hadn't meant to say anything out loud. He shook his head and Mitch just shrugged and squeezed him again.

And what did he mean when he said it's like juggling? Where did that thought even come from? His mind started turning the statement into metaphors on color and dexterity which then turned toward showing off and wanting applause.

"So," the Monster turned and started walking backward, "did you get away this time? It's all very individual to the person and I never can tell beforehand how far it's going to go. I leave it that way because the surprise of it all makes it that much tastier."

Chapter Nine

The dead swarmed. This was no shuffling zombie apocalypse. This was a human tidal wave that happened to be dead. On his few trips through the city James had seen few people, and the masses of them surprised him when they came boiling out of the houses. It made sense when he thought about it. The world had been around for a long time and that meant there were a lot of dead people hanging around waiting for the end. Even so this was supremely impressive.

Back in college he'd sat through a talk given by a survivor of the Korean War. He talked about the Chinese joining the fight on the side of North Korea, and the Americans had tried to hold one of the crossroads, which was key to accessing the northern part of the Korean peninsula. The Chinese had come at them as a human wave. It wasn't a metaphor, he told them. They had crashed onto the American position like the ocean hitting the shore, and shooting at them had about the same effect as shooting at the incoming tide. What James was seeing here must have been something like that just jacked up on steroids and with special effects added by Michael Bay.

James' new friends had put him back into the hole in order to stop any suspicion only to fish him out again an undetermined amount of time later. The strategy they'd worked out was simple. It relied on the unshakable reality of this place. Reality number one; everybody here was already dead and as such didn't need to worry about dying in a fight. Following up on reality number one came reality number two; there are a lot of dead people. That was the extent of their strategy. It was nothing compared to battle plans of generals and kings like Patton against Rommel or Alexander against Darius. On top of that, the vast majority of the people in Purgatory were not, and had never been, soldiers. The beauty of their entire battle plan was it really didn't matter if they were soldiers. If you get enough of them you can just overwhelm your problems.

The guards went first. They, of course, couldn't die and so had to be subdued in some way. James and his friends hadn't really specified how they should be subdued so the people just came up with things. Large rocks were used to pin them, they were thrown into pits, some were smashed or chopped into an unrecognizable mess, but mostly they were just knocked down then ignored, because what were they really going to do to stop the onrushing tide of humanity? After the first wave most of the guards either got out of the way or switched sides.

Then everything changed. The ground bucked and cracked knocking them off their feet. James had climbed to the top of a building to watch the attack and was blinded when light flared from inside the citadel. When his eyes cleared their victory had turned into a confused rout.

The angel Jah-diel, the overseer of Purgatory, was angry. His anger burned like the sun and made him almost impossible to look at. His sword burned an arc across the sky with every swing and his voice turned buildings to dust. Uncountable numbers of dead flew from him in pieces as he made his way from his seat of power.

James pulled his eyes away from the carnage when he heard footsteps behind him. The look on Mishael's face was one of amazement mixed with horror. He stared past James and said, "We are lost."

James had the overwhelming urge to agree with him. He glanced over his shoulder at the glowing embodiment of righteous anger and thought how do you fight that? When the answer occurred to him.

"Mishael!" Mishael didn't even blink. James stepped between Mishael and his view of the angel, and slapped him.

Mishael rocked back on his heels, "What was..." he looked back at the angel then at James pleadingly, "how do we fight that?" Then he raised his hand to his face, "And why did you hit me?"

James poked Mishael in the chest, "What did you think would happen?"

Mishael looked confused for a moment, "When what?"

"When you attacked an angel," James said. "Did you think he would just let you overrun his guards and then surrender?"

"Well, no."

"And did you forget he was an angel somewhere along the line?"

"No, but..." Mishael stammered.

"But what?" James waved his stump at the unutterably amazing scene, "You had to expect something like this."

Mishael sucked in a deep breath, "Yes, we did expect him to enter the fight. We just didn't expect..." and he too waved a hand at the angel.

"A giant flaming sword, and a voice that shatters rock."

"Exactly." Mishael shook his head, "How do you fight that?"

James nodded, "All together. Look at him, my friend. He looks so angry, doesn't he? But what right does he have to be angry? Now look at your people."

All across the open square they saw the citizens of Purgatory getting back up. James had been sure they had been sliced or blasted into oblivion but there they were. He wanted to ask how that was even possible, but he doubted Mishael knew. Maybe it was just the unchanging nature of this place, maybe it was a little help from a higher power, but for whatever reason they weren't staying down. "Our plan is still working. We all attack together, we drag him down, we take away his stupid flaming sword, and we chop little bits of him off with it."

Mishael looked at him, "You are insane."

"Most likely," James said. "Will you be crazy with me?"

Mishael nodded, turned on his heel, and headed down the stairs. James could hear him yelling to be heard above the noise, but couldn't make out what he was saying. Whatever it was got picked up by others and James could see it spread around the square like ripples in a pond. Moments later the citizens of Purgatory poured out of buildings and holes and streets from all sides and attacked. Jah-diel screamed. It was the scream of an Eagle before it struck. The air rippled with the power of it and the people were thrown back.

It didn't matter. The dead couldn't die, and once they had gotten over their shock at the sight of a seriously pissed off angel, the outcome of the battle was a foregone conclusion. They didn't just climb onto the now giant angel, they swarmed. Without visible communication they started acting as a single entity. Some pushed, others pulled, and from who knows where another group of them emerged from the citadel with chains. They held him down while they looped length after length of chain over Jah-diel's arms and chest. Each time they nailed it into the bedrock of Purgatory until he resembled nothing more than a very pretty version of Gulliver in the land of the Lilliputians.

James finally came down from the tops of the buildings and walked through the crowds congratulating them as he went. When he reached the center he found Octavian arguing with another man who was dressed in a very dusty but well-cut modern day business suit.

"A trial?" Octavian shouted, "are you crazy?"

"Look," the man said, "if we are going to be any better then he was we need to do this right."

"We need to be practical," Octavian replied, "and we need to think about why we're here."

"What does that have to do with anything?"

Octavian sighed, "I have been here for a long time, friend, and I know, just like you know, that we are here to reflect on ourselves." He shook his head, "Let me guess, you were a judge in life, right."

The nicely dressed man nodded, "A supreme court judge of the United States of America."

"I have no idea what that is," Octavian said, "and it really doesn't matter. What does matter is getting this whole thing over as fast as possible and getting back to doing what we're meant to be doing."

James stepped up and placed his hand on the shoulder of the Supreme Court Justice, "Trust the old Roman soldier."

Octavian looked at James, "Who you callin' old?"

The judge sighed, "So be it. I believe we all can see he is guilty of misuse of power and dereliction of duty, among many other things. So what should we do with him?"

James walked away as they discussed the best way to dispose of an undying angel. He had to push his way past more crowds of people but eventually he made it to his goal. Sitting down on a rock he looked at the face of the deposed angel. "I just wanted to let you know what I'm going to do." The angel glared at him and James had to fight down the urge to get up and run away. Instead he looked down at the stump where his right hand used to be. "An eye for an eye, and a hand for a hand." James looked up into the angel's eyes. "I figure that's fair." His father had taught him that sometimes an eye for an eye is the wrong thing. Sometimes all that does is lead to reprisals and violence and escalation, but as he walked away from the angel looking for that special thing he would need all he could think about was his hand.

When he finally found it he was amazed it was just lying there unguarded. Maybe no one had noticed it, but then again how do you miss a giant glittering angelic sword. James looked at the mass of people milling around him and wondered why no one had picked it up. It struck him, after all his conversations with the people here, that they really had no use for a sword. Octavian was right. They all just wanted to get back to what they were here for. They weren't here for a sword. They were here to contemplate their lives in the quiet and stillness of Purgatory.

Nobody stopped him as he grabbed it with his left hand, wrapped his right arm around it, and then hefted the giant sword off the ground. It didn't look amazing. James thought the battle sword of an angel should look a certain way. It should crackle with lightning or have fire dancing along it. At the very least it should have crazy swoopy lines to it or look like an aspen leaf designed to kill monsters. But this was just a sword. The handle was wrapped in leather and thin wire to give it a good grip. It was double bladed and reminded him a bit of a Scottish claymore, like the one famously used by William Wallace. It was too big to hold with just his one hand so he had to rest it on his shoulder. Even then it was hard balancing the thing as he made his way back to Jah-diel. It was at the wrist, James thought to himself, as he lined up with the angel's arm. It took him a few tries of falling over and almost taking his own foot off but finally he figured how to start with it on the ground and use it like an axe chopping wood.

Jah-diel screamed. James was thrown from his feet, the thousands of people around him fell like wheat before the reaper, and the very ground rippled as if a stone had been dropped into the still water of Purgatory. James rolled onto his chest and pushed himself up with his one good hand. The first thing through his mind was that it didn't bleed, but then it hit him, of course an angel doesn't bleed. James reached down and picked up the severed hand. Glancing down at the angel's sword he momentarily thought about taking it with him. It would be useful to have along when going to face a monster of unknown power in an unknown place. Finally he decided it was just too unwieldy and he really didn't know how to use a sword. He'd taken fencing lessons as the local YMCA with his best friend during college, but James was fairly sure those experiences wouldn't really translate into using a giant angelic claymore in some unknown world. He'd be more likely to chop his own foot off than do any damage to his enemies, unless they were chained to the ground.

Walking up to Jah-diel's head James had the overwhelming urge to wave at people with the hand. He felt giddy in a way that you only feel when you see someone get what's coming to them. Like that moment when someone almost runs you off the road and there just happens to be a police car there at the right time to pull them over. Now take that, James thought, and multiply it by not just bad driving but by cutting off body parts. Looking down at the stump of his arm, his giddy grin turned into a teeth-grinding glare. James looked up into the eyes of the chained angel and the thoughts flew like dragonflies through his head. He wanted to claim an eye for an eye. He wanted to accuse the angel of being evil and this was a right and fitting punishment. But James knew it wasn't any of those things. It was revenge.

In his mind he screamed, *this thing claiming to be an angel cut off my hand! I don't care what reasoning you give it. I don't care what you have to say to make it seem right, or justified. He deserves it, and that's that.*

James nodded, "Yes."

Malice poured from Jah-diel and pooled in his words, "Now what, little dead human?"

James smiled at this, "It's amazing, after all this you still don't understand."

Daggers shaped like words slipped from the angels lips, "Enlighten me."

James had to resist the urge to slap the angel with his own severed hand, "First off is the simple thing. I am not dead. And second is that what I do now is not something you need to worry about. You should worry about your own future. But you know what," James looked down at the angelic hand, "I might as well try. You never know what might happen." James pressed the stump of the angel's hand to the stump of his right arm and warmth instantly flowed up his arm then was gone.

His view of the world shrank until he was staring at the hand through pinholes poked through the blackness of his mind. The world started swaying and the noise of thousands of people suddenly hit him like a wave. He breathed out and swayed on his feet. He took a deep gasping breath and held his arm up so the hand was directly in front of him. He reached out and pinched the flap of skin between the thumb and first finger, jumping and giggling when the pain of it hit him. He bit off the laughter and just concentrated on opening and closing the hand one finger at a time. Finally he looked up at the chained angel.

"What, no blinding flash of light?"

He looked back down at the now attached angelic hand, "Well, other than the bizarre fact that it's now the exact right size, and it works," he flexed the fingers on the new hand, making a fist, "I guess it's no weirder than anything else that's happened so far."

James heard Jah-diel say something, but the words didn't register as he turned and walked away, opening and closing his new hand. His new angelic hand, he corrected himself with a giant grin.

Chapter Ten

Stepping out of the city walls, the valley of Purgatory stretched out before him and for a moment the only thing that crossed his mind was how much it reminded him of his cat. Logan had been an orange and white house cat he had rescued from the animal shelter. When Logan was just a little kitten, James had been amazed at how long his tail was. He could wrap it completely around himself when he curled up to sleep, and then he had grown into his long tail. He easily weighed thirty pounds and loved to put all that weight right on your chest when he snuggled up to you. However, when it came right down to it, Purgatory was like his cat in really only one respect, they were both the same shade of ginger.

Cats were so much smarter than dogs, James thought to himself as he looked out over the endless Martian landscape. You couldn't really train a cat, but that was why he thought they were smarter. The easier you are to train the smaller your mind must be, he thought. He remembered watching a cousin of his try to show off how she had trained her cat when he was over at their house for Christmas. She held a treat over the cat and told it to sit up pretty. The cat looked at the treat, popped out its claws, and scratched the hand holding the treats. His cousin had dropped the treat and the cat calmly picked it up and walked away with it. A perfect example of how a cat was smarter than a dog.

Sighing, James wished he was smarter than he felt right now, and that was saying something because he was feeling pretty darn good about himself. For what had to be the four thousandth time James looked down at his new hand.

"You know what?" James said out loud to no one but himself, "I think I did well considering all that was involved." He picked a small hill a short ways away and started toward it. "I mean think about it. I end up in a strange world that ends up being part of the afterlife, I get trapped and put on trial by a ticked off, and possibly insane angel who chops my hand off," his boasting trailed off as his mind started flitting back through the almost paralyzing depression he had felt while laying in the hole.

Losing part of himself had been devastating. He remembered joking with his friends in college and asking them what they would rather lose if they had to, an arm or a leg? Would they rather be blind or deaf? It all seemed so harmless. You always lived your life with that sense of, not really invincibility, but just the sense that it wouldn't happen to you.

"Nope," shaking his head, James mentally shook the memories from his head, "I don't have time for this, and besides I helped overthrow the previously mentioned insane angel, and" again he looked at his new hand, "even dished out a bit of karma."

"Now all I have to do," James said as he crested the rise and looked around, "is figure out where in all of Purgatory a single demon would go with a group of kidnapped teens."

Yeah, his brain replied, *that should be nothing.*

"Well, we just have to think like a crazed shadow demon with no compassion, empathy, or..." James trailed off.

And while we're doing that let's just hope the crazed demon doesn't get hungry and start eating the teenagers.

"Right. Let's not think about that. Let's just pretend for my sanity's sake that something completely different is actually happening." He continued to look around at the landmarks, such as they were. "Where would he go? And for that matter why would he even come here in the first place?"

To his right the valley of Purgatory slopped up toward distant mountain peaks that looked sharp enough to cut the sky until it spilled its invariably raw umber blood. Conversely, everything in the valley looked soft and smoothed down. It was all dusty and rounded off, but up there it was edges and solid stone. His eyes were drawn to a single point where the folds of the mountains came together. There, as far away as it was, James could easily see the silver metallic reflection of what he assumed was the gate. He shook his head slightly and decided the actual description would be opalescent, and he knew without even being able to see from here that on each side of the gate stood an angel. James could feel them in his hand, and that struck him as odd. He looked down at his new right hand, raised it, and waved at the distant angelic guardians. It overwhelmingly reminded him of the end of Indiana Jones and the Last Crusade where the knight waves goodbye as the temple collapses around them.

"Not that way," James said to the dusty orange air. "So if the good guys' gate is over there, and it's, to the best of my knowledge, not the place a demon would go, then the other one would be over...” and he looked to his left.

Purgatory stretched away flat as west Texas to his left. There were no trees or shrubs to break up the expanse of nothing continuing on into the unimaginable distance except one thing. There was a shadow, and in this place of no sun a shadow stands out more than almost anything.

“Now if I were him, and I’m not, but if I were, I would head for someplace familiar, and to a shadow demon that thing over there looks very familiar.” James nodded to himself and started walking.

It was a long walk.

James realized halfway through the eternity of his walk across the Sahara of Purgatory that he didn’t need to pee. It was an odd thing to cross his mind but when the black dot you’ve been walking toward for the better part of the length of human existence doesn’t get any bigger you start thinking odd thoughts. Such as he didn’t have to pee, and wasn’t that odd in and of itself?

“But on the other hand,” he said to the swirling dust on his right, “I haven’t had to drink anything either while I’ve been here in...” He paused and waved his hands around, “what should I call this place? Just Purgatory? Because... You know when you’ve said a word too many times and it loses its meaning?” He turned to the dust on his left, “You know what I’m talking about right? I think I just said Purgatory about a million times and it really does fit this place but at the same time I really feel like Orangeatory would be better.”

James walked some more and tried to do something useful. He tried to figure out his pace count. He had to assume certain things about himself since he really didn’t have any tools on hand to measure things, but in this case he was sure a little fudge in the numbers wasn’t going to bother anyone.

“All right people, here’s the deal, and yes I know I’m the only one here but at this point in the game I feel there’s no harm in going a little mad.” With that he stopped. He looked directly at the black dot on the horizon that was his destination and thought for a moment, if it really was what he thought it was, it should be easier to get to. The road to it should be paved with all kinds of good intentions and not orange dust.

"But I digress. My normal step is about a yard, give or take. There are, as you all know from elementary school, three feet in a yard. I think there are five thousand something feet in a mile." James paused and waved his right hand in front of his face, "Why, hello, new angel hand. Do you happen to magically know how many feet are in a mile? What was that you say? You think it's five thousand two hundred and eighty? That's great. Now let's do some mental math since we have all of eternity here and I don't have to use the bathroom any time soon."

James hummed to himself for a while then knelt causing puffs of the ubiquitous orange dust to fly up around him. He wrote out the division problem of over five thousand feet divided by three to get the number of yards and decided that one thousand seven hundred and sixty would do.

"See," he said as he stood up, "you can go a bit mad and still do math. Not bad, if I do say so myself."

As he started walking and counting his steps, he realized he was narrating everything he did in his mind with a voice that sounded very much like the narrator from the classic Winnie the Pooh cartoons. That almost made him lose count. Finally, however, after thirty-six miles the narrator in his head had nothing left to narrate.

"I have decided that Orangeatory is not a good name either. It makes me feel like Orangutans should be running the place. Like it was the afterlife of the apes." James took a few more steps, paused, thought about nothing for a moment, sat down in the dust, and let himself fall back with his arms outstretched. He let the dust slowly settle on him like an old cardboard box in your grandfather's attic.

Staring up into the endless ginger sky he felt a wave of hopeless panic ripple through him. He stopped his breathing and closed his eyes. His heart was the only noise in that entire dead monochromatic world. No birds chirped. No breeze ruffled any leaves or grass, just the steady thump of his heart. It was the steady beat that finally pushed away the panic. He was still alive. He was still doing something.

"But you know," he said to the sky, "I could use a little help here. I think I've done a darn amazing job with what I've been given. Got my hand cut off, and yes I did get a new one, but still it doesn't change the fact that it did get cut off. Now I'm stuck in the desert that seems to be an actual metaphor for everything people say about deserts." He paused to wiggle some dust off his nose before he breathed it in. "And sure I thought it was a little funny to be a bit crazy and talk to myself for the first eternity, but, honestly, by the time the second eternity rolled around I got sick of myself. I may have said some things to myself I might regret when I get out of here. But in all seriousness I could use a little help here."

This whole situation came from his belief. He'd gained his powers because he could do something not many people could. He could really and truly believe in crazy unbelievable things. Sure there were a lot of fanatics out there, and some people would call that true belief. In fact it was true belief. It was so true it could change the world. But true power, the kind that could not just change the world but warp the fabric of reality itself, came not just from true belief. You had to anchor that belief in something first. You could believe your roses talked to you, or your pet rock was really Roger the god of all rocks. Praise be to Roger for he has the power to smite his enemies, but only once, and only if you help him out by giving him a good throw. But in the end, if your belief, your life, wasn't anchored in something fundamentally true then your belief was just a dead leaf in the autumn wind.

James' anchor point started with his father. Always do what is right his Dad had taught him. Especially when no one is watching. Doing what is right when people are watching is nothing special, even crooks do that. If you do what is right when no one is around, and when no one will know about it, then you have something special. The best part about his Dad was how he never needed to repeat the lesson. He just lived it. And in the living of it, James had watched so many good things happen. People would help his Dad for no apparent reason. His Dad had so many friends it was really almost ridiculous. In an age where you could easily have over three hundred so called friends on Facebook his Dad really did have that many. It became the anchor point for James. When the winds of crazy had blown into his life during his junior year of college that anchor had saved him.

James had been recruited, if you could call a crazy dream a recruitment pitch, and had gained power. He could not just metaphorically change the world but realistically change it. Sunlight could be bent and used as a stick. Fire could be sucked from the air itself. Broken bones would heal. Anything was possible as long as James truly believed it was possible. And

94

after seeing the crazy events of a few years ago when he first encountered the Darkness, James truly did believe anything was possible.

But as he chased the Darkness across the United States, and parts of western Canada, James had finally taken a few moments to wonder where the power actually came from. His first teacher, or tutor, or whatever you would call someone who taught you how to warp reality, had talked about a deity his people had called the Great Flame. At first James had just brushed off the notion of some god allowing him to change reality, but now here he was in Purgatory. He'd just fought an actual angel. It was what he could truly call an honest to God angel.

So in this moment with no power and no end to this horrid orange desert all he could think about as he lay there in the dust of Purgatory with his eyes closed was that someone up there needed to help him. He felt like adding something about how he deserved it after everything from the last few events, but he just decided it wouldn't be a good idea to get on any supernatural beings' bad side at a time like this.

"Uhm, excuse me, but are you dead?"

"I didn't say that," James said to himself.

"No, you didn't."

"That's odd," James said again, "I didn't say that either."

"Right again."

James' eyes popped open and he sat straight up ramming his head into the face of whoever was looking down at him. "Ouch." He grabbed the top of his head and rocked forward rubbing at the pain.

"My thoughts exactly." Came the voice again but sounding a bit more perturbed.

James looked around and a shiver of something like surprise mixed with awe rippled through him, "I know you."

"And I thought you were dead," The little juggler replied.

"Isn't everyone here dead?"

"Well, you said you weren't," the juggler rubbed his face, "and I said something to the effect about how going into that town was going to make you dead if you weren't."

James nodded, then stopped and said, "No, you didn't."

"I'm fairly sure I told you it was a bad idea."

James shook his head, "No, actually you told me it would be a good place to start looking."

"And I also said you would never catch me going into a place like that."

James just stared at him.

"The point is," the juggler continued, "you should have been able to imply from my unwillingness to enter the town that it was a bad place to go." The juggler leaned toward him and whispered, "I heard they had a crazy angel in charge of that place."

"Well," James started dusting himself off as best he could, "they did have a crazy angel in charge."

The juggler smiled, "And they say things never change here. It's like I always said back in Rome, you should always listen to the juggler. We may look like clowns but…"

"Seriously?"

"What?" the juggler looked around himself like he must have missed something in this land of orange nothing.

"First off," James said, "I'm already in the middle of the largest physical metaphor known to the living and dead and you want to talk about clown metaphors?" The juggler started to say something, but James raised his hand to stop him, "And secondly what are you doing here?"

"The real question is what are you doing here?" The juggler replied.

"Why is that the real question?"

"Because I followed you here, so in fact the question is what are you doing here?"

"I'm…" James paused. "At the moment," he continued, "I'm having a mental breakdown and going slightly insane. I think I miss the sky." And at that moment it dawned on him how true that statement was. It was so big and blue and amazing, yet he'd taken it for granted all his life. Thinking back on it, he understood why so many people had written poetry about the sky. At night the stars looked down on you with their endless mystery. During the day the sky had so much personality that multiple religions had assumed the sky itself must be a god. The sky could be happy, sad, angry, gruff, or just plain mean.

"Uhm," the juggler broke in on his whirling thoughts, "there really is no time here, but still I thought you should know you have been just sitting there for a while. And I'm still wondering why you were laying on your back out here?"

"Right," James rolled his shoulders trying to loosen up muscles that had become sore from tension. "Well, the short version is I'm chasing a thing that looks like a shadow with lots of white eyes because it kidnapped some teens when I tried to kill it."

The juggler nodded as if that was a statement he heard on a regular basis, "Right, I think I remember your telling me that before you went into the village which I implied you shouldn't go into. That still doesn't explain why you're here."

"I lost him in the town." James sighed, "Actually I never saw him in the town in the first place so I guess I can't say I lost him in the town."

"The town I told you not to go into?"

James rolled his eyes and was about to disagree with the little juggler but then thought better of it, "Yes."

"How'd that turn out for you?"

He looked at his new right hand and decided he didn't really want to talk about everything he'd been through in town so instead he said, "Where'd your rocks go?"

The juggler looked at James for a moment then broke into a smile, "I'm glad you asked." And three rocks jumped from his sleeve, pocket, and somewhere else James didn't see. Soon the three smooth rocks were spinning and twirling in mid air.

"Anyway," James continued, "I figure he might have gone through the black-looking gate."

"I did say," the flying rocks formed a perfect circle in the air, "you had two choices, and you decided to go with the town instead of the gate."

"Well, now I'm trying to get to the gate."

The circle shifted to two loops over the juggler's hands, "I sense a but in there." He chuckled to himself, "That, my lost friend, would have been the start of a great joke on the streets of Rome."

"I'm sure you used it on the Pope himself."

"No," the juggler said vehemently, "Pope Alexander the sixth would chop off very intimate things if you joked about such things around him." The juggler caught the rocks for a moment and, scratching his head with one of them, said, "Very hypocritical of the Borgia's if you ask me. Chopping things off poor jugglers for telling poo jokes while at the same time..." he paused, tossed one rock in the air, and caught it. "Anyway that is not relevant now is it?"

James stared at the juggler for a long moment before saying, "You juggled for the Borgia Pope?"

"And you met a crazy angel."

"Yes," James nodded, "point taken. I guess the real point is that I can't get to the gate."

"Why not?"

"That is a wonderful question."

The juggler extended his hand, helped James up, and said, "I don't understand."

"What's hard to understand about it? I can't get there."

"But you did get there."

"Where?" James' voice rose in frustration.

The juggler pointed over James' left shoulder, and for a moment James understood how every character in a movie felt when the monster, or teacher, or love interest was behind them the whole time they were talking and never knew it. He understood why they hesitated to turn around, because at first you didn't believe them, and then you also didn't want to look stupid if they actually were right and it had been behind you the whole time. So after a moment James sucked in a deep breath and turned around.

The gate hunkered down between two small dunes of rusted dirt. Protruding from the top of the dunes he could just make out two solid stone pillars to which the gate itself was anchored. The gate was, to James' surprise, boringly plain. It wasn't at all what he had expected the gates into Hell itself to be. He had expected insanity or dark grandeur. They should be made of swirling iron in the shape of thorns or skulls, or heck it should be made of real skulls, or even better it should be made from the squirming remains of the damned. But no, it was plain. James had seen gates into suburban neighborhoods that looked fancier than this thing. It was made of straight vertical iron bars about six feet high, and that was it. No screaming demon faces. Not even a sign with something cryptic like in Dante. "Abandon all expectations," James muttered to himself.

"What did you expect?" The Juggler said.

James shrugged, "Something a bit more imposing and..." he waved his hand at it vaguely.

This time the Juggler shrugged, "Have you ever heard the expression the road to hell is paved with good intentions?"

James nodded, reached out with one hand, and lightly touched the iron gate with one finger, tensing up as if he expected to be shocked.

"Well," the Juggler continued with a small smile, "for most people the gates of hell are," he waved his hands at the gates, "just this. They are plain everyday things. Most people enter hell through boring ways, and it's what they didn't do in life that brings them here, not what they did." The Juggler raised his eyes from the gate to the expanse of Hell beyond and his normally jovial expression turned sad and pensive. "If the gates of Hell were always big, scary, and obvious I expect most people would avoid them, but as was once famously stated, most people live lives of quiet desperation. They go to work everyday, get a two-thousand calorie Frappuccino at Starbucks, and go to the gym at night to work off the Frappuccino. All the while ignoring people around them. Ignoring the poor and downtrodden. Saying to themselves that someone else will take care of the problems of the world."

James looked quietly at the little man for a moment then said, "You're not really a juggler, are you?"

The Juggler tore his gaze away from Hell and looked at James. The smile returned to his face, "I am the greatest juggler of all time. Yes," he nodded to himself, "I am."

James raised an eyebrow. "Anyway." He turned back to the gates and pushed one side a little bit harder. It creaked and swung just enough open for him to squeeze through. "You think the Darkness went this way?"

The Juggler nodded, "It's the only way he could've gone to get out of Purgatory."

"But where could he go from Hell?" James looked skeptical, "I thought you could only get into Hell not out."

"Things get out of Hell all the time. People these days are very quick to say it was nothing really, just an accident, or mental psychosis, or just a shadow where it shouldn't be, but in reality things get out all the time."

James looked horrified, "Are you telling me people really do get possessed by demons?"

"Ha!" The Juggler punched James in the shoulder, "Are you telling me you're chasing a demon through Purgatory and about to walk into Hell and you don't think demons possess people?"

"Well, yeah, but when you put it that way..." James trailed off and turned back to the gate and pushed at a broken spot where the two halves of the gate would have met. "So, on a different but highly related topic, are there monsters?"

"Uhm?" The Juggler looked around the vastly empty desert of Purgatory.

"In Hell." James pointed over the gate. "Are there big scary things with rows of teeth and those teeth have little mouths with more teeth and they'll try to eat me with those teeth?"

"Actually, there is one called the Corinthian that has pointy teeth filled mouths instead of eyes." A shudder ran through the Juggler, "Now his fall into madness is a story not to be told in the dark of night. If you want to hear it though, I can tell you."

"That would be, uhm, no." James just stared at him for a long moment, "You're just kidding me right? There's no such thing. Right?"

"Keep telling yourself that kid. It'll help you sleep at night."

"So there are monsters."

"Yes," the Juggler said with a very definitive nod.

"Well," James raised his new right hand and flexed it, "I'm sure this thing can handle anything that comes along."

"Why would your hand be able to, uhm, do anything special?" The little Juggler asked.

"Because," James waved it around as if his hand was a sword, "it was the hand of an Angel." He pointed it at the gates like a gun, "It must be able to shoot lightning or fire or something."

"I doubt it."

"Seriously?" James looked from his new hand to the Juggler, "That would just be, well, amazingly unfair."

"Why?"

"Because he chopped my hand off and threw me in a pit is why. And because he was doing amazing Angel things."

"That's because he's an Angel."

"Well." James hesitated.

"Look," the little man said, "you are James because of who you are not because of your hand. When your hand got, as you said, chopped off, did you stop being James? Could someone else pick up that hand and become James?"

"When you put it that way..." James looked down at his new right hand and twiddled his fingers. "Then why did it just attach right onto my arm like magic?"

The Juggler smiled and shrugged.

"So, in other words," James started pulling on a broken length of iron on the gate, "no magic hand to smite demonic monsters with."

The Juggler smiled at him, "Nope."

"And of course my powers don't work here."

The Juggler cocked his head to the right like he hadn't heard James correctly, "You have powers?"

"Had." James corrected him, "I had powers. But the nature of Purgatory is immutable it seems, so my powers don't do anything."

"Oh." The Juggler looked confused, "So, what?"

James continued pushing and pulling on the length of iron, "My powers are based on belief. If I truly believe something can happen then I can make it happen. But it seems that no amount of believing will change the unchangeable existence of Purgatory."

"Ah," the Juggler nodded, "but where does it come from?"

With a final twist and pull the length of iron broke from the gate. "Great question. I have no idea." James hefted the three foot length of solid wrought iron, "I think there's something, or someone, out there, but I haven't figured out the details." He swung the iron bar like a baseball bat, "It seems as long as I do, well, the right thing, I have access to the power."

The Juggler nodded, "Maybe you need to spend a little time thinking about the source of things."

"I'm a bit busy chasing demons into Hell right now."

"Just remember," the Juggler put his right hand on the gate, "the gate of Hell is plain and boring and Hell is filled with people who didn't have the time to figure things out."

James and the Juggler locked eyes for a long moment then the Juggler smiled, "But you do have a demon to catch and some kids to rescue. And it seems you finally have something to fight off the monsters."

James nodded at the makeshift weapon in his hand, "So Mister Juggler do you have any advice about which direction a crazy demon with some teen hostages would go?"

The Juggler pointed to a shape in the distance of Hell, "There's a tower. Run straight for it. I think there are doors he might head toward."

"Well, the good news is," James struck a sword fighting pose and swung the bar around a few times, "I took fencing for a year or so."

The Juggler gave him a worried smile and tilted his head toward the gates of Hell, "No time like the present."

*****

James ran. And he wished for a moment he'd brought the angel's sword with him, but knew he'd probably have just dropped it in the desert. The tower was a long way away and he wasn't sure if he could keep up a sprint so he settled into what he thought of as a three mile pace.

The first thing James noticed about Hell was the distinct lack of people. He'd always expected it to be crammed full of the damned, screaming in lakes of boiling lava while demons flourishing pointy tails poked at them with tridents. But all he saw was a vast empty expanse of nothing. Well, not exactly nothing. There were rocks. And that was the second thing James noticed about Hell. It had color. Not a lot of color, mind you, but more than one, and after the single minded monochromatic assault of Purgatory, Hell was like a color explosion.

The plain of Hell wasn't like anyplace James had ever seen. He guessed that was kinda the point. But if he was going to liken it to something he'd have to put a few places together. Maybe if you crammed together the desert of the American Southwest with the rocky shoreline of the Pacific Northwest, then threw in a few randomly placed three to four foot high rocks that looked like ancient Aztec obsidian sacrificial knives you'd get close.

One of those rock knives rose up just ahead of him and James thought he saw movement behind it. Something poked its head out and without breaking stride James swung the iron bar and felt it connect with a crack. He didn't look back as the whatever it was started wailing, because the once empty plain of Hell had started to move. Figures rose up out of the dirt and rocks. Some he thought were rocks slowly rose onto whatever it was they stood on.

James made it a point not to look closely at anything. So far nothing about Hell had been what he expected but he wasn't going to stare at something that could very likely give him nightmares for the rest of time. So he ran. Nothing was moving toward him yet, so he tried to remain calm and keep his pace steady. If he kicked it up into a sprint now, he was worried he'd be out of gas when the real running needed to happen. His imagination started to take over, and he pictured an overhead shot, like in a blockbuster movie, where he was running along, oblivious to the screen filling with the hordes of Hell closing in on him from behind. They would be so numerous, one group would have to crawl over the top of another in their headlong rush to get at him. His mind couldn't quite settle on what the majority of them would look like, and it jumped between classic zombies and crazy bug-faced monstrosities.

Finally it got to be too much and he tore his eyes away from the tower in front of him and looked over his shoulder. Twenty feet behind him something leaped, and James tripped over his own feet. He hit the ground hard but did his best to roll and come up swinging. He felt, rather than saw, the iron bar thud into something solid. He looked around in a panic for the tower as the rational part of his mind tried to override the automatic flight instinct. He knew if he just started running, he could end up going deeper into trouble. If he was going to run, it had to be in the right direction. He caught sight of it just as a group of things with no discernible heads caught up to him.

He gripped the iron bar like a baseball bat and started swinging. There was no finesse or skill involved. Just try to hit something while at the same time trying not to get hit by whatever that something was.

James ducked under a rock covered arm, swung the bar at what he hoped was the thing's knee, then automatically dodged to the right assuming something else would be trying to hit him. A puff of dust from where his expectations had been confirmed. He fell into a routine of sorts. Dodge, smack something as hard as possible, run toward the tower till something got in the way, and repeat. The battle wasn't anything amazing. He didn't leap over monsters or do rolls through the dust just to come up and stab something through the face in a sort of graceful finishing move. He just hit things and tried to run away.

Part of his mind was pleasantly surprised that nothing tried to shoot anything at him. No stingers shot out of twisted versions of scorpions, which he'd seen a moment ago. He'd decided running was a great idea when faced with six-foot tall scorpion things. Nothing tried to vomit any type of acid or sludge of any kind onto him. They all seemed intent on punching him or stabbing him with sharp parts of whatever kind of body they had.

A green spiky arm shot past his face and James used the iron bar to knock aside the serrated praying mantis arm of a gorilla-bodied thing, then reversed his swing to smash in the side of its head. He was momentarily distracted as the gorilla face tore apart and he thought he saw a human face underneath. In that moment of startled stillness, James saw something in his peripheral vision. His body tried to move but was too slow. A solid object the size of a tree trunk impacted his left side at about the speed of a bullet train. Pain flooded through his body as he was tossed through the air. He didn't roll or tumble when he hit the ground, he just slid, face first, over rocks and dirt, finally coming to a stop against one of the jutting stone pillars.

James groaned and pushed himself up, still clenching the iron bar in his right hand. He spit out gravel and almost screamed when he tried to take a breath. When he put his hand to his side he could feel his ribs bending in the wrong place. He looked around for the monster, switched the bar to his left hand and flexed his fingers. He had been gripping the bar so hard it felt like his fingers couldn't uncurl. After a second his whole hand started to tingle like he'd been sleeping on it wrong all night.

James watched the monstrous nightmare lumber toward him and muttered, "Great, not only do I have to fight off the demonic version of something from a Godzilla movie, but now I've got gravel embedded in my chin."

He shook his whole arm and sharp pins and needles climbed from his new hand past his elbow and through his shoulder. He clenched his teeth and tried to ignore it when he realized all the little buggers who'd been trying to bite his face off were forming a ring around him and the newly arrived big guy.

"I think I'll call you Bob," James said.

Bob raised bark covered arm like things and roared. The crowd of Hell screamed back and James twitched in surprise as his ribs popped back into place. He looked at his stolen angel hand, "Well, that's a bonus."

Bob started pawing at the ground like a bull about to charge and James said, "Not as good as being able to shoot fire or something, and the tingling part is annoying."

His brain was racing as the words slid out of his mouth, *witty banter with your own hand aside, there is a really big, ugly thing literally from the pit of hell about to stomp us into a squishy puddle.*

"Yes," James said to his brain, "and your point is?"

We should probably do something about that.

Bob charged. James hoped Bob was stupid. He doubted anything down here was really bright or else it wouldn't be down here. So he ran toward it. Bob swung his massive arms too late and James ducked under, whipping the iron bar and getting a solid hit on the back of Bob's leg, which did nothing.

"Right." James ran a few more steps and looked over his shoulder to see the big guy stumbling to a stop on top of half a dozen smaller monstrosities. "We could do that I guess."

Do what?

"You're my brain. You really need to keep up." James spun in a quick circle, "Now where's the tower?"

Little to the left and directly past the thing with all the eyes.

"Good, so..." the world whumped and James staggered to the left. He crouched and looked around just in time to see something else flying at him. He rolled forward and heard it scream as it flew over his head. Looking up from the dust he saw Bob scoop up some poor little Hell spawn and chuck it at him like a baseball. For a moment James thought about taking a swing at the thing as it went by but decided that would be overdoing it a bit. What he needed was to get Bob to charge him again, and he knew it wouldn't take much because all Bob's ammunition was currently running away.

"Hey, ugly!" James paused, "You know what?" He looked at the demons circling around him, "That's really not an insult down here, is it?"

He decided he didn't need to waste any more breath yelling at the giant as it bent at the waist and started toward him.

As he picked up speed, Bob lowered his head and spread his arms wide. James could tell it wasn't going to try to hit him this time. He was just going to turn himself into a demonic snowplow and scoop him up. James had planned for this so he did exactly what he needed to do and ran.

The smaller monsters around him had the exact same idea. They might not be smart Hellspawn but they had seen what Bob had done to the others and they didn't want to be anywhere near him. James had thought he might need to smack some of them to get away, but none of them paid attention to him as they all ran from the oncoming train of destruction. James looked over his shoulder a few times and saw he was outdistancing the big guy. Bob must have realized what was happening and started trying to scoop up more little monsters as ammo. James dodged them easily and had a slight smile on his face when he reached the tower.

Chapter Eleven

Grace leaned over the edge, the gray stone pressing into her palms, and watched the fight far below. He was smart and didn't stand still. After the few interactions she'd had with him she really hadn't been sure what the outcome of this trap would be. In the church he'd stood his ground and done things she never dreamed possible, but then on the plains of Purgatory he'd snuck and hid. Her conflicting emotions were sandpaper rough in her stomach. She'd so desperately wanted him to stand up and do something amazing at that moment. Fling fire from his hands or pull a glittering sword out and cut the monster in half. Instead he'd sunk down and hid, letting them go.

She blinked a tear from her eye. It never turned out well if she showed emotion in front of it. She refused, just like the others, to call it by name. The refusal was a small thing, but when you feel like there's nothing you can do, you do the only thing you can.

Her mind was drawn back to the ground below and the last click of the giant mouse trap. She watched as something truly gigantic rose from the ground and some part of her was disappointed that she couldn't hear it roar from all the way up here. That's how it worked in the movies. No matter how far away the monster was, you could always hear it roar. Barring that, something should have shook or been blown away by the ferocity of its vocal assault. Here, however, it was just a bigger ant in a field full of ants. She'd watched as he'd run and fought his way across the plain below, and from her vantage point it all looked truly hopeless. From the moment he'd set foot through the gate, the things had risen up around him. They'd slowly, unstoppably, worked to close in around him and cut him off, until finally they'd stopped him.

"Useless."

A hand grabbed the back of her shirt, lifted her away from the edge, then tossed her against the tower wall. Pushing herself up she rubbed her back and shoulder where she'd hit. Ray stepped toward her and extended his hand to help her up. As she rose she couldn't help but stare at the monster looking out over the battle below. After every nightmare they'd woken from, he'd gotten bigger. Every time they tried to escape and failed he grew stronger. Each argument, scared jump, or depressed thought just seemed to bring out puffs of smoke for him to breathe in. They'd become meals for him. His own traveling buffet. And now he stood before them resplendent in his grace and power. She didn't want to think of him that way, but it was difficult to phrase it differently with him standing there. He went barefoot and bare chested with loose fitting dark red pants that flowed around him more like smoke than cloth. Thick, dark hair crowned his head, and when he looked at her his eyes were a field of stars, sparkling motes of light spread across black velvet.

"I knew he would be somewhat formidable, but..." He leaned forward, focusing on the fight, "Scratch that. I think it has more to do with the quality of help I recruited. That one just tossed the little one... Missed terribly. Now they're all running..."

Shaking his head he turned to them, "Well, that was a colossal waste of time."

As he shoved them up the stairs Grace noticed Ray, looking like a whitewashed fence with almost all the paint stripped by wind and rain, leaning over the edge, watching the progress of their unknown but possible savior.

"Why?" She heard him whisper.

Then silence stretched over them, weighing them down like a too thick blanket on a summer night. The tower had a way of doing that. Sound was lost in it without even the echo of a tomb. It rose, a massive pillar of gray stone, seemingly forever. The stairs wound around the outside, clinging to it like cracks in the bark of a giant tree.

Mitch put his arm around her waist and pulled her in front of him, switching sides to put her next to the wall and himself at the edge. "What is this place?"

She looked at the monster to see how he would respond then looked back at Mitch. His face twisted up bracing himself for the inevitable blow.

"It's Hell." The monster's voice had been steadily changing since they passed through the iron gate, and as much as she hated to say it, or even think it, it'd taken on a musical quality.

"Actually," he continued, "it's not quite Hell, but as close to it as your rational, and still living, minds can get."

"So," Grace was unable to help herself, and her curiosity, "Hell is a tower?"

"No, and yes." He chuckled at his own irritating answer. "Hell is a place and an idea. The seed and spark of it starts out within each of you. It's that spark I was hoping to use to get me here rather than having to go through the dead imagination of Purgatory. The tower is, for lack of a better term, a useful fiction."

They came to a landing and Grace slid her finger tips along the rough wooden surface of a door. "And these?"

"Those," she could hear him stop behind them, "those are my salvation, and possibly that parasite's death."

Looking back she saw him staring at carvings in the stone above the door. He spoke and the words were drops of lava in her mind. A flame dancing over a gilded crown. The world in ruin at her feet. The stars fell like snowflakes leaving an empty void above her.

She wobbled, the stone stairs rose up, and for a moment she thought she was flying. Cold slate rapped the side of her head. The words and visions blurred and floated away leaving her feeling empty.

"Ahh, it's been too long since I've had cause to speak the music of the spheres." Kron'ael stepped back and looked over the now open door like a chef checking the wedding cake for the last time.

Pushing herself up to her knees Grace heard a shuffling beside her and looked over to see Mitch staring at the open door and taking slow steps toward it.

"Now, now," Kron'ael reached out and pulled Mitch back toward the stairs, "you're mine. He can't have you. It won't stop him. He's too bloody single minded for that little sideshow to do that, but it's a change of scenery and that in itself will convince him to take a look. It should buy some time for me to set up the real show."

He pushed them up the stairs and on they went. None of them wanted to stop. It had come as an unspoken agreement between the three of them. When they stopped bad things happened to their minds. They didn't talk about escape anymore, at least not to each other, and here on the stairs there really wasn't an escape option.

"There's the doors." Mitch whispered at her, reading her mind.

"No." She didn't have time to explain her feelings, but she knew it would be a bad idea to go through one of those. Not only were they in Hell, and walking through a random door was a bad idea in itself, but the feeling she'd gotten when he'd opened it still draped around her neck like a broken noose.

Their best bet, in her mind, was to wait it out. She knew he was still coming. She could see the monster was worried about him, which was a good thing. Eventually he would catch up and then... Well, she didn't know what would happen then. The man had beaten the monster back at the church so there was no reason to suspect he couldn't do it again.

"Stop."

Grace twitched and looked around the unchanging staircase.

Kron'ael pushed past them, "Stay here."

He continued up until he was lost from view. She assumed he was going to set up another trap. Maybe open another door, and he didn't want them collapsing in a heap or accidentally getting sucked into whatever was there.

"Why are you here, wanderer?" The monster's voice carried down the steps.

"Does it matter, fallen star?" An unfamiliar voice answered.

"Don't call me that." Grace heard his voice tighten.

"Or what?"

"How did you even get here?"

"Give a man enough time..."

Kron'ael's face appeared at the edge of the stairs ahead of her, "Come on you three, and ignore the old man."

They walked up the stairs and saw the owner of the voice sitting cross legged, leaning against the rough cut wall of the tower. Tattoos covered every piece of skin like a disease making him a frightening figure of a man. Nothing about him seemed old. His hair was solid brown and the skin not covered in ink seemed unlined with the muscles underneath almost as solid as the stone he leaned against. However, there was something else. The space around him seemed compressed, and the more she looked the more convinced she became that he could compete with the tower itself in sheer age. Then, for a broken sliver of a moment, looking in his eyes, Grace thought he might try to help. Everything in her wanted to cry out and run

110

for him. Maybe he could protect them. The monster seemed, if not scared, put off by him. The comment he'd made seemed to imply there was nothing the monster could do to him.

"Don't think about interfering murderer." Kron'ael stopped between the three of them and the tattooed man, "I might not be able to kill you, but I can pitch you off this tower and happily to see what happens."

The old man gave a slight shrug and settled himself back against the wall, looking out over the plains of Hell toward the deserts of Purgatory. What was he, Grace wondered? If they were in Hell, or even just on the metaphorical edge of Hell then what did that make him? The monster called him a murderer so it would make sense his being here, but he didn't seem to be locked up.

"That is actually going to be very helpful." Kron'ael said.

Grace wondered if the monster always talked to himself or if it was just because he liked having an audience.

"You see, that nut job chasing me is going to be searching for answers by now, trying to figure out what this place is and what to expect from it. He doesn't have a built-in tour guide like you three. He's going to talk with the old codger back there and give us all the time we need to set this up all perfect."

"Set what up?"

"Now, now, it's no fun to spoil the surprise. You'll just have to wait like everyone else."

Up the stairs. No pause, no rest, no change, just up. Her mind wandered. Her Mom staring at her when she'd come home with her hair bright purple. Yelling at her about how she was presenting herself. She'd been so upset when her Mom wouldn't just let her make her own choices in life. And yet, the silence of the tower pressed down on her, squeezing the truth from her memories. There hadn't been yelling, and if there was it had been her doing it. Maybe her Mom was justifiably worried about how people would look at her little girl. Maybe she'd wanted to protect her for a little bit longer from all the comments and stares. Right now, Grace wiped a tear from her cheek so the monster wouldn't see it, she could really use her protection. A night on the couch snuggled against the warmth of her Mom. The cold stone steps seemed to laugh at her and she pulled her eyes up not wanting to dwell too much on the past.

Glancing around she looked at Mitch and was amazed again at how such a quiet guy could end up being... What? Solid rock. At first she hadn't wanted to lean on him, but he'd made himself impossible to ignore. At every chance he'd challenged the monster, spoken up to cheer her, as much as possible in this place, and always tried. What he tried didn't really matter, what mattered was that he'd done something. Was it going to get him killed? Most likely, but that didn't seem to phase him. At this point she wouldn't be surprised if he refused to stay dead. He'd been visibly shaken by the nightmares the monster sent during their breaks, but he was also the first to shake it off. It was like he could recognize what was important and decided those dreams didn't matter.

On the other hand, raising her eyes to the next landing, there was Ray. She shook her head. Ray was a mystery. With all his bravado back in school you'd think he'd be the first to pick a fight, but no. Since the last nightmare Ray hadn't talked unless necessary, and lately she'd started noticing him talking to himself. She never caught what it was. Each time she got close enough to hear him he'd notice her and stop.

"Here we are kiddies."

Grace and the others stopped on the landing and looked around. It was the same as all the ones before, minus the one with the old man. The edge dropped off on the right with a birds eye view of the afterlife, and a wooden door was framed by a stone arch on the left.

"All right, let's hope Mr. Angry back there is distracted for long enough. Now then," Kron'ael turned to the door and placed his hands on it, "just to make sure..." He leaned toward it and laid his right ear on the wood, closed his eyes, and waited.

Grace looked at Mitch and wondered if there was something they could do while he was distracted. Their eyes met and he nodded at her. She wasn't sure what it was supposed to mean, but she took it as an acknowledgement of her intentions. Which was what? She looked back the way they'd come and considered running down the stairs. This offered a little benefit because going down was easier than up, and those were their only options. Also, if you tripped you would still be going in the direction you wanted. Separately, she didn't think running back was a good idea with all the monsters they'd seen attack the guy following them. He'd been lucky, or something, to make it through them. She didn't harbor the same thoughts about the three of them. So up? She looked at the upcoming stairs and couldn't decide. She thought anything would be better than staying with the monster. Not knowing what was ahead, however, meant she didn't know if that statement was true.

Again she looked at Mitch. When she caught his glance she motioned to the stairs with a twitch of her eyes. He shook his head and looked at Ray. Right, Ray, she thought. There he was sitting on the landing with his back pressed to the wall and his legs pulled up, arms wrapped around his knees. His fashionably distressed jeans were more hole than denim now, and his grit streaked face was hidden behind his legs.

Leave him. He hadn't helped, ever. Back in the real world he was a bit of a jerk, and here he was useless. It wasn't the best feeling she'd ever had, that was for sure, but leaving him was getting to be necessary at this point. Cut off your hand to save yourself from Hell. Leave Ray to the monster and make a run for it.

She sighed. If only the math was that easy. If she knew leaving him behind and dashing up the stairs would really lead to her escape then... What? Would she really leave him behind to save herself? Her shoulders dropped, she let out another sigh, and lowered herself to sit on the stair at the far end of the landing. It was a moot point. There was no way to know if ditching him would lead to a clean getaway, and more than likely it would lead to nothing but more pain when they were recaptured.

Kron'ael turned from the door with a smile on his now angelically handsome face, "Nice. Granted I almost couldn't hear over all the teen angst from you." He pointed at Grace and she instantly felt invisible coils wrap around her. He raised his hand and she was pulled into the air. "I think I've been ridiculously patient with all of you, but especially with you little missy."

The coils tightened until she felt all her air, hot and moist, pressed out of her lungs. A part of her brain started blathering and her diaphragm twitched uncontrollably trying to draw a breath. "But I'm not doing this out of frustration or spite. Have I done things just because I was angry? Yes, but rest assured this is not that. In this case it has to do with usefulness."

He flicked his wrist and Grace flew through the air slamming into the door. The coils released and she slumped to the ground sucking in gulps of air. She looked around at Mitch and Ray wondering what they would do, while at the same time hoping they didn't do anything. Throughout this trip she'd watched the monster toss them around with the consistency of a tax accountant. This was nothing new. Insults fell from his lips like leaves from an autumn tree. They'd been beaten, broken, and stabbed over the course of this journey. Philosophically she still wasn't sure how real this all was. Meaning, she was still holding out hope this was some kind of nightmare or existential meltdown. Even if they were really in Hell, part of her still believed only her mind would be here and not her body.

"Now then..." Kron'ael reached over her and rested the fist of his right hand on the door, "I need material." He pressed and Grace could feel the door vibrate through her spine. A light dust began to fall around her and for a moment made the sky of Hell take on the pink hues of sunset.

Glancing up she saw a hole in the door and the monster repositioning his hand. Time passed and more holes appeared. All the while dust drifted down piling up, sad and quiet, against her legs.

"There." Brushing dust off his hands, Kron'ael stepped back and looked at the now pockmarked door. "Can't make an omelet without breaking some eggs and in this case can't make things without stuff." He pointed to the piles of dust and twirled his finger like stirring a drink. The fine sand rose in a small whirlwind and piled itself in his outstretched left hand. "You know what Hell's made of? Well, whatever you're thinking it's wrong. It's not made of the screams of the damned, or piles of bones. There's no great demonic elephants standing on the back of a giant skeletal damned turtle swimming through the emptiness of time and space. It's reality." He reached out and rapped his knuckles on the wooden door, "The fundamental building blocks of reality. In the right hands this stuff is like play dough. You can make anything from it."

Reaching above the door he rubbed some dust into the keystone. After rotating it a few times he brought his hand away. A solid metal ring was screwed into the center of the stone. Taking the rest of the dust he rubbed his hands together and reached up to the metal ring attaching newly formed ropes.

"It would be nice to do the something from nothing trick, but that one He kept to Himself." Looking down at Grace he said, "Now, I bet you're wondering why I would have ropes attached to a door with holes in it?"

Suddenly her mind blossomed with realization. She'd been so caught up in watching him do the impossible that the reason for any of it had simply not crossed her mind. Now the ropes stood out like beacons against the dark Hellish background. Instinct took over and before rational thought could intrude she found herself running up the steps leaving the landing.

Laughter followed her, wrapping around her it became real and started pulling her back until it was suddenly cut off with a thud and a grunt. Her feet had left the ground for a brief moment, but after dropping and placing a steadying hand on the stairs, she regained her momentum. Reflexively glancing over her shoulder she saw Mitch wrestling with the monster and paused. Her breath caught and her mind stopped. His eyes locked on her for a moment then he shouted, "Go! Damn it, Grace! Go!"

Her feet slipped and her knee scraped across the edge of the next stair as her mind whimpered... Mitch doesn't swear...

She was up a stair then four. She took them two at a time, the best her short legs could do. She'd lost count when it wrapped around her again. Solid as iron and pulling with the inexorability of death itself, she was pulled back down the stairs. Mitch was pressed against the wall next to the door by the same force which dragged her toward those ropes hanging noose like from the top of the door. Tears dripped from her chin as the monster wrapped their perfect ends around her wrists leaving her arms stretched above her head.

"Now," Kron'ael looked from her to Mitch, "I expected the running, and honestly was looking forward to it. That pleasant taste of dreams and hopes denied when it seems so close... But you," he reached out and poked Mitch in the forehead causing a knocking sound as his head bounced off the stone wall, "I did not expect the flying tackle." He flicked his wrist and Mitch flew to the right falling on top of Ray's huddled form. "I'm actually impressed. Honestly, Mitch, you've been the most worrisome of the bunch, and really if I was going to feed someone to these things," his knock on the door elicited a faint hum, "it would be you. My point, in this case, is not to get rid of one of you. I need to get rid of him, and with what's happened between us in the past he's more likely to act rashly with our lovely Grace hung up as food for the little pelle comedenti. You like my Latin?" He smiled, "It means skin eaters. Now then," he turned and patted her on the cheek, "you be a good girl and try to stay in one piece until he gets here. Hopefully they understand what I want them to do and won't eat you before then, but," he shrugged, "you never can tell in Hell."

*****

Mitch had never intentionally wanted to kill someone. In fact, until his attempted tackle of the monster he'd never actually been in a fight. He'd always looked down on those kinds of people. The kind that felt punching someone was the best solution to whatever problem they were facing. Mitch deeply disagreed. There was always a better way to deal with a situation, even if it meant just walking away and letting the other person win, because in reality it meant he won.

Now, he burned. A flaming salamander curled around his heart tried to turn his insides to ash. All his strategies were used up. All his good will expended. He'd believed, religiously in fact, that people could be dealt with politely or simply ignored. He was wrong, and he wanted to kill him. If it wasn't for the invisible bands holding him and dragging him up the stairs he was sure blood would finally add color to the endless gray stone beneath him.

"Still brooding Mitch?"

Mitch tore his eyes away from Ray and looked at the monster.

"You gave it your best try." Kron'ael patted him on the head, "You should be proud of that. Not many have caught me off guard, and beyond that you knocked me down and kept me down for a good while. Unpredictable. That's what that was. Now Ray here," he poked Ray in the back causing him to stumble up a step, "he huddled in the corner like the true coward he is. Totally expected that. Grace almost came back for you. Again, totally expected that. You, however..." Kron'ael nodded at him, "Well played."

As the monster chuckled to itself, Mitch looked at Ray not noticing the streams of mist rising from him, dark exhaust from a burning engine, and the monster breathing it in. "Now then, part two of my little fun time."

They'd come to the mouth of a tunnel leading through the tower. The path of the stairs turned ever so slightly, yet the angle when looked at directly made the mind ache. It continued on but not. It went ever so lightly to the left and cut into the heart of the tower where after a few steps nothing was visible. The entrance vanished around the bend and as they entered Mitch felt he'd been slapped in the face by darkness.

"I need to go and talk with... Someone." The voice of Kron'ael floated back to them from the darkness. "You two be good and stay here. I understand the desire to run back and try to save her, but I would caution you not to wander off in this place. As strange as it may sound, I'm the only thing keeping you alive."

His footfalls tapped away and Mitch felt the confining bands drop away, leaving him free. "Ray?"

A mumble answered him slightly to his left, he reoriented himself in the darkness of the tunnel, and swung. It was a wide swing and his forearm connected hard. That was enough to give him a solid location. With his left hand he grabbed cloth and pulled. Snarling, he swung blindly. Two, three times he connected with something and heard grunts.

Hot words poured out tasting of bile, "You're a waste of human life." His fist drew back then hammered down, "Shaking in a corner, always whining and shaking in a corner." He grabbed Ray's shirt with both hands and pushed, dragging him through the darkness hoping to run into the wall, "She might've had a chance if you could've, just for a second, stopped thinking about yourself and done something worth the air you suck in."

Ray's hands flailed, trying to break Mitch's hold, "And what could I have done?"

The impact with the wall in the dark vibrated up through Mitch's arms and drove the breath from Ray, "What could you have done!" Mitch leaned forward and screamed in his face, "Anything, Ray!" He lifted him off the wall and punctuated the statement by slamming him back again, "A few more steps could have gotten her far enough away. There was a split in the path, Ray." He punctuated the name with another bone rattling slam to the wall, "He wouldn't have known which way she went."

Ray let out a barking cough as his back impacted the wall and managed to say, "He would have killed us."

"And yet here we are. I tackled him and literally," Mitch brought his arm back, and in the utter darkness of the tunnel realized he didn't care if he missed, then slammed it forward, "punched him in the face. I'm still alive, we're still alive. He needs us, you idiot."

Letting go he heard and felt Ray slide down the wall to the floor. A whisper floated butterfly thin in the darkness, "I can't... I don't know..."

Mitch kicked out and felt something softer than the wall connect with the toe of his foot, "I know you can't. I've been made well aware of that fact over the last few weeks. At every turn she was looking for a way to get us out of here, but you couldn't. I was just trying to keep the monster's eyes away from the two of you so you would survive long enough for something to happen, but you couldn't help with that either could you?" He kicked again and a part of him shivered in horror when he heard Ray start to vomit, but he couldn't, wouldn't, stop now. The words had taken on a life of their own and flew raptor quick to their target. "Back home all you cared about was how you looked, how other people thought about you. Here all you care about is yourself." He squatted down and reached out only to have his hand batted away.

"What's wrong with wanting to survive? What's wrong with wanting to be home?"

"Nothing." Mitch settled back on his heels, "But I swear Ray, if Grace dies down there, you're going home in a body bag."

Chapter Twelve

It was old stone, gray and rough cut, with an open stairway clinging to the outside. It was a stone pillar stabbing into the sky. The stairway wrapped around the outside, open to the swirling storm cloud skies of Hell. There was no banister or even a low wall on the outside of the stairs, and just looking up at the unprotected climb caused his heart to climb into his throat. He took the first steps at a run. Once he was up a dozen or so he paused and looked back. The plain of Hell was empty. No monsters with too many eyes, or praying mantis arms. As he shook his head James wondered what Hell really was.

The good news was he was fairly certain the Darkness had come this way because there was nothing else. Why the demon had brought the teens here was a different question, and he looked up the tower wondering what he would find there. Was this place like a hotel for demons? Did the Darkness have a room here where he dragged poor kids off to devour their souls?

"So on the bad side," James raised his left hand palm up, "I have no idea where I'm going or what I'm looking for. On the good side," he raised his right hand, "I'm not hungry, thirsty, or have to go pee, so I think everything's coming out pretty even."

He started walking up the stairs again and after a few moments looked up the stairway and said, "And actually I guess I do know where I'm going since there seems to be only one choice."

*****

As James climbed he tried to occupy his mind by detailing his location. He attempted to figure how big around the tower was by counting the number of steps in a single circuit, but without a reference point it was hard to know when he was back around to where he'd started. It wasn't just the lack of reference points, because the land was dotted with a cornucopia of distinctive rocks and weird mountains in the distance to keep track of, it was the problem of how none of them ever showed up again. He picked a mountain, which reminded him of one of the towers in the Lord of the Rings, and after counting one hundred and five stairs and never seeing it again he began to question his eyes. So the next time he picked a rock formation fairly close to the tower. It looked faintly like a flower opening with the rocks being the petals. This time he counted five hundred steps and still the rock flower never showed up again.

"I think this place is crazy," James said aloud.

Really, you came to that conclusion all by yourself did you? His mind answered back.

"Look, you," James said as he ran his fingers over the rough stone on his left, "I'm just saying either this tower is really, really, really, big or..." he trailed off, not knowing quite what to say.

Or, his brain continued for him, *this is Hell and the normal rules of absolutely everything don't apply here.*

"Yeah, I suppose there is that."

James tried to keep counting the steps but gave up after one thousand six hundred and fifty three. He decided there really wasn't much point to it. He'd figured the steps were about twelve feet wide. He'd done this by laying down, putting his feet against the tower wall, and marking where his head came to then laying down again and seeing the edge was still a few inches away from the top of his head the second time.

"What?" He said to the nothing around him as he got back up. "It turns out Hell is really boring." He looked around after he said that to see if any monsters were about to pop out and try to eat his face. "Not that I'm saying you should make it more exciting."

Famous last words. His brain chimed in.

"You're not really helping," James said as he started back up the endless staircase.

Maybe this is what Hell is. It's punishment by boring staircase.

"Yes," said James. "I can see how that would be great eternal torment for someone like Pol Pot. Kill off a few million people and get the stairs of eternal boredom."

Looking up from the endless gray stone stairs, James saw something ahead was different. He took the next few steps in twos then stopped in front of a door. The steps had leveled out into a landing area of sorts. It was about the length of ten steps made up of the same gray stone. On his right was the normal drop off down to the plain of Hell and on the left was a door. At the end of the landing the stairs continued on. The door was, James supposed, more rightly a doorway because there was no actual door. It was an arched stone entryway made of the same stone as the rest of the tower. The keystone at the top of the arch had a single unrecognizable pictogram carved into it. The whole thing looked like someone had tried to merge a Chinese symbol with the cursive letter Z then capped it all off with a right leaning accent mark.

"What'd you think that means?"

Well, let me get out my Hell translator guidebook and I'll let you know.

"You really think Hell has its own language?"

No, I think you should stick your head into the mysterious Hell portal and ask whomever you see in there if they know how to speak native Hellish.

"Personally," James said, "I bet it's some twisted form of the original angelic language."

Kind of like the difference between British English and American English, right?

"Exactly," James paused, "except I think you just compared the English to angels and Americans to demons."

Most Europeans wouldn't think I'm too far off the mark.

"Oh, I bet the French would beg to differ."

Yes, but no one listens to the French.

James put his left hand on the doorway and started to lean carefully to peek just around the edge of the door.

I wasn't serious about sticking your head in there. His brain yelled at him.

James ignored it and carefully moved his head around the edge of the doorway. The room stretched away for what James estimated was at least the length of a football field. He calculated it was at least thirty feet high by mentally stacking three basketball hoops, and the whole thing was lit by circular windows set high in the walls. Gray marble pillars veined with black lined the walls and at the far end he could just see what he thought was a high-backed stone seat.

As he stared trying to make out the details, a figure stepped out from behind the farthest right hand pillar. Its skin was the red of fresh blood and a tail curved out from rough black pants with hooves visible as he climbed the few steps to the stone seat. Its right arm ended in an overly large and blocky hand. Two horns curved up from its forehead with a small flaming crown floating in the air between them. A tidal wave of fear and panic physically slammed itself into James, followed by an almost overwhelming urge to kneel and cry out that he would do whatever it wanted as long as it didn't hurt him. The thing lowered itself into the stone seat but before it could raise its eyes in James' direction, he jerked his head back around the frame of the door.

Panting and leaning against the wall of the tower James wiped tears from his cheeks. He didn't remember crying and he realized in that moment he didn't really care. What he absolutely cared about was getting as far away from that thing as possible. He darted past the open doorway and ran up the steps taking them two and three at a time. The monsters on the plain of Hell were like ants compared to the nuclear bomb of that unknown demon. He glanced down at the iron bar clenched in his right hand and remembered how well it had worked on most of the things he'd ran past on the plain, and knew it would have done so much nothing against that thing as to be laughable. It would have been the proverbial spitting into the hurricane.

James ran until his lungs burned and his legs felt like they would stop moving of their own volition. He slowed to a walk. In his flight from the thing, he remembered running past at least three more doors. Two had light flowing from them and one had been sealed with a wooden door stripped with iron and a huge lock.

"What kind of thing needs to be locked up in Hell?" He said out loud, "And why didn't Mr. Scary back there chase me?"

He shook his head, "Never mind, I don't want to know." He looked over his shoulder just to make sure it wasn't doing the creepy slow walk up the steps.

"Was that the Devil?"

"No."

James jumped backward and involuntarily swung the bar. Being on stairs at the time, jumping backward did not turn out well. Trying to stop his fall he scraped his palm and fingernails along the rough stone of the tower wall. The bar clanged as it hit the floor and the knuckles of his right hand smashed into the steps as he tried to catch himself and hold onto his only weapon at the same time. His breath exploded from him in a grunt and he had to lie there for a moment before the world came back into focus.

When he realized nothing had started chewing on him, he decided to take a moment to figure out his situation. He slowly rolled onto his back and took stock of himself. His left hand hurt where he was sure he had lost a few fingernails. He didn't want to lift it to check because something might jump out and try to bite it off. His right hand throbbed but he'd managed to keep the iron bar firmly in his grip. His hip and right shoulder hurt where he'd landed on them, but other than those he thought he was all right. That changed when he tried to push himself up with his right hand. Pain shot up his arm and he felt something in his hand click where nothing was supposed to move much less click. He gritted his teeth, shifted his weight to his left hand, and forced himself to get the rest of the way up. After all, he was in Hell and he couldn't afford to stop moving.

Finally he decided to face the fact that something or someone had spoken to him, and again, since he was in Hell, he could only assume it was a bad thing. It was implied in the definition of Hell that nothing in it would be a good thing. Looking at his immediate surroundings, he didn't see anything he thought could talk. That didn't really mean much in a place like this. He might have stepped onto the only talking stair in existence. Maybe that was someone's eternal torment, to be a conscious stair so you knew everyone was walking on you.

Looking around more he saw the stairs flattened out into another landing just up ahead. His immediate thought was of another door but this one must have something coming out of it. Maybe it couldn't come down the stairs and get him, but it would once he was on the landing. He paused at this thought and realized he really didn't have any options at this point. He had to keep going and this was the only way forward. He wasn't going to be stupid about it, however, and wanted to get a look at whatever the It was that was on the landing before charging up. Hoping there was room to sprint past whatever it was, he tried to remember the size of the previous landings and thought, at a flat out run, he could cross it in about three or four steps. The main problem, as he saw it, would be if he had to dodge anything.

His mind filled with octopus-like tentacles whipping out from some dark portal and his having to jump over and dodge around them. If he did have to dodge, he might end up dodging himself right off the edge of the stairs. James leaned and looked over the rim of the stairs. He knew he'd come quite a way up, but what he saw was another reminder he wasn't in the real world anymore. It felt like he was looking out the window of an airplane. He almost expected to see clouds drift by below him, and for a moment felt a tug of vertigo as his stomach tried to crawl up his esophagus and his mouth watered involuntarily. Leaning back he decided any dodging would have to be very discreet.

His angel hand had been tingling while he looked down on the plain of Hell, and James waited to see if it would do what it had done in his fight with monster Bob. After a count of fifty-six Mississippi's James felt the broken bone in his hand pop into place and the pain simply went away. He looked expectantly at his ripped up left hand hoping to see the scratches close up and the fingernails grow back. When nothing happened and the tingling feeling stopped he realized it wasn't going to happen.

So, he thought to himself, it must only work on stuff that's really necessary. "Still," he whispered to himself, "not too shabby. Now about that demon octopus." He lowered himself to his hands and knees and slowly crawled up the steps until he could just peek over the top one and onto the landing.

A man sat cross-legged with his back against another locked door. Well, James thought, he could be a demon octopus in disguise. The man looked dark-skinned but it was hard to tell because of an almost total covering of tattoos in different colors and shapes. Some were recognizable, while others seemed to be changing while he was looking at them. They morphed from words to pictures of animals that looked hungrily at him.

Again James counted. This time he waited for five minutes. If time had any meaning in Hell, which James didn't think it did, he wanted to see if eventually this guy was going to do anything crazy. He couldn't see any weapons of any kind and the guy was barefoot and only wearing some khaki cargo shorts. None of the cargo pockets bulged like they were concealing a knife or gun of any kind. Would a handgun even work in Hell James wondered? Even if it did, where would you get the ammo to reload it? Maybe they had Hell ammo. Tiny little demons would be stuffed into the shell and when you fired it they would scream through the air and attack you. That sounded like a great set up for a Japanese anime. The gun would,

124

of course, be carried by some monk of a secret society determined to save the world from some unknown horror. But if you think it's hard to find normal ammo where would you find tiny demons to reload your magic gun? You'd have to take the time to pick them all up after every battle and shove them back into the shell casings, but be fast because if you wait too long they run and hide under bushes.

After five minutes of his mind wandering and trying to keep count James tried to decide on his next move. Going off his previous thought that, by definition, there was nothing good in Hell, he should try his best to just get past the creepy man as fast as possible and continue on with his Quixotic journey. Because, honestly, if ever there had been a windmill to tilt at this tower was the perfect example of a big one. On the other hand the man had said something to him and not tried to kill him. Maybe he could get some info about the tower and where he needed to go. But on yet another hand, this might be a situation like Kaa in the Jungle Book and if you give him a chance to talk he could hypnotize you and swallow you whole.

"Are you going to say something?" The man's eyes didn't open when he spoke.

No, James thought to himself, because you're a creature from the pit of Hell, or rather the tower of Hell.

The man sighed, "I guess I can't expect anything different considering where we find ourselves." His voice was deep and had the distinctive accent tones of the Middle East. He stretched his neck from side to side popping it, rolled his shoulders to loosen them up and started to stand.

James was sure this was a warm-up to an attack. He gripped the iron bar and thought he only needed to knock the man off balance enough to get by him and up the stairs. Maybe, if he got lucky, he could just knock him off the stairs.

"To answer your first question, no, the thing you saw down below was not the devil, at least not in the sense in which you think of the devil. I assume from your clothes," the man gestured at James, "and what language you spoke, you're from the United States and your idea of the devil would be a Protestant Christian Biblical one."

While he spoke the man straightened up, pressed his hands to his lower back and stretched backward until James heard a loud pop. "Ahhh," the man smiled, "that's better. What you saw, if it's the same as what I saw when I came up, is a glimpse into another possibility. The devil of a different world, I guess you could say."

James almost blurted out one of the many questions randomly popping into his head but decided to stay still and be ready for the attack he knew was coming. He knew about other worlds because of the doors he'd found a few years earlier. He'd seen a burning desert through an open door. And he knew from his mentor's descriptions some of these worlds had fallen into the control of darkness. He remembered Rupert telling him of a world where angels and demons were in open conflict and humans scrambled at their feet like so many bugs being crushed by tanks. Rupert had told him of his otherworldly empire's attempt to save the people of that falling world, but it had only led to disaster in his own.

It was, in fact, an escaped demon from that very conflict James was now chasing. Escaping through open doors between worlds, it had made its way to Earth where it found little to oppose it. James didn't want his world to become like the battleground of the other so he was determined to find this thing and end its existence. After years of tracking it, he'd managed to corner it in that little church only to have it use its last option and escape back here to where, James now assumed, it had come from in the first place.

"I could just tell you I'm not a threat," the man continued, "but we're in Hell and honestly why would you trust anything someone, or something, tells you in Hell? Am I right?"

The man pulled a small red Swiss Army knife from his pocket, folded out the smallest blade, and started to trim his fingernails. "I haven't talked to anyone in a long time so you'll forgive me if I start to ramble. First I suppose I should introduce myself. I'm Cain."

He reached up and tapped a tattoo on his forehead.

When James looked at the tattoo he realized he couldn't kill this man. In fact he couldn't remember why he'd even thought it was a possibility. James shook his head violently as if to fight off the strange reaction. He was in Hell, he reminded himself, and he would do what he needed to get those kids back. Even if he couldn't kill this Cain, he could still take out his kneecaps with an iron bar.

"I know you may not believe me but I'm not going to hurt you. I'm an outsider here, like you."

"Why would anyone..." James started to say and stopped himself. He realized, after the fact, he'd stood up and was in full view of whatever this man really was.

"You really don't know the story of Cain?" The man said. "I know it's been a while since it happened, but the Bible is still the best-selling book in the United States year after year."

Cain frowned slightly at James, "What are they teaching you in school these days? Seriously, what good is reading about Huckleberry Finn if you have no grounding in the stories of the Bible? Where do you think all other European and American stories originate? What do you think they mean when the ESPN guy says it's going to be a David and Goliath game tonight on Monday Night Football? Or, what about when a character in just about every murder mystery says they don't know what happened to the victim because I'm not my brother's keeper?" The man shrugged his shoulders, "That one always hits a little close to home."

Don't do it. James' brain warned him. *He's just trying to lure you into a conversation for some Hellish purpose. We're in Hell, remember?*

Yes, James mentally replied to himself, I remember. But what harm can he do with a conversation, and he might give something away about where the Darkness went.

Oh, I don't know, maybe suck your soul out? Or trick you into stepping onto his platform so he can change into a terrible thing and suck your insides out through your left eyeball.

I'm going to have to cross the platform anyway, James concluded. "You can't really expect me to believe you're Cain. The real, I murdered my brother Abel, Cain."

Cain closed up the Swiss army knife and returned it to his pocket, "On the one hand I have no reason to lie to you."

"On the other hand," James broke in, "We're in Hell and I'm not inclined to trust anything you or anybody else tells me here."

Cain nodded, "Point taken." He raised his hands palm out in a placating gesture, "I just want to talk to someone."

James shook his head, "I'm in a bit of a hurry so..." he trailed off.

"Time doesn't exist here." Cain said, "We can talk for what would seem like hours and..."

"And the thing I'm chasing would get farther and farther away." James pointed up the stairs with the iron bar, "I have no idea how it works but the fact that he's getting away and I'm chasing him means some form of time passage is going on here relative to me at least."

Cain squinted at him, "Is that a piece of the gate?"

"Yeah," James looked down at it for a second, "so what? I needed something to hit monsters with."

Cain nodded, "And I bet it's worked well so far, but I thought only He could break the gate."

James thought extra emphasis had been placed on the word He, "Who?"

Cain's eyebrows went up, "Who? You mean to tell me," he paused, then shook his head. "You know what? If He didn't want to tell you then far be it for me to interfere."

"You already interfered, so either spit it out or get out of the way."

Cain laughed, "A second ago you didn't even want to pause here, but sure, I'll tell you something."

James momentarily hefted the bar wondering if he should just hit him and run for it.

Cain raised a hand, "This is going to be annoying but it all comes down to what you have decided about yourself and where you stand. Something started you on this chase, and something has constantly been there to point the way when you've gotten lost, right?"

James' mind flashed back over the choices and paths leading up to this point and a pattern started to emerge.

"You questioned yourself at some point didn't you?" Cain continued, "You wondered why? And to tell you the truth that is the most normal human thing to do. It doesn't make you special. However, you must have something special to do because the response to your question has been abnormal. He normally doesn't take a direct hand in these things; in helping people figure things out. If you survive all of this, I hope you come out the other side with all the answers you could hope for."

Gritting his teeth and deciding he didn't have the time to think through everything running through his head right then James said, "That was very unhelpful and slightly time wasting and while it's been lovely chatting I really must be going. So if you are not going to eat me or try to suck out my soul..." He tentatively took a step up onto the landing and paused expecting something to happen.

Cain laughed, "I'm not here because I'm part of Hell, or even because I've died and been condemned to Hell. I'm here because it was the last place I hadn't explored."

James looked at the tattoo-covered man and couldn't help himself, "Why would you want to explore Hell?"

"I've been alive for a long time," Cain said. "I watched the pyramids rise. I walked the length of the Mongol empire. It was my curse to walk among people, to become friends with them, to fall in love, and to always watch them die while I lived on."

Cain walked over to the edge of the stairs and looked over. "All those stories about crazed scientists, or wizards, or the queen in Snow White. All of those where they're trying to live forever? I pity them. They don't understand mankind was not meant to live that long. That's why He hid the tree of life from my parents. He wasn't trying to be mean. He wasn't scared they would become gods. It's because when you live forever you only get to see death over and over. I've watched my children grow old and die. My grandchildren grew old and died. Eventually the loss leads to depression and the depression leads to insanity."

He waved his hands at the universe in general, "Everyone but me has gone on to something else, and I wanted to see what it was."

James looked at Cain, not sure whether to pity him or just assume he's lying, so instead he said, "How'd you get here?"

Cain cocked his head a little to the right, "How'd you get here?"

"Simple," James said, "the demon I was chasing ripped a hole in the fabric of space and I followed him through it into Purgatory. Then bing, bang, boom, and Bob's your uncle. Well, actually Bob's a really big angry monster out on the plain a few hundred yards before you get to the steps, but that's beside the point."

James looked Cain in the eye and his curiosity again got the better of him. He knew he should be moving on, chasing after the Darkness, but it wasn't like he was just one turn of the staircase behind him. In fact James had no idea how far away his quarry was. And it wasn't like he needed to worry about which direction to go since there seemed to be a limited amount of choices. After all the time he'd spent in the pit in Purgatory, followed by the unknown amount of time it took him to cross that empty desert to get to the gate of Hell, he actually had no concept of how long he'd been chasing the Darkness. So what was the harm in a short conversation with someone who could possibly be the real son of Adam and Eve?

"The point is," James thought about it then continued, "how did you get here?"

Cain looked down at himself, his body covered in tattoos, "The first real lesson of my life was about power." He looked up at James, and James realized he was standing with his back to the edge of the stairs and shuffled nervously toward the next set of stairs. Cain gave a sad crooked smile, "Yes, I did kill my brother." He took a deep breath and continued, "Jealousy is a powerful thing, but the lesson I learned wasn't about the power of jealousy it was about this thing." He reached up and tapped the tattoo on his forehead.

James stared at it for a moment and the feeling of not wanting to kill Cain again settled over him like an itchy wool blanket, "What exactly is that?"

"It's my punishment," Cain replied. "It's the mark God left on me for killing my brother. For a long time I wondered how letting me live while at the same time making it so nothing could kill me was a punishment. Then I lived for a thousand years, and I realized God wanted me to learn a lesson. So I learned."

He turned his back on James and faced the locked door behind him. Reaching up he traced the symbol on the keystone at the top of the arch. "I learned symbols have power. A single shape can hold entire lifetimes of memory, and can convey those memories in a glance." He turned back to James and gestured at him, "You, as an American, should be able to recognize a plethora of logos and brands because you've grown up with them. The shape of a bottle lets you know what drink you're ordering. A multicolored square or a bitten piece of fruit lets you know what operating system your computer is using. And those are the simple things."

Cain reached into his pocket and James tensed for a moment until he saw Cain was pulling out a pencil. He knelt and drew a symbol on the stone landing. James looked down at the crudely drawn swastika then back up at Cain. Cain shrugged, "I know it's a bit of an obvious example but sometimes the more obvious the better."

130

James nodded and tried not to be too obvious when he shuffled his feet a bit closer to the stairs leading up, "I get your point, but what does that have to do with how you got here."

Cain raised his tattooed arms, "They have power." He twisted his arms so he could see the ones on the underside, "Some of these are from people and places no longer in existence. They were made in jungle villages, desert wadis, or monasteries on the tops of mountains, and once I had the right combination I was able to use that power to open a way here."

James raised an eyebrow at him, "You're telling me you have magic tattoos?"

Cain grunted out a low laugh, "And you're telling me you're standing in Hell having a conversation with the son of Adam and Eve while you hunt for a demon, and you don't believe me?"

"Well," James paused and thought about everything that had happened to him over the last few years. From the invisible door, to Rupert's world opening and the Darkness coming through, to James learning how to use the power, it had all been a series of unbelievable events. The only reason he still held onto any thread of sanity was because he had, in his own American way, been conditioned to see the impossible as just another thing.

His favorite comic book character growing up had been Green Lantern. The idea he could just will something into existence had been intoxicating. James had wanted to believe magic was real. He'd started with the Hobbit and worked his way through so many fantasy and Science Fiction books, he couldn't possibly keep track of them. All of that, in its own way, had prepared him to look upon the impossible situations he'd encountered in the last few years and accept them. Each and every new event James had come at with the attitude he would hope and believe it was real until something proved it otherwise. It was why he'd been so nicely suited to the power.

His capacity to believe, to truly believe, had made all of this possible. Because he believed, he had been able to call down lightning, throw fire, and heal himself from wounds that should have crippled or killed him. So why not believe what Cain was saying? Why not believe tattoos could make something happen? Because. Because it was easy to believe in something when you'd seen it happen, but lately James had been ignoring the large elephant in the room. Where did the power come from? What was he believing in? It was all well and good to say you were going to do what was right and not what was wrong. It was even better to say that you stood for something and really believed in it, but his problem was defining what that was.

"Well," James continued again, "I understand symbols have power, but there's a fundamental difference between the power of a good advertising slogan and the power to open a doorway to the tower of Hell."

"You must have power of some kind," Cain said. "There must be something you have at your disposal or you wouldn't be here doing what you're doing."

"True," James replied. He didn't want to freely give away more about his abilities than he had to. He was still in Hell, and he still wasn't completely sure this person in front of him was exactly everything he claimed to be.

Cain nodded as if expecting a short response, then continued, "After all my millennia of traveling, I'm going to assume something about your power. I'm going to assume some part of the access to that power has to do with believing in something. We can go into long discussions about true belief being able to move mountains, or start revolutions. True belief can lead a man to salvation or damnation depending on what he believes in, but what is the bedrock of the house of belief you're building? There comes a time when you have to look closely at that. Are you just blindly flinging your belief like a fisherman tosses his line hoping to catch something? Or are you throwing it like a spear at the bull's-eye knowing exactly what it is you're aiming at?"

"Wow," James said. "I didn't think it was possible to fit that many different metaphors into so few sentences."

Cain smiled, "You would think a sense of humor would be rare in Hell, and you would be right. My point of all of this is that belief can be packed into something. A symbol. And the same way in which your belief or someone else's can physically make something happen, so, too, can a symbol of whatever it is."

"I get it," James said, "but you don't believe in those symbols, so how can you access whatever power is available to be accessed?"

"Because of what I was trying to get at with those last few, and may I say awesome, metaphors. What truly matters is the source of the power. What is the bedrock? I know what it is." He reached up and tapped the ever-shifting mark on his forehead. "All of these others," he tapped different tattoos on his arms, "are trying to get to that true source. Some come closer to the truth than others."

"Are you telling me," James' voice creaked under the pressure of cynicism, "there are many ways to get to where we're all eventually going?"

"No," Cain replied quickly, "but there are many attempts and some come closer than others. When the truth is all around you in the world, it's hard not to have at least a little bit of it in what you believe."

James looked around, taking in the rough gray stone of the tower, the strange swirling storm cloud sky overhead, and wondered how he'd gotten into a philosophical discussion with some crazed tattoo man in Hell. "Look," he said, "this is all well and good, but I have things to do." He started to turn away, fairly sure nothing would be attacking him if he turned his back on Cain.

Cain said softly, "Have you ever heard the story of the flood?"

James let out an exasperated sigh, "I really don't have time to talk about Noah right now."

"No," Cain replied, "not the story of Noah."

James took a deep breath and hated himself for his need to reply, "Then which flood are you talking about?"

Cain looked up thoughtfully for a few moments, "I think it was in Missouri a few years back, but where it was isn't really the point."

"Then what is the point, Cain?" James said in his best patient voice.

Cain gave him a slight smile and said, "So the flood came and this man prayed to God to save him. A police car came by and offered to take him to safety. The man said no thanks, because God was going to save him. Later when the floodwaters had gotten higher a boat came by and offered to take him to safety. Again the man said no thanks, God was going to save him. Finally the man was on top of his house with water lapping at his feet and a helicopter came over him offering to take him to safety. Once again the man said no, God was going to save him. The man drowned, and when he got to heaven he asked God why He didn't save him. God looked at him and said, I sent a police car, a boat, and a helicopter, what more did you want?" Cain finished the story with a smile like he had been waiting for years to use the story in the perfect situation.

James just stared at him for a long moment then said, "And what was the point of that?"

Cain let out a true belly laugh, then said, "Sometimes people are put into strange situations for a very good reason, even if they don't know it at the time." He shook his head, "I thought I went through the search for all these," he waved his hands at the tattoos on his chest, "to get here. I thought figuring out this place would somehow make everything different, or all right. Maybe I could understand the meaning of my curse if I could just understand all of this. But now I realize I'm the helicopter pilot."

"What?"

Cain nodded as if it was all sorted out, "Yes, or maybe the boat driver. Either way I need you to give me your hand."

James just stared at him. There was no way on God's green earth he was going to let this crazy man from Hell touch him. It just wasn't going to happen. He and Cain locked eyes in a strange staring contest. Cain looked at him expectantly as if it was all a foregone conclusion and he was waiting for James to get with the program. James looked back at him thinking, if I just run up the stairs, could he catch me?

James broke the silence, "Why?"

"For the exact purpose of a symbol," Cain replied.

"Not much help there. So, again, why?"

"A symbol is meant to hold power even when you're not aware of it. There are times when you don't have the ability, or just the general wherewithal, to do anything, but a symbol doesn't need to think. It doesn't need to take time to believe or do anything. It just is what it is."

"Cain," James raised his hand to interrupt, "if that really is who you are, I just have to say you are terrible at this."

Cain grinned at him, "I am rambling a bit aren't I, but it's hard not to when you've discovered your purpose." Cain took a quick step and grabbed James by the wrist of his right hand. James twitched to pull his arm away and found Cain's grip holding him like a vise.

He looked down and twitched again. The black lines of a tattoo were sliding over the back of Cain's hand. When it reached the point of contact between James and Cain he felt it slide onto his skin like a spider

134

walking on his skin. He yanked harder trying to get his hand away as the tingling spider leg sensation wrapped itself around his wrist. Finally he raised his left hand and balled his fist determined to get this madman off him, but before he could throw a punch Cain let go and jumped back a few steps.

"Done," he exclaimed.

"What did you..." James looked down at his right hand and saw a black tattoo made of stylized thorns wrapped around his wrist.

"Same hand," James mumbled to himself. "What is it with this hand?"

He flexed his fingers half expecting something strange to happen, and then looked closely at the tattoo. It was made up of three separate strands woven together in a braid. Each stand had a different style of thorn. Some were done to look like they were sticking into his flesh while others looked three dimensional enough to actually poke up from his wrist. One strand started at the ring finger on his right hand and led down to his wrist where it wrapped around the other two. The second strand led from his wrist up his arm following the vein on his forearm up to his elbow. The final strand tied them all together at his wrist.

"It's a very old design," Cain said.

"That's great," James shivered with the memory of it sliding onto his skin.

"There was a tribe," Cain paused. "That's not really important, what is important is it stands for memory. Do you know why you Americans wear your wedding rings on that particular finger?"

James blinked at him like he was looking at a mad man.

Cain continued nonplused, "There was an old belief that the vein from your ring finger led directly to your heart, and thus you placed a ring on it to symbolize the connection to your heart. This tattoo design obviously predates that but it's supposed to illustrate the same sort of idea. When your heart lines up with your hands your actions will line up with your heart. From the overflow of your heart your actions will be defined as good or bad, and you in turn are defined by your actions. The people who designed this tattoo thought of a man's actions as a living memory."

James just stared at him, flexing his fingers trying to decide if he was going to punch him in the face just for good measure when he realized he'd dropped his only weapon. "And why do I need a tattoo for memory," James said to distract him while he searched for the iron bar.

Cain reached down to his feet, picked up the bar, and held it out to James, "I don't really know where this all is going to lead, but I do know you'll need to be able to hold onto who you are and what you believe."

James cautiously took the bar from Cain's outstretched hand, "And how is this going to help with that."

"It's your memory now." Cain nodded as if this should all be clear now, "You may not be able to take the time to think, or even be able to remember, but a symbol doesn't need time or be able to do something. Now," Cain turned to the door in the wall of the tower, "I'm going to be a little busy trying to figure out how to get out of Hell so if you don't mind," he trailed off and continued to stare at the door.

"Really," James said. "Really? That's it? You slide a creepy tattoo onto my arm and then just expect me to head off on my merry way because you say we're all done?"

"Well," Cain glanced over his shoulder at James, "you did say you were in a hurry, but I guess I could give you a little practical advice." He pointed to the stairs, "Eventually they'll split. Some landings have a path that leads straight as well as a one that goes up. For your purposes you need to keep going up."

"Seriously? That's it? You magically put a creepy tattoo on my hand after some weird conversation and think that some driving directions are going to make it all good?"

James looked a the iron bar in his hand, "I have half a mind to knock you over the head with this just on sheer principle."

Cain half turned and leaned his left shoulder against the door, "You can thank me later, if we ever cross paths again. But for now I bid you Godspeed, and good hunting."

James glared at him for a moment, gritted his teeth in frustration, turned, and started, again, up the stairs.

Chapter Thirteen

The stairs were eternity. The stairs were all and all was the stairs. James named them the stairs of death because they had most likely destroyed his sanity. He'd again tried counting, but this time just counting the landings. When that got to be like counting leaves on trees he switched to just counting landings with doors, and when he couldn't remember if he was on door number two thousand and sixty three or two thousand and sixty five he decided to give that up too.

He tried making sense of the markings at the top of each door, but they were never similar enough to even form a coherent pattern. Each was an esoteric symbol from completely different languages and cultures with no connection to each other. Once he came to that conclusion it actually made sense. Cain had mentioned something about the devil of a different world, or a different possibility. James had no reason not to believe after his previous experiences with the doors and other worlds. Here in his world, or rather back there in his world, the being known as the devil was thought to be a fallen angel. A being of immense power that for whatever reason had decided to rebel against God and try to take over for himself. The story said a full third of the angels fell with him.

James had always imagined a third of the angels being a few thousand or if he was really thinking about the population of earth then maybe a few million angels, but now that he knew there were many worlds out there with huge populations his estimation had to change. So possibly billions of angels had fallen and rebelled, and quite a few of those would be very powerful beings. They would spread out and try to take a piece of the pie for themselves rather than work together as a cohesive unit. Teamwork always seemed to be hard for greedy angry people no matter if they were humans or angels. In fact James bet the Darkness he was chasing was trying to do just that. He was trying to find a nice, open, unspoiled world and take it as his slice of the pie. Mr. Crazyfist back down at the base of the tower with the blood red skin and flaming crown would be one of the powerful ones from a different world.

James wondered if each of these doors led to a different world, and if that were true then the universe was a lot bigger than he'd ever imagined.

Was each one of these a different universe, or were they all in the same universe and each door led to a different planet in a faraway galaxy?

His brain started humming the theme song to Star Wars and then got the tune mixed up with either Indiana Jones or Macgyver when he stepped onto another landing. Ahead of him the path split. His mind tried to wrap around the possibility of it but absolutely failed. It was one path winding around the tower, and there was no room for one to go straight and the other to go up, because to go straight you would have to walk through the stairs leading up. His brain was starting to hurt just by looking at it when he remembered what Cain had said. Upwards and onwards. Unless he didn't trust Cain. He hadn't tried to kill him so that was a plus on his side. On the other hand this might be the place where he did try to kill him. Maybe up was a really bad choice and Cain was just the kind of horror who liked to set things up and watch them happen. Some bad guys didn't like to get their hands dirty.

Walking closer to the split in reality that was the stairs James decided to trust the word of the crazy guy. It was just a gut thing, and since that was really all he had to go on then upward it was.

A step away from the stairs something changed, and in a place like this, which was quite literally Hell, any change was ultimately suspicious. Freezing for a second then dropping to a crouch to make himself a smaller target James tried to figure out what exactly it was that had changed. The tower was still just plain stone. He looked around and couldn't see anything charging him or even sneaking up on him. Unfortunately if some broken faced monster really was sneaking up on him then the actual point of it sneaking was to not be seen so the fact that he didn't see them could be proof something was there. That line of thinking was a slippery slope to paranoia and James was about to dismiss it when he realized that being paranoid here was really a great idea.

So he started with the idea that something was sneaking up on him and moved on from there. If he couldn't see it then he should use his other senses. He tried taking a deep breath through his nose, assuming that anything from around these parts would smell like some mixture of poo and a really bad tree shaped car freshener designed to smell like leather. What he got wasn't a smell, it was a sound. That was why the basic part of his brain

138

had triggered the automatic defense response before the rest of him knew what was going on.

The tower was quiet. His footsteps on the stone had been the only sound for what seemed like a few connected eternities. Now, something was... He tilted his head around hoping to somehow pinpoint where the sound was coming from, or determine what it was. What worried him was the possibility that anything around here might sound completely innocuous and turn out to be a baby with a thousand teeth wanting to bite all your toes off. And he liked his toes.

He strained his hearing as much as possible without going toward the sound and a metallic clicking sound like dozens of tiny padlocks opening and closing caused him to freeze. Instantly and with no hesitation he started toward the stairs to get as far from whatever it was as possible, but something made him pause. His body and his mind agreed that he should simply keep heading up the stairs and avoid any crazy sounds but something was out of place. The idiocy of the statement dragged a smirk across his face. Of course something was out of place. It was Hell, everything was out of place. Or maybe, more to the point, he was out of place. What he really meant was that for Hell, where you expect crazy metallic noises, there was a background something or other that just wasn't right. It was like the smell of salt water and the sound of the ocean when you're in the mountains of Colorado.

He tried to filter the sounds. First, and loudest, was the clicking. It wasn't loud except when held in comparison to the normal, actual unearthly, silence of the tower. Below that was something else, something familiar. A voice.

Looking at the choices before him, and ignoring as much as possible the physical unreality of the two paths sharing the same space for a while, he knew he had a decision to make. He could continue up. That was the safe and smart bet. As far as anything here was safe, and he was fairly sure he'd left smart behind a while back. On the other hand he could go straight and figure out what the sound was. That was neither safe nor smart, but as he'd just pointed out to himself was he really one to judge those categories.

"Why am I even considering this?" He mumbled to himself.

Because you're still trying to figure it out.

"Figure what out?"

What you're doing here.

"Listen, brain, I know why I'm here." He glared at the stones in front of himself, "I'm here to catch the monster."

Why?

"Because he killed Katie."

Really?

"Well..." He trailed off. Thoughts crashed around inside his head like broken planks left over from a sunken ship.

"Because I have to prove something to myself."

His brain didn't respond. So he scratched at the stone with his fingernail and spoke quietly to the world around him, "I believe and make things happen, but what do I believe? I tell myself it's all about doing the right thing no matter what, but how do I judge that? On what rock do I build the castle of my beliefs?"

He clenched his jaw and started forward. The upward path of stairs vanished like a heat mirage. "I guess I just need to know that I won't always do the safe and smart thing. Sometimes you just need to do what needs to be done and stop questioning yourself."

"But..." James crouched down and pressed up against the side of the tower, "there's no reason to just charge ahead like an idiot."

As he rounded the tower the path continued to stay flat and the sound grew louder. The voice he thought he heard became more distinct and eventually he was able to filter out the clicking as much as possible and heard a simple word repeated over and over.

Peeking around the bend he saw her, and her lips matched what he'd been hearing. Grace's arms were tied above her head to metal brackets set into a stone lintel above the wooden door. He could tell she was straining, attempting to pull free, but all he could focus on was her voice.

"No, no, no, no, no..." Her head swung back and forth and a drip of blood splashed onto her forehead from the ropes biting into her wrists.

The need to run out and cut her free was so strong it made his muscles twitch, but the other parts of his mind held him back. He may have thought Cain was a trap, but this, this was undoubtedly a trap.

Scooting around the tower until he could get a good look at the situation he knelt down and looked for anything out of place. He gripped

140

his iron bar, and looked slowly around Grace. She hadn't seen him and continued to pull at the ropes. It wasn't something small he had to search for, or something just a little out of place, the wooden door behind her was broken. James revised his first impression, it wasn't broken as if someone had kicked it down and left it splintered and hanging from its hinges. It was broken like something had drilled fist-sized holes in it. The clicking sound was emanating from those holes along with a sound of little cymbals, not like pretty wind chimes but more like a drum set from the pits of hell.

His brain immediately got into an argument with itself about the best course of action. One part said to move as quickly as possible because, obviously, something was waiting to spring this trap on him. Maybe it was behind the door, or farther up the pathway, but it was there. It might be the Darkness or he might have moved on and just left her here for whatever else was lying in wait. Since he didn't know what was going on, part one of his brain said, the best course of action was to simply go as fast as possible. The second part said to be cautious and to scope things out as much as possible before acting. James figured he could merge those two points of view and try to get the best of both.

He slowly came to a crouch and started to inch forward, all the while looking for anything that might be trying to bite his face off. After a few seconds his movements caught Grace's attention and she looked his way.

Her eyes went wide and she immediately started shaking her head and saying, "Shhhhh, shhhhh..."

He nodded to her to let her know he understood the whole idea of being quiet. He hadn't planned on giving out a good old war whoop before rushing in to get her, but sure he would try his best to not make any noise. He continued to creep forward, now not because he was trying to sneak but because he was trying to be extra quiet. She must have seen something before he got here so he was going to be Mr. Silent for the time being. Fine particles of dust and small rocks crunched under his feet as he tried every trick he'd learned as a teen on how to sneak up his parent's walkway without being heard. Getting the car into the driveway had been the first problem since it would be obvious he'd gotten home later than he was allowed if the car was parked in the road. The sound and sight of the car could easily be taken care of by turning off the ignition and the lights and just letting the car coast into the driveway. The next problem had been the motion sensing lights. That thought made him pause and look over at the door wondering if whatever was behind there could sense him in some way. Sharks, for example, have one more sense than people and can tell if something is around them without being able to see it or smell it. In the case of his parent's motion sensing lights James had learned that the slower you moved the better your chances were. The closing of the car door was the most difficult because it could be loud and the motion of it could set off the lights, so you held up the car door handle and leaned on the door so it was in place then let the handle go and there was no clicking sound. The crunch of the dirt under his feet reminded him of pop rocks. There had been an urban legend that if you swallowed a bunch of pop rocks and cola at the same time it would make your stomach rupture. In this case he just wished it would be quiet. He couldn't remember anything being on the millions of stairs and the thousands of landings he'd passed on the way up. But now it seemed he'd stepped onto the dirtiest landing on the whole tower.

A bit of amazement trickled over him when he reached her without something trying to kill him. Very slowly he reached out and touched her cheek. He wanted to say that he wasn't trying to be weird or anything like that. It just seemed like he'd been working toward this for so long. She leaned into his hand but didn't smile. She was, after all, still tied up like some fictional princess waiting for the dragon to eat her.

James realized there was a problem when he looked at the ropes. They weren't anything special, but he also didn't have anything special to cut them. He had a round, mostly smooth, length of iron bar. Not the best tool for cutting through rope. He thought about finding a rough spot on the bar and using it to saw his way through the rope, or maybe he could wedge it into the knot and use the leverage to undo the knot.

Glancing behind Grace, James' mind swirled around pictures of what could come creeping out of fist-sized holes leading to a locked door in Hell. If it was so bad it had to be locked up in Hell he really didn't want to meet it. He decided whatever means was the quietest and would be the best. Trying to saw through the rope would be loud and, most likely, wouldn't work. So he started trying to undo the knot itself. He couldn't get the rope to budge with his fingers, which made him think his angel hand could be a little more helpful at times like this, so he started poking at it with the iron bar. One end was a bit more jagged and broken than the other and it was having some success getting in between the coils that made up the knot.

He figured he was halfway through the first knot when the little cymbal sounds turned to scrapping. At first it sounded like the cymbals were being rubbed together, but James paused and looked when it changed from a metallic sound to a wooden scraping. A black beetle the size of his fist crawled its way out of the hole in the door. It paused at the edge and fluttered its wings a few times as if stretching for the first time in quite a while.

Whew, it's just a bug. His brain let out a sigh. *No deformed Hell spawn. In fact it looks a lot like the one from Missouri.*

James had frozen in the hope he wouldn't be noticed and his brain continued to blather on about Missouri and how unimpressive the beetle was that had just come from the door. Then it looked at him. His heart rate jumped so high he could see his pulse in his eyes because it didn't just look at him like any bug would. James let out a little squeak as he looked into the face of the beetle.

It has a face! His brain tried to scream, but the still logical part of James kept his mouth shut in hopes the crazy beetle would just ignore him.

Its wings flickered again and it tilted its head slightly to the right blinking its eyes, and all James could do was stare. It was an iridescent black color that reminded James of an oil slick. Its body did roughly remind him, as his brain had said, of a beetle he'd come across in the Mark Twain National Park in Missouri. He thought it had been called a Hercules beetle. Bugs had never really bothered James. He wasn't arachnophobic or anything like that. He did have a healthy respect for many of the creepy crawlies in the world because they could seriously hurt you. One time he'd been crawling under his grandfather's house to help put down some visqueen as a moisture barrier and had to pause while his brother was navigating a right hand turn. As he lay there a spider had crawled along its web about two inches from his face. That was about the closest he'd ever gotten to screaming at a bug.

This thing, however, was on a different level. Along with the normal creepiness of any large bug, it had a human face. His brain had no problem processing what it was looking at because all that had been done was the normal beetle head had been removed and replaced with a tiny little face. Its eyes were all black with no iris, and it blinked a few times before opening its little mouth and screaming.

James involuntarily stumbled backward and watched as each hole in the door filled with a little face, and for a moment they all simply stared at him. Some part of his brain tried to tell him to stop looking and to just run. It babbled at him about all the silly horror movies where the kids get killed because they just stood there and stared at whatever horror was coming at them. But he froze. His mind had been prepared for the crazy things on the plain of hell, even for Bob the really big crazy thing, but this was different. Hundreds of tiny faces stared at him from the holes in the door, and for a brief butterfly wing beat of hope nothing happened. Then the silence of Hell was shattered by hundreds of screams. The noise struck James like tiny needles. It was enough to finally break him and get his body to realize what his brain had been trying to tell him. He ignored the impulse to run and swung as hard as he could for the ropes holding Grace to the wall.

The bar bounced off with no effect so he swung at the metal bracket holding the ropes. The screams multiplied and were joined by the low thrum of hundreds of wings. An almost irresistible urge came over James to run but he couldn't leave her. All his doubts and his self incrimination over the death of Katie rushed over him and he tossed them over a mental cliff. He couldn't leave her.

He lifted the bar again to take another swing when Grace leaned back against the door, lifted her legs and kicked him in the chest. He stumbled back and heard her screaming over the bugs.

The voices in his mind blocked out her pleas for him to run. He couldn't let her die.

But, you could do something more useful than having you both die.

The calmness of his mind cut through the screams of the beatles. If he stayed he would die and so would she. If he ran and took them with him at least she would have a chance. In the clarity of that moment he saw the Darkness. In the shadows of the holes white eyes seemed to look out at him, and James hated him.

The beatles shot toward him and he turned and ran screaming until his voice was raw. A few steps later the stairs started up again and he thought about looking back, but, his brain reminded him, he was running up a curving set of stairs and the chances of falling were ridiculous.

144

He reached the next landing and on the relatively flat surface he took the chance and glanced over his shoulder. Expletives flew from his mouth in an attempt to verbally stop the progress of what he could only call an unholy swarm of evil beetles. They flowed up the stairs like a shimmering oil slick scraping on the stone and screaming. In that moment James learned that some four letter words could be used as just about any part of speech. Any English teacher would be stunned to know that a single word could be a verb, noun, adjective, and adverb all in the same sentence. Unfortunately there didn't seem to be any evil Hell swarm English teachers so his tirade of swear words did nothing to the speed of the oncoming buzz saw.

James stumbled as the stairs restarted and the leading edge of evil brushed his back. A few pricks were followed by a weight tugging on his shirt, which was then followed by one of the most disturbing experiences of his life. James could feel them crawling up his shirt. Each little step a pin prick of pain as the beatles grabbed on. He tried knocking them off with his iron bar but only partly succeeded and was rewarded with another stumble as his swings threw off his balance. James thought momentarily about pulling off his shirt but didn't want to trek the rest of the way through Hell shirtless, and from what he was feeling it was fairly certain they would grab onto his back, shirt or no shirt.

More of the tiny hellions latched onto him, and while he could keep them from climbing up into his hair for the time being he couldn't keep them from tearing holes in his shirt. He stopped trying to swat them off and started simply hitting himself in the back in an effort to squash some of the little buggers. It hurt since he was beating himself with an iron bar but he did feel a few of them fall off after repeated blows. Then a knife stab of pain shot through his right ankle. The twitch was involuntary. The human body simply reacts to pain without the need to consult with the mind first, and when something hurts its first reaction is to get away from that something.

He tried to stop the fall with his left hand but that only led to him turning and slamming the right side of his face into the stairs. He didn't skid or tumble, his entire forward momentum simply punched his face into the stone steps with an audible crunch. Pain shot through his head and his brain shrieked.

The stone scraping, buzz sawing, screaming of the beatles washed over him. They covered him as they all tried to attack at the same time. His brain made the decision to temporarily ignore the horrendous pain shooting through his face in favor of the much more pressing need to escape.

James rolled and swiped out with the iron bar in his right hand. He ignored a sudden throb of pain from where he landed on his shoulder and continued to swing wildly. Twice pain from his head injury almost caused him to black out, but a mental image of the tiny monsters biting at his eyes kept him conscious. Bringing his left arm up to cover his face he continued to swipe at them with the bar but he could feel his wild swings doing nothing. It was like he was trying to fight off mist; an evil, screaming, biting mist. He rolled hoping to squish the ones that had latched onto him but he couldn't find a flat enough surface on the stairs and his blithering mind told him he was going to fall off the side. For a moment through the biting and stabbing and pain flaring through his face he wondered if that wouldn't just be the best possible outcome. Choice one, be eaten by a swarm of hell beetles or choice two, fall who knows how far and go splat on the plains of Hell. The problem with choice two, he decided, was they would most likely keep biting him as he fell so it really wouldn't help much at all.

His body started reflexively slamming his head into the stairs to try and dislodge the beetles that were biting through his hair when his left shoulder ran into the wall of the tower. James pushed himself up scrapping along the wall trying to dislodge or possibly crush some of them all while waving his hands in some kind of attempt at keeping them from getting to his face.

Stumbling up the stairs he was constantly rubbing and scraping along the wall trying to dislodge the beatles. Their screams grew louder as they bit into his ears. Blood ran down his back and into his pants, or at least he thought it was blood. If he was lucky maybe he'd squished some of them and it was Hell bug guts running down. He gagged and dry heaved time and again from the overwhelming smell of sickness. It was the smell of being bedridden and closed in a small room for days. The individual spots of pain merged into one body covering mass to the point where he almost didn't realize when his face stopped tingling and the pain from the broken bones under his eye stopped shooting through his skull.

This led to a faint glimmer of hope that if he could just survive long enough the strange healing power of his angel hand would keep him going. On the other hand, metaphorically speaking, that would be the worst way in the history of worst ways to climb this tower. He might survive but it would hurt, literally, like Hell.

A person's internal clock loses all meaning when pain is involved. Moments stretch on into eternity. Your brain stops processing the majority of external stimuli to focus on more important things, like how much it hurts. Smells and sounds become something you vaguely remember later, or wake up in a sweat with the dream lingering behind your eyes like a parasite. Some people connect the experience to random objects or other smells and can never drink Sunny Delight again because the taste reminds them of that eternal moment. The smell of diesel exhaust brings the memory of Humvees and Helicopters. In the eternity of James' pain the hum of the bug's wings triggered a memory of the fan in his dorm room, and as he staggered up the stairs blindly ramming himself into the wall some part of him knew he would never be able to fall asleep with a fan running again.

The rough wall of the tower caused little fingernail scratches along his shoulder as he blindly stepped up for the next stair and missed. The fight or flight chunk of his brain kicked in and told him in eloquent ways as he landed on his hands and knees that if he stayed where he was he would die. The screaming bugs with their little faces and rows of sharp little teeth would tear him into something most resembling uncooked stew meat. James' body didn't argue. It handed control over to another wilder part of the brain, which decided rolling would be the best option at that moment because it would deal with multiple problems. In a small conference room in his head there was a little table surrounded by neurons and they were all watching as one neuron used a white board to explain how rolling would not only keep them moving long enough to, hopefully, get the feet back where they belong and continue normal locomotion but would also have the added benefit of squishing some of those horrid bugs. The neurons took a vote and it was unanimously decided to continue with this course of action.

James rolled. Multiple parts of his brain were designated to worry about different things all at the same time. One part was sure he was going to roll off the edge and fall to his death. This worry was moved up the priority list and he subconsciously rolled a little more to the left to make sure plummeting was less of a possibility. Other little worries such as jamming the pinky finger of his right hand were given such low priority that he couldn't have even told you it happened. The largest section was, of course, given over to worrying about the bugs. Were they still trying to eat him? Were they trying to pick him up and carry him back to feed some sort of demon bug queen? It was this section of his brain who, very tentatively at first, informed him the bugs were gone. All the other parts of the brain immediately dropped what they were doing and ganged up to say he'd lost his proverbial mind, but it insisted they all get together and check things out.

The hum was gone. James scrambled, slowly, to his feet and blinked his eyes open. Taking a deep breath he tried to process the situation as best he could. First he needed to make sure the bugs were actually gone. Looking around he realized he was just inside the mouth of a tunnel. Looking down the stairs he could just make out the last of the bugs disappearing around the bend of the tower. He mumbled a few choice words to them followed with the only really rude gesture he knew then decided he needed to take stock of his own bits and pieces. The personal medical inventory was overridden momentarily by the reasonable suggestion of his brain to get a little bit farther away from the bugs.

A smaller part of his brain tried to tell him that staggering into a dark tunnel in Hell was most likely a bad idea, but given the choice between the demon bugs he knew about and the dark tunnel, James chose the dark tunnel.

Putting his left hand on the wall James stumbled ahead until he'd gone around the curve of the tower enough to lose sight of the tunnel entrance. He figured, through the fog of pain, if the bugs didn't want to come in then he should be safe. Forgetting the fact that anything able to scare away a swarm of Hell bugs should be something to worry about. He lowered himself to the floor and decided it would be better for all involved, which was just himself after all, if he laid down for a moment. He pressed his right hand to the rough stonework and lowered himself down. Stifling a scream as the bleeding bite marks pressed against the stone he prayed his angel hand would fix it all before he went insane. Assuming the pain would keep him alert he gingerly laid flat on the stones, pressed his right side against the wall for some semblance of protection, and folded his hands on his chest. Closing his eyes he started to mentally check all his parts and pieces starting with his toes.

The Darkness would know he survived. He didn't know how, but he would know. That meant he still needed the hostages, and as he lost count of his wounds he forced himself to have a small glimmer of hope. This all pointed to the Darkness trying to get somewhere in particular, and since the kids had been dragged along this far he would continue to drag them along. Hope, there was still hope.

Chapter Fourteen

The beeping started in some existential place outside of himself and slowly worked it's way up in the hierarchy of importance until James pried his eyelids open for the sole purpose of finding the source of the noise and killing it. His alarm clock squatted on the other side of the room and glared at him. Rolling out of bed he again regretted the idea to move the stupid thing across the room while at the same time congratulating himself on it. This way he actually had to get out of bed to turn it off instead of just rolling over and beating it into silence then going back to sleep. He'd only missed class the one time but it had been enough to cause him to implement drastic measures.

Looking around his dorm room he struggled to remember the dream he'd been having but only got snippets. Images of rust colored sand and the strangest feeling connected with his right hand. He shrugged, grabbed his bathroom bag, and headed down the dorm hall to the showers.

Guy's bathrooms are quiet places. At seven in the morning it doesn't matter if you're a crazy college guy or just a plain history major, all you do is quietly take care of your business. Males don't normally talk to each other in the bathroom anyway. In fact it's a sort of American taboo. You can get yourself seriously hurt by talking to another guy in the bathroom. Normally the worst that could happen in the dorm bathrooms was a dirty look reminding you to keep your business to yourself because it's too early in the morning. Things changed a little bit later in the day. If you wanted to take a shower at nine in the evening you were just opening yourself up to pranks and who knows what, but at seven in the morning the showers were a sacred place of solitude and silence.

As James woke himself up in the shower, the previous day slowly came back to him. His memory ran hard into the mental wall of his first kiss with Kate. He let the warm water wash over him while he mentally savored the taste of her lips. There were other memories trying to intrude about their date but they didn't really matter. It was the rush of butterflies in his stomach, and the look in her eyes at that exact moment that mattered. He didn't like to admit it to his friends but he'd only ever kissed two girls before last night. Well, three if you count that time playing truth or dare on the marching band trip to Oregon. He didn't count that one because she smelled weird and she'd tried to French kiss him and ended up basically slobbering all over him. Not a good truth or dare experience.

His first class wasn't until nine but he'd told Kate he'd meet her for breakfast in the University food court. He wasn't sure if she was technically his girlfriend now or what, but he was still bouncing on his toes as he walked the trail from his dorm to the dining hall. He was thinking of getting off the food plan to save some on tuition but he wasn't quite sure how he was going to feed himself if he didn't have access to the food court. It wasn't exactly gourmet but it was food. A good bowl of Captain Crunch in the morning, or maybe a waffle with strawberry topping, then, if you timed it right, a burger for lunch and whatever they had for dinner. If you missed the normal meal times you had to just make due with whatever they put out in the buffet. Usually he just went for another bowl of cereal since it was always available.

When James opened the door to the food court his mind was swirling with possibilities. He didn't know what to expect and was filling in the blanks with gusto. In one scenario she was just waiting for him at a table and when he walked over she stood up and gave him a good morning kiss. In another she wasn't there yet and after he found a place to sit she snuck up behind him and kissed him on the cheek from behind to surprise him.

He narrowed down his possibilities when he saw she wasn't there yet. It meant he would need to figure out how to greet her, and he was a little nervous about it. Since he wasn't quite sure what their relationship was yet he couldn't quite settle on the exact way to say good morning to her. Could he kiss her good morning? Or was it too soon for that? Should he just give her a big smile and pull a chair out for her like a traditional gentleman? That was the safe bet, but should he be safe? Girls liked dangerous guys right?

He looked around and wished there weren't so many people here. It would make it easier, and nicer, if they were more alone rather than surrounded by a gawking crowd. This was one of the irritations of being a guy. American culture dictated that you had to always make the first move. If you, as an American guy, sat back and waited for the girl to do something she would see that as indecisive and weak and move on to a guy who actively pursued her. So you always had to do something. You always felt like you were getting ready to jump off a cliff. James thought it must be so much easier to be a girl because you could just sit back and watch the poor guy fumble around trying to figure out what was going on. The girl never had to put herself out there in those emotional jump-off-a-cliff situations.

By the time James had his Captain Crunch and a place to sit he'd settled on a mix of flirtatious and gentlemanly for his morning greeting, while at the same time trying really hard to determine if he could move in for a good morning kiss. If she had a bunch of friends with her it would be less likely, but he could always hope.

Each time the door opened James looked up ready to wave so she would know where he was sitting, and when it finally was her he totally forgot to wave. As she stood in the door looking for him a chopped movie real piece of his dream fluttered by his mind's eye. Sadness pressed his heart back into his chest and looking down at his hands he could almost see blood.

"Hey you."

James' head jerked up at the sound of her voice and all his words stuck in his throat. His great flirtatious plans to call her beautiful, and pull her chair out for her fumbled away. He tried to salvage it all with the best smile he could manage, "Hey."

He stood up and pulled her chair in the hopes it would cover his awkward greeting, "How'd you sleep?"

"Well," she smiled back at him while she sat down, "I was a little bit worked up," she paused there to let him realize what she was talking about, "so it took me a while to fall asleep."

James grinned at the realization she'd been laying in bed thinking of him. His brain queued up a great reply about how he'd found it easy to fall asleep so he could dream about her but it all got stuck when he realized he couldn't remember. He couldn't remember getting to his room, or getting ready for bed, or laying there thinking about her. The entire evening should have been permanently burned into his mind with the edges tinged by a glorious haze of happiness.

"Uhm, James," Kate's face slipped from happy good morning to worried, "is something wrong?"

"I," James looked across the table at her and tried to mentally grab onto any memory of going to bed last night.

152

Kate reached across the table and took James hand in hers, "What's wrong babe? Did something happen last night?"

James shook his head, "No, it's just this really disturbing dream."

"Oh, you wanna talk about it?"

James smiled at her, "Nah, if I don't think about it then it should just fade away."

She nodded and smiled at him encouragingly. "So what've you got going on today?"

Good, James thought, change the subject and get away from the weirdness. He chuckled to himself mentally when he realized he knew exactly what she would be doing today because he'd memorized her schedule a few weeks ago. He wanted to accidentally bump into her more around campus, but to do that he needed to know where she was going so he'd taken the time to figure it all out. It'd taken a while since he didn't want to seem like too much of a stalker, but it hadn't been too hard. Just pay attention during conversations and mentally note any time she mentioned what classes she was taking, or what activity she was going to. That way he could accidentally, on purpose, be in the right place at the right time to see her more often.

James smiled at her and looked down at the table to lace his fingers with hers, "Well, my first class," he paused and stared at something on the back of his hand.

"Yes?" Kate said.

James ignored her for a moment, reached out with his left hand, and pulled back his right sleeve.

Kate looked down, "I didn't know you had a tattoo."

"I don't." James stared at the thorns pressing into his wrist. His arm twitched involuntarily to get away from the pain of them digging into his flesh. "Where did," he trailed off and realized he'd knocked over his chair and was standing. Kate was saying something but his whole world was the tattoo.

His head started throbbing, and when he looked up at Kate she had blood pumping from her chest and running down her shirt. He remembered. The crisp air of that night two years ago drifted by and sent a chill across his skin. He hadn't realized in his hurry to catch up that she would be at the church. It was just supposed to be the Darkness and his henchman Professor. James had finally gotten a grip on the reality of his powers, finally come to truly believe and understand he was chasing a real monster. His small previous victories gave him confidence and he was more than a little cocky with his newfound power. Having just blasted two evil lackeys with lightning from his very own hands he was so sure he could stop these two from setting fire to the church and touching off devastating city wide riots that he didn't pay attention to anything else around him.

If he'd only stopped for a moment in his headlong rush to be the hero maybe he would've noticed how strangely she'd been acting. Maybe if he would have taken the time to check in with her instead of just rushing off to fight the Darkness, but no, it'd all happened so fast. James had known the Professor was part of her schedule, and for the last two years he'd beat himself up for not thinking of that. He should have realized with the Professor and the Darkness after him they would have tried to get him by using the people he cared about, and if there was anyone he cared about on campus it had been her.

She hadn't known what she was getting into, and even if he'd thought about it he would've told himself she was too strong to be suckered in by the bad guys. In the end, though, it was strength that brought her into it. You don't need to do much convincing when someone already has a strong set of morals, you just need to tell the right lies. Make them believe what you're doing lines up with their beliefs. Once you get them going they'll do the hard work and convince themselves they're on the right path, because who wants to admit they made a mistake. They would rather rationalize what they're doing and not admit they were duped.

So there she'd been, his brand new girlfriend. They'd only shared one kiss. He'd never made it to breakfast with her like he'd promised. He didn't expect her to be at the church that night so when he saw her he'd been so taken off guard he hadn't seen the shadowy form of the Darkness laying heavy on her shoulders. The realization that she was being controlled didn't come until later. She'd yelled something at him and pulled the trigger. He'd deflected the bullet back at her with his newfound powers by reflex, and as he cradled her the blood pooled in his hands. In his nightmares he still watched her life flow onto the pavement.

James looked up from the tattoo at her standing there, alive, in the dining hall. He tried to freeze the image of her in his mind. He wanted to remember her like this, smiling at him and alive, not bleeding and confused in the parking lot of a church.

"I'm so sorry Kate."

Confusion flickered across her face, "James, what are you talking about?"

James stepped around the table and hugged her. Burying his face in her hair he breathed her in trying to memorize the scent of her shampoo and the living warmth of her. Then with a deep sigh he pushed her away and closed his eyes. In his mind's eye he saw the tattoo wrapped around his wrist, the thorns pressing in reminding him of who he was and what he was supposed to be doing.

Are you sure? His brain whispered to him.

Sure of what?

Are you sure you want to let go of this?

Trade in a trip through Hell for the comfort of getting her back?

Yes.

And what good would that do?

Well, for one, I'm tired of getting chopped, bitten, and all the other painful things from the last two years.

James remembered the sheer soul shattering agony of having his hand cut off, the overwhelming pain of a thousand bites by crazed bugs, and he wondered if he was making the right choice.

We can stay here. It's nice here.

Why is it nice here?

Well, let me count the ways.

No, really, why is it nice here? We're in Hell right?

Right.

I know it wouldn't turn out well. Nothing in Hell turns out well.

But even if it was nice for a little while...

And we got that little bit, didn't we. Now it's time to get back to work. It's time to figure out what I believe, and who I am. She had been tricked and lied to, with her beliefs twisted to suit the ends of others. James knew he needed to find that metaphorical granite bedrock to set his feet on, but to do that he needed to keep going. So he blocked out the whispering voices of doubt and focused on the image of the tattoo.

Chapter Fifteen

James twitched and sucked in a deep breath as his eyes popped open. In a primal way he was sure he hadn't taken a breath in a long time. He tried to sit up and his left side refused to move. Feeling mentally fuzzy after the dream he thought his arm had just fallen asleep, so reaching over with his right hand he poked blearily at his left arm with the iron bar. Looking at the offending arm he tried to figure out why there was white stuff stuck to him, and at the same time a separate part had just realized something was breathing, and it wasn't him.

The human brain can only act so quickly, and when it only has partial information it tends to slow itself down even further in order to make the best possible decision with what is available. His mind however immediately put unknown breathing together with being in Hell and decided something needed to be done immediately.

He rolled and brought the iron bar up to defend himself, or at least that's what he intended to do. The white material stretched like a rubber band then yanked him back onto the floor. Looking down and realizing it was covering more than just his left arm he started to panic. In the dim light of the tunnel the stuff looked slightly opalescent and covered most of his legs up to his waist and extended up his left arm to just above the elbow. Looking out into the darkness of the tunnel he'd stumbled into after the bug attack he realized something wasn't just breathing anymore. Wooden clicks like a walking cane tapping on the stones accompanied a shift in the darkness. James pulled at the sticky white substance but without being able to move his legs he didn't have enough leverage to pry his arm loose from the paving stones. The clicking and breathing had come close enough now that he knew whatever was out there would be visible if he looked up but looking at it was really the last thing he wanted to do.

The breathing turned into a strange dry coughing. James involuntarily twitched as the stagnant air moved and a whiff of rotten fruit drifted past his face. Splitting into two options his brain froze in indecision. He could try to use the bar from the gates of Hell to saw at the stuff in the hope it would somehow cut through, or he could wait for this new horror to jump at him and hope he could do some damage with a well-timed swing.

The tap tap of wood on stone moved closer and stopped. Realizing his decision had most likely been made for him he looked up and tensed to stab or swing at whatever was going to come at him. His brain translated the wooden tapping and told him he was about to be attacked by a pirate with two peg legs and he almost started giggling. In that fraction of a second a part of him was amazed at how people feel the need to classify things and give some semblance of normalcy to even the most horrific or bizarre. The human condition seemed to be able to deal with tragedy better if it was in a recognizable or somewhat understandable shape.

The thing hunkered down in the semi darkness. Slowly a wavering red light began to glisten as her hair began to glow, floating about her head as if she were underwater. The dance and flow of it caused the shadows to slide across the wall of the tunnel. Her back hunched over, with black broken nubs sticking out from her shoulder blades, causing her arms to dangle and the backs of her hands to scrape the stone floor. Her legs continued to shift and move with the wooden tapping coming at each step. Covering her emaciated body was a rag of a dress whose original color was hidden under rust red stains. Her face, highlighted by the twisting of her flickering hair, was strangely childlike. Over large unblinking eyes stared at him while the mouth curved down in a little girl's pout. She rocked back and forth as if she was trying to get up the momentum to move. Eventually she seemed to fall forward onto her hands and her legs rushed to keep up. A furious clicking sounded from her feet and she opened her mouth to show a row of small sharp teeth. At the last moment she swung her hands up and struck at him with sharp dirt crusted nails while her mouth hinged farther open and white fluid seeped from the tips of her shark like teeth.

With his right side not attached to the floor James was able to twist away from the wall in time to hear one of her clawed hands strike the floor where he'd been laying a moment before. Whipping his arm up he felt the bar connect with something and at the same time heard a crack. Bringing his arm back down as quickly as possible he struck at her torso hanging over him as hard as he could with the limited movement his predicament allowed him. His mind wished he could get the bar turned so he could stab at her, but at the moment the best he could manage was hitting as hard as his limited motion allowed him.

Twisting and swinging he felt something cut a burning furrow in his shoulder then his thigh. Yelling out involuntarily he continued hacking away. Finally, his wiggling and hitting caused her to overcompensate. She struck out at him with her nails extended but missed and ended up with some fingers wedged into a crack in the tower wall. With the slight pause in her attack he was able to get room for a good swing. The hand split away at the wrist with the sound of a dry twig snapping. Immediately the sickly sweet smell of rotten peaches spilled over him and she let out a scream.

Trying to scuttle back into the darkness of the tunnel she swayed and fell, rasping, to the stone floor. She stood and, from the corner of his eye, he watched the red dancing light of her hair disappear into the darkness of the tunnel.

Chapter Sixteen

Ray hurt. Despite the darkness Mitch had landed some serious shots. But what hurt more was the confusion. There was a day, before Hell had come to greet him, back home, when he'd been sick and stayed home from school. Lying in bed everything had seemed somehow slightly off, and for a time just being there with his eyes closed, focusing on his breathing, he could pretend that things were fine and he was lucky to be getting a free day. However, he couldn't shake the feeling that everything was twisty and aches crept up on him from lying in bed for so long. Getting up eventually, he wandered the empty house. Looking out the window he was momentarily shocked to see the world came to an end at the edge of his yard. Gray-white fog encircled the house, its nothingness pressing in, and for a moment his sickness and the world mirrored each other.

Now, here he was again. Something was wrong on the inside, and the fog had come to swallow his world. What was worse, laying here in the darkness of the tunnel, he didn't know why. Why were they all so different from him? What did Mitchell expect from him? Self-sacrifice was all well and good in the stories, but in the here and now, where it wouldn't accomplish anything, it was pointless. Could he have helped hold down the monster? Of course he could have, but what would it have gained them? Nothing.

Could you? His mind whispered back at him.

Have you ever really stood up for anything?

The words grew louder and pushed at the paper thin wall of his bravado.

"That's not the point." His whisper didn't reach farther than his own ears, "It wouldn't have changed anything."

Maybe that's what you're really confused about. Angry about.

A smell of rotten fruit drifted by along with ragged breathing and a strange clicking. He crushed himself against the wall, hugging his knees. This was proof. Something sliding past him in the darkness. Some horrible monstrosity was only feet away from him, and there was nothing he could do.

Not true.

The voice was so loud in his mind. He was sure the thing passing by would hear it and come after him.

There's always something you can do.

But it wouldn't make a difference, and, he added to the conversation in his own head, and it would hurt me. Isn't the point of all this to survive and not get myself killed?

Realy? Is that what you think the point is?

The sound of the thing, and the smell, faded into the darkness of the tunnel.

Why? He asked again to the voice in his head. Why is that man coming after us, why is Mitch trying so hard to save us, and why do I feel so bad? Isn't the real world proof? Everybody loved me there. I was popular. Isn't that proof I was doing the right things?

And yet when you were sick did anyone call to check on you? When you really needed help...

A memory sprung to his mind unbidden, he'd been coming home late one night after a youth event at church. The Suzuki he'd been driving hit a patch of ice and went off the road into a muddy farm field. Nothing had been damaged, and he hadn't been hurt, but he did need help getting out. Calling around he'd gotten a lot of "I would if I could" answers but not a single yes. Finally he called back to the church, just in case someone was still there, and had been lucky to get the youth pastor before he'd left for the night. A few minutes later there he was along with Mitch. Ray'd always assumed Mitch had come along because he was getting a ride or didn't feel like he could say no to the youth pastor's face...

"I'm scared." Ray whispered to himself.

Of course you're scared. You would be insane if you weren't scared.

The sound of metal ringing against stone echoed through the tunnel.   A man's scream cut through the darkness followed almost immediately by a shriek like a pick stabbing into the nerves behind his eyes.

Ray tried to make himself even smaller as a flickering red light rounded the bend of the tower. SqueezIng his eyes shut he thought, then what is the point? I'll admit my friends weren't the best, and sure, he inwardly groaned at this, I'll even admit Mitch is a better person than me, but where does that get me?

You asked why? What difference does it make?

He hunched forward and rested his head on his knees. "I just want to understand, you know? I just want to..."

Be amazing?

"Yeah." He whispered into the darkness.

You don't think Grace trying to keep your spirits up was amazing? Mitch standing in the way so you didn't get hit so often wasn't amazing?

"That's not what I meant."

Yes it was. Don't lie to yourself.

"Those things are so small."

Voices, real ones, rose up somewhere ahead of him. A hissing, coughing, that he didn't want to listen to was answered by the monster's clear tones. Ray blocked them out and sunk into himself.

A steady review of events passed through his mind. He tried to focus on his life before all of this, but that became more and more difficult. It became a grand metaphor of a basketball game to him. His thoughts boiled down to simple statements. You train hard so when the game comes you win. Training takes longer than the game itself, but it isn't the training that's important, it's the game. He finally had to admit he hadn't trained well for this game. And now, when it was all on the line, he found himself out of shape and unprepared. To his defense, no one had told him this was the game he'd be training for. How was he supposed to train for something when he didn't know what it was?

"On your feet, munchkin." The monster hauled him up and shoved him forward, or at least what he assumed was forward. "I have to say, I am duly impressed by that man back there. He is seriously giving me an ulcer. Well, I can't really get an ulcer, but you know what I mean." A dim light flickered to life just ahead of them. It floated over the outstretched hand of the monster. "Mitch carry Grace if you have to but we're moving now, and let me be clear, I don't need all three of you so don't go all hero on me right now. I'd be perfectly happy to just leave her here in the darkness with my friend."

Ray looked over and saw Mitch supporting Grace. His right arm was wrapped around her and she leaned heavily on him. She was covered in small cuts, each leaking out a trickle of blood. He had no idea when she'd gotten back. The monster must have gone back and gotten her while he was laying on the floor after Mitch beat him.

"He's going to get you." Grace said quietly, "He's right back there, and..."

Kron'ael backhanded her across the mouth and she staggered into Mitch. "That will be enough of that. I put up with some unpleasant attitudes from all of you, minus Ray, because I wasn't feeling quite myself. Now, either move on or be food for her." He gestured toward the flickering orange light, which they all very deliberately refused to look at.

"See," Ray whispered to himself, "there's nothing I can do."

A monster compliments you, the voice echoes in his mind, *and you don't find that wrong?*

Light ahead marked the end of the tunnel, "Yes, but..."

"You," Ray jumped, thinking the monster had finally heard the voice, but when he looked he realized the conversation was directed at the thing the monster referred to as Her. Looking around, Ray saw Mitch and Grace leaning against the wall talking. He assumed Mitch was apologizing for not saving her, or blaming Ray for not helping. Who was he kidding, Mitch wouldn't blame him even after the fight they'd had. Not consciously thinking about it, Ray moved closer to the monster so he could hear the conversation. After all, no one expected him to do anything, so what did it matter if he overheard what they were saying?

"Look, I don't really care what he did to your hand..."

She bubbled something back at him and raised her arm. Ray didn't really want to look at her close enough to see what it was.

"I need you to do one more thing, and it will work this time."

Again she responded, and again Ray didn't understand.

"I would, but you know the conditions for me to even be here. It has to be someone here, and you are the best here. It's simple, he'll head for the tunnel opening, it's the only way out. You wait for him to get through the door where he'll be distracted by the statue, and the rest is up to you."

She barked something at him, turned, and started toward the tunnel opening.

Watching this spawn of humanities nightmares, Ray's mind froze. Thoughts started trickling like slowly thawing ice. A bit of a sentence about the man following them dripped down, a mental image of his favorite basketball game from the year before slid in, and underneath the jumble a soft question.

Do you want to be amazing?

He heard a noise and realized it was his own breath whistling through his nose. His heart was beating hard enough that he could feel the pulse in his neck. "What," he whispered through clenched teeth, "am I supposed to do?"

You know.

In that moment all the clutter was swept away. It was true. He did know, and really he was the only one who could, because no one would expect him to.

His feet started moving, he focused on lifting up onto his toes which forced him to lean forward giving him greater momentum, and in that moment he smiled. "This," he said to himself as he cleared the last few feet, "is how it's supposed to be." He finally understood. He did have a part, and it did matter.

He locked eyes with her the moment before he lowered his shoulder. The impact lifted her off her feet, he locked his arms around her, and with two more strides he launched himself off the edge of the tower taking her with him.

Chapter Seventeen

James wasted no time and tucked the iron bar under his hip. With his one free hand he quested around up the wall until his fingers found the severed hand dangling from the wall. His arm dripped blood from his wound onto the paving stones. Not able to get a good look at it he purposefully blocked the injury from his mind, filing it under the heading of after surviving this. If he let little worries like being poisoned by a monster get to him he'd never get anything done, and right now getting free was the most important thing in his personal universe. The very blood he spilled proved what he hoped would be true as he sawed at the white material with the fingernails of the demon's severed hand.

He tried to look into the darkness while at the same time watching where he was cutting, and finally he freed his arm and was able to sit up. Pausing he strained his hearing, listening for any breathing or the tapping of her legs, and putting pressure on the bonds holding his legs down he continued to saw until he broke free.

Tossing the hand away in case it decided to try for him by itself he got to his knees and squinted into the darkness hoping to find a small source of light ahead showing the exit, but the only twinkling came from the entrance. In front of him there was only darkness and the possibility of more monsters. Putting his hand out he found the wall right where he'd left it and levered himself to his feet. Standing James did a quick inventory of his person. He rolled his neck, flexed his hands, bent his knees, and was happy to find that all his parts and pieces were not only in the right places but seemed to be in working order. The cuts he'd received from her were already beginning the now familiar tingle of healing. The tunnel must have been her lair. He wasn't sure if he'd fallen asleep because of something she'd done, or if he was just exhausted after his flight up the stairs. Seeing as how he hadn't slept a single time since entering Purgatory he was leaning toward something unnatural rather than just exhaustion. After he was asleep she must have come out of the darkness and begun to wrap him in her silk. He would have remained trapped in the dream, unknowing of his true fate, until he died.

His fingers told him what his eyes couldn't see about his clothes. Gauzy threads were trailing from him in what he could only think of as cobwebs. Underneath those he could tell the little demon faced beetles had really done a number on him, and while his amazing angel hand could eventually heal him, it was doing nothing for cotton.

"Great." James said to the darkness, "Now I have to trek through the rest of Hell in tattered rags." He barked out a laugh, "At least I'll fit in."

He worried for a moment about his voice alerting something in the darkness to his presence, but after the attack he'd just survived he didn't think it really mattered.

"Now then," he paused and realized he didn't have his iron bar any more. "Great." He knelt down and started patting around on the ground hoping it hadn't rolled away when he stood up. He honestly couldn't imagine making it this far without it. It could have dropped from his hand back when the beatles first swarmed him, or it could have bounced back down the stairs when he fell and rolled into the tunnel, and yet somehow he'd held onto it. Now it was almost as much a symbol of hope to hold onto, as it was a weapon. He slid his fingers over the stone floor and finally felt something cold and metallic. With a sigh of relief he wrapped his hand around his only friend in this terrible land and stood.

Pressing his left hand to the wall James tentatively walked forward. He was sure this was the right way but he wasn't sure of anything beyond that. He stopped and looked back wondering if there had been some kind of fork in the road and he had taken the wrong turn. With all the beetles after him he'd simply been pressing on with his eyes shut. The normal staircase could have continued on in one direction and he stumbled, literally, into this tunnel. At the thought of going back to check his mind and body rebelled. Logically speaking he was sure the beatles had gone back to their door. He remembered, faintly, seeing them flying back down the stairs, but this was Hell and logic really didn't have a place here. For all he knew they could all be waiting for him. After all, how many times does a nice tender meal wander right by your evil door in Hell? He wanted to go back to check on Grace, but he was almost sure she wouldn't be there any more. The Darkness would have taken her and gone the fast way while he was forced to take the tunnel of doom if he survived the beatles.

"All right," James told the dark, "forward it is then."

After a few steps he said, "You know, I probably shouldn't be talking should I?" He looked around and saw nothing in the pitch black, "There could be something else in here just waiting to eat me up."

After beating back the attack he couldn't help but tease the thing in the dark, "Look, if you are out there could you at least let me know? We could have a nice chat before you grind my bones to make your bread. Oh, and you smell terrible."

He stumbled on for a while longer, taking each step carefully in case there was a sudden drop or maybe the resident monster had left an ottoman or couch in the way for him to trip over in the dark.

"Ha, but seriously, I've been chased by monsters, hit by something that resembled a living demonic tree, tattooed by a nut job who might really be Cain, almost eaten by a swarm of really ugly beetles, and lured into some sleepy dream death trap only to wake up to Ms. Nasty trying to eat me. So if you're going to jump out and try again could you at least give me a heads up? I'm seriously tired and there's a fifty-fifty chance I wouldn't even run."

James paused, leaned against the wall, and started to close his eyes for a short break. Jerking himself off the wall he shook his head, "Nope." His voice louder than he intended, "Not going to fall for that again."

The cliché about catching more flies with honey flitted through his mind followed by the realization about the eventual outcome for the fly. Sure it might be happy for a second with the free honey but it would still end up dead in the end. Its guts would be liquefied and sucked out by some sneaky spider who kept a cupboard full of Winnie the Pooh style honey pots.

"Sure," James said to the tunnel, "why not. I'll call you a giant spider because that would just top things off wouldn't it?" He gripped his iron bar and waited for a count of ten. When nothing happened he stumbled on.

After running through the opening song to the classic Winnie the Pooh cartoon twelve times, and being seriously amazed he remembered all the words, he saw the light at the end of the tunnel. The closer he came to the opening the easier it was to see the makeup of the tunnel. It was simple gray stonework just like the rest of the tower. No monsters, or monster furniture to trip him up. He was secretly hoping for a cheering crowd at the end, or at least a big sign saying something like, "congratulations", or "you survived the tunnel from Hell".

Looking down at himself he was amazed by how bad he looked. When he'd fallen through the door ripped in space by the Darkness and landed on the orange sands of Purgatory he'd been wearing Sunday go to church clothes. Now his white button up shirt was blood stained and shredded. His Dockers had the knees torn out and he was sure the darker spots were more blood but it blended nicely with the khaki material. His shoes, thankfully, had survived mostly intact. They were scuffed badly but there were no holes he could see. If there was one thing that would make this trip worse it would be doing it barefoot.

Stepping out of the tunnel and into the diffused light of Hell James paused to revel in having survived. He knew this was just another step along the way, and he knew he was still in Hell, but some part of him wanted to do a little dance just because he was still standing. His heart dropped as something moved out of the corner of his eye. Not knowing what it was his body decided the best course of action would be to simply drop. Glancing up James saw something swing over his head and turned his drop into a forward roll. A brief mental image of Indiana Jones trying to make it to the Holy Grail flashed through his mind and a slight smile tugged at the corner of his mouth.

Without getting to his feet James swung his iron bar at kneecap height and realized, as it crunched into a statue of a knight, that Hell really was what you brought with you. In a literal sense he was in Hell, but in a deeper sense he had been in his own personal Hell ever since Kate had died. He'd blamed himself and had been looking for redemption. Anyone could be walking around trapped in their own version of Hell. The stone knight tipped on its broken leg and took an overhand downward swing at James who lunged into the statue and shoved. With a crack the other leg broke and the stone knight tipped over the edge and tumbled to the plain below.

James steadied himself on the edge of the stairs and tried to watch the statue as it fell. He might be here now but, he decided, he wasn't in Hell. People ended up here because of what they already were. It was the end result of that old proverb, wherever you go there you are. If you were a terrible person in life then you brought that terror with you to Hell and it became your Hell. His memory of watching Indiana Jones had brought a smile because he'd had a good life. He might not always have been the best person, or made the right choice every time, but what he brought with him to this place was a head full of happy memories. Maybe the trap back in the tunnel would have been worse than a gut wrenching guilt trip if he'd been a murderer.

The memory of what he'd seen in the tunnel pulled the smile from his face. Kate's death had been his fault. Sure she'd been mentally worked over by some demonic thing, but that never would've happened if he'd been paying attention. He'd been confused and frightened by everything at the time, but he couldn't see it as an excuse for letting his friend down. Sometimes you just have to ignore the confusion and focus on what you can deal with, and he felt deep down that he should've been able to protect her.

James looked up the stairs and realized he was doing exactly the wrong thing. He needed to let go of the confusion and guilt and focus on what he could actually do right now. He could go forward. He could figure out where the Darkness had taken the kids, and he could get them back. If he happened to find a way to destroy the soul sucking parasite that killed Kate along the way then all the better.

Chapter Eighteen

Nothing had changed about the stairs. They still went onward and upward. They were still broken only by the occasional landing. Again some had doors and some were just blank. And again he was lured into a false sense of overwhelming boredom by the trudge up the endlessness of gray stone.

The landing was just like all the rest as he stared down at his feet until they settled onto the gray stone and the sound hit, rocking him sideways. He immediately dropped onto one knee and turned to face whatever monstrosity he assumed would be coming to eat him this time. His brain quickly hoped it would be something big and solid, like the stone knight. Something he could actually hit, and not like those beetles just swarming around every swing.

What he saw confused him. Light spilled from an open archway. No door covered the opening and look as he might he couldn't see if one had ever been there. The marking above the arch looked Latin to him, but he couldn't tell what it stood for. He'd always made fun of some of his relatives for making their kids take Latin. No one spoke Latin anymore and the only time you'd ever need to know it was if you were planning on becoming a doctor, and in that case they would teach you the parts of Latin you needed to know in med school. Well, James thought, now he could tell them he'd found a use for the Latin they were spending all their time on. Unfortunately, if they ended up using it here, it would mean they were in Hell and that would be sad because he liked his relatives.

Light spilled from the archway in the reds and yellows of fireplaces and torches. It danced across the gray stone trying to remind it of other colors in the world. James crouched there and silently counted to one hundred to make sure he hadn't alerted something to his presence. His curiosity pulled him toward the door but his brain had other ideas.

No. Absolutely not.

What?

Don't what me. I'm your brain, I know what you're thinking.

I'm just going to take a peek.

After everything that's happened you really want to peek into another doorway in Hell?

Think about it. The one time I did peek nothing happened, and the one time I tried to sneak by bad things happened.

That proves nothing.

What it proves is I don't have to listen to you.

If we die I'm going to be very angry with you.

If we die I'm hoping we won't be here any more.

James squeezed himself against the wall and inched his right eye out from the edge until he could just see into the room beyond. Wooden tables were placed end to end down the center of the room with Greek columns holding up a vaulted ceiling thirty feet above. The walls were lined with torches making soot black streaks on what once was white marble. At the end of the room a giant fireplace audibly crackled as logs the size of small cars transformed to ash. The table was filled with plate after plate of unrecognizable meat, and James decided he didn't want to look any closer. He was certain whatever people ate in Hell wouldn't be what he would want to get a closer look at.

What he could only label as humans in filthy togas staggered around the room picking up pieces of food biting into it and wandering off behind the columns. James started to look behind the columns when one of the people stopped and started sniffing the air like a predator picking up a scent. James froze, knowing somewhere in the back of his mind that it was movement which gave people away. Unfortunately nasty toga guy didn't care about most of the time and turned directly toward James, pointed, and screamed out something in what sounded like Latin. For one brief moment James wished he knew what had been said, but when he saw them all turn toward him he decided he could do without knowing.

He realized as his feet hit the first step that he'd been doing a lot of running lately. He preferred to call it a strategic retreat, or the better part of valor, or even surviving to fight another day if that other day was against normal people in a normal world and not against crazed toga guys in Hell. Oh, and also he wished he had a gun. Glancing over his shoulder he decided a rocket launcher would be better. It would be like all those Quake matches he'd played on the computer in college. What you really wanted was to aim the rocket closer to their feet to get the best collateral damage from the blast.

If you aimed it at their torso or head you had a chance of missing, and in this case missing would be unhealthy.

The toga guys streamed up the stairs and despite their portliness were gaining on him. He wasn't sure how they moved so fast but then again this wasn't exactly a normal place. Hitting the next landing and seeing it didn't have a door to worry about he decided to make a stand where there was less chance of tripping on a step. He braced himself at the edge of the landing facing the downward steps hoping it would be harder for them to fight uphill.

He didn't have to wait too long for them to come into range knowing the iron bar gave him greater reach. When the first one's head was level with his swing he started in. Normally he would have felt horrible about hitting someone in the head with an iron bar, but this situation didn't really fall into normal. He didn't know who these people, if they even were people, were. They might be in Hell for something they did back in ancient Rome, or they might be the demons who tormented people living in ancient Rome. Either way James figured they were fair game for a good head whacking with his iron bar of doom.

The first one's head crunched and he dropped, rolling down the stairs and taking out the legs of other crazy toga guys behind him. Unfortunately the stairs were wide enough and they came at him three at a time. His backswing from hitting the first one wasn't very strong and just pushed the next one into his Hell buddy. This knocked them both a little off balance and James took advantage of this to kick out at them hoping to knock them off the edge of the tower. One fell and the other stumbled back, windmilling his arms to keep his balance and knocking two others off the edge in the process. Three more pushed ahead and James took a wide swing with the iron bar hoping to hit more than one.

"Crunchy on the outside but soft on the inside," James muttered to himself as he connected with another toga head. The remaining crazy togas retreated a few steps down and seemed to be waiting for something. James wondered if he should take the opportunity to run again but hesitated when he remembered how quickly they caught up to him the first time around.

After a few moments he saw them passing things up from the back of the line. When they started throwing food at him James wondered if Hell wasn't just evil but simply crazy. He'd always thought of Hell as a really big volcano with bubbling pits of lava and screaming people in them. Now he was fairly sure it was just weird.

James dodged the food just in case it was going to burst into flames or explode on contact, but all it did was just thud, or splat, on the stone landing. Backing up a few steps James took a closer look at the crazy toga's ammunition and was surprised to see that it was just food. The meat wasn't someone's arm or leg and he even saw a dinner roll thrown in from time to time. When the togas realized their not so deadly barrage of food wasn't going to bring James to his knees in fear they started walking back down the steps.

"Really?" James said aloud. "I almost get eaten by a swarm of angry Hell beetles and you guys just want a food fight?"

Looking around the landing and seeing nothing more frightening than a few suspiciously fuzzy dinner rolls James put his back to the tower wall and slid down till he was sitting with his arms resting on his knees. He took a deep breath and blew it out trying to expel the exhaustion and fear that had been building up.

"Quork?"

James fell to his left and swung the bar toward the sound but hit nothing.

"Rrrack, rrrack rrrack!"

Rolling onto his knees James tried to find whatever demon had sprung from the fuzzy dinner rolls of Hell. He'd thought they looked suspicious.

Another "Quoorrk?" drew his attention farther left where he saw a raven standing two stairs up from the landing. Only those who live in the frozen north of the world really know what a raven is. The birds most of the world calls ravens are really crows or rooks, just the little brothers of a real raven. A real raven, like the one cocking its head at him, was big. The only thing bigger in most northern nations would be an eagle, and James had seen ravens fight off eagles. In his time attending the University of Alaska he'd come to regard ravens as some of the smartest animals in the wild.

They got a bad name throughout history because they were scavengers and would regularly show up to eat the eyes of the dead after a battle. It was one of the reasons they were depicted as representations of death or war gods from the old religions of the north. The Irish goddess of death was actually a crow, but you couldn't blame the Irish since they didn't know ravens were better than their silly little cousins. The Vikings had gotten it right, however, when they picked ravens to be the earthly representation of Odin. They were his eyes in the world keeping track of all that people said and did. You knew if ravens were watching you Odin was also watching.

The names given to groups of raven kin also said what people thought of them. A group of crows was a murder, a group of rooks was a parliament, and a group of ravens was called an unkindness. The parliament of rooks had thrown James for a bit until someone told him that rooks would gather together in a group and one of them would squawk and give a rookish speech. At the end of his speech all the other rooks would either fly away happy with the measure he'd proposed or they'd all jump on him and tear him to little bits. Sounds just like parliament, or congress for that matter.

"Quork?" The raven hopped down one step and looked at James.

"So," James replied, "are you going to turn into some strange beast and try to kill me now?"

In response the raven hopped down to the landing and watched him with one black eye.

James looked around the landing at all the food laying there, "How bout this? I wasn't planning on eating any of this," he gestured to the feast on the ground, "so I will gratefully give it to you, but in return you have to remain a good raven and not try to peck my eyes out? Sounds like a deal?"

The two stared at each other for a few moments until the raven made his decision, hopped over to a bite size piece of meat, and ate it in one gulp.

"Good," James said, "I'll just sit here and rest a bit if it doesn't bother you."

The raven hopped over to a pile of food and started picking through it.

"You know Mr. Raven," the raven looked up from his food, "I always wanted to go on an adventure." The raven seemed to nod at him as if telling him to keep going, so he did, "After I got these nifty powers I thought everything would be so much more awesome. I mean, honestly, who wouldn't want to have superhero powers? Am I right?"

The raven said, "Rrrrock," and went back to eating.

"Ya, tell me about it," James nodded. "Sure I can throw lightning around and refill my gas tank for free but there's a downside to adventuring."

The raven looked up at him and distinctly gave him a look like he was crazy.

"No, seriously, I can throw lightning, and fireballs too. All this," James waved his iron bar at the smashed toga guys on the stairs, "was just because my powers don't seem to work in this wonderful place."

The raven continued to stare at him.

"Adventures should be about getting the pretty girl and saving the day, but so far I killed the pretty girl and the bad guy got away. I ended up here and some really bad things happened," he set down the iron bar and looked at his new right hand.

"In adventures you know the good guy is going to win and everything will turn out alright in the end. To tell you the truth, I don't even know where I'm going much less if it's all going to turn out."

The raven hopped closer and nudged a dinner roll toward James then looked up at him with a, "Quork?"

"Thanks buddy," James smiled, "but I gotta admit I'm not too keen on eating anything from Hell. No offense to you or your generosity."

He sighed, "Well, part of the reason I was given these powers was because I choose to do the right thing." Having just looked at his new hand his mind played back over the events after the fall of the angel. Had it been the right thing when he'd taken the angel's hand? He hadn't stopped moving long enough to even let himself think about it. Maybe he'd done it out of anger, and a need for revenge, but maybe it had been justice. Sometimes, he decided, the bad guys needed to be punished; a hand for a hand in this case.

"And I'm stubborn, so I think it's time I got on with my impossible quest. I may not know where I'm going, but I don't want to waste any time getting there."

Scooping up his iron bar James stood and realized, in a place like this, a little bit of politeness would go a very long way so he bowed slightly and tipped an imaginary hat to the raven, "It was a pleasure making your acquaintance Mr. Raven and if ever our paths should cross again I hope it will be as friends."

The raven looked at him, bobbed his head once, and went back to eating.

James stepped politely around the raven and started back up the stairway on the tower of Hell.

Chapter Nineteen

The stairs ended. The tower ended. After climbing for so long, the end of the stairs felt momentarily like the end of the world. James had almost come to believe they would stretch on forever, that the tower was a representation of the endlessness of Hell.

He could see above him the end of the tower but after taking so long to get here he knew he couldn't waste all that effort by just rushing up and getting his head taken off by whatever horror would live at the top of the tower of Hell. Dropping down so his palms rested on a step a few up from his feet James climbed up the last few cat style. Before the last step he flattened himself out and peeked over the top trying to be sneaky while also remaining ready for something to try and take a swing at him.

The top of the tower was flat; no temple, or grotesque skeleton altar, just flat. The same gray stones of the stairs and the landings continued on. He'd expected some change in scenery and again was surprised by the simplicity of Hell. In the middle of the giant flat circle of the tower top was a desk. From what James could tell at this distance it was made of some kind of dark wood with what looked like some kind of animal feet carved at the bottom. Maybe, James thought, it was a trap and the desk was actually a dragon. Maybe, it was just waiting for him to get closer to change and squish him.

On the other hand a desk that changed into a dragon would be almost the strangest thing he'd seen so far in Hell. Why not just be a dragon James thought? It's not like he had an escape route from the top of Hell. With that logic bouncing around in his head he decided a trap would be of little use here, unless it was simply to torment him. While tormenting was, in all reality, the purpose of Hell he realized his range of choices was severely limited. He could either move forward or he could sit here and do nothing until something showed up to kill him. Having survived this far he decided there really was no choice. So with what little bit of confidence James could muster up he clutched his iron bar from the gate of Hell itself and stood up.

Stepping onto the top James paused waiting for something to trigger. Something had to happen. He'd just climbed all the way to the top of this blasted tower, and if something didn't happen he would be slightly cross. He hadn't found the Darkness, or even a clue as to where the evil thing had gone. He'd assumed, since there was only one way to go, that it had gone this way. The only doors that were open on the way up James had looked into and the Darkness hadn't been hiding in any of them. Now here he was at the end of the tower and no Darkness.

Before he realized it James was walking toward the desk. As he got closer more things stood out to him. The desk was dark wood and visibly heavy. Swirls in the wood gave it a natural feel, but James wasn't sure where you could get real wood in Hell, and who you would hire to carry it up the stairs. Maybe some poor wood demon like Bob down on the plains of Hell had been harvested to make this one singular fixture. The top of the desk was black and looked slightly padded around the edges. There were feet carved into the bottom of the legs but they looked like what you would see on the bottom of an old freestanding bathtub and not so much like the dragon he'd imagined earlier. The top of the desk held two wicker baskets, one on each end of the desk, stacked full of papers. On the right hand side of the desk was a silver metal cup full of pens and a second silver cup next to it for pencils. James glanced around and could see no way to sharpen the pencils, and for some reason it bothered him. Finally, next to the right hand wicker basket there was what looked to James like a basic black plastic stapler.

It wasn't the desk, however, that caught the majority of James' attention. Sitting behind the desk was something James had only ever seen once before. It wasn't the wings he was most interested in. He actually found himself, as he walked up to the desk, wondering about the chair. How did a man with wings that big sit in a normal chair, James thought? It must have chunks cut from the seat back.

The angel, because James couldn't think of another word for a man with wings, sat bent over the desk intently writing on an off white piece of paper. He was dressed in a gray three-piece suit with a white shirt and black tie. His hair was brown and his skin was slightly tanned, like he was the kind of guy who got outside as much as he could but didn't tan on purpose.

As James got to the desk the angel raised his left hand in a gesture that clearly said he was a bit busy and would you mind waiting until he was done with this last bit here on this very important document. It was at that moment, looking down on him, James realized this must be the Devil. He was at the top of Hell, and there was no one else here, so this must be the Devil.

Looking around the top of the tower again James wondered at the lack of guards or monsters or something to protect the lord of Hell. Hadn't he always heard of things like Dukes or Princes of Hell? Weren't there supposed to be Arch-demons huddled around trying to get the Devil's favor?

"Actually," the Devil spoke without looking up, "you would be surprised by how few people actually come up here." He glanced up at James, "As an example, you are the first guest I've had in about one thousand nine hundred and eighty years, give or take a few depending on what calendar you use."

"But," James looked around again, "you're the Devil."

"That is correct, in a way." The Devil looked back down and pressed his thumb onto the bottom of the document leaving a strange print in the place of a signature.

"In a way?" James said. "How can you be the Devil, in a way?"

The Devil placed the piece of paper in the left hand basket, pushed his chair back from the desk, and stood. In that moment James realized he was actually a little taller than the Devil and the thought poked him in the brain, how could you be the Devil and not be over six feet tall?

"Well," the Devil started around the desk, "I am The Devil," he placed emphasis on The, "but I'm not the only Devil."

"What does that…"

The Devil raised a hand to stop him, "First, I understand it's been a bit of a trip to get here, and since I so rarely have guests," he gestured expansively with his hands and a table with two chairs appeared, "would you care for a cup of tea and some snacks?"

James looked down at the table, at the sight of a plate of sliced meats and cheeses, and he realized, for the first time in the eternity of Purgatory and Hell, that he was hungry. He assumed the Devil didn't get hungry, and yet here he was offering him a snack. The fact that he hadn't been hungry all the way here and now his stomach was growling didn't surprise him. He just had to keep reminding himself he wasn't in reality land anymore.

Seriously? His brain said, *You're going to eat something given to you from the Devil himself?*

Look, James thought back, if he wanted to kill me why would he resort to poisoned tea?

Because he's the Devil. The father of lies. Etcetera, Etcetera, Etcetera. He might get a kick out of watching you choke on a cracker made out of sharp stuff.

Sharp stuff?

You know what I mean.

"James?"

James looked from the table to the Devil and back.

The Devil sighed, "I understand you don't trust me, and it's completely rational with what you've been taught all your life, but really I'm not going to kill you with some sliced ham and Havarti."

Father of lies. His brain whispered to him, but he sat down anyway.

"First," James said, "what exactly did you mean by you're not the only Devil? I thought there was just one."

"Of course you did because that's what you've been taught." The Devil reached out, took a cracker, and spread something that looked and smelled a lot like salmon onto it. "First, let me ask you a few questions to narrow down what you know and what you don't." He took a bite of his cracker and James almost died of hunger watching him chew. After he swallowed he asked, "Can the Devil be everywhere at the same time?"

James blinked at him a few times, "Uhm, I, uhh…"

"Exactly," the Devil replied. "The correct answer is no. The Devil, or myself if I may say so, am a singular being. I have exceptional talents and can travel rather quickly if the need arises, but I am just me and I can only be in one place at one time."

James didn't really know where the conversation was going so he decided the best choice, when talking with the Devil, was to just sit, listen, and try to not be tricked.

"My actual title," the Devil continued, "is not the Devil. I am the Accuser. Or I suppose in your modern day American language I would be called the Prosecution."

"You're a lawyer?" James just looked at him for a moment then added, "That would explain a lot about lawyers."

"Ha," the Devil let out a single laugh, "Yes and no. Yes I suppose you could call me a very, very glorified lawyer, but no, that doesn't explain much about American lawyers. They're their own problem, and I had nothing to do with that."

"But, aren't you a prowling lion waiting to devour those who go astray?"

"No. Well, I'm not. That's someone else's job, the whole devouring thing."

"You have jobs?"

"Of course." The Devil finished off his cracker. "You see, we were created much differently than you were. Each and every one of us was created with a specific purpose. Some are guardians, some work with weather, and some have very specific jobs, like Death. My job is to accuse."

"Accuse?"

"Have you ever read Job?"

"Uh, a long time ago."

The Devil leaned over to his desk and flipped through the paperwork in the right hand basket. Pulling one out he read it quickly and said, "Tut tut," in a very stereotypical British gentleman sort of way, "you haven't been to church in ages. The last time you read Job was," he ran his finger down the paper, "in fifth grade."

"Well, you know, things come up."

"Oh," the Devil put the paper back onto the pile, "Don't worry it's not my place to judge how often you go to church. Oh wait," he grinned at James, "actually it is."

"So..." James trailed off.

"So," The Devil continued, "I spend about half my time over in Heaven petitioning for the rights to certain people, and the other half of the time I'm sitting here writing dispatches for my deputies."

"Wait," James leaned forward over the table, "What do you mean by rights to people, exactly?"

"The traditional way of saying it, and believe me Heaven is very much about holding to tradition, is to sift you like wheat."

"That doesn't actually tell me anything."

The Devil smiled, "To put you through the wringer, to bend you and see if you'll break, to test you, and try you."

"Let's say," he leaned back in his chair and again James wondered how that worked with the wings, "there's some big shot religious TV personality. People are flocking to him by the thousands. My job is to dig into his life and see what's really there. Then I take that information to Heaven and put in a petition with the big guy Himself for permission to, how would you say it these days, mess with him and prove he isn't all he claims to be."

"Like?"

"Get a little rumor started over in one corner and soon you find out he's been sexting with girls in the youth group, or it turns out he's secretly addicted to painkillers, or hookers, or he's using the millions in offering money to pay for a giant yacht docked in Monte Carlo. Or, let's say there was a boy who, through some amazing set of circumstances gained incredible power over reality. Is he right for that? Will he do the right thing when the time comes, or will he be like so many others and convince himself he's doing the right thing while actually just finding excuses to do what he wants?"

James looked into the plain brown eyes of the Devil and sighed, then said quietly, "What if he doesn't know?"

He slumped back into his chair and raised his hands palms up, "What if he's asking those same questions?"

The smile on the Devil's face was simple and unassuming, "That's the point of the test, and not every test is the same. Some are tested to see if they can maintain their stance in the face of the hurricane. Others are tested to see if they'll ask the right questions or listen to the right advice."

"And the point of all this?"

"To show who they really are. To show the world that those high and mighty self righteous people are all just the same, frauds. Or to show that someone is worth the time and effort. To see what the powerful do when the power is taken away. To see if they are only doing the right thing because people are watching."

James looked at the Devil for a moment. He took in his perfectly combed brown hair and noticed a sprinkling of gray in it. Could the Devil get gray hair? Did angels feel the passing of the centuries? The one in

Purgatory certainly had noticed how long he'd been there. "You do this because you like seeing them suffer?"

"Not really," the Devil reached out for his tea, "I do it because it's my job, and I like to do my job well."

"But, aren't you Lucifer? The Angel that tried to become God and was kicked out of Heaven for his hubris and pride?"

"Me?" The Devil laughed, "No, no, I'm not the fallen star." He took a sip of his tea, "Remember James, The Devil, any devil, is a singular being. We can only be in one place at a time, and while Lucifer is a very powerful and very persuasive being he is only one being in a multitude of realities."

"So Lucifer's not in charge of the demons in the other worlds?"

"Good heaven's no. Do you have any idea how many other worlds there are?"

"I know about three." James said.

"Well," The Devil replied, "there are a whole lot more than three I can tell you that."

"So do you work in all of them doing this accusing thing?"

"No, one world is more than enough for me."

"But," James paused, "I thought," questions tumbled through his mind like an avalanche.

The Devil smiled, "Most people don't actually think. They think that they think, but they really are just repeating what they've been told by society and pretending to think."

"Uhm," James' brain temporarily locked up while trying to digest everything.

The Devil leaned forward a bit, "Take some poor hunter gatherer from four thousand years ago in central Asia. He would never believe it if you tried to tell him how big the world really was. He would be sure it all ended just past the river, or the ocean, or that range of mountains in the distance. It's the same thing today. Go talk to some poor science teacher at a local high school in Middle America and try to convince her that other universes exist in a vast multitude and they'll tell you to stop reading so much science fiction."

James' brain decided to rebel against the current line of conversation out of sheer irritation and momentarily take control of the mouth to blurt out, "But where's the Darkness?" He waved his arms around and pointed at the edges of the tower top, "This is the end of the path. The top of the tower. Where did he go?"

The Devil raised an eyebrow in a perfect evil genius impersonation, "What?"

James sighed, took control of his mouth, and tried again, "This has been a very nice conversation, and much more helpful than the one with Cain, but I still have a job to do. I'm starting to understand I'm being tested, but I can't just sit here and wonder about it all while he gets farther away."

"While who gets farther away?"

"The Darkness with all the eyes. I was tracking it through Purgatory and up the tower here in Hell. I thought it didn't have any way to go but up and yet when I got here..." he trailed off and looked around meaningfully.

"I hate to remind you of this but I'm not all seeing or all knowing." The Devil let the statement hang there waiting for James to fill in the details.

"It's a demon of some kind that blends into shadows and gets into people's heads. I haven't seen a real body on the thing except for a twisted version a while back in Purgatory. It gets stronger when people around it make contradictory or chaotic decisions," James paused and tried to think of any other way to describe the Darkness. "It came through the doors between the worlds into my world from the one just before."

"Ah," the Devil nodded knowingly, "did he come from the up door or down door?"

James shook his head slightly, "I'm not even sure what that means."

The Devil spoke slowly as if to help a small child understand, "Did he come from the side with a doorknob or without?"

"Uhm," James resisted the impulse to reach across the table and slap the Devil figuring it wouldn't turn out well and thought for a second, "If I remember correctly they pulled the door open and the Darkness came through, so he would have been on the side without a doorknob."

"Good," The Devil reached over to his desk and picked up a blank sheet of paper, which hadn't been there before, and selected a pen from the silver cup, "and how many worlds away did you say he came from?"

"He came through two doors."

The Devil wrote something down on the paper, "And you said he feeds on contradictions?"

"Chaos," James corrected.

"Remember," the Devil wrote more down, "I'm a glorified lawyer. It's not really chaos but simply a mass of contradicting choices leading to disastrous outcomes." He finished writing, pressed his thumb to the bottom of the paper, and placed it in the left hand basket.

James looked from the basket to the Devil, "What good did that do?"

"I should get a reply from my agents momentarily." The Devil motioned to the table, "You really should try the tea."

James decided to ride out this newest in a long line of strange situations and settled back in his chair, "What kind of tea do they serve in Hell?"

"Ha," the Devil let out another laugh, "They don't serve tea in Hell, but to answer your question this is a nice Oolong. I thought the caffeine of a dark tea might help you."

James' brain latched onto the Devil's statement, "Wait, if this is tea, and we're in Hell, then what do you mean they don't serve tea in Hell?"

"Oh," said the Devil, "I see the confusion. You're not in Hell."

James looked around then back to the Devil to see if he was making a joke, "After what I just went through," James started and stopped when the Devil nodded knowingly at him.

"You did touch on Hell, yes. I suppose a better way to say it would be that you brushed up against the edge of Hell."

"But," James stood up and pointed off the edge of the tower, "the monsters, and the beetles with the faces, and the guy in the room with the horns and the glowing crown, and" he paused, looked back at the stairs, and shivered, "and the beetles with the faces."

The Devil put his teacup down and folded his arms, "You mentioned the beatles twice."

"There were a lot of them, and they hurt," he sat back down, "a lot."

"Yes, my initial report said you ran into some nasty things on the way here."

"Some?" James wanted to hit something, "Just how long it took to get up this tower was a torture."

The Devil cocked his eyebrow again, "Tower?"

James looked around at the obvious tower they were sitting on top of, "Yes, tower."

The Devil smiled at him, "So you see a tower? That's interesting."

"What are you talking about?"

"Hell isn't a tower James."

"Then what did I just climb?"

A chuckle escaped from between the Devil's perfectly white teeth, "Hell isn't a physical reality, it's a spiritual one." He raised his hands to stop James' questions, "I know everything you've ever read or seen about Hell talks about lakes of burning fire, etcetera, but how else do you expect people to describe something spiritual except with metaphors?"

"So you're telling me I didn't just climb a tower?"

"Let me guess," the Devil settled back into his chair, "it was a long journey filled with trial and tribulation and along the way you encountered places where you could vaguely see into the heart of things, but mostly it was closed to you."

"Yes." James was starting to see where he was going with this.

"It is the journey of man," the Devil said.

"But I came through Purgatory and passed into Hell through the actual iron gates." James knew he was starting to get defensive and whine, but he'd been through so much lately it just didn't seem fair if he wasn't really in Hell.

"You have to understand there's a difference between where you are and the concept of being in Hell. You have to die and be the right kind of person to end up in Hell. You, James, are neither of those."

"So where am I?"

"I suppose you could call it Hell's backyard, or if you're British it's the garden of Hell." The Devil leaned forward, "You're standing on the doorstep of Hell and looking through the windows. Every once in a while something slips through an open window and bites at you, but you aren't actually in Hell." He glanced down and brushed some crumbs from his suit, "And be glad you're not. What you saw, whatever it was, is only a faint shadow of Hell."

James let out a deep sigh, "I guess where I am is neither here nor there, it's where I need to go that's important."

"And where do you need to go, young James Patterson?"

"That's just it," James stood and looked around the top of the tower for anyplace the Darkness could have gone, "I'm not sure where the Darkness went."

"Ah yes," the Devil reached over to his desk and picked up a piece of paper from the middle of his desk. He ran his eyes over it, "Ah, I see."

"What?"

"He was a minor functionary in a separate world, and it seems he thought he could make it better on his own."

"Ya, ya," James leaned on the back of his chair, "so where is he?"

The Devil set the paper back on his desk, "He is no longer in Hell."

"What? But how," James stopped and looked around hoping to see something, anything that would help.

"There are many roads and many doors leading to Hell James. As was once famously stated, wide is the path and easy is the way that leads to destruction. It seems your nemesis has taken one of those paths to another world."

"How could he do that?" James started to pace, "all the doors were locked, and the open ones were places in Hell not other worlds."

The Devil shrugged, "Remember, what you saw on your way here was simply your mind trying to make sense of the senseless. You were trying to apply reason to an unreasonable situation. The doors you saw might or might not have been locked, or even real."

James gestured to his tattered clothes, "I don't think this is a figment of my imagination."

"No," the Devil nodded, "those were real."

"So where'd he go?"

The Devil pushed himself back from the table and stood, "I really hate to say this, but it's not in my job description to help wandering souls."

"Well," James immediately countered, "it's not in your job description to not help either. Which means for once in your existence you have the free will to make a choice."

The Devil stared at him for a moment then moved around his desk. He opened a drawer and scooped up an old inkwell and pen from inside and walked back around toward James. "You make a good point."

The Devil dipped the pen into the inkwell thoughtfully, "Most of what you see in life is cloaked in different layers. Some are harmless or even helpful, but other times what you are seeing with your actual eyes is simply a covering for something else entirely. What you need is to be able to see the truth, and you can't see that with your eyes. Sometimes the only way you can truly see is to close your eyes."

He looked at James and said, "Close your eyes."

James' initial reaction was to not trust this being. This thing had admitted to being the Devil, and had confirmed that if he wasn't in the heart of Hell he was at least in the direct vicinity of it. Why should he trust anything from this angel, or demon, or whatever it was?

"What have I got to lose?" James said, "If you were going to kill me you'd have done it already. And there's nowhere else for me to go."

Nodding slightly, the Devil added, "Very rarely do I get the opportunity to make a totally free choice, and I have to admit that I like a good story. If I help you, and show you the way, your story will only get more interesting. So," and he gestured to James' eyes with the dripping in pen.

Taking a deep breath James closed his eyes. The sharp metal tip of the pen pricked onto his skin above his right eyebrow then scraped its way in a rough circle around his right eye.

"Not quite done," the Devil said and James could hear him dipping the pin into the inkwell.

The tip resumed its scratching creating rays out from the sun circle of his right eye.

"There," the Devil said with a bit of triumph in his voice, "all done. And not too shabby if I do say so myself."

James opened his eyes and was disappointed when the only difference was the slight smell of the ink lingering in the air around him. "Uhm," James looked around himself again to see if anything would glow or change shape, "nothing's changed."

"Right." The Devil reached up and smacked James' right eye with the palm of his hand like he was adjusting an old TV set.

"Ouch," James staggered back a few steps. "What was that for?"

"Had to transmute the ink."

"Right," James said sarcastically. He looked around again and still saw nothing different.

"You can't look with your eyes," the Devil said.

James closed his eyes and saw nothing but the darkness of his eyelids. Concentrating on anything he hoped he could activate it in some way, while part of his mind giggled at him that the Devil was pulling a prank and he'd be wandering around for the rest of his life with the word dork written on his face. Finally the darkness resolved into a kind of black and white version of the world around him, and with a little more effort it slid into a kind of false color version of reality. It reminded him, in a way, of footage you'd see from those thermal cameras all the ghost hunting shows used.

He looked around and saw the top of a tower, "I thought you said Hell wasn't a tower."

The Devil's voice came from behind him, "I said it was a metaphor, and I said Hell isn't a physical reality but a spiritual one. It's not lying to you. How you see it just happens to be different from how I see it."

James turned to look at the Devil and saw a brief afterimage of something huge and bright moving very fast.

"No, no, no," the Devil said. "This is the first time you've used this. You look at me as I really am now and it might just burn out your brain."

James opened his eyes and turned to the Devil, "You really think you're all that eh?"

The Devil just nodded, "I'm a creature of fire and light born of the word of God himself in the moment of creation. So, yes, I think I'm all that."

James swallowed an unexpected lump in his throat, "I cut off an angel's hand."

"And it's a good thing you didn't have this to see the reality of the situation at the time." The Devil walked back to his desk, pulled out his chair, and sat. Looking across the wooden expanse of the desk at James he said, "Thank you so much for having this chat with me. I doubt something like this will happen again for thousands of years and it's nice to take a break from time to time."

"Right," was all James could think to say at the moment. He turned and started back toward the stairs to start his search for the Darkness.

"Not there." The Devil smiled at him and pointed to his right, "over there."

James looked and didn't see anything but the edge of the tower then nodded to himself like he was a bit of an idiot and closed his eyes. The false color version of the world slipped into place and as he got closer to the edge of the tower he saw a second set of steps.

Chapter Twenty

Everything looked different. The stones of the tower glowed with an individual light, and the stairs seemed to move under his feet like an escalator. He saw statues lining the stairs and open doors, which he was sure he didn't want to look into. He paused not knowing what to look for in this visual overload.

Normally he would close his eyes and take a few deep breaths to settle himself and figure out what needed to be done, but in this situation that wasn't going to help. He opened his eyes and looked around at the gray stone tower.

"Okay," he said to the air, "I need to focus."

But on what? His mind asked.

"Well," he realized it felt better to talk out loud in this silent place, "there has to be a way to track it with this eyeball thing I can do or what would be the reason for giving it to me?"

The Devil thinks he's funny?

James snorted, "Ya, because the Devil never gets to play pranks on anyone. But seriously, there has to be a way to track it."

There's the oil slick.

"The oil slick?"

You know.

And he did.

James closed his eyes again and watched the strange colors of the truth fade into existence. He ran his closed eyes over the stones of the wall and the strange moving stairs. He remembered each time he'd come up against the Darkness how things had felt different. If you took an oil slick on the parking lot of Wal-Mart and turned that into a feeling, you would know what it was like to stand around the Darkness. It wasn't overwhelming, just a little bit oily.

Once he knew what he was looking for it jumped out at him. It was on the stairs, the wall, the statues. James didn't have to slowly follow the trail like an old Scotland Yard inspector with his magnifying glass. He could run down the steps, taking them two or three at a time. Finally he came to a door. Through the lens of his new eyes the door looked as simple and wooden as any of the others he'd come across.

Maybe, he thought, it was like the Devil said and the door was just a door. It wasn't lying to him. On the surface of the door he could easily see the oily sheen of the Darkness and to cement his suspicion the door was ever so slightly ajar.

The door itself was flat with no handle or lock. If it'd been closed all the way there would be no way to open it. But somehow, whether it was the Darkness who'd done it or something else, the edge of it was a finger's breadth out from the arch surrounding it.

James set down the iron bar and pressed the fingertips of both his hands into the edge and pulled as best he could. Nothing happened. He tried putting one foot up on the archway and trying to use that as better leverage for his fingertips. Even more nothing happened. He picked up the iron bar again and wedged it into a spot where the stones of the arch had lost some mortar holding them together. It created a gap just big enough for his bar to slide in. Using the little leverage he had James pushed it sideways and pulled at the same time. The door moved an inch.

It was tedious, irritating, and left some serious scrapes when he slipped and rammed his knuckles into the wall, but eventually the door opened far enough to grab the inside and pull it open.

Looking through with his new sight James saw nothing but darkness. He really didn't want to walk through the strange door in Hell with his eyes closed, no matter how cool his new power was, so he opened his eyes and with as much confidence as a fly going to tea with a spider he stepped through the door.

His foot hit something and he stumbled forward catching his elbow on a wooden pole. It fell and tangled in his legs stopping him from stepping forward and turned his stumble into a fall, which ended quite suddenly on a very solid door. Steadying himself as much as possible on the door and waiting for the proverbial clattering to stop James silently cursed at himself for such a stealthy entrance. He doubted the Darkness would be standing here waiting for him, but he could be walking into its evil lair. He counted to twenty and once his eyes had adjusted to the darkness he found himself standing in a dusty janitor's closet.

"Great," he whispered to the dust, "I stepped out of Hell and into a closet."

He wished this were one of the video games he'd played where you could turn on a super vision mode and see if any people were in the next room. In some he could have cast a spell to detect life signs, while in others he could turn on some technical goggles and see their heat signature through the walls. He did remember his own special vision but that would be worthless in this situation. It would show him the truth of the things around him like the mop bucket and broom, and he seriously doubted they were anything other than exactly what they looked like. On the other hand if they were different he wasn't sure he wanted to see the true spiritual essence of a mop bucket. It was probably dirty and depressing.

"Ha, ha, I made a funny," James whispered to himself as he felt along the door for a crack to peek through. His fingers came to rest on the keyhole just beneath the door handle. He could tell it was metal of some kind and it seemed to be big enough to actually see through.

Kneeling down he pressed his right eye against the hole in the hope of seeing something on the other side. It was dark. So while one part of his mind was a little bit giddy about actually having peered through a keyhole for the first time the majority of his mind was irritated by the fact that he would, once again, be walking blind into a room.

James gripped his iron bar and opened the door with his left hand. He was still trying to decide if he should only open it a crack and peek through or if he should just pop it open and jump out when the decision was made for him. The broom he'd bumped into slid off the door, where it'd been resting, and fell to the floor with a sneak destroying crack.

His breath caught and adrenaline surged through him making his fingertips tingle. With the element of surprise out of the question James threw the door the rest of the way open and readied himself for a fight. When nothing jumped from the semi darkness after several seconds he started taking stock of his situation.

Moonlight filtered into the room through curtained windows and showed chairs and tables all facing a wall covered with a blackboard. James had been in enough classrooms throughout his life that he knew one instantly just by the feel of it. What he hadn't been in for a long time was a room with a chalkboard. His institutional memory stretched back to about the fifth grade. Before that it was all just a blur of images, and he wasn't sure if those were his memories or just pictures he'd seen in his parents photo albums. But in all of his memories of school from elementary all the way up through college he never remembered seeing a chalkboard.

Granted, he thought to himself, I'm fairly sure I've stepped into a completely different world.

Maybe, his brain replied, *maybe they haven't even invented markers and white boards yet. You could introduce that and become a millionaire.*

So you're telling me, he replied to himself as he walked as quietly as possible toward one of the floor to ceiling windows, that you know how to make a marker?

Well, not exactly. But I'm sure if we described it to someone they could figure it out and we could still take all the credit.

James ignored himself for a moment and looked around. The dimly lit room was a simple rectangle with six simple wooden tables and a door on the far side leading to what James assumed would be a long hallway with doors to other classrooms. Each table had two solid wood chairs and all of them faced the wall on his right. In front of the blackboard was a simple podium and James could see a book resting open on it. He was curious what the book was about, but decided looking out the window was the higher priority.

Reaching out James pulled the curtain back just enough to see out with his left eye. He realized his new, and quite awesome, seeing power would be useless like that so he switched to the other side of the window and pulled the curtain back again.

Thinking about how he really needed to give his new powers names he looked out over a moonlit stretch of lawn. Cobblestone pathways created a cross in the grass and led to large stone buildings on three of the four sides. The fourth side, the one directly in front of him, was bordered by a head high stone wall with a gate set in it. Through the gate James could see a road of some kind. He couldn't tell if it was paved or just packed down dirt. At regular intervals along the cobbled pathways were statues. James leaned toward the window hoping they would give him a hint of where he was. He could tell they were all in billowing robes of some kind and most of them wore octagonal hats with what looked like a feather sticking up from the right side.

The obvious classroom he was standing in coupled with the statues of what could only be professors led him to an inescapable conclusion. The Darkness had invaded a university.

"Well," he no longer felt the need to whisper in an empty classroom, "if there's one place that's easy to create chaos it's a university campus."

Weaving through the tables and chairs toward the door he decided on a fairly simple plan of action. Turn on his Devil goggles, he wasn't sure if he was going to stick with that name or not, and keep on tracking the Darkness through the university.

The door flew open in front of him and the room flooded with light. Through his light blinded eyes James could just make out three people running into the room. One was holding what James' brain could only think of as a lantern while the other two were waving some kind of wooden carving. All of them started shouting immediately and James reacted on pure, I just literally went through Hell, instinct.

He dropped low assuming whoever it was would react like a normal person and swing for his head or chest. Lashing out with his iron bar he caught the first one on the meat of the calf muscle between the knee and the ankle. James had hoped to hit the knee since that would be a more instantly crippling blow, but was happy with the reaction as his unknown assailant dropped to the ground, gripped their leg and started yelling something that sounded a lot like, "Ow, ow, ow."

James grabbed a chair with his left hand to use as a shield, raised his iron bar, and stood up. Stretching himself to his full six feet two inches to make himself look as big as possible he advanced toward his attackers. He felt confident he could handle anything after surviving the beatles, and nasty tunnel monster from Hell. Instantly the song "Hard Days Night" started running through his head.

One of his assailants grabbed their injured member and tried to drag them back toward the door while the other one waved the lantern at James in what seemed like a false hope the light would scare him away.

After standing there for a few long seconds and realizing they weren't going to attack him, James took a moment to really look at the three of them. They were all dressed alike in black robes, and in the flickering light cast by the lantern James could just make out that one of them might be a girl. Other than that, their most striking feature was how unthreatening they were.

Cracking a little bit of a smile James set down the chair and lowered the iron bar. Holding out his left hand he said, "It's all right. You just startled me."

The one holding the lantern said something back to him in a language James didn't even pretend to recognize. It had the deep rough tones of German but sounded about as much like German as a raven sounded like his sixty eight year old Mother. On the other hand when she was nagging him to clean his room she did sound remarkably like a raven.

"Sorry," James spoke in the most comforting tone he could summon, "I didn't get that. If you could just repeat it in a language I actually understand that would be helpful."

The one still standing stepped between James and the injured one. The man took up a protective posture and raised a wooden carving in what seemed like another hopeful gesture to fend James off. He started saying something and by the monotone of his voice and the cadence of it James assumed he was quoting something.

James barked out a laugh as he realized they were trying to exorcize him. Then something occurred to him. He wasn't in Hell anymore, or Purgatory for that matter. Those places might have been immutable points in time where his power of belief couldn't affect anything, but this was a world. It might not be his world, but that didn't matter. These people obviously believed in something, which meant his power should work here.

Concentrating on the words James closed his eyes and believed he could understand them. He was starting to get the feeling from all of these events that there was more to this power than he'd previously understood, but for right now it was enough to believe it would work. He didn't just believe he could understand what was being said, he knew it, like he knew water was wet and somewhere someone would be complaining about paying taxes. He knew he could understand this language.

"By the power of the Almighty and his hundred names I cast you back..."

"Excuse me." James raised his left hand like a schoolboy wanting to ask a question, "If you haven't noticed, I'm not a demon."

The boy stopped in mid exorcism and stared open mouthed at James, who gave a polite cough to cover up the embarrassed silence then gave his best smile. Through all his concentrating on the language James hadn't noticed the girl get up from helping her injured compatriot and do a fairly good sneak around to his left side where she promptly picked up a chair and hit him with it.

Staggering to the side James dropped the iron bar and grabbed his ear, "Son of a..." He started hopping in a little circle, "Mother of a monkey goat pissing..." He clinched his teeth and felt the pain go from his jaw to the top of his head, "Ow, ow, stupid little," He felt something wet and sticky under his fingers and was fairly sure he was bleeding. The only reason he didn't crumple like wet newspaper was his recent hellish experience with pain.

"What the..." James really wanted to curse but he knew it wouldn't help. He turned and looked at the black robed figure and with her hood now falling back and he could see her long dark hair spilling over her shoulders. Taking his hand away he looked at the blood on his fingers then waved with his right at the chair she was starting to raise again, "What would make you do something like that?"

She stared at him in confusion for a moment and James took the now available time to grope around behind himself for a chair he could sit in rather than be hit with.

"Seriously? What did you think you would accomplish with that?" He stared accusingly at his hand, disappointed to not see it soaked in Stephen King amounts of blood.

"Seriously." He looked back up at her then quickly over at the others to make sure they weren't about to hit him with a bookshelf. "Is that how you deal with evil spirits around here? Hit it with a chair and hope it goes away? Because I have to tell you it very rarely works."

The girl started to open her mouth and James raised a hand, "Shush you. Just put down the chair and back away from it." He turned to the others, "and you two, sit down, you're making me nervous."

James felt his right hand tingle and remembered. It was strangely easy to forget now that he was sitting in a solid normal chair, surrounded by

196

solid normal things. Even though he knew this wasn't his world, or his home, it was still a normal world and someone's normal home. That tingle in his hand pulled him back and he could see in his mind a crazed angel held down by chains and the souls of Purgatory. He shook his head and felt the last bits of pain fade away under the influence of the angelic hand.

James took a deep breath and looked around at his three attackers, "All right. Now that I'm calmed down and less likely to do something rash, like, let's say," he stared at the girl who was now sitting on her weapon, "hit someone with a chair. I'd like to know why you attacked a random stranger in the middle of the night?" He figured by turning the situation around and interrogating them he could put himself into a position of authority, even if it was false, and avoid some unanswerable questions about what he was doing here in the middle of the night.

The three stared at him in silence.

"Are you kidding me?" James shook his head, "I know you can talk. You were just chanting at me like I was," he paused and took another breath.

"You," He pointed at one of the boys, "Why are you here?"

"Uhm," The girl to his left started to speak.

Without looking at her James raised his hand and pointed at her. "You, I don't even want to look at you right now so shush until my head stops ringing and I don't feel like punching you in the nose." He could see her shoulders slump from the corner of his eye. "But you," he pointed at the boy again, "I asked you a question."

The boy fidgeted in his chair and finally looked up at James, "We, um, tracked it to this room, and, um, thought you were it and so..."

"Whoa," James held up both his hands, "Slow down there. First, what should I call you?"

"Oh," the boy looked at his companions, "well..."

James raised an eyebrow at him and looked around at the others, "You're thinking if I'm some evil thing from the pits of evil land and you give me your name I'll have some crazy power over you right?"

He watched them all shuffle uncomfortably in their seats and mutter things under their breath.

"Fine, then here's how it's going to work," James pointed at the boy, "I'm going to call you Stinky," he pointed at the other boy, "you are Fart, and you," he pointed at the girl, "I'm calling you Pain in the Ass."

"Hey," she straightened up in her chair.

James waved a finger at her, "Shh, Pain in the Ass, I'm talking to Stinky right now." He shuffled his chair so his back was to the girl and he was only facing the boys. "Now let's try again, Stinky. What is this thing you think I am?"

"Well, uhm."

The other boy reached up and put his hand on his friend's shoulder, "Look, there were some kids who thought they could fix a problem by," he waved vaguely at the air, "calling something up to deal with the problem for them. Ever since, things have been going wrong and people have been getting hurt. We narrowed down the origin of the," he paused again and looked around the room like the right words would be painted on the walls, "thing to this room."

"And you thought," James continued for him, "that you could, somehow, send this thing back to where it came from."

"Yes."

"And I'm assuming getting into a fistfight with an evil spirit and hitting it with a chair wasn't exactly how you saw this all going down?"

"Not exactly, no."

"So why do you think a normal person like myself would be here, in this exact room?"

"Are you from the Church?" Stinky asked.

James tried to look intelligent and raised an eyebrow, "Who would be sent to investigate strange occurrences like you've been having, and might figure out the origin of those events?"

The three looked at each other and slumped a little in their chairs. The girl spoke up, "You are from the Church."

"And you just hit me upside the head with a very hard chair." James turned and looked her directly in the eyes, "And, might I add, it hurt quite a lot."

When James turned back to the boys, the one who'd been speaking extended his hand, "My name's Ren."

James took his hand and was glad this world didn't have some strange form of greeting like rubbing knees together or something, "My name's James."

The other boy extended his hand, "I'm Todd."

James nodded and shook his hand as well then turned in his chair and faced the girl again, "Do you have a name my dear swinger of wooden chairs?"

She nodded at him, "Aubergine, but my friends call me Abby."

"Well," James smiled a little at her and noticed, now that the pain had subsided, that she was very cute in a chair killer sort of way, "now that we're all being a little more civil why don't we try to fill in some gaps."

James waved his hand at the chairs in front of him suggesting Abby join the others. Once she was situated he looked them over, "could you lose the hoods please. It makes me feel like you're about to try and exorcise me again."

As they pushed the hoods back James tried in the dim light to make out some details. His eyes lingered on Abby with her long dark hair and light complexion. She had a rounder face and pretty lips. He also decided if he looked any longer he might get himself in trouble so he shifted his gaze and almost fell out of his chair. Ren reached out a hand and steadied him. James mumbled something about feeling a little dizzy while trying not to absolutely stare at the two little horns poking out of Ren's short-cropped hair. They were about two inches long and even with all the shadows had a slight red color to them, which contrasted with Ren's blonde hair. As much as a small part of him wanted to stare at the first pretty girl he'd seen in the eternity of his trip through Purgatory and Hell the entire rest of his brain absolutely wanted to do nothing but reach out and touch the pointy little things on Ren's head. The fact hit him that no one else seemed in the least affected or surprised to see a normal looking kid with little horns poking up like tiny volcanoes about to explode. He tried to check out Todd but found himself trying to look at the horns from the corner of his eyes and couldn't really focus on anything else. Finally he focused and tried to get a good look at the final member of the threesome. He wasn't short but gave the impression of being so when you put him next to the almost waifish Ren. His shoulders filled out the black robe and James could easily see him in a rugby uniform. After catching himself glancing back at the horns he shook his head at the simple oddity of it all and decided to get back to business.

"So," it crossed James' mind that this whole thing wasn't even close to the weirdest thing to happen to him in even the last few hours, "I'm going to make some guesses and you all can tell me if they're right or not. If so, it should save us a lot of time."

"Sure," Ren said, and James promptly categorized him as the leader of the little group.

"First guess, people have been talking about whispers in the dark."

Ren and Abby looked at each other, Todd nodded and said, "Yeah, weird huh."

"Not if there's someone actually there whispering to you Todd."

"But that's just it," Todd added, "Everyone who's heard it says there's never anyone there."

James then categorized Todd. He seemed to be shy but when he gets going the shy goes quickly away. He still didn't have a category for Abby, aside from hitting people with chairs. People always tell you not to judge the book by the cover, or not to stereotype people, while at the same time doing just that every day of their lives. He bet teachers were the worst at this. Every year a new group of kids comes into class and they have to figure them out quickly to know how to deal with them. So they judge them. Or to put it more politely they categorize them. The boy with the long bangs pulled over his eyes wearing all black and sitting in the back of the room isn't likely to be the outspoken one. The girl wearing all name brand clothes most likely isn't going to be the nicest kid in class. Granted there were always exceptions and hopefully really good teachers would never let the students see the categories and should always be willing to change their inner view of you once they got to know you.

People label each other all the time. Sometimes those labels have names like Emo or Goth. Sometimes they are connections to what you do like Jock. Other times they're just feelings like she talks too much or he never talks at all. But no matter what we say out loud we all categorize and judge.

So far Ren was the leader and Todd was the follower who was eager to be helpful. Where that left Abby he would have to see.

"Were there ever reports of seeing eyes? Not normal eyes but just white spots in the darkness that looked like eyes?"

They all nodded at him.

"Has anyone said how many eyes they saw?"

Ren shook his head, "The number always changes, and we can't be sure if that's because there is more than one of these things, if it's changing, or if people are just exaggerating the story as it gets passed around."

James nodded, "Right. So in the stories you give the most truth to what is the largest number of eyes you've heard of?"

"Six-ish," Ren answered.

"Six eyes," James said, "if that's true, it means it's getting stronger. The more it can manifest itself the more it can see and so more eyes show up. Granted if someone really did call it here, and give it a free pass to get in, it would start off with a ready supply and not have to hunt for food."

"Food?" Abby's voice squeaked a little.

"Well, it," James paused and thought for a moment before continuing on a different tack, "has anyone been acting out stronger than they normally would? Like you knew they were a little irritated but it went beyond that to violence which normally wouldn't happen?"

All three of them looked at each other and gave little nods. Ren turned back to James, "It started out as a fairly normal boy girl problem. Everybody goes through it at one time or another." He shrugged and looked to the other two for confirmation of his point. They nodded slightly at him and he continued, "Except when the confrontation happened between the two guys who were both trying to date the same girl it went nuts. They both ended up in the hospital and the girl..." Ren's voice trailed off.

"Did she die?" James' voice was barely enough to break the silence of the room and none of them answered except with a nod.

James stood and walked to the window, "That's his pattern." He looked out at the manicured lawns and seeming perfection of a college campus. It would be the perfect feeding ground. Just like the first time.

At the time he'd been confused. He couldn't understand how getting people to go on marches against tolerance or for tolerance could be part of an evil master plan. One student had died, riots were brewing like a bad witches' cauldron, and his girlfriend at the time had gotten involved believing it was the right thing to do. When he'd finally confronted the professor behind it all James thought it was all over. The bad guy had gone down, the crisis was averted, and to top it off he had cool new powers. The downside, of course, was his girlfriend. Her death in the middle of it all had haunted him right up through the tunnel in Hell. The situation had taught him what sadness and grief really were. Up to that point he'd never had someone die on him. It was a teenage cliché sure, but they were supposed to be invincible. And then she was dead. He really hadn't been sure what to do. Grief can play out in so many ways, healthy and unhealthy, but James hadn't done anything. For weeks he hadn't gone to class, and any time his friends asked him out he found some excuse to get out of it, which really isn't that hard when you're a card carrying introvert. He'd done so many things on his own anyway before the night of her death that no one was fazed when he disappeared for days on end. What he didn't realize was he was looking for a way to vent.

With his new powers he could have crushed cars or knocked trees down, but none of it felt right. And, after all, he'd been given these powers on the premise of doing the right thing. So day after day he wandered, surfed the web, read books, watched movies, and in short looked for a way to deal with his grief.

Then it happened, another school having the same problems as his had gone through. Normally a college having student protests wouldn't make any page of the news much less front page, but when a student dies in the protests things change. The situation hit home and James found himself using his powers to persuade an attendant at the airline counter to print him out a ticket. No one was going to use that seat anyway so what difference did it really make, he'd said.

When he walked onto campus the truth hit him. The professor hadn't been the mastermind. Tolerance hadn't been the issue. Just like a runny nose isn't the flu and black bubos aren't the plague. They were just visible signs of a deeper problem. The Darkness causes the conflict, feeds on the hot energy flowing off it, and grows stronger the worse it gets. Sometimes it's as simple as a difference of opinion, but it inevitably leads to something bigger, something violent.

"Whose pattern?" Abby had walked up behind him at the window and stood looking up at him.

She wasn't short but at a bit over six feet James found himself looking down on most people. The top of her head came up to his chin and the moonlight played color tricks with her hair turning it a silky dark purple.

Again James found himself shaking off the momentary attraction. He was in a different world hunting something he was now sure was a demon. The last thing he needed was to be fantasizing about a pretty girl. He didn't even know what color her eyes were after all.

"Sorry," he said, "my mind tripped and fell on memory lane."

He turned back to the small group, "I'll have to get more details about how it got here, and how long ago it was, and details about specific students so I can put together a precise timeline. On first glance, however, I'm fairly sure this is the same," here he paused, not quite sure what to call the Darkness. He looked around at the three. They watched him with expectation as if he was somehow an expert and he would fix whatever problem this was. He chuckled to himself for a moment realizing he was the expert. He had, in point of fact, gone through Hell to learn the truth of things.

"Well," he continued, "to be frank with you, it's a demon." He paused to see how they would react to the news. Would they think he was crazy? Would they think the church that sent him regularly sent people after demons?

After a few beats Todd nodded vigorously, "I told you guys." He turned to Ren and poked him in the arm, "Didn't I Ren? I told you it was a demon, but no, no one believes Todd. If you need help with your math Todd's your guy, but matters of philosophy..."

"Okay," Ren patted Todd on the head like a puppy, "you were right. I'm not sure that's a good thing."

Abby nodded, "I was hoping they'd just hired some tough guy to scare kids and spread rumors."

Todd crossed his arms looking pleased with himself, and Ren turned to James, "So what do we do?"

"Well," James looked at each of them and realized he'd never had someone help him. The first time, back at his university, Rupert had been there, but he really hadn't been much help. In fact Rupert had kinda been the reason James had almost died a few times.

One of his guiding principles throughout this chase had been to get no one involved. If James let people get involved the Darkness could use them, could hurt them like Kate, and he wasn't sure he could watch anyone else die. On top of that he'd never thought anyone would believe him long enough to get involved. After all, how do you tell someone about a living shadow running around possessing people and causing problems? If he thought about it in a certain way it reminded him of Peter Pan's shadow running around the nursery at the beginning of the movie. If the shadow had been a psychotic murdering monster.

In this case, however, James realized he could use the help. There really was no way to avoid them knowing about it since they were already here, and they'd already figured out the main points on their own. Also he wouldn't need to convince them about anything. A demon running around campus trying to kill students? Why not? Plus he was in a completely different world and at the best he would need directions to get around.

"Fine, I could use the help."

They all smiled at him, excitement playing across their faces like kids at Christmas. Did they even have Christmas here? Did they have kids here or did they pop out of eggs fully grown? This could be weird, and problematic.

"But you do what I say. No running off on your own to try and catch it in a dark classroom with nothing but a chair to hit it with."

A veritable chorus of agreement echoed off the walls of the classroom and James decided to start thinking of them as his gang. He'd briefly considered labeling them as the Scooby-Doo gang but that would mean he was either the dog or Freddy and neither of those really set well with him. Plus that would make Todd Velma and that was just weird.

"First things," James looked at them and decided then and there what was important at this very moment, "I need sleep, lots of it. Oh, and a place to get cleaned up and some other clothes so I blend in a bit better here on campus," he looked down at his torn up and bloody clothes, "and don't look like a deranged hobo. But really sleep is the top priority right now."

"But," Abby put her hand on his arm and a little tingle shot all the way up to his scalp, "that thing is still out there."

"Yes, it is, and if I, or you, go out there right now tired and unprepared," he pointed at the chair she'd hit him with, "all we're going to do is get killed. I went through a lot chasing this thing down. And when I say a lot I mean more than you can possibly imagine." He pulled at one of the many holes in his shirt caused by the beatles, "Unless you have a really bizarre imagination, which includes screaming death beetles. So I want to be prepared and well rested."

Ren stepped up and put his hand on Abby's shoulder, "There's some unused dorm rooms in the guy's wing, you can use one of those. The best we can do for cleaning up is the bath house, and as far as a change of clothes I guess you're about the same size as me so I'll get you a spare set of robes on the way to the room."

James nodded and almost fell over in exhaustion just from the effort of it.

Chapter Twenty One

Sleep is a wonderful and blessed thing. As James lay looking at the ceiling of the dorm room he understood why the Bible sometimes referred to death as falling asleep. It was just so nice. He tried to remember the last time he'd woken up and had the time to just lie around and look up at the ceiling. It'd been years, and technically he shouldn't be doing it now. He wasn't sure how much of a head start the Darkness had on him in this world. The absence of time in Purgatory and Hell had really thrown him off, and what Ren and the others had said made it seem like the Darkness could've been running around this world for weeks at least. Relaxing here wasn't a luxury he could afford. On the other hand the Darkness had been here for a while now so what difference did fifteen minutes make in the grand scheme of things?

That demon, which he was certain now it was, most likely thought James hadn't made it through Purgatory much less Hell. It would have its guard down. From what the others said about the events it also sounded like the Darkness wasn't in any hurry to leave campus. However, the reaction of the students might be enough to drive it in an easier direction. This seemed to be some kind of religious institution and depending on the level of the belief centered on the students the Darkness might find it hard going here.

Clichés are irritating but in this case one seemed to fit the situation, the greatest trick the Devil ever played was convincing the world he didn't exist. Maybe in that sense the Darkness would find this a useful hunting ground. They didn't know he was here and so wouldn't find any reason to fight him off. That idea was shot down quickly by the chair James had taken to the side of the head. It proved they were willing to fight. Beyond that James knew belief was a truly powerful thing and if this really was a religious institution there must be a general overwhelming belief keeping most dark spirits out. That belief, James had found, wasn't really focused like his own, but could create a kind of protective shell around groups or places. The only reason James had followed the Darkness into that Alaskan church in the first place was because someone had let it in.

It was a truth which had stuck around in myth and legend eventually bleeding into even modern day tales of dark spirits like vampires. They couldn't get you unless you let them in. This was specifically true and generally true of just about everything. You wouldn't be a meth head unless you let it happen. You wouldn't have problems with a soul sucking darkness demon unless you let it in. And that was the point here. Someone had let it in. It was why James' three would be assailants and now allies had been in that room in particular. For some reason they believed students had let the Darkness in. There may be a bubble of protective belief around this school, but they poked a hole in it. They let the hyena into the hen house, the dingo into the daycare, the bull into the china shop.

James sat up realizing without needing to be told that his mind was running amuck. Resting was good but he was seriously out of practice. If he didn't get up and do something he might be overpowered by random metaphors and drown in his own ocean of mental stupidity.

He slid his legs off the side of the bed, sat there in his Green Lantern boxer shorts, and looked at his clothes. Purgatory and Hell may be immutable and unchangeable points in the universe but they'd really done a number on his stuff. Granted it hadn't exactly been expeditionary gear in the first place. He'd dressed himself in slacks and a button up shirt to blend in with the other church goers, and instead ended up going to Hell in a pair of Birkenstock dress shoes. His Dockers were stained and ripped, his dress shirt had bite marks and dried blood. There was no way he was going to pass unnoticed wearing those.

Thankfully while he was passed out Ren had dropped off a change of clothes just inside the door. A pair of black leather shoes, black slacks, and a white button up shirt sat folded next to where a long black robe hung from a hook by the door. After getting dressed he looked at himself in a small mirror and decided he looked like he was going to a graduation ceremony.

Stepping out of the dormitory James shaded his eyes. The sunlight was crisp and brittle and shattered fragments of yellowed light cut into the nooks and crannies of the campus. The warmth shivered his scalp and for the first time in a minor eternity James looked up into a blue sky. He stared until echoes of clouds moved across his vision, and the tear rolling from his eye was full of thoughts. He wished he could stuff all his recent memories in that single drop and wipe it away; rid himself of the memory of a burnt orange sky stretching on to insanity and a gray staircase full of screaming horror.

He sighed and wondered if he would ever be able to look back on that time with anything other than sheer panic and hopelessness. Time would surely dull the memories and the sandpaper of life would smooth the bloody edges of a cut off hand, but now in this moment of sunshine and a cartoon crisp blue sky he would rather just forget.

In his short life, one of his fondest memories was of running over green fields and jumping the stone pasture walls, scattering brown British hares and laughing with his brother. Here looking out over the fresh green commons of the campus and the perfect short stone walls hemming it all in, the only thing he wanted to do was lay down and watch the clouds compete in a never ending race. He wanted to sink into memories full of laughter and simple companionship and never come up for air, but he could feel the history of a hand on his shoulder and could almost see his Dad from the corner of his eye. Even in this, after literally going through Hell, he had to consider what was the right thing to do. His Dad had never said as much, but it wasn't always what people said that made the best example. Over the years he'd watched his Dad, and even when he should have stopped to take a rest, not just to smell the roses but to recuperate, he still did what needed to be done.

"Yes," he whispered to himself, "but what's the benefit?"

Does there have to be a benefit? His mind shrugged it's non-existent shoulders at him.

"If there's no benefit to all this then why do it?"

After everything, you're complaining now?

"I didn't really have the time or opportunity to complain recently."

What too busy dodging screaming headed beetles? What kind of excuse is that?

"A darn good one if you ask me."

The benefit, silly man, is all around you.

"Great now my own brain is being all hard to understand."

First off that's not even a word, and second off take a moment and look around you.

208

"It's a word if I say so. This is my own head after all. And what am I supposed to see around me?"

Just look.

"Students, grass, buildings, trees that I just realized have blue leaves."

What? Seriously? Blue leaves?

"Yeah, right over there."

Cool, but not the point. Life, peaceful life, is happening all around you, and why do you think it's possible?

"Because," James nodded to himself, "people made the right choices instead of the easy choices."

Right.

"Still, I wish someone else could be responsible this time." He looked around the campus again and started toward an interesting looking building. "Well," he muttered to himself, "you can poop in one hand and wish in the other and see which one comes true first."

James had no idea where he was going, and no idea what time it was, but he assumed with the sun being just over the top of the buildings that it must still be morning, and unless this world had a totally different astronomical set up than his, he still had time before the planned meeting with his new team at lunch. He wanted to get a feel for the campus so that when they explained things in more detail he would have some reference points for what they were talking about.

The building he finally stepped into felt like a cathedral, but with the style of this campus reminding him of his medieval studies class he wasn't sure he could rely on that. The solid wooden door opened into a large room filled with round tables. Stepping out from the door and letting it close behind him James tried to take in as much as possible. He couldn't be sure what things were actually used for unless someone told him, but he could make some general assumptions based on the fact that most everything seemed to follow a very earthly pattern. They had doors and windows. They slept in beds at night. Everything was basically human sized and shaped. So using basic social norms and his own university experience as a filter he looked around the room.

Each table had six to seven black robbed students seated around it. They all had books out in front of them and seemed to be actively discussing something. At regular intervals an older gentleman with a very impressive four-cornered hat came around and seemed to be checking on them. So maybe this was a kind of study hall or extension of another class, like a lab for a philosophy class.

He walked along the wall quietly noting the building's simple rectangular shape and unimpressive interior. The walls were covered with tapestries and paintings, but none of them were anything exceptional or interesting. He stopped and looked at a few of them hoping to gain some insight into this new world, but found the vast majority of them were simply portraits of people in black robes wearing fancy hats of one kind or another.

Stepping out the door on the far side of the building he decided wandering silently through random buildings wasn't really going to be helpful. He needed to know the names of the buildings and their functions. He needed to know where people hung out for fun versus where they simply sat and studied. If he was going to hunt he needed to know the lay of this wilderness.

If all things held to social norms eventually the current class would let out and students would come through the commons heading to the next thing on their schedule. Hopefully if he waited in a good spot he could find one of his new friends and talk them into skipping class to give him a tour. With this new plan in mind he felt fully justified in finding a prime piece of grass and lying down.

Eventually a bell sent its bronze voice across the lawn and James opened his eyes. He listened to doors opening and conversations filling the air. He wasn't sure how he was going to tell any of the three he'd met from the multitude of black robe-wearing students, but if worse came to worse he could use the power to help out. He preferred not to use it for mundane things like finding someone in a crowd. No one had really been around to explain the power to him so he really didn't know if there were limits or problems that came along with it. Maybe if he used it too often it would give him brain cancer.

A face came into view and looked down at him. Brown hair spilled down and framed a familiar face. "Ah," James smiled and extended his hand, "wishes do come true."

Abby took his proffered hand and helped him up, "Were you wishing to see me?"

At least three very flirtatious replies bounced through his mind. Each rejected at the last moment. Finally James just smiled and settled on being normal, "I have no idea how to get around this place. I went looking around and that," he pointed to the building he'd walked through, "is one of the most boring buildings I've ever been in."

Abby laughed and shook her head, "Don't let Master Prensly hear you say that. He believes two hundred year old theological arguments are the most fun anyone should be allowed to have."

"So," James looked around, "give me the basic layout."

"Well," she pointed behind him, "you should recognize the boys' dorms." She glanced at him, "how'd you sleep?"

"Like I just came back from the dead."

Abby looked at him for a moment and tilted her head slightly, "And how's your head?"

"My head? Oh, you mean where you hit me with a chair. Right in the ear. With a really heavy wooden chair. In my ear." James pointed to his ear, "right here. After you took a really big swing," he pantomimed grabbing a chair and raising it over his head, "and hit me in the head with it."

"Yes, I get the point. I hit you with a chair. I said I was sorry."

"Still hurts a little," James lied. "Every time I rolled over onto my side it woke me up."

"Look, I feel terrible, all right," a blush turned her cheeks rosy, "but what else was I supposed to do?"

He chuckled and before his internal filter could catch it he said, "You're pretty when you're flustered."

Her cheeks brightened again. She turned and waved a hand at the grass, "What were you doing just laying on the grass? Isn't that thing still out there?"

"Yes, it is. But in order to understand the layout of the problem I need to understand the layout of the school and I couldn't do that without a guide. I assumed you would all be in class so rather than stumbling around disrupting the school I decided to wait."

"Now then," he turned and started walking across the commons, "you were giving me the grand tour weren't you?"

She caught up with him in a few strides, "The theological science and mathematics building is to the right, the historical theology department is to the left, and straight ahead is the doctrinal college."

"Right," James paused and looked at the buildings she'd pointed out. "Right." He turned and looked at Abby, "Whoever designed this place must have a masters degree in architectural theological boringness. How do you tell any place apart? That building is square and redbrick, the other one is square and redbrick."

"Yes, but they have different crenellations on top, and that one," she pointed to the doctrinal college, "has gargoyles."

"I see." James raised his eyebrows and nodded dramatically.

"If you want to see some amazing buildings, there's the observatory behind the science building, and the cathedral back behind the doctrinal building has beautiful stained glass."

James turned slowly taking the campus in. His description of the buildings had been a bit harsh but basically true. The main buildings on campus were simple and solid. Each had a variety of pillars or, as Abby had pointed out, gargoyles to differentiate them from each other.

Picking a direction James started walking. Following one of the stone pathways through the buildings he started mentally cataloging all the places the Darkness could lurk. It was a good word, lurk. Over the years he'd been tracking the demon James had begun mentally using words like lurk because it made him feel like he was in a comic book or a fantasy novel. It helped him cope with the strangeness of the situation. He'd learned quickly to adjust his worldview. If he'd tried living through the last two years hanging onto his previous way of looking at things he couldn't have done it. His old way of thinking didn't involve power, demons, or anything even remotely associated with those unless he went to the movies on a Saturday night. The ability to adjust your mindset was one of the great things about humanity, and in some cases the inability to adjust was the downfall of parts of humanity.

A very large iron bound wooden double door stopped his musings and he glanced at Abby expecting her to say something about wherever they were. She looked back at him saying nothing. He twitched his head at the door and she raised an eyebrow. James realized non-verbal communication was getting him precisely nowhere, "Uhm, and this is?"

She gave him an even more quizzical look before turning back to the doors and looking up. He followed her gaze until his eyes came to rest on a beautiful circular stained glass window.

"Cathedral," he said, "I was just, well, a bit lost in my own head I guess."

"Or maybe it's brain damage." She turned and headed toward a smaller door farther down the side of the building.

James snorted a laugh, "I guess I deserve that, but if it is, you're the one who caused it."

The single door opened onto a massive vaulted interior space. The columns supporting the arches high overhead instantly made James think there was nothing new under heaven.

"I suppose there's only so many ways to hold up a really big stone roof."

"What?" Abby looked sideways at him.

"Sorry, just thinking out loud." He gave her a bit of a smile, "I've been doing this by myself for so long I forget to leave the dialogue on the inside sometimes."

Abby gave him a little smile as if to say everyone talked to themselves from time to time, "So why'd you want to see the chapel?"

"It's," he paused and looked around, "comforting." Octagonal stone columns seemed to throw the heavy wooden pews out to anchor themselves to the marble floor. Scrollwork wrapping the pillars drew your eyes upward following the pattern until you were met with the glory of light coming from massive stained glass windows. Along the nave there were three spaces between the columns each filled with a picture in stained glass. Some told a story in themselves with the window divided up into scenes, while others were simple flowers or pastoral scenes.

James stepped out into the main part of the nave and turned to see the window above the door they'd entered through. Staggering back he bumped into the edge of a pew and sat down hard. Looking down at him in shimmering stained glory was a juggler. The larger than life figure was wrapped in cream colored robes. A smile radiating with sunlight shone through a brown beard while his hands were held palms up at waist height. Between them spun, in a great circle, balls of every color. At the very top of the circle a golden ball seemed to glow as the rising sun shone through it. Below the juggler's bare feet floated script in a language James couldn't read.

A hand touched his shoulder and he twitched, "Are you all right?"

He looked up at Abby blankly for a moment then back at the window, "What does it say?"

She looked curiously at him, "Roughly translated it means, He holds the universe."

"I know him." James whispered.

"What?"

"I," James looked up at her and remembered he was supposed to be someone who knew all these things, and not a stranger from an alternate universe, "I, just have really always liked this version, and with the sunlight hitting it like this, well, it takes the breath away."

"I'm glad." Abby sat down next to him and looked up at the juggler with him, "I've always liked it too, but lately there's been talk of taking it down and replacing it with something," she paused and waved her hands vaguely at the air, "something more serious."

"Serious?"

"Personally," she leaned toward him and lowered her voice, "I think it's the smile. Some of the more conservative members of the church don't think He should be..."

"Happy?"

"Well," she looked back up at the juggler, "it isn't really a happy smile is it?"

James looked into the eyes of the juggler and knew from personal experience what she was talking about. He'd seen that smile before, the exact same smile, just less windowish. "No," he replied, "it's a bit more mischievous than that isn't it?"

"That's exactly the word I would use. But I like it because of that. It reminds me He's not worried. He's got it under control. The universe spins in His hands and He doesn't even need to concentrate. In fact He's actually thinking about something that makes Him smile."

Yep, James thought, He's thinking about how He talked me into going through the gates of Hell. "So He's God."

"Well," she looked at him seriously, "no one has seen God, and so we make pictures to teach about the attributes of God. It must be

214

understood this is not the actual physical representation of God because He has no actual physical being."

"Ah," James winked at her, "right, because He wouldn't want to get His hands dirty mucking around with us down here now would He? But what if," he paused to collect his thoughts, "what if he still wanted to get involved."

"Of course he wants to get involved. He loves us and wants us to have a good life."

"Right, right, but what if he really needed something amazing to happen?"

"Like a miracle?"

"I guess you could call it that. Uhm," he realized he wasn't making much sense and the giant smiling visage of the juggler was throwing off his train of thought.

"What are you trying to get at?"

James snorted. What was he trying to get at? He'd been given his power under unusual circumstances, and because of that no one had really been around to explain anything to him. The best he'd gotten was a crazy dream that somehow took place in his old high school auditorium letting him know, in no uncertain terms, that if he used this power for the wrong reasons he would be held accountable. The overwhelming questions which had been dragging at him this entire chase hit him again. Why had he been chosen in the first place to have this ability? What was he supposed to do with it all? Was this all just a test like the Devil had said? Had that little juggler back in the desert of Purgatory really been...

He looked up at the image of the smiling juggler and some things hit him from his interaction with the little juggler. He'd constantly been talking about choosing the right stone, and yes a person could read too much into things, but in this situation James didn't think it was too much of a reach. When all had seemed lost the juggler had pointed him in the right direction, and had offered him words of encouragement. But at the same time if he really was this towering figure in a stained glass window then why hadn't he taken care of the problem instead of making James do it? Why hadn't he stopped the Darkness since he'd actually been there in purgatory? Why hadn't he done something about Mr. Crazy angel back there?

Looking up at those worlds spinning through his hands James realized he had to come to a decision. Is this what he would believe in? Would he believe this person, this God was putting him through a test for some reason? He'd taken away his power and sat back to watch what he'd do. What was the point of all the pain, his lost hand, the vision of Kate and the guilt accompanying it?

He looked down at his new hand and realized the guilt he'd carried with him for so many years was gone. If a strange man had simply walked up to him and told him to get over the guilt would he have listened? No. Would he have been strong enough to do what needed to be done if he hadn't gone through the pit in Purgatory? Once upon a time he would have said yes, but that younger version of himself would have been wrong. His comrade in the pit said he wouldn't have done anything different because we are who we are. Well, maybe, like this stained glass window we're actually just a great multitude of things all put together, and he'd needed this to add the right pieces to make the best picture possible.

He shook his head realizing Abby must be wondering what was going through his head, and a statement jokingly poked it's way through his head; you never learn to ride a bike if Dad never takes off the training wheels.

So what was he getting at? Out of all the chorus of why's singing in his head, what question could really matter right now? Should he keep searching for the teens to save them from the Darkness? That one was easy. A harder question had been asked of him more recently. He knew he had power, but what he hadn't known was where it came from.

"To put it bluntly," he looked up at the multitude of worlds spinning through the juggler's hands, "do you think if you believed in him enough you could make amazing things happen?"

After a few moments of silence James looked down from the stained glass smile radiating above him to see Abby raising an eyebrow at him, "You're the specialist from the church and you're asking me?"

"Yes, I'm asking you." He felt in his heart he already knew the answer, but he wanted to hear someone else say it. "Here in your university, focused on the dealings of God, surrounded by the wisdom and teachings of generations, do you think belief can tap into the power of God and physically alter the world?"

216

She pursed her lips and tipped her head a bit to the left, "I do." She held up a hand before James could say anything, "I'm not sure how consistent it would be, or even if God would choose to act in that way every time, but yes I think it's possible."

"So, your well thought out, university trained answer is," he paused for effect, "maybe."

Abby stared at him for a long moment, "I can't tell if you're being serious and testing me or if you're being sarcastic."

Giving her his biggest smile he stood up and extended his hand to help her up from beside him, "And you'll never know. Now," he squeezed her hand, "I've had enough calmness and wonderful stained glass light. On with the tour."

She stared at him, then, with a sigh and a shrug, headed back toward the door.

As they walked away James looked up. A small cloud passed, for a moment, in front of the sun and the juggler winked at him. "I'm glad you think this is funny."

Chapter Twenty Two

Todd and Ren met them at a nondescript brown wooden table in a long room filled with matching brown wooden tables. Metal plates, silver ware, and cups had been waiting for them along with food piled on trays in the center of each table. It was simple fare with bread, meat, cheese, and some kind of fruit James had never seen before but found it had the gritty texture of a pear mixed with the flavor of a banana. The bread was amazing and there were two kinds of cheese with one being orange and solid while the other was khaki colored, slightly squishy, and spreadable.

"I love cheese." James spread some on the rough brown bread, "My brother on the other hand could kill a small group of people with smell alone if he has too much cheese."

Todd coughed, "Man, don't do that I almost shot water out my nose."

James laughed, "Better than what my brother shoots out his..."

Abby punched him, "Shhhh, you need to keep your voice down."

"But it's," James looked around what he was thinking of as the lunch room and realized most of the students were perfectly quiet while the one that were talking did so in very hushed tones, "Wow, you guys need to loosen up a bit here."

Ren stared at him from across the table, "Is that an official statement of the church? Because the most recent Bull stated that meals are provided by the grace of God and should be respected as such."

James looked at Abby, "Now I get why they don't like the juggler very much, and no it's not an official statement just a personal response to the fact that you all are swinging much too far on the pendulum of seriousness. Moderation is better than fanaticism in most things, especially when it comes to Todd shooting water out his nose."

Nodding, Ren looked over to where some professors were quietly having their lunch, "Just don't let them hear you say that."

"Anyway," James said around a bite of crumbly cheese, "Abby gave me the tour this morning."

"You skipped classes?" Todd whispered as loudly as he could.

"It was important." She looked from Todd to Ren, "He needed to know his way around so things would make more sense."

"Well..."

James held up a hand to cut Ren off, "No. She did the right thing. End of discussion. If she gets in trouble, so be it. Some things are more important than others, and finding this thing is the very definition of more important." James put his hand down, "So, we need to figure out either a pattern so we can trace it, or a person it's connected to so we can follow them. First, how did you figure out the room was the place it all started?"

"This is a small campus," Ren started, "We have, maybe, seven hundred students here full time with another dozen or so who come every once in a while. After a few years you get to know most everyone."

"We became friends," Todd gestured at the group, "because of how smart Ren is."

"It started out as a study group. Anyway, you figure out rather quickly which students are the study hard type or the lazy type."

Abby leaned in, "Or the stuck up and bully you type."

Ren nodded, "Exactly. Most of us just learned how to avoid them or at least how to not get on their bad side."

"They're rich kids mostly." Abby sliced off another piece of bread, "They're only here because their parents want them to have a good name attached to their education."

"Sure," James shrugged, "They're like pigeons or rats, eventually they show up everywhere."

"Exactly." Todd nodded.

"At first," Ren looked at Abby and Todd to see if they were done with their silly statements, "it was just your normal irritating stuff, but some of them started getting rough and really serious. A few kids ended up getting hurt and one was expelled from school."

"One of the bullies?" James asked.

"No," Abby cut in, "This kid stood up to the bullies and was threatening to bring the issue up before the school board."

"Then, all of a sudden," Todd stuck his knife in the bread for emphasis, "the kid gets expelled and all the professors would say is he was endangering the harmony of the school."

James raised an eyebrow and looked at Ren, "And?"

"And," Ren continued, "things started going wrong a few days later. Fights breaking out over silly things, students who'd once been friends accusing each other of cheating or lying about random things."

"Then it really got bad," Todd said around a mouthful of bread.

"The girl you told me about?"

"Right," Abby answered, "I knew her. She was a nice normal girl."

"It seems to me your lovely institution here would frown on boy girl relationships."

Abby nodded, "True, but it still happened."

Todd made a wood cutting motion with his hands, "They used an axe."

"We don't need to go into details," Ren said.

"Really," he made eye contact with Todd to see if he was joking, "an axe?"

Todd held eye contact and slowly nodded while making small chopping motions with his knife.

"Well," James paused for a beat, "What I need is to know how you knew it was that specific room."

Todd leaned forward conspiratorially and whispered, "One of the boys involved in the fight was also a victim of the bullies and when the authorities came to get him all we could hear him say is that someone needed to put it back."

Abby nodded, "At first we all just assumed he was ranting and crazy."

"Maybe talking about the axe," Todd made the wood cutting motion again, chopping into his bread.

Ren sighed, "But when rumors started spreading about the eyes I decided to ask one of the other kids to see if he knew anything."

Todd patted Ren on the shoulder, "Ren is taking a class in exorcism."

Ren shrugged, "None of the kids who were being bullied would talk to me but I was able to put together pieces and trace back events to that room. I'm fairly sure of the events, and also because of a book that was checked out and never returned."

"By the guy who used the axe," Todd interrupted.

"Yes," Ren sighed, "I was able to figure it out because of the book together with things they've said, and because of the random cleaning the school did in that specific room. They were definitely trying to bring something through."

"And use it to get back at their tormentors," James finished.

"Exactly."

"Yeah," It was James' turn to sigh, "and it turns out it doesn't work that way does it?"

Their shoulders slumped. James could picture it. The picked on kids had found their champion, the one student willing to stand up to the bullies, and he'd been kicked out of school. After that their lives were getting worse and worse and now they felt there was nothing they could do about it. If they went to anyone they would end up expelled like their friend. Then one of them must have stumbled onto the book. It was most likely a description about how to get rid of evil spirits, like the exorcism class Ren was taking. But they figured if you could just turn it around couldn't you use it to get one? And if you could get one then you should be able to control it and send it, like an angry attack dog, after your enemies.

The Darkness, already looking for a way into a new world, had found not only a crack in the wall but a full invitation wrapped in ribbon. Once he was through he found willing helpers with their defenses down, easy prey to a thing such as him.

"But what about the teens?"

"What?"

James looked around at the tables full of students. "You would have noticed if other kids were here." It wasn't a question. The reason he'd done any of this, gone through Purgatory and Hell, was to save some kids he'd never met. Yes, in a greater sense, this whole chase was just that, a chase. He needed to catch this demon and remove it from the world, or as the case may be, all the worlds, but in the immediate sense he was trying to save some teens. They were caught up in something they weren't intended to be a part of. He knew without having to dwell on it much that he was really just trying to save one of them. Grace didn't remind him physically of Kate, and he couldn't explain why she made him think of his dead girlfriend, but he did know he had to save her. He'd failed Kate, and his forced trip down memory lane back in Hell had cemented that fact in his mind. This time he was determined not to fail. He needed to save Grace.

Who knew what had happened to them on their journey through Purgatory and Hell, and up to this point James couldn't even be sure they'd survived. Maybe the Darkness had sucked them dry like some modern day Shelob and then tossed them aside on the plains of Hell where big nasty Bob the tree thing decided to use their heads for the demon's soccer league.

As the images played across his mind James realized that might be the best of the many possible scenarios. Throughout his journey he'd lost all track of time, and other than the few hints which had led him to this point, he hadn't seen the Darkness for the entirety of the evil circus he'd just experienced.

"Teens," James said looking directly into the eyes of each of them, "do you know about any teens that might have shown up at about the same time as the demon?"

All three of the others looked at each other then back at James. Ren shook his head and slightly shrugged his shoulders, "No, I can't say that we've noticed any new students."

"Any unknown kids wandering around campus?"

Again all he received were confused looks and shaking heads.

"Well, I suppose that doesn't really prove anything." James drummed his fingers on the table, "He wouldn't just let them roam freely around the campus after all. He took them originally as protection."

"This thing took hostages," Todd's knife made a metallic sound as it hit the floor. "God's blood man, why didn't you say so?"

"It doesn't change anything. We still need to figure out where it's holed up, and if anyone is helping it. If, and at this point I'm leaning heavily on if, the teens it took are still alive we can grab them at the same time as taking it out."

Todd nodded sharply and James made a new mental note on the sheet marked Todd in his brain files. Todd could get angry, but was this a useful, I'm focused on catching the bad guy thing, or a running around crazy and getting nothing done kind of thing. Either way Todd looked like a solid lump of stone under those black robes and James was sure he wouldn't want that coming after him with angry eyes.

First things first he thought, and he closed his eyes. His skin tightened around his right eye like being hit by a cold breeze on a warm day. The darkness behind his eyelids turned gray. Taking a deep breath he looked at the group around him through his new filter. The truth is an interesting thing, and when you translate that into some kind of visual stimulus it changes from an interesting thing into a new kind of psychedelic monkey. When someone lies to you what does that look like? To a normal person a lie could be not making eye contact or crossing their arms defensively. You might see a tilt of the head or tapping of fingers, which are out of place for that person. In poker they call this a tell and the better the poker player they better they are at reading another person's tell while hiding their own. All of that, however, is seeing a lie. What does the truth look like? Then extend that thought to what does a person truly look like, or what does a place truly look like. Some places, like the dining hall, James was sitting in look just like they do every day. They truly are a dining hall. The table is so truly a table that it couldn't be anything else.

People are a different case. Around him James truly saw people for the first time in his life. At first he didn't focus on his immediate co-conspirators. He needed to learn how to filter the results before he decided to judge them. Across the room an older gentleman leaned against a doorframe. On his shoulder perched a gray little imp. It was digging sharp claws at the end of its little hands into the soft flesh of the man's neck and scalp while leaning over and whispering something into his ear. Next to him was a table full of shifting shapes. At one moment they would solidify into men and women then shift into green pillars of flame then into crying children sucking their thumbs.

Turning to the left James twitched as a blue light pierced into his closed eyes. James wanted to throw his hands up to filter the brightness but remembered in time this would be a strange gesture for someone with his eyes closed. He mentally squinted and looked into the light. The figure easily blocked the floor to ceiling window and the illumination shot from his chest like a lighthouse keeping watch. At his side the figure had a sword the like of which James had only seen once before and the memory of it caused his arm and hand to ache. They locked eyes, and for a moment James wondered what this thing was going to do. He felt an urge to raise the hand he'd cut from the angel of Purgatory and twiddle its fingers at him. Lookie here, he wanted to say. What'cha gonna do about it? But the figure just nodded slightly and turned its attention elsewhere.

A poke in his arm brought his attention back to his immediate surroundings and James looked through his closed eyes at his new friends. Part of his mind wondered if it was wrong to look like this at people you were trying to work with. Was it in some way an invasion of their privacy? People keep their true self hidden for a reason, or was that only true if you were trying to hide something?

Todd was immovable. He was a tree with unreachable roots and unbreakable bark. He was a monolith carved with words of fire spelling out friendship and persistence.

Ren burned. He was a pillar of flickering fire, blue hot and unwavering. At its center was an unmoving white light.

Abby was at peace. She was a river and a willow tree. The wind would blow and the bank would crumble but the bending willow and the curving river would continue in peace. Unless she thought you were a demon, in which case she would hit you with a chair. But, in all fairness, rivers, no matter how peaceful, would destroy your world if you were in the way.

He watched through his closed eyes as Todd slowly raised his hand and poked him in the chest. James rocked back and opened his eyes, "Sorry bout that."

"You were, uhm," Todd looked at his friends for some help then shrugged, "looking around with your eyes closed, and I'm pretty sure you flinched once."

James laughed and looked over Ren's shoulder at the simply dressed professor by the window. He wanted to walk up to him and ask some very pointed questions, but he was sure no useful answers would be forthcoming.

"Also," Todd leaned into his line of vision, "I think I saw something around your," he waved his finger in a circle vaguely toward James' eye.

"What?" James smiled at him, "You think I have some sort of magical power? Maybe I can look around with my mind and figure things out?"

Todd's eyes widened and he stared at James for a moment before Abby backhanded him across the chest. "Well?" He looked at her, "You've heard the stories about the exorcists from the church."

"Besides," James swung his legs over the bench and stood up, "if I do have a tattoo around my eye I most definitely didn't get it from the Devil himself. Cuz that would be weird."

Todd just stared at him and Ren rolled his eyes, "Come on Captain Gullible." Ren stood up and started gathering their plates, "I'll clean these up and meet you all outside."

Outside James looked up at the clouds in their ever shifting game of tag. He was sure of one thing now, none of them were evil. "So how long exactly has it been here?"

Abby looked over at him, "It's been, exactly, fifteen days since we think they called up the demon."

"A lot can happen in fifteen days."

"A lot has happened. Someone has died, multiple fights have broken out, and the entire feel of the school is," she trailed off and looked at Todd.

"Brittle." He added.

She nodded, "Brittle is a good way to put it. It feels like everything could shatter if someone twitched at the wrong moment."

James watched a bunny shaped cloud chase after a series of puff balls before dissolving into nothingness. "It's a chase."

"What?" Ren said as he came through the door.

"It's a chase," James looked down from the clouds and at the three of them, "and when you're chasing something you need a trail to follow. So..."

"So," Todd leaned toward him and whispered, "we need to figure out who to follow."

"Exactly."

They all looked at James expectantly, and he looked back at them expectantly. A few moments passed before he poked a hole in the floating balloon of silence, "So I don't know anyone around here..."

"Right." Said Todd, "That's why you need us."

"To point out," James waved his hand in little circles trying to help Todd along with the train of thought.

"To point out..." Todd trailed off.

"Seriously?" Abby shook her head, "Come on." She grabbed Todd and James by their voluminous black sleeves and pulled them along the path.

"What?" Todd tugged slightly at her hold on him, "Can't he just close his eyes and use his trick to figure out where the demon is?"

James shook his head slightly, "It doesn't work like that."

"Ah ha! So you admit you do have some special thing you do with your eyes when you're not looking with your eyes."

"That was overly complicated."

"You know what I mean, and don't change the subject."

Abby pulled them to a stop, "Hang on. Do you have some special sight?"

"What?" James had to decide fast. He'd seen with his second sight the truth about the three with him, and none of them were bad. In fact they all seemed to be good people. The problem with what he saw was the interpretation. The truth may be the truth but you still had to figure out what it meant. You could show the truth of a firecracker to an ant but he wouldn't understand it. Sometimes the truth was absolutely useless without the framework to know where that truth fit into the wider scheme of things. For example, in the dining hall he'd seen a group of students and from the truth swirling around them he could deduce they were childish but trying to be grown up. A lot could be inferred from that. Maybe they were petulant and prone to acts of childishness, or maybe they were just learning to grow up and were finally acknowledging their childish ways in order to better understand themselves.

His compatriots could be easy to understand or he could be completely misunderstanding the truth about them. What did the flame of Ren mean? Was he burning for knowledge? Did he secretly have a really bad temper? Was he an arsonist at heart? And Abby; a flowing river could mean any number of things. In Taoism it was a good thing. The river didn't let life beat it. It always found ways around problems without getting angry. But at the same time water wasn't exactly what he would call the picture of reliability. It shifted to fit whatever situation it found itself in. The only one James was sure about was Todd. Todd's truth was unambiguous. A solid stone with the words friendship and persistence carved in flame was a good sign he could count on him. But all in all James hadn't seen anything about them to scare him. No shadows hiding on their shoulders or tentacles waiting to grab him. All in all they might be complex but they were good people. Well, Todd wasn't complex, but that's probably what most people liked about him. Too many complex people in your life made things difficult and irritating.

"Well?" Ren looked at him with his head tilted slightly to one side.

James took a deep breath and let it out slowly through his nose. "Look, it's been a long time since I've felt like I can tell anyone around me anything of the truth. I've been hunting this particular demon for years now, and the people I normally run into in this business aren't exactly open to the idea of, well, any of it. Many people, or to be honest with you, entire groups of people, frown on much of what I can do and would gladly group me right in with the demon if they knew half of what's happened to me."

"So you did get a tattoo from the Devil." Todd looked at James just like a golden Labrador looking for a treat. It made James smile.

"The tattoo around my eye helps me see things as they really are. Demons are tricky and can hide or look like random other things. Sometimes this one latches onto a person and rides them. Using them without them even knowing he's there. I needed to know for sure he wasn't in the cafeteria listening in on us. So, yes, I took a look around through my special magical tattoo."

"That's so cool." Todd leaned closer to James trying to see the now invisible markings.

Ren gently pulled Todd away, "Trafficking with Magic is strictly against the deepest held precepts of the church."

"It's not magic." Abby's voice was barely more than a whisper.

Todd and Ren looked at her. James fiddled with his black robe trying to decide if there were pockets. He never knew what to do with his hands in awkward moments so normally he would stick them in his pockets, but he couldn't for the life of him figure out if this giant wizard robe had pockets.

"What do you mean?" Ren said.

Abby stooped a little to put her face into James' line of vision. Their eyes met, "it's not magic is it?"

James smiled and gave a little shrug. He could sense the wheels turning in her mind. She was thinking back to their strange little conversation under the mischievous smile of the stained glass juggler.

"It's belief." She broke eye contact with James and looked at the other two. "It's not magic, it's belief."

"What's that supposed to mean?" Ren's tone of voice didn't just suggest Abby was crazy.

"What it means," she took a step toward Ren, "is that God acts in whatever way he sees fit, and if he sees fit for one of his servants to do miraculous things, who are you to question him?"

"And how are we to know he is not the demon in our midst?"

James laughed. He couldn't help it. He just laughed. For the first time since this chase had started he'd decided to trust people with the truth of it all, and what did he get in return?

"You know what?" In his mind a memory blossomed of him sitting at a coffee shop in a Barnes and Noble. Across from him was a tubby balding man who's asthma made him sound like an overworked steam engine. Rupert had tried so hard to convince James about all of this. He'd told him about the demons, and about the power. James, being a rational American college student, just couldn't bring himself to believe the crazy talk coming from the strange man sitting across from him sipping on a frapachino. And now here he was. Now he was the crazy man ranting about power and demons. Rupert would have laughed.

"What?" Ren said.

James held his hand out palm up and believed. He'd told Rupert seeing was believing and so Rupert had levitated him a few inches off the ground. He'd also instantly fixed his flat tire and filled his car with gas, which was much more helpful but not as cool as the levitating trick. But now it was James' turn, and now, for the first time, James knew what he was believing in. He wasn't just believing that this power he'd been given could change the world, he had something concrete to believe in now. And it made him laugh. He could see the little juggler digging in the dusty orange soil of Purgatory for the perfect rock as clearly as if it was happening right in front of him.

His belief took form and a perfect white rose grew from his hand, blossomed, and with a slight breath of wind each opalescent petal opened wings and butterflies lazily danced away on the breeze. They all held their breath as flickering white wings rode the sunbeams between the emerald green of the grass and the sapphire blue of the sky.

"If you don't believe," James' eyes followed the erratic path of the butterflies, "it isn't my problem. I have a job to do. Help me or don't."

James looked up and the three of them were spellbound, watching the white wings flit their way across the open lawn.

Ren's voice cracked slightly, "I," he took a deep breath, "I'd always hoped to be a part of something." He looked over at Todd, "But after a while you stop believing anything real will happen."

Todd gave a little nod, "They all end up being stories, you know. You hear of miracles, but only like you would tell a bedtime story. And, eventually, you start to believe nothing like that could ever happen to you."

Abby reached up and touched Todd's cheek, "I think what they're trying to say is yes." She dropped her hand and turned to face James, "Yes. Of course we'll help you."

"Well," James reached over and poked Todd in the arm, "back to the point at hand."

Todd tore his eyes away from the few lingering butterflies, "Wha?"

"Who do we follow?"

"Oh, right. Uhm," Todd looked to Ren, "who do you think?"

Ren looked around at the campus. His eyes finally stopped on one of the many brick buildings. "We start there."

"Right," said James and he started walking toward it. Looking over his shoulder at them he raised an eyebrow, "So what is that building exactly, and how will it lead us to anything except terribly boring architecture?"

"That," Abby said as she caught up to him, "as I told you earlier, is one of the Historical Theology buildings."

"Sorry, I got it mixed up with the Theological Theology buildings. Or was it the Theology of the grand Theological Theopholis buildings I was thinking about?"

Todd snickered and Abby shoved him, "Don't be heretical. Or does the Church allow its operatives to profane good teaching?"

Ren looked sideways at Abby, "I'm not sure I would call the history department good teaching."

Todd snickered again, "We're all pretty sure the history books have been, shall we say, revised a few times."

James nodded sagely, "Of course they have. They wouldn't want you finding out most of the great teachers liked to tell fart jokes."

Abby gasped and Todd burst out laughing and grabbed Ren's robe to keep himself from falling over.

"Really?" Ren looked from James to Todd, "Is this really the time for," he reached out with one finger and poked Todd slowly between the eyes, "all of this?"

James grinned, "If you can't find time to laugh, the enemy has already won. Because what good is saving life if that life doesn't really live."

"Wow," Todd had stopped laughing, "that was deep."

Abby pushed Todd and James until they started walking toward the History department again, "And you two, are not helping this process."

James leaned over and whispered loudly to Todd, "She's pretty when she gets flustered isn't she?"

Todd covered his mouth and snorted, then whispered loudly back, "don't let her hear you say that."

"Why not?" James faux whispered back.

"Because," Abby's voice rose up from behind them, "I might just hit you both with a chair."

James grabbed Todd's arm and laughed as they walked along the path. He knew it wasn't the best time to be joking, but he couldn't help it. He needed to laugh right now as much as he needed to breathe. Everything in his life had been so serious for so many years that he didn't realize how much he missed being with kids his own age and just laughing. After Kate had died he really hadn't had a chance to appropriately mourn and get back to a normal life. He'd gone straight from mourning and huge amounts of guilt to tracking the Darkness, and when you track a demon there really isn't much time to make friends and tell jokes. Even his internal humor had grown dark, cynical, and sarcastic.

This moment, with the laughing, and the leaning on someone who laughed along was more beautiful to him than any amount of sunlight glittering on wings of miraculous butterflies. He'd said it glibly but now he was convinced of the truth of his own statement. If he didn't take the time to live, to laugh, then what was all of this for? Why stop the Darkness if you weren't going to live in the light?

Ren walked beside them shaking his head, "There's a teacher's aid for the history department who was one of the students I believe assisted in the summoning of this demon."

James took a deep breath to settle himself, "And you think he still has some attachment to it?"

"Yes. In point of fact I believe his very demeanor has given away his connection with the demon."

"What do you mean by that?"

"He's grown much more self assured."

"And that's a bad thing?"

"No, not in and of itself, but in this case his new poise has come from nowhere." Ren turned and looked back at Abby, "Wouldn't you agree?"

Abby nodded, "Normally I would compare him to a very bland color of paint. You couldn't point him out in a crowd if you knew who you were looking for. But lately things seemed to have changed, and like Ren said it seems to have no apparent reason."

"So," James glanced over his shoulder at Abby, "to sum it up, a kid who is constantly bullied all of a sudden has an influx of confidence. And you believe it's because of his association with the demon?"

"Yes."

James nodded to himself. They were exactly right. The Darkness would need helpers. At first he wouldn't be able to act on his own without being found out, and in a place like this, where they taught classes on how to get rid of demons, being found out would be a very bad thing. So, he would need to teach these kids some tricks. He would call it the power of belief, and in a sense it was. They would be able to do many of the things James could with his power, and seemingly they got the power from the same place. He'd always wondered how it all worked, but being the only one he knew of that could do it he'd never really had anyone he could ask about it.

He knew belief didn't always depend on the truth, and for belief to have true power truth, again, didn't really need to play a part. In fact misplaced belief could be one of the most powerful things imaginable because people who tended to hold onto untenable positions were usually the ones with the strongest belief. If you were going to believe a blue light bulb was a god it required a much larger amount of belief than believing water was wet.

In the case of the Darkness and his henchmen all he needed were some practical examples for them to see in order for them to believe. Once they had been convinced, and in this case it wouldn't be hard since they had summoned him for this very purpose, he could use them for his own purposes. They would walk around feeling more powerful, because they were, and presto you get a transformation from bullied wallflower to confident lady's man.

"So how are we going to track him?" Todd asked as they neared the entry. "Are you going to use some miraculous thing to see where his footprints lead? Will there be some dark shadow hanging off him that only you can see with your tattoo?"

James stopped walking and looked around at the three, "You realize it's the middle of the day right?"

Confused looks bounced from face to face and finally Todd spoke up, "Isn't that the best time to face demons?"

"It's also the worst time to follow someone. And beside that isn't he going to be in class right now? What are we going to do stand outside the window and peek in for the next few hours? Isn't someone going to notice, and aren't you all supposed to be in class right now? You'd think with as strict and cranky as this place seems to be that someone would have noticed you're not in class."

"Wait a second," Abby put her fists on her hips and faced him, "first you want our help and now you're telling us to get lost?"

"Actually I just realized we were going about this in a bit of wrongheadedness."

"That's a big word," said Todd.

"Yes, yes it is, and it's appropriate for this situation. We can't just walk into a class and sit around, hoping he'll ignore us even though we aren't supposed to be there, waiting for him to lead us right to his demon boss. We have to be a little sneaky."

Ren nodded, "He's right. We've been charging around hoping no one would notice, but I know for a fact my professor will call me out for not being in class today. What am I supposed to tell him? I've been hunting down a demon?"

"Right," James put his hands on the closest shoulders and pushed them away from the building, "you all go to class and think of some plausible reason you weren't there on time while I sit around and wait for class to let out."

"But you won't know who to follow," Abby said.

"Which is why I expect you all to be back here as soon as possible to point him out to me. I'm also assuming he's not going to scuttle off immediately to wherever the demon is holed up. You said he seemed to have a newfound sense of confidence. Well, let's hope he puts that to use and hangs around campus for a bit before heading out to do nefarious things."

Todd nodded and leaned toward him, "You were just looking for a reason to use the word nefarious weren't you?"

"Maybe," said James, "and with all that's going on I have high hopes for working in the phrase, roaming band of ne'er-do-wells, at some point."

Abby rolled her eyes, "Just stop you two."

"Well," said Ren, "I'm off to concoct some story for being late to class. Shall we all meet back here at the end of the day?"

After nods and general assent the three headed off in different directions. Todd was the first to disappear among the other students, while Ren's little horns marked him out even at a distance. James found himself watching Abby the longest and wishing for just a moment things could be more normal, but for this moment he would be willing to take a quiet moment by himself on a blanket of perfect grass.

Chapter Twenty Three

A lot of spying on people is waiting. And a lot of waiting is trying to not be conspicuous just standing around in the same place. James had no idea how long the classes lasted, or when the school day ended. He didn't know if a rugby team was going to come and practice on the field where he was standing, but to be truthful he was fairly certain no one did much of anything on the grass because it was a perfect carpet of green, either that or they must pay someone really well to take care of it. He quickly realized he couldn't just hang out on the grass and watch the world go by. No one else was sitting on the grass, which he found really weird. Sitting on the grass and doing homework on a sunny day was a required cliché of every college or university in the world. Granted this wasn't his world, and this did seem to be a much more uptight university than he was used to, but still it seemed like a serious tragedy to have grass this nice and skies this blue and not be allowed to sit out here and get your work done.

He really wanted to take advantage of this down time and just kick back and watch the clouds make funny shapes, but he couldn't risk standing out and calling attention to himself, so if no one else was hanging out on the grass then, he decided, he shouldn't either. So for a few hours he set up a giant circle that led him around the main buildings of the campus while still allowing him to keep an eye on the spot they were supposed to meet up.

Eventually a bell rang and students in black robes flapped their way from one building to another. He looked at them fluttering by and tried to pick out Abby or Todd but had no luck. He'd hoped one of them would come and at least let him know some kind of a timeline, but at the same time he knew he was keeping up a charade where he was already supposed to know all these details. He was, in their eyes, a member of the ruling elite with knowledge of all things. He didn't feel like lying to them anymore but really couldn't figure out a way to break it to them.

James looked at his reflection in a passing window, "Hey, Todd, you know how I told you I was part of the Church, well actually I came from another world to catch this demon, not the Church. How'd I get here you ask? Well, you see, that's a funny story. Have you ever heard of Hell? How about Purgatory?"

Yep, his brain replied, *That would go over well.*

What? No witty metaphor for how that conversation would fail?

Uhm, like a fail cake baked with fail flower and covered in fail frosting. How's that?

Awesome.

He saw students coming into the class he was looking through the window at and moved on. After a few more loops of the campus the bells rang again and James headed back to the meeting spot just in case. The three of them were waiting for him when he arrived.

"Fun classes?"

"Sure," said Ren, "I just love lying to my professors about why I'm late."

"Good, it makes it easier if you love it." James turned away from Ren before he could respond to the sarcasm. He wasn't really in the mood to hear the sad sob story of lying to a favored professor. His feet were tired from walking in circles and he wasn't sure how the rest of this night was going to progress.

"What now?" asked Todd.

"Well, is this kid going to head out right away or does he have things to get done before he goes back to the lair of his evil overlord?"

They looked at each other before Abby answered, "We have no idea."

"Great." James looked around and realized the crowds of students were starting to thin. "We can't just stand here and wait for him to come out. Speaking of which, do any of you know which door he's going to come out of? It's easier to follow someone if you know that kind of thing."

Again James watched them all look at each other. They were obviously waiting for someone else to say they knew exactly where their target was going to exit the building, but after a few empty seconds James broke the silence with a groan. "Seriously, we need to work on this whole planning thing, and the fact that we don't have one."

"Well," said Ren, "you're the special agent with miraculous powers. Why don't you think of a plan?"

"Right." James thought for a moment. "Here's the thing, we can't all just stand around together, and we can't all walk around the same building over and over together so we're going to have to take shifts."

"So how do we let the people on shift know if something happened and which direction he's gone?" Ren asked.

"You don't have cell phones do you?"

"Have what?"

"Of course not, because that would make it too easy."

"Why don't you just miracle up something?"

James laughed, "I wish. I have to be able to completely visualize what's going to happen, and then I have to be able to maintain that in my mind while it's happening. It doesn't really matter how complicated it is, that's the miraculous part, but I do have to be able to get it to fit in my head. So sure I can make a way for us to communicate with each other, but I don't think I can maintain it for more than a few minutes before my mind starts playing tricks on me.

"So we only take short breaks. We always have someone with us so they can stay behind and let anyone else know what's going on. We walk around the building all nice and spread out since we don't know where he's going to exit.

"First thing, I really need to go to the bathroom. Where's the nearest one?"

After his trip others went to get something to eat or use the restroom. People came and went from the building but never the one they were looking for. A few times James had to warp reality a bit to keep professors from bothering them. It was never anything severe, more a bit of mind trickery to keep them from thinking about the group of students constantly circling the same building.

Night fell and James finished a sandwich Todd snuck for him. They watched lights go on in windows and he started to wonder if there was a way out of this brick palace of boredom they didn't know about. Finally when he'd almost convinced himself to head into the building and make sure the kid was still there he saw Abby waving her arms from the corner of the building.

"Finally." Todd groaned next to him. "This secret demon chasing stuff can be really boring."

James smiled and flashes of Purgatory and Hell flicked through his memory. "Don't complain too much. Exciting only means you're about to get horribly injured."

They quick walked to Abby who silently pulled them down a side path. After turning a corner they spied Ren at the far end of the walkway. He looked as if he was reading a book and trying to walk at the same time. The good thing about this place and these students, James thought, is that no one would ever suspect them of anything.

As quickly as was reasonable they caught up with Ren. He pointed out a black robed figure walking purposefully toward the edge of campus and James wondered how you could tell the difference in the dark between one black robed guy and all the other black robed guys. He assumed Ren knew what he was doing and concentrated instead on making sure no one noticed a group of four students obviously following another.

The lights of the campus eventually faded behind them and James started wondering why the kid they were following didn't try to hide where he was going. They'd said he'd seemed more confident in recent days, but there was a difference between confident and stupid. If you were going off to see the evil demon you'd summoned up from Hell you should at least be a little bit sneaky about it.

The student ahead of them paused to open a gate in a long fence and James hesitated when his brain realized it was the entrance to a cemetery. "Really?" He whispered to himself.

"What?" Abby whispered back.

"Is he really going into a cemetery?"

The others stopped and looked at him. James waved at the now open gate and gave the others an exasperated look.

"What?" Todd said, "It makes perfect sense to me. Where else would a demon build a lair?"

"First off, a smart demon would stay away from obvious places like these so people like us couldn't find it. And second off, did you really just use the word lair?"

Todd shrugged and looked a little embarrassed, "Well, it is a lair if you think about it."

Ren pointed at the gate, "We're going to lose him."

The three of them hurried ahead of James. He held back the feeling this wasn't the way it was supposed to be. Why hadn't the kid tried to hide his destination? Why would he go to such an obvious place? The only answer to all the questions and bad feelings was a trap.

James immediately pushed a pulse of force in front of him knocking the three off their feet. He wasn't sure what this particular kid could do but the last acolyte of the Darkness he'd run into could seriously toss around some power. That time hadn't been like this at all. Aside from the sun being down in both situations the two encounters were as different as night and day, and yes, he said to himself, he was aware of the silliness of the metaphor in that situation. This time he was in a grassy field leading into a dark and, yes, slightly creepy graveyard. With the other one he'd been in the well-lit parking lot of a Catholic church. It was where everything had fallen apart.

The Darkness had convinced one of his university professors that he could change the world. Looking back on it now James was amazed by how much of a cliché the entire encounter had been. The professor was convinced the world was going down the wrong path and he could fix it, but to build a new world you needed to destroy the existing one. In his rush to fix everything he saw wrong in humanity he'd decided the ends justified whatever means were needed, and so had killed a student and convinced James' girlfriend to help him burn down the local Catholic Church. The professor had ranted on about intolerance and the need to be the spark which would start the worldwide conflagration. It had been one of those monologuing bad guy moments.

In the end his girlfriend had died in his arms and his anger had led him to kill the professor. He'd worried for months afterward if killing him had been the right thing to do. Wasn't killing him just as bad, in some way, as what the darkness had been trying to do? Eventually he simply had come to the conclusion that no it wasn't the same. He had killed him out of anger, but it had been justified anger. Sometimes the bad guy needed to pay the price for his actions. The thing that angered James the most about all of it was how the Darkness, the demon they were chasing, had simply sat back and fed on all the nasty emotions like a putrid leech.

In a standup fight the professor could have taken James. He'd been using the power longer and understood better how to apply it to the environment, but the anger burning through him after the death of Kate coupled with the flow of this new power through him tipped the scales overwhelmingly in favor of James. He'd believed and the righteous fire of his belief had pulled lightning down from the sky. Since that one encounter he hadn't met anyone else with the power, and had only fought the darkness face to face once. And in James' mind that'd been a clear victory, minus the fact kids had been kidnapped and dragged, literally, through Hell.

James held his three new friends flat on the ground, convinced he wasn't going to lose anyone this time, he took a moment to survey the scene. He could tell they were trying to yell at him but with their faces being pressed into the grass not much was coming out but random grunts.

"Maybe this was a bad idea." He whispered to himself. He'd thought having people with him would be a good thing, but maybe he'd just been starved for company and now he was putting them in harm's way. He realized this situation and the people involved in it were nothing like Kate and her death, and he realized simultaneously he was having a hard time even thinking her name since the encounter in Hell, and the direct reminder of the part he played in her death. Even so he didn't want the agony of more people's death on his conscience.

The gate in front of him was a simple gap in a long stone wall ringing a standard graveyard. The metal gate momentarily reminded him of another gate in a burnt orange desert, and James flexed his fingers wishing he had the reassuring weight of the iron bar. He'd left it sitting next to his bed that morning thinking since he had the use of his power again he wouldn't need anything like a metal bar to hit the bad guys with. Maybe it was why wizards carried things like staffs or wands. You could still do magic without them, but it was nice to have something to hang onto and point menacingly at the bad guy. Without them it was like sticking up a bank with a finger gun.

James released the binding holding his new friends down and put up a shield. He knew his mental limitations and knew he couldn't maintain the mental picture needed to hold them down while dealing with a possible attack. He held his hand up in the shape of a gun for his own mental sake and leaned through the gate. The ground under his feet erupted sending him flying. His shield was pointless against stopping the earth itself from moving, and he quickly abandoned the effort in favor of a mental bulletproof full body airbag. He felt the impact of another attack coupled with the impact of hitting the ground, but wasn't sure what form it took. As he rolled to his feet he struggled to maintain his protection while expanding the personal bubble out. He wasn't sure how well it would work against another ground attack, which meant it wouldn't work at all since the entire point of his power was the firm belief in something working. James realized this as a flaming ball struck his barrier.

A smile spread across his face. The fireball had done more to help him than the crazy teachers aid he was chasing. It'd given him the location of his opponent and provided him with enough time to adjust his mental landscape. Now instead of worry and doubt causing the ground to literally and metaphorically crumble beneath his feet he had time to recast the world in iron. He rose to his feet and shrugged off another fireball attack. He physically planted his feet and in his mind the ground became an extension of his belief. His mind spun out metaphors and rejected them just as quickly. It was more solid than rock, it was more immovable than a mountain. For a moment the image of the juggler in the stained glass window flickered in his mind. A smile of pure surety on his face as the world's spun between his hands. In that fraction of a second James nodded to himself. That's how solid the ground was beneath his feet. As solid as the smile on God's face.

James moved forward into the graveyard dragging his mental solidity with him. He had no idea if the student tried to toss the ground again. If he did he must have been surprised when nothing happened. Another fireball arced from behind a large stone tomb and James reached out with his mind and his hand and grabbed it. Smiling to himself he split it into three separate balls and sent them all back at the tomb. One went right, the other left and the final one leaped over the top. There was a whump followed by a very satisfying scream from the far side of the tomb.

Not being able to see the student James still wasn't sure of his fitness so he maintained his personal defenses as he rounded the tomb. The black robed student was crawling away and trying to pat out a small fire as James approached. James released his personal shield and pressed the kid into the ground.

"I suggest you calm down." James paused at the sound of people coming up behind him. He wasn't really sure how long the fight had actually taken but it couldn't have been more than a minute. Obviously long enough for his friends to get up and come after him.

Rather than deal with all their questions and comments about whatever it was they thought they'd seen, James looked over his shoulder and raised one hand toward them hoping they would get the hint and be quiet for the time being.

"Now then, my new friend, I need you to answer a few questions."

The kid spit at him, "I'm not telling you anything. You're just a lackey of the corrupt institution that's pushed me and my friends around for so long."

James mentally put a gag on the kid before he could get into full rant mode, "Well, I see this is not going where I'd hoped, so let's try again." He leaned forward and put his finder on the kid's forehead, "I could care less about your sad emotional life right now. I do sympathize with you getting pushed around and all that, but, seriously, you crossed the line from sympathetic character to minor idiot when you called that thing up from Hell. Now, and I've always wanted to say this, we can do this the easy way or we can do this the hard way. I'm looking for some teens who were kidnapped and dragged off by a demon, the same demon you called up. You are going to tell me where the Darkness has taken them. If you decide in your idiocy not to tell me I'll simply," James poked him again in the forehead, "pull it out of your head."

In the back of his mind James had been maintaining his firm belief about the unchangeability of the world around him in the hopes this would stop the kid from trying anything silly, like lighting him on fire. He was rewarded with a satisfying look of confusion on the students face.

"Look, if you're trying to do something with your amazing newfound powers forget it. What I believe in," again the mental image of the juggler twitched through his mind, "is stronger than the Darkness you believe in. Now, I'm going to remove your gag."

The kid scrunched up his face in a mix of anger and confusion, "You can't pull thoughts out of my mind. My mind is my own. I believe it's not possible so it's not."

James nodded knowingly, "Actually I've never tried to read someone's mind, and I have no idea how it would work, but I've always wanted to try. It could be messy. My belief in getting the thoughts out would collide with your belief in keeping them in. I have no idea what that would actually do to your mind. We could end up scattering your gray matter all over this lovely graveyard." James shrugged then smiled his best insane smile, "But I'm really willing to give it a try." He leaned back away from the student, folded his hands together and cracked his knuckles.

The kid's eyes went wide and James could almost see his thoughts spin across his wide open pupils. Finally the reality of the situation won out and with a sigh he mumbled something.

James leaned closer, "I'm sorry I didn't quite catch that?"

"It's in the old Olsen house."

James raised an eyebrow and looked over his shoulder and the three behind him. They nodded knowingly at him. Todd was obviously trying to look menacing and nodded his head like he was sentencing someone to death. James chuckled to himself and turned back to the student.

"Well, I can't just leave you here to stab me in the back so I'm going to have to kill you."

The kid's eyes went wide and James let out a laugh, "I'm just kidding. I wouldn't kill you. But seriously," and with that he mentally bonked the kid on the head.

After making sure the teacher's aid was out cold James stood and turned to the three behind him to find Ren glaring at him. "What?"

Ren shook his head disapprovingly, "A man of God should be good in all he does."

"And?"

"You obviously took pleasure in scaring him."

"You're darn right I did." James bent over, brushed the grass and dirt off his knees, then straightened up. "That idiot called up a demon from Hell, gained unholy, and I use that word literally, power from it, and tried to kill us. So, yes, I think he deserved a little bad karma from the situation even if you don't know what karma even means."

James looked at the three of them and realized he had a decision to make. He didn't like the idea of any of them getting hurt because of this little adventure, but having backup in a tough situation could be useful. However, how realistic was that idea of them providing backup? Against what the Darkness could do would they really be any help? When they had run into him in a dark classroom they hadn't exactly been effective, unless you counted the now infamous chair attack. On the other hand they hadn't been effective because he wasn't a demon, and how effective was an exorcism against a normal guy? Answer, not very.

"Ren," James looked him in the eyes, "this class you're taking on exorcism, how realistic is it?"

"Well, these methods and prayers have worked over hundreds of years."

"Right," James nodded, "but realistically do they work every time?"

Ren gave him a slightly scandalized look, "You of all people should know not to doubt the power of prayer and belief."

"Sure, sure, but I also know not to trust in mumbo jumbo and random words some guy read from a book written a thousand years ago and never actually practiced."

"These are not the words of some charlatan." Ren's voice raised and he took a step toward James, "these are the words of God himself spoken through his chosen prophets."

Todd placed a hand on Ren's shoulder, "Calm down. I'm sure he knows that." He turned to James, "Right? You're just testing our faith before the final confrontation with evil, right?"

"Of course." James nodded and looked out into the darkness of the cemetery. But no mater what he couldn't stop his inside voice from yelling at him.

Faith is all well and good, but will it protect them against normal things like rocks and pointy sticks not to mention fireballs and lightning strikes.

It protects me doesn't it.

Yes, but that's different.

Really? How so?

Don't mess around with me man, you've got magic, and what do they have? Really nice graduation robes.

They have faith, and true faith can change the world.

Yes, great, and you heard them earlier. They never thought miracles would happen to them or even anywhere around them. How much faith is that?

But now? They saw me do stuff, and seeing is sometimes the best way to convince the unbeliever.

Really? You're going with seeing is believing again?

Yep, but I'm not stupid. They may have faith like a really big mustard seed, but they have no experience.

"So," James turned back to them, "here's the deal, and you will not argue with me." He waited until all three had nodded at him then continued, "You will show me where this house is, you will then plant yourselves outside the house and do the most major, bad ass, excuse my language, exorcism you can come up with. Most likely everything inside that house, except me, will be in dire need of a good existential flushing so you will keep up the exorcism until something amazing happens or I come back out."

"Something amazing like what?" Abby asked.

Todd elbowed her in the side, "Like glowing lights, or angels coming down, or the whole building imploding in on itself until nothing remains but a hole in the ground." He looked at James seriously, "Right?"

James shrugged, "For all I know those could all actually happen simultaneously. This is a bit of a unique situation. But no matter what, you will not come into the house, and if anyone other than myself comes out you will not attempt to fight them."

"But,"

James held up a hand and cut Todd off before he could continue, "You stink at hand to hand combat with demons, we all know this, so if I don't come out and something else does you run back to school and get that guy from the cafeteria."

"Who?" They all asked in broken unison.

"He was leaning up against the really tall windows watching the cafeteria like a human lighthouse."

Abby looked at Ren, "The janitor?"

Ren shrugged, "He's the only one allowed to lean up against the wall during lunch, and I suppose a human lighthouse would be a good description for him."

"Great," said James, "If I lose this fight and something else comes out you tell the janitor everything and he'll take care of it."

Todd slightly raised his hand, "Uhm, why the janitor?"

"What else would be a better disguise? A janitor can go anywhere without being questioned and do just about anything he likes without anyone noticing he's even there. Like you already said he's the only one allowed to lean on the wall, which I have to add is a little overly strict."

Ren looked at James like he'd lost his mind, "Disguise for what?"

James grinned, "Get to know him. Become his friend, and maybe, just maybe, he'll tell you. But in this case I'm absolutely sure you can trust him."

He hoped this would be enough to keep them out of harm's way, and if everything went wrong maybe the glowing figure he'd seen in the cafeteria really would take care of it. He hadn't confronted the thing in the first place because he wasn't really trusting of them after the whole chopping off his hand thing. And besides, that crazy juggler wouldn't have put him in this situation if he didn't think he could handle it. Right?

"Well my friends," James turned back toward the cemetery gate, "lead on to the haunted house and let's get this over with."

Chapter Twenty Four

For the entire walk to the abandoned estate all James could think was what to do about the kidnapped teenagers. The entirety of this entire trip, adventure, torture session, whatever you wanted to call it he'd been focused on catching up with the Darkness. The fact of the teenagers had been a bit of a sideshow. He wanted to save them, that was a given. No one deserved to be used by a demon. But on that same note James had no idea what shape these kids would be in. Were they even salvageable? Would they be zombies doing only what the Darkness wanted? Were they all dead with their bodies being food for the crazy denizens of the steps of hell? James remembered the unknown food they'd thrown at him as a kind of weapon and wondered for the first time if those chunks had been all that was left of the teens? He mentally ran away from that thought and into the arms of unreasonable hope. The only reason for taking hostages was to use them as a shield of some kind and that would be pointless if you ditched them along the way. Sure the Darkness couldn't really know James was still on his trail, but after all these years of cat and mouse it could reasonably expect him to show up eventually. In that case he might have kept the kids around to use again.

He'd have to content himself with hope in this case, and would have to plan accordingly. If they were still alive and in a condition to be saved he needed to save them. Hopefully that could happen before he confronted the Darkness, that way he could get them away and they wouldn't be in the line of fire. It would be a bit pointless to save them just to have them grabbed and used as human shields again.

So the amazing plan was to break into an abandoned house, save the kidnapped teenagers who'd been dragged through Hell, and destroy the demon he'd been hunting for years. Don't forget the fact there might be minions. The question he had to ask himself now was do you save the minions because they're being used against their will, or do you assume they're in this of their own free will and who cares if they happen to catch a fireball in the face? From what the others said earlier, and from what he'd seen from the student in the graveyard, they seemed to be in this of their own free will. He mentally shrugged to himself and thought whatever happened, happened, and if they tried to kill him he was going to defend himself. You can't hesitate when fighting a shadow demon from Hell and his collegiate minions. Maybe he could even think up some good one liners like, class is now in session, or, you got schooled. But every time he thought of those he ended up sounding like Arnold Schwarzenegger in a Terminator movie. Seriously, however, he would be happy just coming out of it alive.

They crested a small grassy rise and a run down home came into view. The three of them knelt down so as not to be seen from the house.

"I assume the creepy place is where we're heading?"

Two of them just nodded and Todd leaned towards him to whisper, "The couple that used to live there died and the kids have been in court fighting over who gets it."

"So," James leaned toward Todd, "no ghost stories or crazy killings happened here to scare intrepid college students and keep them from sneaking into the place and having a party?"

"What?" Todd looked at him like he'd talked about licking cows for fun, "Didn't you hear me say it was in court? You know what church lawyers do to trespassers."

"Right, right." James nodded his head knowingly while at the same time wondering what religious lawyers would do if they caught trespassers. Would they burn you at the stake? That's what they'd done to Joan of Arc and all she'd done was wear trousers instead of a dress.

The home had nothing really sinister about it. It was two stories with a pointy roof. From the number of windows it looked like there were a few rooms on the second floor and a separate attic with an octagonal window. The first floor had two big windows on either side of the main entrance, but the drapes blocked out any view of the inside, along with the fact that it was totally dark. There was a waist high stone wall around the whole place reminding James of a trip he'd taken to England with his brother a year before all this madness had started.

Those were good times. Any time he wanted to think of a perfect day he would think of his brother and himself running through English fields trying to find Hadrian's Wall. They would leap a short stone wall and scare a few thousand rabbits. The green of the fields and the blue of the sky had been so perfect he'd based his assessment of all other colors on that day. That day was full of the joy of being young and able to run all day without a pause coupled with the continuing hilarity of watching so many rabbits run for their tiny fuzzy lives.

This place, on the other hand, wasn't going to be full of fun and life and bunnies. It was going to be full of demons, and black robed minions. Well, one demon for sure and some minions. But you can't forget the minions.

"All right," James stared at the house trying to see anything out of the ordinary.

"Why don't you do your thing?" Todd whispered.

"My thing?"

"You know," Todd pointed to his own eye.

James looked at him for a moment like he'd lost his mind then remembered he did have a thing he could do.

"Right. Sometimes I forget I even have that."

"I wouldn't."

James ignored him and closed his eyes. He focused on the world around him and the darkness of his eyelids resolved itself into a grayscale picture. The house still looked like a normal house, but with one main difference. There were vines of darkness covering the structure like an out of control greenhouse. It was like an evil scientist had merged crude oil with creeping jungle vines then tossed in a healthy dose of creepy. They extended out to the stone wall and in a few places ventured beyond onto the grass of the field. The windows and door were covered with a thin network of the dark vines preventing anything from coming and going without alerting the inhabitants.

He could see small gaps in the network that something small like a mouse could fit through, and for a moment the thought crossed his mind. If the power really could do anything he could think of then why not turn into a mouse? James quickly tossed that idea aside. While it might be theoretically possible to do it, he didn't think he could maintain the presence of mind to sustain the transformation, much less even understand what needed to happen well enough to do it in the first place. The human mind thought of itself as human automatically. Everything about you, every experience you've ever had, all of it put together set the fact in your mind that you were human. James could believe in throwing fire, and speaking another language, but he wasn't sure he could believe he was a mouse. That left only one real course of action. He would have to just barge right in and hope for the best.

"There's layers of protection all over the place." He said as he opened his eyes and looked at the others.

Ren leaned toward him, "So what's the plan?"

James took a deep breath and let it out through his nose. "Have you been thinking about that exorcism?"

Ren nodded.

"Can it be done from farther away than the stone wall around the place?"

Ren seemed to think for a while, "Does the power of God have a specific range?"

James smiled. That's what they needed; blind faith. Sometimes blind faith was the worst thing. People would charge in and get torn to pieces because they believed something would save them. But in this case true pure belief was the Rolaids to the evil stomach problems of the demon. He shook his head and wondered about his own state of mind.

"You two," James gestured to Todd and Abby, "do what he tells you. And you," he poked Ren in the arm, "get that exorcism going as fast and hard as possible then keep it up for as long as possible."

Abby leaned toward him, "And what are you going to do?"

"Me?" James stood up and dusted off his knees, "I'm going to kick down the front door and see what happens."

James started to walk down the hill then stopped and turned back to the three, "Hey," he whispered loudly to get their attention, "how many other students d'you think're in there?"

They looked at each other then whispered frantically for a few seconds before Ren turned to him and gave a little shrug, "Maybe three?"

"Did you just say that with a question inflection?"

This time they all shrugged a little and Ren whispered again, "It's our best guess."

"So there could be more?"

"Or less," Todd whispered encouragingly.

James rolled his eyes as he turned away and started walking down the slope again. Or more, he whispered to himself. It was going to bug him not knowing how many bad guys he was facing, but there was nothing he could do about it.

What he would love to do was stay up on that rise and just blast the crud out of the place, but with the need to possibly save innocent kidnap victims he couldn't do that. It also meant he couldn't just go throwing fire and lightning around willy-nilly either. That meant defense followed by quick precise strikes. After his encounter with the student in the graveyard he knew he would be facing people who could use the power, but had never actually had anything thrown at them so they would expect to win quickly thinking they were amazing with their new found powers. He should be able to shrug off their initial attack and tag them back before they could recover from the shock of not winning on the first try.

Pausing halfway to the gate in the wall James took a moment to set his mind. The solid assurance he'd gained at the graveyard still ran through his bones grounding him. He knew now what he hadn't known for the past few years of this chase. What you believed in was more important than simply believing because eventually someone with a competing belief would come along and you'd have to fall back on whatever it was you actually believed in, and whether you stood or fell depended on the strength of that thing, not on the strength of your belief.

He looked down at his hand and the tattoo running from it up his sleeve. It was designed to remind him of who he was, and in this moment he could use all the grounding he could get. He thought of his family, his mother and father, his brother and sister. Memories of times with friends playing impromptu touch football games flickered through his mind. All of these helped to strengthen his belief and his defenses. In his mind he used his identity and his beliefs to build walls of unseen force around himself and harden the earth beneath his feet. Once he started walking again he was sure nothing could touch him.

He walked purposefully through the gate in the stone wall expecting any number of attacks. After his first encounter he figured some fireballs would come flying from the upstairs windows and maybe someone would try to toss the ground under his feet, but nothing happened.

At the front door he paused for a moment and listened. He expected to hear creeks and unknown sounds of people hiding inside, but it was silent. The vision he'd seen of the house wrapped in dark vines let him know he was in the right place, so all that remained was to do exactly what he'd said.

Taking a small step back James raised his right leg and kicked hard next to the doorknob. A splintering sound led to the door popping open and James couldn't help but say, "Knock, knock. Anybody home?"

From behind him James could just make out Ren's voice. He was saying something very forcefully, and James gave a fierce smile. It had been difficult for him to take those three seriously, after all, in his world the idea of exorcisms had been relegated to bad TV shows or rumors of secret rituals done by strange Catholic priests. But taking a stroll through Hell had a way of changing one's perspective on many things. For starters it had changed his way of thinking of the Darkness. Sure he'd thought of it as vaguely supernatural, but really he'd classified it in the same group as a man-eating tiger. It was something bad that needed to be hunted down for the safety of everyone. But now, after his little anti-holiday through Hell he'd come to honestly think of it as a demon, and if that was true then the idea of exorcism had to be true as well.

Exorcism, James had decided, was a series of motions designed to bring an unbelieving mind to a place of true belief. The person started out thinking that a normal Joe like themself could never defeat a demon from the pits of Hell, but after performing the exorcism ritual the mind space had shifted. Now they knew with absolute certainty that God himself was working through them and nothing could stand against them. So why did some exorcisms work while others failed miserably? Two reasons, he'd decided, first some people just never got to the place of truly believing. They lived in the realm of hope, and while hope is important it doesn't hold a candle to truly believing because hope leaves room for doubt. Second, and James wasn't sure about this one, some demons were just really tough. He thought back to the room at the base of the tower of Hell. He'd just peeked through an open door and seen only a glimpse of the thing seated on its throne, but that glimpse had been enough. The very essence of that thing had shifted reality. James had known beyond any doubt that if it had even looked at him he would have burned. Maybe, James thought, if he'd had enough time to mentally prepare for a confrontation with it he could survive, but by himself he knew he couldn't kill it, or even, more to the point, exorcize it from any place it wanted to be. One of the limitations of the power was being unable to think of more than one thing at a time without lots of practice, and even with practice James found he couldn't hold more than two concrete ideas at a time. One of those ideas had to be simple and solid and unmoving or his mind would lose track of the other idea. He was certain that thing, whatever it was, could do a bit more than one attack at a time.

Maybe someone could exorcize that thing, but it would take serious mental set up and continuous pressure. In the religious community that would be referred to as prayer and fasting. Maybe this was why monks sat around praying and mumbling to themselves. Just maybe they were saving the world from things like that horned king of Hell, and no one ever knew.

At that moment the tone of Ren's voice changed, and James heard the other two chime in. One, it sounded like Abby, was off to the right side of the house while the other, a deep bass voice, started in from the back. A song drifted over the yard and echoed back from the walls. James didn't know the words, or even the language they were singing in, but the very sound of it lifted his spirit. This was right, he thought to himself. And without even needing to check he knew the oil black vines were breaking.

"Well," he whispered to himself, "my turn I guess."

He grabbed the doorframe and leaned forward enough to see around the edge of the door to the right then to the left. The door opened onto a living room. The floors were wooden and covered with thick red rugs. Around the edge of the room were seating arrangements of different kinds. To the right was a couch and two easy chairs while to the left was a small table surrounded by four padded wooden chairs. Unfortunately, and what added to his worry, there was an extreme lack of any people.

It was obviously a trap, and like many things in life, the anxiety leading up to the actual event, in this case someone trying to kill him, was driving him nuts. He solidified his protective barrier in his mind and decided the only thing for it was to purposefully spring whatever trap existed. However, he didn't want to be stupid about it so he closed his eyes and checked the room through his Devil granted truth sight. His mind briefly passed over the idea that the Devil might be messing with him and there could be a really big bad nasty something waiting right in front of him but he couldn't see it because his special sight was just a trick. You can't dwell on things like that, he decided, or you'll just be frozen forever with indecision and he couldn't afford that right now. So you do all you can, you make a decision, and you act on it.

He saw nothing in the room, let out the breath he hadn't realized he was holding, and stepped into the room trying to see everything at the same time. A blaze of light blinded him at the same time as a concussion over his right shoulder sent him flying into the table. Contrary to every movie in the history of humankind tables don't break when you land on them, especially not solid, hand crafted, hard wood tables. James hadn't really thought out what would happen to him inside his nice little protective bubble, he'd just thought about making it as hard as possible so nothing could get through it. In this case it worked exactly like he'd mentally pictured and nothing got through it. On the other hand he bounced around the inside of it exactly like a hamster ball thrown at a solid, hand crafted, hard wood table. The light blinded him and the fall disoriented him, but to his credit he'd spent his alone time over the last two years running through what he would do in different situations. Granted this exact one had never crossed his mind, but ending up on the floor while being attacked had been a fairly constant worry.

He took his bubble and pushed it out from himself in a great shove. This, he hoped, would knock over any attackers and give himself time to get up. With his eyes light blinded all he could count on were his ears and all for the moment all he could hear was furniture scraping across the floor as he pushed it.

He blinked away tears and squinted around the room this time looking up and down and seeing two holes in the floor he'd missed on his initial look into the room. Both his hands came up to throw a fireball at each hole when the floor fell out from under his feet. You can mentally picture the ground being as solid as you want, but if it's not actually present there's really not much you can do about it. His mind momentarily argued with gravity, and if he'd had more time he might have won the argument, but gravity doesn't really give you the luxury of time.

He reflexively maintained his powerful notion of invulnerability, but his teeth still clacked together hard enough to have bitten through his tongue if it'd been in the wrong place when he hit the floor. He rolled two times to the left on the solid stone floor on the premise that he really didn't want to stay still long enough for the bad guys to take easy pot shots at him.

His mind fractured into competing plans. One wanted to send force and fury of many kinds blasting through the unknown space. Mental images of lightning and miniature tornadoes of fire spinning around the room filled his mind's eye while a separate mental voice yelled at him about collateral damage. Would it really matter if a few teenagers got toasted if he was able to take out the Darkness he mentally yelled back? Every voice in his head, some sounding an awful lot like his Mom and Dad, yelled back that, yes, it really would matter.

He didn't take the time to argue with himself and instead set off a series of fireworks around him both to illuminate the area and blind anyone trying to poke him with anything. His eyes quickly took in an empty square basement and a black robed figure just to the right throwing his arm up to cover his eyes.

James swept his right hand up and flicked his fingers throwing off razor sharp shards of ice the size of his fingernails. They hit an invisible field a few feet in front of the person James had mentally tagged as Evil Student Number One. In quick succession James flung a wall of force out from his back just in case someone was trying to sneak up from behind him then draped a layer of blackness over the bubble of protection around Number One.

He started poking at it from as many angles as he could, knowing the same limitations would apply to this kid as applied to him, and hopefully he had more mental training than Number One. On the other hand maybe Number One was the head of the chess club with a mind like a steel trap. It seemed like a possibility for a kid who was bullied all his life.

James unconsciously took up a boxing stance and started throwing little jabs, which coincided with the attacks against the bubble of protection.

Float like a butterfly, sting like a bee.

Hit him on the left, on the left, on the left.

And when he commits too strongly.

We knock him out on the right.

James slammed large, heavy blows to one side of the bubble then quickly followed it up with a needle thin strike to the other side. He knew he'd been successful when he heard a scream from inside the blackness of the bubble.

Again in quick succession he sent out a pulse of force around him and registered for later investigation a small yelp. He followed it as quickly as his mind would shift to sucking all the air out of Number One's bubble through the tiny hole he'd made. The student couldn't keep up the mental images protecting him with his ability to breath severely hampered and the bubble collapsed.

James tossed out more mental flash-bangs and as they lit up the room he knocked Number One against the wall hard enough for him to slump into what James hoped was unconsciousness. At the same time a small, but vocal, part of his mind told him he'd been standing in the same place for too long and that was bad. He jumped to the right then spun, flinging his hand out leaving an arc of flame, which burned its way along the solid wall of the basement at chest height. A stack of wooden chairs, which must have been extras for the dining room table upstairs, caught fire and lit up the empty room. The only possibility of escape for whoever had yelped behind him was the obvious door next to the flaming pyre of chairs.

James took a moment to catch his breath and check for any injuries. He felt sore in multiple places from hitting the table upstairs and then the floor in the basement, but he couldn't find anything more pressing than a few bruises. He didn't want to give Number Two a chance to set up a new trap for him, so other than giving the flaming chairs a smugly satisfied look as payback for one of their brethren hitting him in the head, he charged the door.

He burst through it pushing a protective shield in front of him and found a flight of wooden stairs heading up a narrow stone passage. As soon as his foot hit the bottom stair the door behind him flew off its hinges and hit him hard in the back. The only thing that saved him from having his head smashed in was his forward lean as he tried to see up the stairs. As it was, the solid door impacted his lower spine with a deep whump and his kidneys screamed a few choice words in the general direction of his brain. The force of it knocked him forward and his shins cracked the wood of the next step while his hands tried their best to save his face from a personal meeting with the edge of the stairs.

For a moment his mind lost its focus and his shield slipped into nothingness. Only the poor aim of Number Two saved his scalp from catching fire as a jet of flame roared over him. James rolled to his side and clapped his hands together mentally forcing the stone walls to slam together farther up the stairs. He could feel something pushing back trying to pry the walls apart so he focused on holding that while he picked himself up and did a quick check to see if he could still move. He felt a trickle of blood running down each shin and into his socks along with his back feeling like someone had hit him with a car. He took a tentative step up to the next stair and his shins and ankles told him in no uncertain terms what he could do with himself if he kept this insanity up. He knew he could push himself to keep going, but wasn't sure how long he could keep that up before something just didn't listen to him anymore. Then he remembered his favorite new appendage. If he could just last long enough his nifty new hand should kick in and help him out. After all, if he could survive a swarm of screaming Hell beetles one irritating college student should be doable.

James decided the best thing to do would be a direct attack. Number Two wouldn't be expecting him to charge after getting slammed into these lovely stairs. Sometimes when you're wrestling with someone, and you're both leaning hard against each other trying to overpower the other man, the best thing you can do is let them push themself over. He was fairly sure this was the founding principle of some martial art or other out there, and a part of him thought it might be a good idea to learn something like that if he was going to keep going in this line of work.

He let the walls go and with a spin of his right hand sent a flaming tornado up the stairs as cover. He tried to run up the stairs and decided a fast limp was the best he could do. He didn't want Number Two to have a chance to recover so while the firenado spun its way up the stairs, which on looking back he realized might not have been the best idea on old wooden stairs, he started tossing as many different attacks as he could think of. Ice spikes were followed by lightning and before the crack of thunder had dimmed he bounced fireballs off the walls and ceiling mentally picturing them ricocheting around like red dodge balls of death.

Tossing up an angled protective shield James stumbled up a few more stairs and was just able to see Number Two around the edge of his firenado framed by another door. Parts of his robe were smoldering and

256

he'd just dispensed with the last bouncing fireball. They locked eyes, and for a moment James felt bad for the kid. His face had seriously out of control acne and his head was topped with long thin hair pulled forward to cover as much of the socially embarrassing problem as possible. He was tall and the very definition of gangly and disproportional. On a puppy big floppy feet were cute and a sign it would grow up to be a big solid dog, but on a person big floppy hands just looked, well, dorky. James felt a pang of self-consciousness because no one really had control over those things. He'd been blessed with the physical inheritance of great parents and grandparents. His brother had taken advantage of it way more than James ever had with a constant succession of very good looking girlfriends and letters in every school sport.

Sympathy for your enemy was all well and good, and in the end it was one of the defining differences between good men and evil, but sympathy doesn't stop elemental attacks from burning your face off. James' angled protective shield meant he didn't have to put as much effort into blocking attacks because they naturally slid off to one side rather than putting all their force directly into the shield. As the first attack slid off to the right James countered with invisible punches at Number Two's head. In his mind James sent blow after blow of invisible Bruce Lee chops, but rather than blocking them all Number Two broke the stairs under James' feet causing him to stumble.

They both had to take a moment to recover but within seconds the stairway was like a fireworks display gone wrong. A small blizzard dropped needles of ice. This was followed by flashes of blinding light and an ice slick on the landing in front of the door. Blobs of flaming goo stuck to James and for a moment he had to focus on clearing his mind and using the power to get the stuff off him. This gave Number Two a chance to regain his feet after slipping on the ice and James decided this needed to end.

He cleared his mental landscape and focused his belief. This kid, new to the power, and most likely not sure of his own strength had spent his life being taught by the world that he wasn't strong enough. Now James was going to take advantage of those lessons. In his mind James believed there were no attacks. The stairway was clear and clean. He didn't just believe this as being true, it simply was true because it was the natural way of the world. This mental picture imposed its will on the world around it and no matter what Number Two tried nothing could change the pure surety of James' mental picture.

In the silence James reached out and formed hands from the walls and floor around Number Two. They grabbed him and held him fast. James limped up the remaining stairs and faced the acne covered boy. He wanted to lecture him. To tell him all the things he'd done wrong, all the choices he'd made which led him to this spot. How even if you're dealt a bad hand you still could make the right choices. Your circumstances could be terrible but in reality it didn't matter how bad they were because what really mattered was what you did, and what choices you made. You can't always control what goes on around you, but you can control how you react to it. But as all these things pinged around the inside of his skull James knew he didn't have time, and he seriously doubted the kid would listen. Sometimes you just ended up too far down the road to even see where you made the wrong turn any more.

James reached out and tore a strip of cloth from Number Two's sleeve. He mentally covered it with ether and pressed it to the student's face covering his mouth and nose. After a few moments his eyes rolled back and he slumped forward. James reached out and grabbed one of the stone hands and pulled it like putty around the student wrapping him in ropes of stone. He might not stay knocked out for hours, and the stone might not keep him tied down for long if he did wake up, but hopefully this would all be over long before that eventuality.

A spasm ran through James' muscles and he only saved himself from falling over by catching himself on one of the remaining stone hands. A fierce tingle ran through him and he knew his angel hand was finally doing its thing. He had no idea how long it would take to fully heal everything wrong with him, but at least it was doing something, and it meant he had an even chance of winning this thing.

He took a deep breath and tried to ignore the pins and needles running through his shins and lower back. Staring at the doorway in front of him he wondered what exactly was on the other side. Maybe the Darkness would conjure images of his dead girlfriend to distract him like the flame haired demon had tried to do in the tunnel. Even though he did feel a certain amount of guilt for Kate's death he knew she couldn't really be here, and anything would most likely be an illusion.

The remains of the door at the top of the stairs were scattered and some chunks were even embedded in the walls and ceiling. However, the lack of a door didn't help with seeing into the adjoining room. The darkness itself acted as a physical barrier, and James stood in the doorway trying to see what lay in his immediate future. So far his attempts at defense hadn't turned out well, and the aches and pains of being knocked around and even broken told a very descriptive story of his failure.

Growing up his father had loved to read Louis L'amour books, and the house had been filled with pictures of the beauty of western states like New Mexico and Arizona. In all those westerns James had noticed none, and they emphasized that fact, of the heroes liked to stand out in the middle of the street at high noon and have a gunfight. A smart man would never do a gunfight out in the open, he was likely to get hurt doing things like that. If someone was going to be shooting at you then you moved, a lot. You tried to make yourself as small of a target as possible, or distract the bad guys with something while you snuck around and shot them from behind the woodshed in the opposite direction.

Granted, standing in the middle of an open door wasn't the best way of not being noticed, so rather than trying to be sneaky about it he decided to be confusing instead. He mentally blurred himself then stepped into the room and sent visual copies of himself stepping out to the left and right and one in front of him. He hoped in the confusion of trying to kill his momentary doppelgängers he would get the chance to blast whomever was in the room waiting for him.

Deciding not to wait for someone to shoot at him James tossed out some more of the light flashes he'd gotten used to. He'd learned if he directed them outward it left him able to see the room while at the same time blinding any immediate troublemakers. Nothing happened. In point of fact something did happen just not what he wanted to happen. The little fireworks went off but the only thing they illuminated was more darkness. For a moment James felt like this was actually a nightmare, something would come out of the darkness, and he wouldn't be able to run or scream. The darkness pressed down on him and his breathing started to come in short quick gasps.

Immediately James closed his eyes. The darkness of his mind was a familiar thing as opposed to the nightmare darkness in front of him. He slowly pushed his breath out letting his lungs deflate. Part of his mind screamed at him that he wouldn't be able to pull any air back in, but another part told him this was just a small panic attack. He didn't normally have panic attacks, and truth be told he kind of looked down on people who suffered from them. Yes, it meant he wasn't the best person, but he couldn't help feeling that way. The only time he could remember having an honest, for real, panic attack was when the dentist put this mouth guard suction thing in. He felt like he couldn't swallow or breathe because the suction was pulling all the air out while at the same time he couldn't adjust anything because the mouth guard part kept him from moving. For a few moments his brain had tried to convince him he was about to die, but he knew he wasn't. Many other people had survived the dentist and many more would.

That sentiment might not work in this case.

Just breathe in.

In fact I'm not sure anyone has ever survived this particular situation.

You're not helping.

Oh, am I supposed to be helping?

Yes.

Cuz right now I'm pretty sure I should be panicking.

These are all just mind tricks.

These are not the droids you're looking for.

Ha.

See, see, I can help. Oh and by the way no one's shot at you yet.

Hm, true.

Which could mean any number of things, actually.

Well now, we should take a look shouldn't we?

Your flashy thingies didn't work, remember.

Ah, but you forget I have a secret eyeball.

And James concentrated on the tattoo around his eye. A room slowly resolved into shades of gray around him. He was just inside the door from the stairs and a living room spread out in front of him. Most of the furniture had been pushed off to the sides of the room while two tables stood side by side in the middle. To his right a door led into what looked like a kitchen while another door to his left led out into the entryway where he'd fallen through the floor. At the back of the room a set of large carpeted stairs led up to the second floor.

There was nothing immediately sinister about the room except for the bodies of two teenagers lying on the tables. Where was the third one? He looked around the room and didn't see any sign of the other boy. Black vines wrapped around the two binding each to their table and trailing off to eventually lead up the stairs. The next thing James noticed about them was the missing shoes. None of them were wearing shoes. He gritted his teeth as mental images of them walking barefoot across the desert of Purgatory and up the steps of Hell throbbed through his brain.

The tall one's once fine black church suit was torn and dirty, and even though he was missing his shoes he'd somehow managed to keep his coat but had at some point lost the tie. On the table closest to him James was able to recognize, even in the shades of gray, the hair of the girl from that Sunday morning in church so long ago.

"Grace." He whispered to himself.

He hadn't been sure she'd made it here after the trap was sprung on the tower stairs. He'd assumed with what he'd learned from the students, but it was nice to see she'd made it out without being eaten alive by the beatles. She was one tough kid.

He remembered all the way back to the look in her eyes when he threatened to let the Darkness kill them in the church. She'd been calm. While the others had either fainted or gotten the freaked out look of a deer about to be shot she'd just looked at him and nodded. He'd watched her stand her ground against a powerful woman of her community then not blink at the idea of dying at the hands of some shadowy demon. On the tower stairs even with her life in danger she'd still tried to warn him of the trap. The thought of not letting her die had helped push him out of the hole in Purgatory and kept him going.

"Well Grace," he whispered to her sleeping form, "sorry it took me a while."

He looked around the room again, this time checking above and below for any signs of traps.

"The way I see it we have two options." He tried to see up the stairs without moving any more than necessary.

"Option number one, I go up the stairs and find where the creepy vines lead. Most likely it's to the big demon himself. I take out said bad guy thereby freeing you from captivity."

James had a mental picture of an epic battle between himself and the Darkness. During the battle parts of the building would be destroyed and since they would be fighting on the second floor some chunks would, most likely, fall down into this room. His mental picture then had the entire building collapsing and killing all the teens.

"Right," he shuffled a step closer to the tables, "so maybe option two."

"What is option two, you may ask?" Squatting down he tried to see under the tables hoping his magic eyesight would show him if anything was there. The dark vines wrapped around the tables and crossed over themselves underneath but other than that nothing sinister appeared.

"Well, Grace, since you asked, option two is getting you out of the nasty vines of evil first, then going and kicking him in his glowing eyeballs."

James slowly worked his way to the head of her table and eyed the thick vine leading away to the stairs. "I'm thinking it's like a really nasty Band-Aid. So let's try to get it off as quickly as possible."

With his eyes still closed James conjured a Japanese Katana. It was the sharpest thing he could think of. The tattoo showed him the truth of things, which meant this thing was truly like a vine, so if he cut it, the part around her should be removable. He poured all his belief and will into the blade, raised it over his head, and swung. His momentum carried him forward and when he met no resistance his body couldn't react in time to stop itself from slamming into the floor.

A scream cracked his ears and James rolled onto his back trying to locate the source. His eyes flew open reflexively and were greeted by dancing firelight. The room had changed to a simple concrete box with no windows or doors, and where the tables used to be in the center, a bonfire burned.

The scream trailed off and was followed by sobs filled with something on the edge of being words but filled with too much terror to even make it that far. James rolled onto his knees and looked over the fire. He saw Grace held down by a gang of boys. Three or four of them held each arm and leg while others pulled out knives.

James didn't know he was screaming until one of the boys turned to him. A faceless blob of a head looked at him from under a black sweatshirt hood. Pure rage burned through James and without a mental picture or time to set his power of belief he simply threw the rage out like a weapon.

With a swipe of his hand the bonfire was brushed aside. A roar tore through his chest and his rage wrapped around the faceless mob tearing them apart and flinging them away. Within seconds none were left and Grace lay on the hard floor twitching and sobbing.

Running to her his rage was pushed aside and overwhelming empathy poured out of him like water.

"What do I do, What do I do, What do I do?" He couldn't form a coherent mental picture while looking at her bleeding, but found it impossible to look away. Whole strips of her skin had been peeled away showing the muscle underneath and her once colorful hair was burned and pulled out in chunks.

James wrapped his arms around her and pulled her to him. He looked up at the ceiling and whispered, "I don't know what to do."

He looked down and kissed her forehead and like his rage and desire to destroy had ripped out and tore apart her attackers so too did his caring and need to heal her.

He had no mental picture of her being whole and unhurt. He didn't know how to fix what had happened to her. But he believed someone out there did. Someone out there knew her and loved her. Someone wanted her fixed and perfect. His belief washed over her.

She twitched in his arms and let out a breath. James opened his eyes and realized he was on the table in the living room holding her against him. He leaned back and looked around. The concrete box of a room was gone. He could see with his eyes open and didn't really care to think about why the oppressive darkness was gone. What was important was Grace.

He looked back, and her now open eyes stared at him.

"I..."

Her sobs cut him off and her arms wrapped around him squeezing tight.

A deep breath of relief escaped him as he realized it had all been another mind trick. She hadn't been hurt. He leaned back away from her and looked her over as best he could.

"Are you hurt?"

She sniffled and looked down at herself. He could tell by her expression she was expecting to see horrific wounds, and that one look told him the trick hadn't just been in his mind.

"It's all gone." He whispered to her. "Do you understand? It's all gone."

James looked around at the other table and realized he would have to go through something similar with the other boy.

He slid down off Grace's table, "Here's what I need you to do," he pointed to where some furniture had been piled up against the corner of the room, "I need you to get inside that pile and hide."

She looked at him wild eyed and grabbed his sleeve like she would never let go.

"I'm not going anywhere." James patted her hand, "I just have to wake him up, and I'm not sure I can do it if I'm holding onto you." He wondered if she would be dragged into the mental trap with him, and if she were would she be able to survive the trauma after everything she'd already been through.

Wrapping his arms around her he lifted her down off the table. Setting her on her feet he steadied her until she seemed able to stand on her own. He took her hands and led her to a pile of furniture in a corner of the room.

"Grace?" He cupped her face in his hands, "I need you to squeeze back into that space." He pointed to a space just big enough for her in the middle of the jumble of chairs.

She shook her head and grabbed onto his sleeve. He smiled and hugged her to him, reminding himself she was just a kid. He wasn't much older himself but there's a grand canyon sized gap between an average sixteen year old and a twenty three year old, especially after the last two years of running across the country trying to kill off the Darkness.

"I don't want to leave you alone, but I have to get your friend over there." He tipped her head up and locked eyes with her, "I need to know you're safe while I get him. No one will look in there for you, and I promise I'll only be over at the other table for a few seconds."

She let her breath out in a little huff and shook her head.

James nodded, "Believe me, I understand, but I can't leave him there. And I need to know you're safe out here. So please, Grace..." he gestured at the chairs again.

Finally she looked from the prone figure of her friend to the stacked furniture and gave a little nod. Squatting down she squeezed herself back into the gap in the furniture and attempted to make herself as small and inconspicuous as possible.

"All right, you stay there and I'll go see about waking him up."

As he turned he felt her grab his pant leg. He turned to look at her and she motioned for him to lean down.

Her voice cracked as she whispered, "What took you so long?"

James smiled, glad to see at least a little of her spirit coming back, "Well," he shrugged a little, "I had to chop off an angel's hand then have a word with the Devil."

She gave him a weak smile and in his gut he knew however hard his trip had been, hers had been worse. Maybe, hopefully, it would be like a dream and fade after time. He doubted that. His worst dreams from childhood still held a place in the dusty closets of his mind. He could always try using the power to help her forget, but he wasn't sure what accidental damage he might do.

Turning from her, he focused on the boy still laying comatose on the table. Closing his eyes he saw the vines wrapped around him and was surprised to see nothing else. He'd assumed after his attack to free Grace something would show up to try and kick him in the teeth, but maybe the big ugly upstairs wouldn't notice his evil soul siphon had been cut until it was too late.

James again drew his mental katana and took aim. This time he knew what to expect. There was no way the Darkness could ignore all the vines being cut, especially after the explosions and fireworks from the fight against his minions.

Taking a more careful swing so as not to end up landing on his face again James felt reality shift into the mind space Grace had been trapped in. The tall boy was strapped to the wall surrounded by the faceless things which had assaulted Grace in the other dream, except here they weren't torturing the boy. He was frantically pulling at his bonds, yelling, and staring at the other side of the room. James looked over the heads of the faceless and saw the other boy he'd expected to be with them. The faceless tore at him and over his screams James could just hear that the tall boy was yelling a name over and over.

Putting away his Katana James knew his first target needed to be saving Ray. He assumed it was the blonde boys name the other one was yelling. Unlike the rage he'd felt at finding Grace being tortured all he felt here was disgust. Now he knew it was all a mind game, and the fact that anything with a mind could think these kinds of insanities up was wretched.

When fighting a human there were certain attacks James couldn't bring himself to use. Normally he tried to incapacitate his enemy or scare them enough so they wouldn't fight back anymore. He'd found this attitude was normal with the vast majority of humanity. Even generally bad people were loath to automatically kill another human being. They would threaten and scare as much as possible long before they would actually kill someone. But here, with a bunch of faceless mind monsters, James had no compunctions against simply tearing them apart. It was easy. He just pictured them like play-dough. He swept the majority of them to the sides before dealing with them because the ones he wasn't personally destroying would continue attacking Ray as if nothing else was happening. This single mindedness helped James deal with the situation much faster since he could destroy the majority of them before the rest even realized someone was there. They were simple creatures with only one goal stuck in their play-dough heads.

Once they were all dealt with James pulled the taller boy down and wasn't surprised when he ran to his friend and cradled him like a father might hold his injured son. This might be all in the mind, but the pain was still real to them. He wasn't really sure how he'd woken Grace up, or even if he was the one who'd woken her up. She might have snapped out of it on her own, or some part of his power might have pulled them both back simply because he'd willed it. This time he knelt beside them and placed a hand on their heads. Nothing happened so he closed his eyes and tried to will them all back to the room. Still nothing happened. He thought back to what he'd done with Grace and knew there was a difference. With Grace he'd felt devastated. Rage and sympathy had crashed through him and the emotions themselves had acted instead of his own power. Here he just didn't feel that. He was impatient because he knew he still had to walk up those stairs, and he was angry these kids had been taken advantage of like this. But in reality he just didn't feel as strongly for these two boys as he did for Grace.

His parents had raised him with an old fashioned sense of chivalry. He could remember times his father had pulled him aside and reminded him to open the door for someone, or how to act around girls. Boys weren't treated the same as girls in the standards of middle class American chivalry. Boys were target dummies in football practice, boys opened their own doors, and boys brushed themselves off and got on with life. It was a social outrage if a girl was taken advantage of. On the other hand, if a boy was hurt the general feeling was he should've stood up for himself.

James sighed and tried to push those thoughts away. A thought flashed through his mind and actually made him chuckle, which in this situation wasn't exactly what he was looking for. He remembered back in high school a fad had passed through his school. All the religious kids started wearing these blue bracelets with white letters spelling WWJD on them. What would Jesus do? James opened his eyes and looked around the strange mental prison. That sentiment wouldn't help him here, but what would help him is what was hindering him in the first place. What would his father do? Yes, dealing with girls had been different, but in every memory he dragged up about his father he was always helping someone. It wasn't always because they'd been friends, or colleagues. His dad hadn't even really liked some of the people he'd helped, but he still did it. James knew beyond a shadow of any kind of doubt if he'd asked his dad why he'd done it he would have gotten a simple response, it was the right thing to do. It wasn't always the convenient thing, or the easy thing, but it was always the right thing.

James nodded to himself, realizing this time would necessarily be different than when he'd brought Grace back. So taking a deep breath he heaved the injured teen up onto his right shoulder then kneeling down he lifted the other onto his left. He knew this wasn't humanly possible, but he had super powers so it didn't really matter. Once they were settled into a kind of manageable heap James rocked back and forth a few times and ran at the wall. Pressing with his mind he lowered his head and crashed through like the Hulk in a bad cartoon.

Shaking his head he saw with a good level of joy that he was standing in the middle of the living room and the two tables lay broken on the floor. Walking over to where Grace was huddled against the wall James smiled at her like he did this kind of thing every day. As he went to lower the two down he realized there was only one of them. The weight on his other shoulder was gone. Looking around he expected to see the other one laying on the floor accidentally dropped in the strange dash out from the mind trap, but Ray was nowhere to be seen.

Behind him he could hear Grace whispering to the taller boy, "Mitch," James looked and saw her grabbing Mitch's face and looking into his eyes, "it's okay," she whispered, "I don't think this is a trick."

Mitch let out a breath, nodded, then pulled her hands away from his face. Turning slightly Mitch looked at James, "Thank you."

James knew he should take some time to talk with them and reassure them everything would be fine, but he really didn't think he had the time for that. The Darkness had slipped away from him so many times in the past, and this time he had him surrounded. Well, he thought to himself, as surrounded as he was ever really going to get.

Leaning past Mitch he reached out to the chairs piled up around Grace and pulled off two chair legs, laying them down one next to the other. He touched each one and, for lack of a better term, weaponized them. In his mind they were now a combination of holy water, magic torch, and shock stick. He wished he'd thought of this before now, but he'd leaned so much on his own ability to use the power that he'd never thought of making a weapon for himself. If something happened and he didn't have time to activate his power he might need something like those now magical chair legs.

Cain sitting on the stairway of Hell came to mind. Now he understood at least a little of what he'd been saying about symbols. Maybe it was why Cain had covered himself in so many. Each one was ready to do something. It was the sentiment many ancient cultures had about swords. The sword wasn't just a piece of shaped metal. It was a symbol waiting to be activated. It hummed with anticipation to do what it had been created to do. Maybe, James thought, if he made it out of this somewhat whole, or

268

at least alive, he would take the time to make a weapon for himself. It would be a holy sword with some kind of cool name. He would use it to hunt other demons. Shaking his head he chuckled to himself at his ability to ramble in his own mind.

He looked up at Grace and Mitch, "I'm sorry to do this but I'm going to need you two to look after yourselves for a bit. That thing up there needs to be dealt with, and if I wait too long he might slip away again." He gestured to the chair legs. "Do you believe I have power beyond a normal person?"

They both nodded at him.

With a thought and a wisp of power James made his eyes glow an electric blue, "Do you truly believe I can fight the demon who trapped you here?"

Their eyes widened and again they nodded.

"Good," he needed them to believe him or they would never try to use a chair leg to defend themselves if something came. "I've blessed these and given them power over anything that may come after you."

He glanced at the stairs and knew any time he'd had was quickly running out. Reaching out with his left hand he patted Grace on the shoulder in what he hoped was a reassuring way then with a smile to add to the everything-was-under-control feeling he stood and headed toward the stairs. At the bottom step he closed his eyes and took the time to look at them with his special vision. Nothing seemed out of place until the top step and that wavered a bit like a heat vision on a long stretch of desert pavement.

He took a deep breath, readied a fireball in each hand, and took the stairs two at a time. At the top a long hallway emptied into an open door at the end. He assumed the Darkness would be down there, but wasn't about to go past the other doors leading off the hall without at least making sure nothing was going to sneak up on him.

To his growing amazement each room was just a room, and no one was waiting for him. No monsters crouched behind the doors ready to eat him, and after checking the third and final room he realized he had to go through the door at the end of the hall. Closing his eyes again he looked through his tattoo and saw a door of a different kind. The simple wooden house door was gone and in its place stood a stone archway, which made his skin attempt to crawl off his bones. The stone was gray and etched in the keystone at the top of the arch was a rune. James couldn't read it, but he didn't need to. He'd recognize the setup and the placement of that rune for the rest of his life. He was sure he would see those gray stone doorways in his nightmares along with the unknown things ready to crawl or fly from them.

"Well," his voice echoed back down the hallway, "back into it then."

He stepped through the door. The room seemed to bend away from him. Gray hard walls led up to a vaulted gothic ceiling supported by black veined marble pillars. He knew if he opened his eyes all he would see would be a plain bedroom with a curtained window and some old dusty bed. At the end of the pillared room was a man and the throne he sat upon was made of the twisted broken forms of people clothed in black college robes. He lounged with his feet spread out before him and his arms draped over the heads of the captured students. He was tall and bare from the waste up with loose dark red pants held on with a leather cord. His body would have been the template for any photo shopped movie star, and long black hair hung around his face like an angelic version of an eighties rock star.

"James," he leaned forward and waved for James to come closer. "I don't think we've ever properly met. I am Kron'ael also called Kochbiel or Kabaiel and once, long ago, I was the angel of the stars. And you," again he gestured for James to come closer, "you are James my pursuer, my hunter, my thorn in the side."

He looked down the long hall at James, "What? Nothing to say? After all these years of back and forth, of almost killing each other and living to fight another day?"

James slowly shook his head. He'd mentally prepared himself for so many eventualities, but this wasn't one of them. He'd expected a shadow thing with whipping tentacles, but not this. He needed a moment to change his expectations and think of a way to deal with this.

So talk to him.

I don't want to talk to him.

Look, this is classic bad guy behavior from every movie or comic you've ever seen.

Which is exactly why I don't trust it, and I don't want to have a conversation with the nasty demon who was just torturing Grace.

True, true, but we need time to figure this out. Time to figure out his weaknesses.

Do you see him?

Yep.

I'm not sure he has any weaknesses.

Still, no time like the present.

"So," James wondered how real the pillars were, and if they would provide him any protection in a fight, "you look better than the last time I saw you."

"Oh, yes," the demon looked down at himself. His muscles actually rippled under his slightly tanned skin. He lifted his right hand up and turned it to watch his slightly opalescent fingernails catch the light. "Having some free time to nourish myself has done wonders for my personal outlook."

James shook his head and decided this was pointless. Talking would solve nothing, and at no point in a conversation did James see this thing giving away any weaknesses. His best bet, he decided, was to just catch the thing unaware and get the first shot in. Maybe he could collapse a pillar onto it. He decided against that, not knowing if the pillars would react in a manner similar to earthly physics. So blast him really hard in his too pretty chest with something very powerful jumped to the top of the list.

He figured if he tossed something it needed to be a surprise so the middle of a sentence would give him the best chance.

James nodded at the demon, "So I was right, and the stronger you got the more solid," he didn't raise his hand to throw the lightning like he normally would. Instead he just mentally tried sending it straight from his chest. Nothing happened. His teeth clenched as a wave of terror rippled through him.

The demon smiled, "Is something wrong?"

This time James did raise his hands. Again his mind solidified the image like he'd done it so many times before. He believed the power would send lightning and fire wreathed like the DNA of death into the bare chest of the creature in front of him. Again nothing happened.

This time a single laugh cracked the air like breaking ice. The demon stood and waved a hand at James like clearing smoke from the air, "I'm sorry, but don't you know where you are?"

He raised his arms and two great wings spread from his back. The feathers were gray and faded to black at the tips, and they filled the space around him. "This is my world James. Your belief has no power here. It doesn't matter what, or who, you believe in," spit flew from his lips at the force of the words, "because this is my world, not His."

The demon started walking toward James. His wingtips seemed to tear through the fabric of reality showing only darkness beyond.

"I am what I was. I am what I was meant to be." He raised his arms and turned a slow circle, his outstretched wings carving furrows in the stone, "I am a king, and soon, after I deal with you, I will be a god."

The realization hit James harder than anything had before. He really was back in Hell. He'd hoped this was just another trap like the one the teens were in, and because of that he'd believed his power would still work.

All this time he'd been looking at this hall through the tattoo on his eye and just now the truth of it poked through into his mind. The tattoo showed him the truth, and the truth was that what he was seeing was a part of Hell. He opened his eyes and nothing changed. This was no bedroom on the second floor of an abandoned house. Kron'ael had become powerful enough to open his own door into the tower of Hell. The next thought rocked him back and he almost turned and ran. In Hell he was powerless. The angel hand had kept him alive, and the iron bar from the gates of Hell had provided him with some measure of protection, but in reality he was sure he'd only made it through Hell because no one really dangerous had noticed him. Now that had changed.

Maybe, his mind babbled at him. *Maybe if we run he'll chase us and we can lure him back into the real world, and if he doesn't chase us we can just leave him here in Hell cuz that's where he belongs anyway.*

James didn't take the time to argue with his mind. His body decided on its own that running was the right decision and orders were sent to his legs to carry out a retreat. He twitched and something grabbed him. Darkness wrapped around him and pressed him to his knees. His mind screamed and visions of Grace and the boys being tortured rippled through his mind. Without his power and with no one coming to save him his fate would be that and worse. Now, a quiet part of his brain whispered to him, *you truly will be in Hell.*

Emotions flared up in him. Anger at the little juggler in that orange desert. Anger at the same juggler staring down at him from the stained glass window of the church. If he really was God he should have known this would happen. He should have given him better weapons. He should have warned him. The anger was punctuated with relief knowing at least Grace was free. He'd accomplished part of what he set out to do. Maybe it would be enough to carry him through. It would have to be, his mind whispered.

The darkness pressed him down and whispers filled his ears. They told him of depravities and torments to come. They laughed and sang of his coming pain. Then something touched him.

A hand softly came to rest on his right shoulder. At first James twitched thinking it was the beginning of an attack but when nothing happened he wondered if he was imagining it, wishing some little comfort into existence, but then another hand pressed onto his other shoulder. The weight and solidity of them flared a memory, bright and clear, of his father standing behind him.

A voice spoke quietly into his ear, "I sent you here because I believed in you too."

Whispers of weakness and loss tried to plug his ears, but the hands held him tight and again the voice spoke, "Listen. What do you hear?"

James didn't want to listen. He wanted to shut out the whispers because they were right. He was weak. He'd failed. Without his powers he was nothing but a self-aggrandizing college drop out. He'd failed Kate, he'd failed Grace, and all because he wanted the power. It had been easy for him to believe in the power. It was something he'd wanted all his life, so when he saw it he sucked it up like some bloated mosquito. But it had all been worth nothing because he was worth nothing.

A hand lifted from his left shoulder and came to rest on the top of his head, "No, don't listen to the lies. Beyond them, listen."

He wanted to turn and look up into the eyes of whomever or whatever was behind him, but at the same time he just wanted to stay there with that hand resting on his head. Here he was safe; no more fighting, no more demons and Hell. But even as those thoughts slipped through him he started to hear it.

At first it was just a pressure on the edge of the darkness surrounding him. Then a few notes flitted around him dragonfly quick. He strained to hear it pushing away the whispers, ignoring the threats and lies. The tune came into focus in three layers. A deep pulsing base, like the beat of his own heart, laid the foundation for a strong tenor, and above it all a soprano chimed like the church bells of a fairy tale. The words were foreign to him, but the voices cut into his fogged mind razor bright and sunlight sharp.

The song wrapped around him lifting his spirit and forcing the whispers into nothing more than white noise, the buzz of an ineffectual fly at the window of his mind. James knew those voices, and he knew the strength of their conviction, but more than that he knew the truth of their song. He'd asked Ren to perform the strongest exorcism he could think of and what he'd gotten was a choir of three angels.

James opened his eyes and stared into the darkness. Dozens of blank eyes stared back. He grinned at them showing his teeth because finally he knew the truth. The hand ruffled his hair and James nodded.

"Don't worry," James tossed the words into the darkness surrounding him, "I've got this."

Faith may eventually be lost, hope might fail, belief may be placed in broken vessels, but truth will remain, and the voice of truth had spoken.

His smile widened as the hands behind him took firm hold of his arms and helped pull him to his feet.

James pulled in a breath and sang. The words to hymns he'd only heard as a child came easily to his mind and as they spun out from him the darkness flinched. He pressed on flinging out his song of conquest. He sang of hope and love, he sang of truth and sacrifice, and with each word the blank eyes shuddered. Finally he simply found himself humming a harmony to the song Ren, Todd, and Abby were singing outside the house. Raising his hands he pushed the music out and with a final ripple the darkness tore like cheap cloth.

Shrugging his shoulders and cracking his neck James took a deep breath and looked around the stone hall. Standing only a few feet away the demon's face twisted in rage, but before he could say anything James twisted sideways, took a single step, and kicked him in the chest.